LAVINA

LAVINA

∽∽

MARY MARCUS

The Story Plant

The Story Plant
Studio Digital CT, LLC
P.O. Box 4331
Stamford, CT 06907

Copyright © 2014 by Mary Marcus
Jacket design by Dina Leonard

The selection from "Burnt Norton" by T.S. Eliot, from *The Four Quartets* copyright © 1971 by Esme Valerie Eliot, reprinted by permission of Houghton Mifflin Harcourt Publishing Company.

Print ISBN-13: 978-1-61188-201-8
E-book ISBN: 978-1-61188-202-5

Visit our website at www.TheStoryPlant.com
Visit the author at www.MaryMarcusFiction.com

First Story Plant Printing: April 2015
Printed in the United States of America

0 9 8 7 6 5 4 3 2 1

This novel is dedicated to the memory of Ruth Marcus, Naomi Goodman, and Aline Davis, who was also known as Noog.

ACKNOWLEDGMENTS

I'd like to thank Amos and Joel, for their presence in my life and work.

It is a true honor and a writer's dream to work with my editor and publisher Lou Aronica.

Lisa Haber and Susan Woolhandler read nearly all of the drafts of *Lavina* over the years and gave me council time and again. Bless you both!

Nora Tamada, thank you for understanding dialect and understanding me.

My gratitude to the great Dina Leonard for her taste and talent.

Jennifer Vincent—without you, none of this.

What I never understood to this day, to this very day, was how white people could have black people cook dinner for them, make them meals, but wouldn't let them sit down at the table with them. How can you dislike someone so much and have them cook for you? Shoot, if I don't like someone, you ain't cooking nothing for me, ever.
– Ray Charles

The ordinary response to atrocities is to banish them from consciousness. Certain violations of the social compact are too terrible to utter aloud: this is the meaning of the word *unspeakable*.
– Judith Herman

Blow the horn in Zion,
Sanctify a fast, call a solemn assembly;
– The Book of Joel

M e, I'm guessin' I'm a haint. Don' know another name for what I am. Ain't no angel 'cause I don' have wings. Anythin' that happen since I die, weren't like I thought it would be. Never seen my mother, the pearly gates of heaven, or the baby girl I lost 'for I had Billy Ray. What I sees is what I left behind.

A deep green summer in nineteen hundred and sixty three. Hot it were, but it were always hot hot in Louisiana in August. Some say you could fry chicken eggs on the cement. I died that summer, nearly every colored person in Murpheysfield come to my funeral. Coffin were shut, had to be. Them at the church, they did everythin' but call me Saint Lavina, her who died serving the Lord in the path for freedom. Why there was even a picture of me on the funeral program. Me in my best wig.

I sees two houses. My own, a rundown, no-count place I never finish payin' on with a dirt-poor yard and a broken front step. When it rain, the front flood and when it don', it just set there filled with red dirt and dust. Got too lazy to plant me any zinnias. Go inside and there's that old bathtub a settin' there in the kitchen and the hot water heater rustin' in the corner where the spiders spin them threads. Spider webs on account of I didn't spend near as much time in my own house as I did over at the Long's. It's a big ole white house on Fairfield with fourteen rooms I kept clean with my own hands and knees, lemon wax, and my purple feather duster.

I left two chirrun behind, and them two I can see like it were yesterday. My own boy, golden brown and shinin', comin' soon on bein' a man. A handsome man as you'd ever see. Little harmonica in his hand, he were born to play that thing, funny sound it make, touch you way down in your toes. He Billy Ray Davis, born at the Confederate Charity Hospital, middle of the night in November. Next day I took him home 'cause they needs the bed and we was strong.

Now, my girl, she were white as an egg, born to a sickly woman what never take care a her. She start off growin' like some old weed in the yard. I knows right away she stronger than any of them pretty flowers. She Mary Jacob and she settin' at the kitchen table with her nose in some thick old book. She tappin' on the black-and-white floor. That chile, she love to read. And when she read, she tap.

You can't turn back the hands of time. The seasons they come and go, no matter that you ain't there no more to feel the hot of August and September turn into the cool of October. And you can't feel November in your knee when November come. But you remember what your life was, and a lot of it were full of pain like your knee always was. Pain don' hurt you when you die. That ole blackbird pain, he fly away. You ain't happy when you is dead. But you ain't so sad neither. Ain't like living. One moment you is happy, then you turn around you is sad.

Them that dies watchin' over them that lives and that's the truth. But that's all we can do. Can't reach out and give them two a shake and a talkin' to, like I'd like to. Wouldn't hear me if I did. That don' mean I ain't watchin' to see what happen. I is always watchin' . . . I is always watchin'.

NOW
(THE EARLY NINETIES)

DESCENDING

～～

There's no such thing as a direct flight from New York to Murpheysfield, Louisiana. I'd gotten one of those cheap seats that stopped in Pittsburg and Atlanta. By the last leg, the plane was all but empty; my seat mate, like almost everyone else, had gotten off. I was alone and completely paranoid. I didn't know someone had actually been watching me since New York. I thought I was jumping out of my skin because of where I was going and who I was going to see. I remember hoisting myself up to take a look around the plane. Way in back two old ladies sat alone, bent over their knitting; empty seats all around them. In front, on the other side of the aisle, I didn't see a person, just a fold-down tray with some balled up napkins, a swizzle stick, and three empty bottles of airline booze knocked down like baby bowling pins. A lush, I decided.

I gave him a name right away, even before I actually saw him.

The call had come the week before. I walked into the kitchen, pressed the button on the answering machine and heard her strident voice—distant but familiar—an enemy I'd known all my life.

"Mary Jacob, this is your sister! We're at the Shumpert Hospital. I'm puttin' Daddy on the line."

Then, an earsplitting clunk of the phone being dropped. I cringed even before the real shocker, his deep voice full of sadness.

"Child, I want you to come home. I'm longin' to see you."

"You're *what*?"

Since then I'd spoken to Kathryn twice in one week; we normally spoke maybe twice in five years. I still had not spoken to my father again. My sister's insistent drawl was in my head, like a catchy tune

I didn't want to be there. *"You ever heard of a kidney machine, sister? Poor Daddy has to go on one. We're takin' him home tomorrow. Did I tell you I'm engaged again? My fiancé is up in New York City right now. If you take that morning flight next Tuesday, why, he'll probably be on it too. He's comin' to see me and to help me out with poor Daddy. Why, I don't believe I've ever met your husband or your son."* S-u-uhn like it has three syllables instead of one.

In back of a barf bag, I found the laminated safety card with the little stick figures free-falling into space. I studied what to do if we landed at sea.

Not that there's a sea anywhere near Murpheysfield. Down below were pine trees, farm fields, and red dirt, the color of blood when it dries.

I looked up from the disaster card and saw a big blond man, hands grasping the top of the seats, barreling down the aisle, bringing with him a whiff from the bathroom, the nasty soap, the smell of shit, the lush of the three empty booze bottles. He stopped in the aisle, stared at me pointedly and started doing a kiss-y thing with his lips.

"Mind your own business, dick head." I didn't say that. Nor did I explain myself to the stranger. Why should I?

"Look, I'm not the kind of person who makes out with her seat-mate on an airplane. I was acting out, or more to the point, he was kind and handsome, and he listened." Instead, I stared down at my watch and waited for this stranger to take his seat and quit harassing me. I didn't really care that the red-faced man thought I was wild.

The plane felt like it was sinking. My gut did too. I had a catch in my throat, I wasn't breathing very well. I was halfway hoping Big Daddy would be dead by the time I got there. Yet, I was curious. The old man had never asked for me before; this last wish was his first.

And being down there, I could skip marital therapy . . .

"Tell me a little about your parents, Mary Jacob. What was their relationship like?"

"I don't remember. My mother died when I was twelve. I was sent away to boarding school after that. I never saw much married life."

"You don't remember anything; that's unusual. And is your father alive now?"

"Yes."

"Did he remarry?"

"Three times."

"And what's your relationship like with him?"

"We don't have a relationship."

"That sounds sad."

"We're not one of those close families."

"How do you feel about that?"

"I don't feel much at all; it's the way it's always been."

"Well, it sounds sort of sad to me."

Then the kindly gaze that's seen it all turns on my husband. "And Peter, are you from a close family?"

"We're not close, we're claustrophobic. My father died a couple of years ago. My mother lives in Brooklyn. Sometimes I think Mary Jacob's lucky."

"So your relationship's tough then?"

"She's my mother, she drives me crazy. She drives everyone crazy!"

And so on. As it turns out, according to our therapist, I have no role models. Though even Peter admits I'm a good mother and wife, and described me to Michael as *loving* and *devoted*, two words he normally wouldn't get caught dead using. Michael translated "loving and devoted" as Peter feeling left out of the picture. Maybe he's not in the picture because he doesn't want to be. Did I say that? I must have said that.

My best friend and collaborator Vincent, who is from New Orleans, doesn't see his family either. Maybe this is a southern thing. Still and all, he can paint a pretty clear picture of the afternoon his mother walked in his room and caught him with another boy: the sound of his mother gasping; pulling his pants up hastily, then covering the other boy; the way the light was coming in the window, the smell of new mown grass, the color of the sheets, and the texture of the blanket.

I wasn't so much sent away as dismissed, forgotten. Kathryn, who is five years older, married when she was eighteen and left home. Our mother died that same year. She was hardly cold before my father married my sister's best friend Van—also eighteen—and I was sent away. I was, I've always supposed, nothing more than a classic case of the unwanted child, too close in age to Van. And to his third wife too. When his fourth wife Margaret was alive, though we never visited, she sent my children hundred dollar checks at Christmas time. In turn, I sent them a pot of tulips with a neutral non-denominational greeting and signed everyone's names. After Margaret died, Big Daddy Jack hit the road, until now.

⁓⁓

"And Mary Jacob, when do you start remembering?"

"My memory kicks in pretty clearly at thirteen."

"What do you remember?"

I closed my eyes.

"The hospital bed in my mother's room being taken away. Boarding school. My friends there. My history teacher whose hands shook. The tree outside my dorm window, reading *Jane Eyre* for the first time. Summer camp in North Carolina. Water skiing. The way the boat lifts you up out of the water and you fly."

I opened my eyes. Peter was looking off in the other direction, bored or embarrassed, I couldn't tell. Michael nodded his head sympathetically. In maritial therapy there's quite a bit of sympathetic nodding.

"You remember a lot for someone who has memory problems."

"And Peter, how about you? What do you remember?"

"Thirteen was my Bar Mitzvah. I remember cringing when all the survivors started crying."

"Survivors, as in death camp survivors?"

"You got it."

"That's tough," said Michael.

"Vat you goyim know from tough?" replied my husband in the funny Jewish accent he uses to charm his way out of things.

"Do you think that your being a son of a camp survivor gives you permission to do things other people can't?"

Good question. Excellent question. Three points for kindly Michael. Though now that I had taken a crash course in infidelity, I suddenly could relate to why Peter had cheated. You don't think about death when you're acting out. Not the death camps, not your father's death, or your own fiery one falling down from the sky. Nor do you think about the biomedical instruments used to prevent death (after I spoke to Kathryn, wanting to be prepared, I walked across the park to Mt. Sinai to look at a dialysis unit). Adultery—the turn-on—distracts the mind from its petty anxieties, its dutiful desire to do the right thing. And makes the wrong thing irresistible.

One minute we were total strangers, sharing the two-seat on the side of the plane. We talked for a while. He was handsome, he was kind, he had this gorgeous shiny black hair. Our faces were close together, close enough to smell his breath. His breath smelled good. Our legs touched and I reached up and ran my hand down his face, grazing his long black hair. Yes, I started it. Me, Mary Jacob. To get even? To say I could do it too? Maybe. Or like I said, I was just turned on. Though, Peter's affair wasn't the only reason we were in therapy. Just the excuse. Still, already I knew I didn't have the *sang froid* to be a cheat, because I was more than a little unnerved that the blond, red-faced man had seen us. What a jerk.

"Buckle up, ladies and gentlemen."

We were on the ground in Murpheysfield.

My hometown had a real airport now, not the landing strip I remembered. I was walking in the small terminal headed toward the rent-a-car counter, suitcase in hand. Four men were ahead of me and while I was waiting, someone came up behind, standing way too close. The whistle didn't tip me off (he was whistling along with the Muzak) but the smell of whiskey did. He brushed up against me, horribly familiar. I didn't need to turn around. I knew it was the lush from the airplane.

When it was my turn, I said my name softly so he wouldn't hear. But the woman behind the counter couldn't find my name or any record of my reservation number. Even worse, they'd run out of cars.

It's never any trouble pulling out my southern accent. Like my husband's Jewish one, it's always right there, just below the surface, another personality waiting to come out.

"My daddy's real sick," I said, letting the molasses drip, "and I'm awful worried." I mumbled my local address. The Hertz woman repeated it loud enough for the whole airport to hear. But never mind, the address had worked its magic, as I knew it would.

"Mary Jacob Assure," she said, like she wasn't sure how to say my name. I didn't correct her and say, Ascher. "Miz Assure let me just take care of the gentleman behind you and then we'll see what we can do."

The big blond man approached the counter. I stood a little away, studying him. I saw his red face had once been handsome too. He was so loaded I could smell the whiskey from where I was standing. Still, drunk or not, he had no trouble getting a car. I thought he was probably getting my car.

As he weaved away, toward the exit sign, I couldn't take my eyes off him. When he reached the doorway, he turned and made another face. Not a kiss-y thing like before. He was pulling on his face to contort it. Two beefy fingers on either side of his eyes.

Slant eyes. Ha ha. Very funny. Even though I live in a sheltered world where people would never behave this way, this guy felt really familiar, like a song I hadn't heard in a while, one whose words I knew by heart. I hated that he knew my name. He probably even knew my address. The Hertz woman had shrieked it loud enough to hear back home in New York. And still he lingered there by the exit sign.

"Bye Bye Mary Jacob, toodle loo!"

I raised my arm New York style and flipped him off. Toodle loo to you too, creep-o.

The exhilaration of doing that didn't last. Before I knew it, I was behind the wheel of a maroon econo-box morosely mulling over the last conversation with Kathryn.

"I'm gonna need you to sit there with him. We can't even keep a nurse, Mary Jacob. He pinches the pretty ones and makes fun of the ugly ones and won't do what they say. He's a livin' breathin' terror. I was thinkin' why it's a good thing he's weak as a kitten, or we'd never be able to control him. I was lookin' at him just today, thinkin' Daddy's an old man now."

Strong Jack Long, weak as a kitten? It seemed impossible. Like God or the devil being ill.

At a red light, I stopped and turned on the radio. Just a couple of notes let me know it was Billy Ray singing. There's nothing wrong with my musical memory. It was one of his very early hits, "Diamond Buttons."

I've always loved Billy Ray's music. I read somewhere a long time ago that, like me, he comes from Murpheysfield. We wouldn't

have known each other. Those were the days of Jim Crow, yet the
singer has always felt like someone close. At signings, people tell me
all the time that they feel close to me on account of my books. Perfect
strangers will hold out their hands and call me by name like they
know me. And I'm not even remotely famous outside my tiny little
children's lit circle. But Billy Ray's been famous forever. As long as
I can remember anyway. I even dream about him. Sometimes we are
children in the dream and sometimes all grown up. We're always
kissing in the dream, kissing and holding on to each other like we'll
never let each other go.

Someone was blasting a horn at me. I was afraid to look in the
rearview mirror. What if the lush was following me? I was in the
poor outskirts between the airport and town—why is nowhere
always a skirt?—a part of town that used to be referred to affection-
ately as "coon town" by the local white gentry. African American
Town? Would that be the correct nineties terminology?

The announcer on the radio was saying Billy Ray would be playing tomorrow night in Murpheysfield, L.A., like it was Los Angeles,
not Louisiana. Home of the not-so-great Mary Jacob Long, I was
thinking. But I wasn't Mary Jacob Long. I was Mary Jacob Ascher.
Mary Jacob Long didn't live here anymore. But like it or not, Mary
Jacob Long was coming through loud and clear. And I didn't want to
be inside her skin anymore than I wanted to be inside the crappy
rented car heading toward Big Daddy Jack.

I tried to conjure up Joshua, my son, and Lizzie, my stepdaughter: the two clearest people to me on earth. But they seemed far away,
hazy. Billy Ray playing the harmonica was who I was seeing.

The car was stuffy. I pushed some buttons and the windows
went down. The air outside was soft and spring-like. So different
from the frigid air I'd come from on a New York February morning.
I was still in African American town. In the rearview mirror I saw a
child on the dusty street. He was standing very still, watching me. It
kept running through my head: *Run, run Billy Ray, run!* Then my old
dream flashed before me, Billy Ray kissing me.

Keep going, I told myself, and I knew exactly how to go. To go
straight for several miles, to turn left at the Seventh Day Adventist
Church, a building made of tan-colored brick. Emblazoned across
the back, is a huge neon cross with a Star of David dead center.

ALTERNATE ROUTE

～♱～

Red dirt and pine trees. Rednecks stopping at truck stops, a few cheap motels here and there . . . hundreds of miles of this. Floyd behind the wheel of the van was driving him nuts, sitting there with his thunder thighs open and the big sack of MoonPies wedged in there between his spread. When Floyd wasn't stuffing his face, he was doing rhythm on the steering wheel; those hands of his couldn't sit still for a second. The driver's MoonPies were bringing him back to his childhood, as if heading toward Murpheysfield weren't doing that and then some.

He was always hungry back then. If he'd been lucky enough to get his hands on a MoonPie, it could've been the only food he'd have until his mother came home from work, walking up their rickety step, calling out, "Sugar, I carried us home our supper." She'd be beaming from ear to ear as she set down a brown paper sack on the kitchen table. Inside there'd be a chicken back or neck, sometimes the dry, end piece of roast the Long's didn't want; some biscuit, a piece of soggy pie. Never enough to get really full. Not even close.

"Brothers and sisters, the great Billy Ray live in Murpheysfield tomorrow evening. Just drive over the border into Louisiana and see the legend himself performing at the Riverhouse."

Not bad, he thought, relieved that the radio stations were hip to it. I am a legend, he thought. But legends are old.

Floyd was grinning like a big baboon. He put up his hand to high five Billy Ray, who refused to return the gesture.

He watched Floyd's smiling baby face frown and listened as his hand dug in the noisy plastic bag and found more—he must have had forty of them by now—they were the small, bite-size MoonPies, not like the ones he remembered. By this point on the tour, the singer knew whatever Floyd did was going to get on his nerves and he was trying to control himself. What he wanted to do was shoot him, kick him, piss on him, throw him out of the car, and leave him by the side of the road. He liked skinny blond Steve who was nodding out in the back seat much better. Steve didn't do his stuff in front of him, and he was grateful for that. And he sure wouldn't pull that cheap high five either. Maybe he'd nod his head. Maybe he'd say, *all right*. But he wouldn't high five and pop more MoonPies into his greedy pink mouth. The kid could play too. Usually, when you didn't show off and go into a lot of unnecessary jive, it went along that you could play, though Floyd could play too. He'd have had him out on his black ass day one if he couldn't do that.

"Now when I were backing Cookie and the Cupcakes," he'd say, at least a couple of times a day. Or "Little Anthony, he had to have a box underneath him when he sang, he were that small. Bobby Bland always rests himself between sets; he's old now. Never have played for BB."

He lit up a Kool though he knew it was bad on his voice and for years had been trying to limit his smokes to half a pack a day. Even in the joint, he had tried to do this. But knowing where he was going was hard on his nerves. Behind bars he could take. The shit that went along with making a comeback he could take. His girlfriend giving him the commitment shit—the getting married shit—he could take. But facing a Friday night alone in Murpheysfield, Louisiana was something else entirely. He hadn't stepped foot in the place since he was fifteen years old but that didn't change a single thing. Fine with him to see the whole town burned to the ground and all the white flesh barbecued.

"You come from around here, don't you, brother?"

"Yeah."

"Anybody we can call on your cell-u-lar phone, bro?"

Ever since they had started out on this tour, Floyd had been trying to get his hands on the singer's prize phone. Billy Ray knew it was better to ignore the smiling fuck, but part of him kept wanting his backup guy to understand the rules. That if you were cellular, you didn't have to tell every fool you got one. Showing it meant something; to have one meant you ain't had the thing long enough for it to count.

"No mama, no sistahs, you don' mean?"

"I told you, motherfucker, leave it alone!"

"Okay, man. I was just thinkin' we could have us a meal. This road food is getting' on my nerves."

"Sure ain't spoilin' your appetite any. . . . Look at this floor."

"Man, I'm gonna clean up at the end of the day. I always does that."

The singer laughed. "You'd trade the best trim in the world for a plate of homemade fried chicken, huh boy?"

Floyd grinned from ear to ear and did a little more rhythm on the steering wheel.

"I don't know about that, man. I could use me a nice plate a trim."

Both of them laughed. Meanwhile, the east Texas station began to play a medley of the early songs. The ones that had sent Billy Ray to the top of the Motown charts, then on up the Top Forty all those years ago. The ones that could always get him management, a booking, and a cut of the cover charge but not at the major places anymore. That wouldn't happen unless he came up with a new hit. Unfortunately, for too long a while, he hadn't come up with anything at all.

He didn't remember recording "Billy Ray Loves the Apollo," the track they were playing now. By the time he recorded that album he was getting high as a kite during recording sessions and everywhere else come to that. But even clean, in the car next to Floyd, he could remember the excitement, the heat of the crowd screaming and, when he was up there, how the sound equipment warming up sent body rushes up and down his spine. Body rushes still happened, but not as sharp and sweet as they were when he was young. Maybe, he thought, because no one makes recordings like the one they were playing now. Today even performance recordings sounded smooth and technically perfect. Still, when it all came down, something was missing that weren't missing back in the sixties when he started out.

Sure, it sounded far away and old-fashioned. Sound engineering had come a long way. Maybe too long a way. Back when he was a kid on the road, you had to know your stuff. Hadn't he made his first live appearance on stage with nothing but a dime store harmonica in his hand? A few lousy speakers and a mike no one would use today even to tape a message on their answering machine. Your talent had to carry you back then. There was no MTV with some faggoty Brit with a ponytail and his butt in the air, following you around with that steady-cam. Sound wasn't digital. Sound was sound: you made it yourself, fueled with your own heat and sweat.

The crowd was screaming on the tape. They screamed better in the old days too. He hadn't thought about the song they were playing now for he didn't want to remember how long. "Without Your Love" had been his first slow song, his first love song. No harmonica and minimum backup. His voice had to carry the whole thing and it fucking did, all right. He couldn't have been more than seventeen when he recorded this. Pulled it off so good, a couple of other performers had done more than all right with their version of it.

That was the real test of a song. If a song had enough in it, almost anyone could perform their version of it. You could do it bubble gum or soul. You could do it disco. Disco wasn't his thing, hid out getting high until it was over, though he was as high as a kite when he came back at the end of the seventies with an album that blew them away.

It was a funny thing about the old songs. The notes and words, they felt familiar and close, but no more close than other songs other people wrote. They were part of him, but not connected to him. Nothing seemed connected to him. Sometimes he thought being clean all the time was the trouble. He was more than halfway convinced Sarah and the boy were to blame. Billy Ray had never lived a normal everyday life like the one he'd been living for a while now, with a healthy dinner and regular hours. Part of him liked it though—the two of them were healing his mind and body—though the more he thought about it, the more it was clear that family life wasn't good for the hum, had probably even killed the hum off. Couldn't be anything else.

In the front window, the side window: red dirt, pine trees, and road signs. The inside of a prison cell wasn't a lot worse than Louisiana red dirt and pine trees. He thought anytime now they'd be running into one of them old cotton fields. When his mother was fifteen, she had picked cotton. She used to say she could remember it in her shoulders. "Billy Ray, Arthur, he settin' right here in my shoulders giving me the misery."

Her voice still came back to him even all these years later, soft, musical, and sweet. He could remember her saying "Arthur" like she was right in the car with him. Not ten feet under in a cemetery he'd never been to. That was another thing, should he try and find out where she was buried? Had she been buried? Maybe after they murdered her, they just threw her tired old body in a ditch somewhere and let the dogs get at her.

"Brother, you mean to tell me, you don' even know one chick we can call on yo cellular phone? You gotta know at least one chick in this town. All we need is one, they always got friends."

A chick from Murpheysfield had been on his mind lately. If he hadn't met Sarah and Connor, he'd have never seen her picture as a grownup and, with her name, put it all together. Last year, he had even gotten his manager to get her home phone number; he had not been surprised that she had left the South and lived up in New York. It was in his mind that one day he was going to call her and they were going to talk about what happened. Six-year-old Connor loved her books, had a whole set of them, and was all the time asking to be read one at bedtime. The star of the books was a little black girl named Vina. Lavina was his mother's name. Billy Ray knew the girl in the books was named for her. His mother and Mary Jacob had been close. She had even kept a picture of Mary Jacob on her shelf in her room, right near her good picture of him and the empty frame where she put a little bit of the fuzz from the head of her baby who had died before he was born. Mary Jacob had saved his life, no question about that, though neither one of them could save his mother.

"She don' have to be a fox, man. Them ugly girls, why they is always so grateful when one of us shines our lights on them."

"Suck my dick, brother."

"Okay, Billy Ray. I hear ya. Nothin' we can't handle here."

It's bad for the performance not to get along. Floyd knew this and so did he. Bad enough they were playing Murpheysfield. But beggars can't be choosers. The new manager had arranged the tour without consulting him. Something that had happened in the old days too, but the pay was better. Even a million years ago the bread was better. Fucking blow. All that money up his nose. Using it had made him numb to everything around him, including who was cheating him and of course, cheating on him. What was the joke they used to say in the seventies and eighties? "Blow is God's way of sayin' 'brother you gots to make more money.'" They used to laugh at that. Kept saying it over and over as they sucked up that nose candy. But, of course, the joke was on them. How they hoovered their way through tens of thousands of dollars of the stuff month after month. A million or two easy. Maybe even three.

"Just a few years ago, you were hot shit. This ain't Atlanta. Could be they still think you hot shit around here. Maybe we won't have to call. Maybe they be there waitin'."

Instead of killing him, hands around the thick, black neck, Billy Ray reached over and grabbed one of Floyd's MoonPies, which were soft from the sun, and spread it across his smiling baby face like butter on bread. He could have done more, but left it at that. Unfortunately, now some of the sticky chocolate was on his hands. Sarah called him a clean freak. And he did hate that sticky chocolate being on his hands. He didn't like anything on his hands but soap and water and afterwards a clean paper towel.

"What you tryin' to do brother, get us in a wreck?"

He ignored Floyd and lit up again. Already he was half a pack over the limit. And now there was chocolate on the Kool too. Floyd would have sucked his fingers clean if Billy Ray asked him, just to get at that last bit of sweet.

With the Kool between his lips, the singer leaned over, slipped off his new Italian loafer and wiped the chocolate on his thin silk sock. He took off his other sock, made the two into a ball and threw them on the floor of the van with the sacks from Floyd's junk food— let *him* clean it up. You always gotta make the best of a bad situation.

ONCE UPON A TIME . . .

‿∽‿∽

I was parked in the driveway of the big white house on Fairfield Street. It was the biggest house on the street and the only one that needed painting. Spring was out in all its glory in Murpheysfield, Louisiana, everywhere but here. Nothing soft and sweet grew around my father's house. On his wide front lawn, just the giant live oaks, almost black in color, snaking one into another, blocking out light. I longed to get out of the car and stretch my legs, but it was like the plane all over again, only worse. Now nothing separated me from what I didn't want to face.

Home is where one starts from.

The back door was open. I went warily inside. Soft sunshine poured in from the window above the laundry room sink. I didn't have to glance sidelong to know there was a window there, as surely as I could smell a faint odor of bleach, and a delicious hint of ironing and clean laundry. In my mind's eye, in slow motion, like a black-and-white movie on late night TV, I saw a large dark hand with a heavy metal iron moving up and back, up and back, hissing across the snowy white damask of the dinner napkins. The picture disappeared, went black like the end of a movie, but it left me with a good feeling, like a pebble tossed in a pond, a rippling of happiness. I almost never felt this way in real life. Why suddenly here of all places? Still it was as though the words themselves were imprinted in my brain, the same place where music and poetry lived: *nothing can hurt you here; here you are safe.* And that place seemed to be where I was heading, suitcase in hand. In the kitchen with the old wooden table and chairs. On the black-and-white floor, with the bread box and the icebox and the cake plate with the round glass cover, the sunlight on it making it gleam. Someone was at the kitchen sink. She had a gray uniformed back with a neatly tied white apron bow at the waist. She turned to face me.

"Well, well, Miz Mary Jacob, they is waitin' for you. Miz Kathryn, she at the beauty shop, but Mr. Jack, he upstairs waitin' for you to walk up them steps."

The happy feeling was gone as quickly as it came. I felt my face flushing, a catch in my throat. Then sadness again.

"You don't have to call me Miss Mary Jacob," I told her gently, "just call me Mary Jacob, please."

"Yes'm."

I smiled at her, and she looked relieved and sort of scared—she couldn't possibly be afraid of me, could she? Then, a bell went off, crisp, staccato and she gestured to the oven, the place where the delicious smell was coming from. I was aware then, of standing there holding my suitcase, with a throbbing arm. Meanwhile, the old lady was padding toward the stove, and then stooping to open the oven. The smell was stronger with the oven open and the sweet buttery fruit smell filled the whole kitchen.

I walked toward her, feeling the heat of the oven. She was shorter than I was, thin and wizened, though when I first came in she seemed much larger and solid.

"That's a dewberry cobbler, isn't it? I thought dewberries didn't come out until the summer."

She was smiling angelically. "Now that's the truth. We freezes them, so as we can have them all year long.

"And tell me your name, please?"

"I'm Annie. Annie Hunt."

"Hello, Miss Annie." I held out my hand.

Annie Hunt smiled beatifically.

"Seriously, just call me Mary Jacob."

We were both smiling now. But I was sort of freaked out behind the smile. Had she been working here when I was little? Had I forgotten her too? I've always been friends with my babysitters and I still have my first cleaning lady—fifteen years later. Peter says I am too friendly. I get too involved in everyone's lives. That I overpay. And he doesn't know the half of it. Could it be possible that I forgot all about who worked here? Obviously somebody took care of this huge place. More than one person, considering its size.

"How long have you worked here?" I asked. "We've never met. I'm sure I would have remembered you."

"I been workin' for Mr. Jack ever since Miz Margaret passed. I come here with Miz Margaret when she marry Mr. Jack. I worked for Miz Margaret for thirty years. Woulda been thirty-three years come July. And I promises her I will stay with Mr. Jack as long as he need me."

I was relieved I hadn't forgotten her. "I never met Margaret. She must have been a wonderful woman if you stayed with her for thirty years."

"Miz Margaret were an angel from heaven and she remember you. She were a friend of Miz Lil and Miz Margaret. Why she say, when you were a baby, she come here to this house and bring you a present."

Someone had brought *me* a present? It was all I could do not to grasp Annie Hunt's old wrinkled hands and ask her crazy questions: "Was I a good baby? Did I cry a lot? What was my favorite food? My first word? Did I like teddy bears or rabbits? Did I have a favorite dress? Who am I? What in the world ever happened to me here that I cannot remember?"

I put my suitcase down next to the old wooden table, pulled out a chair and sunk down in it.

"I guess I'm a little scared about going upstairs and seeing my father. I haven't seen him in such a long time. I hope you don't mind if I sit here for a bit."

"Course you are, honey. You sit yourself down, and I'll bring you some cobbler. Mr. Jack, he say I is to make you dewberry cobbler."

For me? He said that? I watched Annie padding around, first to the shelf to remove a dish, then to a drawer and on to the stove top where the cobbler sat. Presently, she set down in front of me a plate of the deep purple stuff in a pretty bowl with pink and blue flowers. The spoon that was in the bowl was heavy sterling and initialed. And no paper towel like at my house; here, a proper white linen napkin.

"Thank you so much," I smiled, taking a bite. The crust was light and crisp, the filling dense and way too sweet: lard and tons of white sugar.

"This is amazing," I said. "Why don't you sit down with me and have some?"

Annie Hunt, who had been smiling, put her hand over her mouth modestly as though I'd said something very risqué.

We both jumped at the jarring noise that was coming from the wall nearest the laundry room.

"Mr. Jack," Annie said, heading toward it.

Annie was engaged with some antiquated device on the wall that looked like something from Alexander Graham Bell's workshop.

"Yes sir," she was saying. "I'll tell her that."

"Mr. Jack says you is to come upstairs. He is waitin'."

I took another bite and chewed elaborately, like it was steak instead of purple mush. I took another, in no big hurry to leave the safety of the kitchen.

All too soon, I got to the last little bite and, when I did, Annie Hunt whisked it away and me out of there.

"Miz Kathryn, she say to use your ole room. I putcha clean sheets on the bed."

"Thank you, Annie."

And now, all at once, I was out of the safe kitchen and into free fall, that's how it felt, like the ground beneath my feet had given way. But I remembered it all: After the kitchen you come to a butlery, a long narrow room where the good china, linen, and crystal are kept. Connected to that, the dining room with the huge antique table spread out, and above it, an ornate chandelier with necklaces of crystal looping down.

My father's house had always come to mind when I played Clue with my children. Only no conservatory, never any flowers. Not even a stiff arrangement on the hall table like there used to be. Mary Jacob with her suitcase in the front hall. Mr. Long with his guns in the library. The library was in back, two huge rooms away, but I didn't have to stand in the library to see the glass front case. I knew what was inside. The shotguns, the deer guns, the bird guns, the pearl handled revolvers gleaming behind glass. Mr. Jack with his guns in the library. Mary Jacob on the stairs with her suitcase. The beautiful old runner was still on the stairs. I was on the large landing after the first set of stairs; it had a window seat with tall windows overlooking the driveway.

The door to my old room was shut. I opened it, expecting to see a four-poster bed, the dark wooden chest of drawers, the flower prints on the walls, the wooden bench. I even remembered my old bear that used to sit on the bed. Unlike the rest of the house, which was virtually identical, everything in here was different. Now there were twins with two suitcase holders at the foot of them. A writing desk, a chaise; soft floral chintz to match the wallpaper and curtains. It looked like a room at an expensive hotel. Any trace of me had been completely removed. Even though I had dumped my family years ago, it stung that I'd been dumped too.

I put my suitcase down. Then I went to the windows that faced the back of the house and opened one up as far as it would go. I stood for a moment looking out at the live oaks in back, taking in deep draughts of the clean fresh air.

In the upstairs hall, I hesitated, knowing it was time to see my father. I was remembering too, what Kathryn had said on the phone. "He's got to go on that kidney machine right away. Maybe you'll take him the first time."

Kathryn had gone on to say, "I was reading this article at the beauty shop that said when you always want to sleep it means you're depressed. He sleeps all the time now, Mary Jacob. I guess that means he's depressed."

"Yes, he probably is," I'd said. "Who wouldn't be at his age, in his physical condition?" What my sister Kathryn probably didn't know is that sleeping is a sure sign of progressive renal collapse. The poisons make you sleepy as they build up in your body. In the final stages you sleep all the time. There's no real pain and it's not a bad way to go . . . but I hadn't come to offer my advice.

By now, I was creeping toward the heavily carved four-poster bed, the same bed where my mother Lillian had repined for most of my childhood. According to Kathryn, Big Daddy's fourth wife Margaret had died up here as well.

The man in the bed was sleeping. I was glad of that because I was shocked down to the tips of my toes. Big Daddy Jack had shrunk.

He was stirring. I was so used to calling my father "Big Daddy" that I didn't know what else to call him now.

His eyes were fluttering open. One long, thin arm reached out for me. I was grasping his hand and that was a shock too. My father, my own flesh and blood, was touching me. I'd imagined everything else but not that I'd be moved by holding my father's hand. Or that he would hold on like he didn't want to let me go.

I'm used to feeling sad seeing women my age walking arm in arm with their mothers on the street. But I've never thought much about having a father. Not consciously anyway. Now I knew I'd longed for a father too. Or maybe just the unbelievable fact that I had one. He was smiling at me as he held on. Deep lines ran down his haggard face. He was very handsome for a man his age, except for the teeth. They were the color of dirty ivory and his breath was foul like an old dog.

"I want to thank you, darlin', for coming home. I've been waitin' for you."

I stared at him, unable to speak. I didn't trust myself to speak.

Jack Long was still holding on. "Help me sit up."

I did as I was told, feeling the slippery silk of his pajamas on my hands, the bones in his thin back. Up close, his body didn't smell much better than his breath. Some of the smell was from cigarettes— there was an almost empty crushed pack and a crystal ashtray filled with butts next to the bed. But there was a prevailing other odor too.

"Here, Mary Jacob, sit yourself down on the bed." I did as I was told and placed myself at the very end of his big old bed, my back against the post. We were staring at each other frankly. Me looking at him, my father looking at me, unselfconsciously, the way children and animals look at one another. Neither one of us turning away, neither one of saying, "What are you staring at?"

He broke the silence.

"You're a fine lookin' woman, Mary Jacob. I'm glad to see you turned out just as you did. Good head of hair, you've kept your figure and looks; I approve of a woman keeping her figure. Tell me, do you smoke?"

"Not anymore."

"Drink?"

"Not much."

"What are your vices?"

"Curiosity, I suppose." And selfish men, but I didn't say that last part. Maybe I didn't want him to know so much about me.

"Eve bit into the apple of knowledge and we've never recovered."

"Men wrote that story."

"But it contained a fundamental truth about the nature of women. And anyway, Mary Jacob, it's still our world."

"Not for long."

Jack Long laughed a bitter little laugh. "Well, I certainly won't live to see it."

"It might do you some good."

My father reached for a cigarette, lit it, and smiled appreciatively. "It figures you're a blue stockin', daughter. But of course, I sent you to college. You're educated, unlike your sistah who has no intellectual curiosity whatsoever. I must say I'm enjoyin' this conversation."

I was enjoying the conversation too. It was certainly a novelty—sitting on my father's bed, shooting the breeze—even if by now I'd figured out the other smell was his necrotic flesh. He was sort of flirting with me; I was sort of flirting back. I wondered, is this what women did with their fathers: A safe venue for the male/female ongoing battle? I've watched my stepdaughter Lizzie try and relate to Peter. She can often be quite seductive—Peter responds to that. Peter isn't the greatest father either. He let me raise Lizzie practically on my own, and he hasn't been all that much better with Joshua. But Lizzie, when she was little, used to sit on his lap and call him Daddy. Joshua too. And Joshua used to say he wanted to marry me when he grew up. I didn't encourage him when he said that, but I knew it meant love and I was grateful that he loved me. I still am.

I couldn't recall ever sitting on this man's lap or running into his arms freely or happily or ever saying, "I love you, Daddy." Or him saying I was his little girl, or calling me sweetheart or honey, or calling me anything at all come to that. For as long as I can remember, when I thought of the man in the bed it was with a hard and rigid heart, knowing there was no possibility of love between us. Now, I wanted to know why. Not everyone was close, but most families were closer than us. Most families at least had their moments. Most families tried to fake it more than we did. Why did Jack Long want me suddenly? Was he trying to settle his debts? Did he believe in hell? Did he want to say he was sorry? Was he sorry?

He was holding my hand, and looking at me with frank pleasure.

"We have much to discuss, daughter, but waitin' for you has made me tired. You'll have to excuse me now. You'll sit with me later, won't you? I'm terribly glad you've come."

ALL FILLED UP
〰〰

He was grateful for the dying light and the quiet in the car. He was even feeling sort of mellow about Floyd, who had kept his mouth shut for a while. By the time the exits for Murpheysfield came into view, Billy Ray was telling himself, just get used to it, same way you got through being inside without going crazy from it. He could get through Murpheysfield, like he got through the state prison outside Atlanta. And the good part was Murpheysfield would be over one hell of a lot sooner than the big house—even if the road food wasn't all that much better. Sarah had spoiled him with all that healthy home cooking. No such thing as a really fresh salad on the road or veggies cooked without grease and salt. If it weren't for his fiber pills and Evian (also thanks to Sarah) he'd be plugged up and farting his way through this whole fucking gig.

By now they were just inside the town limits. No-count American towns, most of them look the same after dark. He was looking at a strip of cheap motels, a row of the usual junk food restaurants, mini golf, a snake farm, a water park with a closed sign, and a church plopped down on the red dirt like it landed there in a storm. He was telling himself, after my next hit, I'll lay some cash on Sarah, then make my way to Europe and only come back here on tour.

As if that was so fucking easy. A hit started with the hum, which was as natural and uncomplicated as the air he breathed once it showed up, but left just as mysteriously as it arrived. He had gone through these dry periods before—you learned to just get through them—but the present one felt bigger and more frightening because so much depended on it. He was broke—jail had all but wiped him out—he was getting old, and he needed a hit the way a starving man needs a bowl of food; it was a matter of simple survival. If the hum required freedom and giving up Sarah he'd pay that price.

The sad part was, the singer liked his girlfriend better than any woman he'd ever been with and maybe even loved her too. It wasn't that he was hooked—hooked was what he'd always been before—this was something deeper than that. And it wasn't because of her looks either. Having surrounded himself with only extraordinarily beautiful women, he had been interested to discover he liked the company of a woman who wasn't always reapplying her lipstick every five seconds. "You look in the mirror more than I do, son," she'd said to him on more than one occasion. Another thing he liked about her, the easy sense of humor that could laugh at things—he had never met a white woman with such a good sense of humor. Sarah was in her late thirties, a little heavy, and though she was still pretty, now the years showed. But Sarah was the kindest woman he'd ever met next to his mother, and generous like his mother had been too. It was her place where they lived and a lot of the time she paid the bills with her raggedy ass paycheck from the job she worked. Paid for all three of them: her son, her man, and her.

Not like his wives, those gorgeous greedy bitches who had taken him to the dry cleaners every single time. Found out the last one was porking his manager. Got rid of them both, though they got the bread. He had gone on a year-long drug binge after he found them out that had ended up with him in the joint. And it had been downhill until he met Sarah.

He might have been able to stay longer if her boy Connor wasn't involved. Not that Billy Ray had anything against Connor; like his mother, the little kid was one of a kind, a classy little dude. Smart as a whip too. What Billy Ray didn't like was the eager puppy dog look on Connor's face when he picked him up at daycare or when they played ball together in the back yard before dinner. A look that said, "I need a man to take care of me. Be here for me, Billy Ray. Be my daddy." Billy Ray knew he was not up to the job. Some of that had to do with the hum, and some of it had to do with who he was and what he'd been through.

Those skinny little white arms—good as they felt around his neck—weren't meant for him. He was the wrong man for the job.

The singer's own father had left when he was Connor's age. He did not know exactly how old the man would be, but he'd be up there by now. He must be dead, because he would have shown up, like other relatives had shown up over the years, asking for handouts. Billy Ray's memory was of a tall, thin man with close-cropped hair and a clean white shirt who laughingly raised him up over his head and cried, "Up you go Billy Ray, boy is flyin' to the moon!" then gently laid him back on the ground again. He could never reconcile that clean, innocent memory with the sight of his mother lying on the floor of their bedroom with a smashed-in face and her arm bent at a gruesome angle the night he left them and never returned. In the years since, the pleasure of that one memory with the pain of the other had melded. When pleasure came to him, he distrusted it—pain was far more reassuring; it was something to count on.

Because he didn't want to be like his father, the singer had decided these past few days on the road to make Sarah a parting present of the only valuable thing he had left: The remaining button on his shirt with diamond buttons that he had performed in at the height of his fame. He had hocked the other three diamonds over the years, once for lawyers and twice for dope. It was in a box at the bank and he was thinking he'd get it made into a necklace she could wear (a ring wouldn't be right since he was leaving) and then he could split, knowing he had left her with something.

He wanted to be fair to the boy too, and also leave him with a good feeling. He had decided he would take him out and buy him a video player—the deluxe model—as a parting gift. Sarah was a good sport and wouldn't take it away, even if she didn't approve of it; that's the way she was. Never stubborn or unkind. Always thought of the other person first. What he was going to say to the boy was another matter. He did not want to just leave the way he had been left all those years ago, waiting for his old man to come back and say he was sorry and to lift him in his arms again. His mother had given him no explanation of the huge thing that had happened to them. Or informed him that there would be less to eat. At night, hungry in his bed, he'd put his thin pillow over his face so she wouldn't hear his crying. He'd hear the same kind of muffled sobbing coming through the cardboard thin wall that separated her from him. The old shack where everything was broke seemed to shake with their mutual misery. Once her swollen eye healed and her arm came out of the sling, she made a joke out of it. Or maybe she was just faking it. "Thought I'd be a one-armed plug-ug for the rest of my life, Billy Ray."

"Connor, I'm leaving," the singer saw himself calmly saying, as they played ball in the back yard. "I'm settling in overseas." This is as far as he ever got in his imaginary conversation with the boy. He'd then start to see the boy as clear as day, looking up at him, sniffing up his tears in that brave way he had about himself—and Billy Ray could not continue, not even in his imagination. It was a good thing he was out on the road for some time, so everyone could get used to him not being there. Truth was, he had to get used to it himself.

"Billy Ray, you sure sure you don' have one sister or cousin?

"No, I ain't got nobody. Only person I know here is Jim Crow."

That cracked old Floyd up and he started beating on the steering wheel again, just when Billy Ray had gotten used to the silence. When the driver calmed down, he asked, "The Colonel, Jack, or Burger King? I'm sick of McDonalds."

"Burger King and McDonalds are the same you dumb motherfucker."

"Tell me something I don't know," Floyd crooned.

They pulled into a Quality Courts just as it got dark. Seconds later, they were pulling out like a bad fuck. Quality Courts with the vacancy sign, all filled up, thank you very much; at least that's what they told Floyd. That's when Billy Ray knew he was in Murpheysfield, Louisiana, home sweet fucking home.

They stopped by a Kentucky Fried and ate their supper under one of those umbrellas on the cement seats. The singer made sure to pull off the greasy top layer of skin before eating the white meat and slaw and the gluey white roll. Steve in the back just had fries and a can of Coke. Junkies don't eat. When they do, it's usually soft stuff. Billy Ray was recalling fondly how it felt to be all coked up and not able to chew. Hum going strong, music pouring out from his heart into his fingertips, the harmonica flying like it had wings instead of hands attached. Floyd was plowing through an entire barrel himself, plus a quart of fries, several ears of their frozen corn on the cob dripping with grease, and at least four rolls. No slaw. Somebody, he thought, ought to give that fat man a couple of lines to kill his appetite. A line of coke might save the fool's life. Floyd had even asked for the skin Billy Ray pulled off and was about to drop in the bag. Afterwards, he ordered Floyd to go back in there to ask for extra napkins. In prison, he had learned to stock up when you could. That way when you needed something, there it would be waiting for you.

It was dark now and he felt tired after doing nothing all day in the car. When he was tired, he wanted the stuff. Being in Murpheysfield made him want the stuff even more. Who wouldn't with his memories? Was there anybody left who even remembered what had happened? The girl would remember. She were there after all. There where he left her with his mother and all that blood. But never mind that. He couldn't remember anything but a sort of red haze, red turning into black. He must have run away, but he didn't remember running. What he remembered clearly was him and Mary Jacob kissing. Clinging to each other like lost souls. And while he couldn't remember the faces of most of the women he'd porked over the years, he knew he'd remember that kiss to his dying day. After that, everything was a blur. The next thing he knew he was on a bus, headed toward New Orleans with all that behind him. Used to think sometimes, especially after he made real money, that he ought to do something about what happened. "And you oughta, Billy Ray," he'd say to the mirror when he was shaving or looking at himself in one of his fifteen-hundred-dollar suits. You oughta go down there with some lawyer dude and put the whole town on trial. Trouble was he couldn't prove anything.

He put the blame on Martin Luther King, someone his mother and her friends at the church had worshiped like he was Jesus Christ himself. When King got himself shot several years after his mother, he watched it on the TV and thought, "Well, black man, it serves you right for killing her." Because of Martin Luther King, Billy Ray never had anything to do with any civil rights shit. Any march on any place, nothing.

These days, he couldn't afford more lawyers. Sons of bitches were still robbing him blind. Anyway, it didn't matter since his mother was gone. Just as the young Billy Ray was gone. If the hum was gone forever—which he feared to the depths of his being—he would have to kill himself, or maybe without it, he'd die. Maybe all he'd have to do was sit and smoke Kools till he went up in flames. The singer put his hand up to his chest and rubbed it around for a while to soothe himself. Then he closed his eyes and drifted off as the motion of the van rocked him to sleep.

Presently, he woke up with a start. They were parked in the dirt front yard of the St. James. Floyd was singing "St. James Infirmary," a song Billy Ray had always detested.

Let her go, let her go God bless her.
Wherever she may be, she can search this whole wide world over,
And never find another man like me.

Outside the van, the insects were making their noises the way they always do in the country. Then a drunk laughing his ass off poured out from some window. It was all so fucking familiar, as familiar as the song Floyd was still singing as he lugged the suitcases toward the light. Instead of getting out right away, he stayed in the van with Steve, who was stretched out in the back seat.

He had warned Steve at the beginning of the tour, "Man, if I ax you for drugs, don't give 'um to me. Not even if I beg, not even if I cry, not even if I tell you I'm gonna kill you with my hands. Don't give me them drugs, you hear?"

The skinny blond boy had smiled his ugly bad-toothed junkie grin and replied, "Hey, I hear you man." So far, the singer had not tested him. He was wondering now what Steve would do if he made the request. The kid was a good piano player. Maybe one of the best piano players he'd ever had, but he didn't have much of a mind left and was as easy to handle as a rag doll. Drugs had definitely eaten a hole in his brain. He'd probably forgotten the warning by now and would be glad to share his stuff, especially if he offered to pay. It's lonely doing your stuff all alone. Always better to get high with somebody else. He was desperate by then, and the desperation was familiar and almost sweet. All he had to do was take his hand and shake the boy's shoulder. Either that or reach over into his pocket. Junkie was so stoned he probably wouldn't feel it. Billy Ray wasn't afraid of heroin. Heroin wasn't his thing. He didn't like needles. He'd use it like blow. It not being blow would keep him safe. And that would be a blessing too.

THE WOMAN IN THE MIRROR

W hat made you move back here, Kathryn? Weren't you living in New Orleans?"

"I certainly was. Didn't I send you a picture of our house on St. Charles Avenue? We were on the cover of *Town & Country* magazine when Christopher was King of Comus. I thought I sent you that."

"No."

Kathryn was at her dressing table, glaring at me in the mirror. "I always wondered why I didn't hear from you," she went on. "Are you sure you never saw that article about us in *Town & Country* magazine? We were very important in New Orleans. I was quite hurt you didn't call me the moment you saw it."

"You never sent it to me. I'd like to see it. I really would."

"Well, I'm sure we can find a copy around here somewhere. Margaret and Daddy came down for the ball. Margaret talked about it for years."

It was in the early evening of my first day in Murpheysfield. Our father was still asleep, Kathryn arrived home, announcing, "Here I am!" and now I was sitting on another bed—a queenly queen—with a tufted headboard and matching silk coverlet. A huge gilt mirror on the wall in front of the vanity table reflected my sister's face and torso, and also her collection of sterling silver and crystal containers holding her perfumes, potions, and powders.

"You were going to tell me why you moved back in here, Kathryn."

My sister took a long pull from her cigarette, put it down, and then reached for one of her tabletop hand magnifying mirrors and scrutinized herself. Smoke curled up in a flattering haze around her face. I thought it was amazing that she looked as good as she did with all the smoking.

"Well, Christopher made me sign this perfectly horrible pre-nuptial. My lawyer told me it was the most disrespectful document he had ever laid eyes on, I never thought he'd hold me to it. Then, of course, Daddy got sick."

"Where are your children?"

"Little Kathryn is in Baton Rouge, Calhoun is in Mobile, and the youngest, Lillian Lynam, is living with her father down in New Orleans. She and I are like oil and water; she's better off there."

"Don't you miss her?'

Kathryn took a pull from her cigarette, "Not one little bit!" she practically hissed at me. "Why should I? She takes her father's side against me. And she likes his new wife better than she does her own mother. After our divorce, Christopher married his secretary practically the very same day. He sent her to law school at Tulane and now she's his lawyer. Those girls of mine are the biggest duds I've ever seen. Did I tell you little Kathryn is having her first child? Imagine being a grandmother at my age!"

"That's what happens when you get married at eighteen."

"And divorced at twenty-three!"

"And married at?"

"Twenty-five!"

"And divorced at?"

"Thirty!"

"And married at?"

By the time we got to the last round we were laughing. But my laughter was more nerves than mirth. I was thinking about Kathryn's daughter, who, like Lizzie, had been left by her mother. You don't get over that.

I was also wondering where I was all those nights in the room that didn't exist anymore. I've never been beautiful like my sister or, more importantly, sure of myself, but confidence is, of course, one of the many gifts of beauty. I like my face now. I look young for forty-two. And with all the exercising, my body is young too. But never in all my life have I sat at a mirror smiling at myself like Kathryn. When we were growing up, everyone always said she looked exactly like a young Grace Kelly, and in fact my sister bears more than a superficial resemblance to that cold ice princess who married her prince. Perhaps that's why her royal distain for a commoner like me has never seemed anything but natural.

If I couldn't remember some things, I knew very well to feel uncomfortable here in her highness's private chamber. When we were growing up, I was never allowed in her room, let alone to sit on this bed. That's probably why I was halfway expecting any minute to be evicted with a sharp word or reprimand. When you are beautiful, when you are wanted and you belong, you can do anything you want to those who are not blessed as you are. When we were growing up, the same gilt mirror had been festooned with dried corsages, their ribbons dangling down, trophies of Kathryn's many conquests. I've never received a corsage or been to a fancy dance. Once I got to college, boys started to like me, though at boarding school I never went to the dances—I was afraid to. My kind of courting was done in blue jeans, smoking dope. I thought maybe that was why I couldn't remember great hunks of my life. Even so, it was coming back to me, listening to Kathryn; the life I watched, anyway. From her description of her life today, it's a continuum of that other time. The years have passed. Kathryn has married, reared children, but it was clear as her looking glass: my sister's real life was here in front of the mirror.

"You know when I moved back in here, I had to sell all my ball gowns to some tacky costume rental place. Do you know I owned sixty ball gowns?"

"How many tiaras?"

I was joking of course.

"I have Mother's and mine. Christopher made me give back the Crowder one; it was the best of the lot, I'm sorry to say. Why, I'm sure the new Mrs. Crowder won't look half as well in it; it has a four carat sapphire that exactly matched my eyes." My sister sighed. "What do you have of Mother's?"

"Nothing." I replied truthfully, "Just a picture of her; I keep it on my dresser at home."

"Well, Daddy, damn him, sold what Van didn't make off with. He saved a few pieces to keep Coco interested. I know for sure she got a cocktail ring I wanted. I didn't get nearly as much as I should." Kathryn blew out a protracted stream of smoke. "You mean to tell me you don't have any of Mother's jewelry?"

"No."

"Not even a bracelet or a bar pin?"

"No."

"Well, you should call up Van."

"Where is Van?"

"She lives in Dallas now, never married again. She owns a dress store, paid for with family money. All my friends get their clothes there; why, it's the new Neiman Marcus. She's quite the success. But I'm warnin' you, don't even whisper her name. It's just a blessing that baby boy of hers died, or Daddy woulda been broke twenty years ago, instead of—"

"I didn't know they had a baby."

"Of course she had a baby. Jack Lynam Long III was born with his cord around his neck. Same year I had little Kathryn. Van and I were both expecting children at the same time. I can't believe you don't remember."

"I didn't live here after mother died; I guess you've forgotten that." I was trying to sound casual, but I was shocked Van and my father had lost a child, a half brother to me. I was hurt too; I hadn't been told. Or maybe I'd just forgotten.

"Well, Daddy was beside himself for months, going down there to that cemetery every day crying over its little grave, saying the devil stole Jack Lynam Long III. By the way, have I told you, I'm gonna be a grandmother?"

"Yes you did. Would you have liked a brother, Kathryn, I would have!"

"No, don't be silly, it would have been the worst thing. Did I tell you little Kathryn wrote me a note. Wouldn't think to pick up the phone and call. Now imagine being a Grandmother at my age."

"You don't look like a grandmother."

Kathryn regarded herself in the mirror, "I never said I did."

Her voice brightened. "Did I tell you I got my boobs done, and my tummy tucked? It was pure hell. I got an infection and was on pain killers for months, but it was worth it."

Kathryn was opening up her dressing gown to the mirror to display her wares. I slid off the bed and onto the floor and started doing pushups on the soft, thick carpet so I wouldn't have to see. Kathryn's friendliness disturbed me even more than her hostility, which I was accustomed to. I certainly didn't want to see her breasts, the new ones or the old. I didn't really think of Kathryn as my sister. Van had been my sister, my nice sister. Not this woman in the mirror.

By then I was puffing from the pushups. I did a few more for good measure.

"I don't mean not to be hospitable. I hope you don't mind," Kathryn said, "that I'm going out with my fiancé alone. John's been up in your neck of the woods and we haven't seen each other in weeks; the man's on fire for me! Besides, like I told you, Daddy's a holy terror with the help. Why, I been cooped up in this house for nearly two days and I've got to get out. Tomorrow, I've got someone comin' in at night to sit with him, and John and I will take you out to dinner."

I was resting on my belly. "That's fine, Kathryn, I'm glad to stay with him. Is there anything I need to know? Like pills and stuff?"

"He can give himself his shots and take his pills. Annie'll be carrying his tray up just about now. And she'll leave your supper on the stove. He's not supposed to eat salt or sugar and if he asks you for the shaker or the sugar bowl, don't let him have it. Thank God Annie's so old and can't get a job anywhere else. We cain't keep anybody here these days with his temper fits about the salt and sugar. Why, he scared his last night niggah so bad she had her whole family come pick her up at three in the morning. You'd think it was a Klan convention instead of poor weak Daddy blowin' his top."

I felt my body go taut. I said softly, "People don't use that word, Kathryn, nice people just don't. If you feel that way you ought to keep it to yourself. It's disgraceful!"

"What do you know about nice people? I wouldn't say 'niggah' in front of Annie or any othah niggah. What do you take me for?"

What was the point of saying, "a racist, a redneck"? I wondered what my sister's reaction would be if she saw one of my books or went to our readings where black children sat together with their arms around white children. Kathryn knew I wrote children's books but had never mentioned that she'd picked one up. Had I seen her and her ex husband in *Town & Country* and had the same response? What was more likely, given our relationship, is she had just not bothered to send me something she valued about herself, as I hadn't. Could it be Kathryn felt as lonely and alienated in my presence as I felt in hers and disdain was the only way to show it? It was certainly something to think about.

I wondered if any bookstore in Murpheysfield carried our books. Maybe I'd go see. That would be interesting to find out whether political correctness had hit the Deep South., Or was it still just Uncle Remus and the Tar Baby even now in the last decade of the Twentieth Century? I sat up and started stretching my legs. For the time being, I decided I'd leave that word alone, though I promised myself if she said it again I'd throw a pillow and break all her crystal shit. Write "racist" on the mirror in bright red lipstick.

"How about Coco? Tell me about Coco."

"Well you didn't miss much. Coco was from the wrong side of the tracks; why, she gave ballroom dancing lessons in the front room."

"What happened? Why did she leave?"

"Same reason Van did. Poor Daddy was old enough to be her father. That's why when he married Margaret, I coulda kissed her feet. Margaret was Mama's age and she was a lady. Why, she kept poor Daddy from the . . . but never mind that. That's ancient history and I've got to get dressed now; we'll have plenty of time to catch up later. What in the world are you doin' with your legs?"

"I'm stretching."

"You're what?"

"I'm stretching my legs, that's all. I do it all the time, and they're all cramped from the plane ride."

Kathryn was now standing over me in her push-up bra and half slip. A tube of flab hung out from under her tight brassiere with its high, fake shelf of breasts.

My sister gave me a disapproving look.

"I wouldn't do that anymore. That must be why your legs look like a football player's. I can see the muscles bulgin' out even through those pants you got on. I hope you brought a nice dress, somethin' you can wear tomorrow night. I'd lend you somethin' myself, but those linebacker shoulders of yours and that flat chest would never work with my clothes."

Kathryn was heading toward her closet when the doorbell rang, four long melodious chimes.

"Oh Gawd," Kathryn called out from the closet. "Mary Jacob, why don't you run get it and introduce yourself to John? But wait, you don't have your face on. You look half dead. Annie will have to get it. Now run scoot and let me get dressed. That precious man is dyin' to see me and I cain't keep him waitin' forevah. Go be an angel and keep Daddy company."

∽∽

Once again I was standing in the doorway of my father's enormous bedroom; it had to be at least twenty feet long. He was sitting up in bed. In his crimson-and-black patterned dressing gown, he looked like a lounging movie star from an old-fashioned movie. I was glad I'd taken Kathryn's suggestion and put on makeup and combed my hair. If I didn't know how to deal with my father, I still didn't want to look "half dead" in front of him either. A tray of food lay untouched on the bed beside him. But the tall glass with the dark brown liquid was nearly empty.

"So Mary Jacob, Kathryn and that chap of hers are gone for the evening. I'm glad of that. Now we'll have a chance to visit. Just the two of us."

I smiled at my father. Apparently, I had nothing to fear from this amiable stranger.

"And how are you two gettin' along? I can't imagine a woman of your intelligence would have anything to say to that hoyden. Have you met her new beau? He's fat as a pig and has a red face and neck. His law firm advertises in the yellow pages. An improvement from the last caller; however, he was in *trade*."

I couldn't help laughing. Listening to him felt like being in a snobbish English novel. But, I've always loved English novels and the snobbier the better.

"I'd appreciate it if you'd fetch me a fresh bottle of whiskey. It's over there by those cabinets under the bookshelf when you first walk in the door. To your right, child, the second set of doors. Now bring me that fine tall bottle and don't go tellin' your sister or anybody else where I keep my libation, you hear?"

"I won't," I assured him, then returned to his bed with a fresh bottle of Johnny Walker red and two tumblers.

"So you're joining me, I'm glad of that. How do you take your whiskey?"

"Not like yours."

"I'm glad of that also. Just go into the bathroom and put some water in your glass. I'm not goin' anywhere."

When I returned, my father motioned to the bed. I never would have thought two days ago that I'd be resting my back against his bedpost drinking scotch like it was the easiest thing in the world, but oddly enough it was easy.

"Have I told you how much I appreciate your comin' down here, child?"

I felt my face turn red.

"You and I got off to a bad start, but that doesn't mean the end has to be like that, does it now child?"

"No," I told him, "of course not."

"That sad and terrible business wouldn't let us be close for a long time. You blamed me, you know; I can see it on your face that you still think I'm guilty."

I didn't answer him, but I thought he was right. I did blame him for my mother's death. Didn't he marry Van shockingly soon after that? Why bring that up? My father was old and he was obviously sick. There wasn't anything he could do to make up for that.

"Have you eaten your supper?"

"No."

"A fine host I am. I told Annie of your love of fried chicken and dewberry cobbler and when you go downstairs you'll see that's what you have for supper. Go down stairs, darlin', and after you're done, come back here and we'll have another drink."

I left his room and walked down the hall. The huge house was so quiet, I could hear something click from rooms away. Peculiar music was now drifting down the upstairs hall. My father was laughing and his laughter followed me down the hall.

The sky was dark outside the windows on the landing as I headed down the stairs. I had felt curiously light and easy in my father's company, but now suddenly I wasn't so happy anymore. It came down on me like a curtain: sore shoulders, a faint throbbing behind the eyes, nothing new, really. It was close to seven thirty. I was cold and the house was huge and depressing. And I had not even been in all the rooms yet. Not the formal front room or the library that adjoined it in back.

I stopped at the window seat and sat knees down on the velvet cushion like a child. I heard a door shutting downstairs. Presently, I saw the small figure of Annie Hunt and her towering shadow, twice as big as she was, walking slowly down the driveway. Annie had a paper bag in her hand and her large purse in the other. I had a strong sense of déjà vu as I watched the small woman and her enormous shadow as they made their way down the driveway, where the long low branches of the live oaks reached out. I had the strangest urge to open the window and shout, "Take me with you." Instead, I followed her old woman's progress down the driveway, till she turned and disappeared from sight.

I headed down the stairs to the huge front hall, past the Grandfather clock that didn't work anymore, past the powder room under the stairs and into the kitchen. The only light on was the small bulb above the range where I saw a foil covered plate gleaming under the light. The old-fashioned kitchen was exquisitely neat, smelling faintly of fried chicken.

Though I was very hungry, I didn't stop to uncover the plate and taste my supper. Something more urgent than hunger gnawed at me. I was moving toward the doors against the back wall. When I opened one up, I saw a broom and mop. I went from there to the vestibule between the kitchen and laundry room, the light outside the back door helping me to see. I was standing in the laundry room, still searching. The linen mangle was gone and the old-fashioned deep slate laundry sink had been replaced by a Formica top cabinet with a small modern sink. But the old maple rocker was still there, nestled under the window. Without knowing why, except that I had to, I went to it and sat down, rocking back and forth with my eyes closed, comforted by the swinging motion of the chair, at peace. Here, at last, was a safe haven in the vast shadowy house. Happy was not a word I associated with this house. Yet I had felt happy when I walked in the back door this afternoon, and now once again in the rocking chair that felt familiar. All was calm and well as I rocked back and forth.

Presently, as often happens, little Vina appeared to me. A character you invent is like a child. And Vina does belong to me. Vina belongs to Vincent too. I've always gotten along with him much better than I do with Peter. But I didn't want to think of my marriage just then. Better to think about darling Vincent who always made me laugh. "Poor little Vina," he had said last week. "Her mother's a jock and her father's a queen—still we love her." And we do. Vina really is our daughter, she's that close.

I continued to rock and felt myself transported from my father's house to a better place, where I never felt lonely or left out. Ideas for books have always come this way. When I least suspect they will, never when Vincent and I are together deliberately trying to create. *The Secret in the Broom Closet*. It was just the kind of mystery I did best. Easy and domestic; the clues, I knew would be fun to come up with. God bless you, little Vina, I thought, God bless you.

ST. JAMES INFIRMARY

~~

He was standing in the downstairs of the St. James. Much as he hated the drab modern roadside motels that went along with vending machine junk food and shitty TV shows, this place was even worse. Worse because it was trying to be something it wasn't. Worse because it was dirty. Worse because it was Murpheysfield. It had a big downstairs with old-fashioned velvet chairs and couches to sit in, a stairway in the middle that went off on two sides, and all sorts of rooms upstairs. The singer thought it might have been a honky whorehouse once. On the walls hung gold-framed mirrors and pictures of white women with half their tits showing in old-fashioned clothes. Coming in from the van, after Floyd had gotten them rooms, the fastidious Billy Ray had winced to see roaches crawling on the floor in the dimly lit front hallway.

This was the singer's first tour under his new management. He had known it was a come down. But how far he had come down had not been entirely clear before this very minute in Murpheysfield. The fucking town was cursed.

He was staring at the walls wondering why you never saw pictures of old-fashioned black women with their titties stuffed into dresses, their hair pinned high on their heads. He was imagining the handwriting on the wall in between the sad pictures and the dull mirrors that once had been bright. "Give it up, motherfucker." "You're nobody no more." "Hum is gone. Hum is gone away."

The clerk behind the desk, a man near the singer's age, with a mustache very like his own and a gold chain around his neck, stood up, gave him a big smile, clapped his hands, bowed, and sang a few bars of "Gonna Come True" in a not bad voice. This made the singer feel a little better. Here at least was a fan.

When he finished (after fucking up a couple of lines) Billy Ray nodded his head in acknowledgement. That made the clerk beam.

"Send you up something to your room, man? Anythin' you want, all you gotta do is say the word!"

The singer knew that meant drugs. Drugs and a hooker if he wanted it.

As always, the idea of coke beckoned him: the cool numbness, the rush, the feeling of great happiness the first few lines always give, especially after a long break. Still, you had to know your source, and he doubted if there was any such thing as decent blow in Murpheysfield. Probably all he'd get is baking soda mixed with roach killer.

"Tell you what, I'll give you a call if I want something. Send me up a bottle of water from the bar. Evian if you got it."

The clerk smiled, "H2O coming right up." He handed him a huge key on a holder so heavy he could do reps with it.

"Your room is up the stairs. Givin' you the best room in the house, man. Your suitcase, why, it's already there in your room. We is glad to have you with us."

Billy Ray climbed the stairs and walked down a hall.

There was no way to stop the flood of memories. Walking down a dusty street in this very town, tired and thirsty, with no hope of a ride. Him waiting for his mother to come home, lonely, hungry, in the summer waiting on the porch with his harmonica; in the cold months, inside fixing them a pot of greens and hoping she'd bring home meat. The way her face looked when she wasn't smiling to cheer him up. Weary she'd been, especially that last summer. Why had she gone and gotten herself involved with that sit-in shit and never told him? Who talked her into that? Probably one of her friends at the church had made her do it. There were plenty of them, believing in Martin Luther King—all of them, in fact. Him, he never had no friends growing up. Just him and his music. Later, music, drugs, and women had taken up his time. All the musicians he played with over the years, they weren't really friends. They were entertainers, same as he was. Too much wanting to outdo the other one. Truth be told, the closest to a real friend he ever had was little Connor. Sarah took a course on Friday nights until ten o'clock. Usually he hung out with Connor, sometimes they went out to dinner to a place they both liked, one Sarah wouldn't approve of. Their last night out together, the boy had asked him what would happen if his mother wrecked the car and didn't come home, who would he go to? The singer had not been able to answer, but the question had thrown him. And made him decide that since he was leaving, he better do it sooner rather than later. Still, it wouldn't do any harm calling Atlanta just to check on Connor. A lot of the time those young girls she got were doing anything but what they should be, which is watching out for him.

He unlocked the door and looked around at the best room in the house. No use thinking about other rooms, though truth be told, even the five-hundred-dollar-a-night places could have bugs crawling in the bed. He made a quick inspection with the small flashlight he always carried with him. Satisfied he was safe, he sat down on the saggy bed, reached for the phone, and hit the numbers for home. Listening to it ring, he remembered how when his mother saved up money she would take him downtown on the bus to shop at the stores that sold cheap clothes. They always had to shop on Thursday. She was off Thursdays and Sundays and back then, stores didn't stay open on Sundays. Thursday was their only real time to visit. Sundays were church all day, at least for her. He told her when he was ten that he was finished with church and it had upset her no end. He never told her why either. He stopped going when he figured out that the God they were praying to was a white man. Never could go after that. He wondered suddenly if little Connor would break Sarah's heart the way he'd broken his own mother's. Probably he would. Though he wouldn't be there to see it happen, the thought of it troubled him.

"Connor, what you doin' boy? You behavin' yourself?"

"Hey, Billy Ray, where you at now?"

"Louisiana."

"Is that far?"

"Ever heard of New Orleans?"

"Mom showed me where it was."

"Well, we go to New Orleans day after tomorrow."

"When are you coming home?"

"Couple of weeks. But I'll have to go on the road again."

"Billy Ray?"

"Yeah boy?"

"I got thrown down in the dirt at school. He laughed at me. He said he was coming to day care and he'd do the same thing."

"How big is he?"

"My size, but he's mean. Everyone's scared of him."

"Tell him you're gonna knock his dick in the dirt. And look at him like you mean it. Then spit on the ground and look at him again. Did you tell your mother?"

"No."

"You want me to tell her?"

"No."

"You sure?"

"You know her, she's not like you."

"What else?"

"Nothing. How long have you been gone?"

"Almost a week. Do you know how long a week is?"

"Seven days. Forever and ever!"

"Seven days ain't very long, Connor. It is when you're six, but not at my age."

"The food's better when you're home. We both like it better when you're here."

"When I get back I'll take you for ribs."

"They made you sick when we went before."

"I'll get something else. And I won't get the pie."

"I'm getting pie! Pie with ice cream on top and we won't tell Ma," the little boy cried happily.

Except for the boy's soft breathing, there was silence. Another thing he liked about Connor. He didn't always have to fill the silence. Two of them could just sit together saying nothing.

"I'm saying goodnight now. Tell your mother I called, but not to call me. I'm going to sleep."

"Night, night, Billy Ray. Sweet dreams."

"Yeah, you too."

The singer stared at the phone for a while, angry with himself for calling the boy and encouraging him.

He went for the TV and tried to get it on. Couldn't see worth shit close up. Probably didn't even have cable at the raggedy ass St. James Infirmary. He fiddled with the knobs but couldn't get reception on even one station. No remote control dingus either. What did he care anyway? TV made you stupid, sitting there watching their white faces and their white lives, and the occasional black show weren't any better. He didn't let Connor watch too much TV. Didn't want him to grow up stupid even if he weren't gonna be there to know how he turned out.

His bottle of Grecian Formula, his makeup and reading glasses were in his small bag. The singer went for them now.

He opened up the carton of Grecian Formula and unfolded the directions. Probably he knew them by heart, though it never hurt to make sure. If you can control the small things, the big things often stayed under control too.

He was back in the bathroom, stripped down because the dye drips. He had come up with his own way of handling the hair dye, which was to apply it with Q-tips. He had brought a huge box of them to take on the road. His mustache needed work too.

In the middle of his careful application, he heard a knock on the door. He dropped his Q-tip on the Formica counter, wrapped a towel around his waist, and went for it.

"Yeah?"

"Room service," a young sounding female voice answered.

The singer opened the door a crack and peered out. As if this small town hooker ever seen a waiter pushing that cart with the cloth over it, carrying any kind of food you wanted, even at three in the morning. This skinny chick didn't look more than fifteen years old. Instead of making her look sexy, her long curly wig made her look even more like a child. Her scrawny little chest had either a titty job or a padded bra on—that kind of build never came with tits. She was holding in her hand a bottle of cheap water that had probably been filled from the tap. The skinny legs aroused him. It could be over in a matter of a minute or two. All he'd have to do is get her on her knees and tell her to go to it. Wouldn't even have to take off those shoes. Wouldn't want her to come to that. Twenty-five, thirty tops in this small town. In the major cities it could be up to a C-note for a few seconds of release.

A thin drizzle of the Grecian Formula dripped down from his forehead. She wouldn't probably even notice he had hair dye on, and if she did, she wouldn't mention it. That was the beauty of bought sex. And anyway, it wasn't like they were gonna kiss or anything. It wouldn't be a bad way to pass the time while the dye did its thing.

"Hold on," he told her. Then he went for his wallet, hesitated for a moment or two, and withdrew a few ones. Back at the door by then, he shoved them through the small opening, took the bottle of water, and shut the door in her face.

Later, after a shower and a futile attempt at watching TV, he was lying in the dark, trying to rest his eyes, calm his nerves. It was too early to sleep, but not too early to relax. He had sworn off pills, which made him dull the next day. With Sarah he could relax. Next to her in their safe, clean bed he could relax and he could sleep, like a weight of ten thousand bricks was on his chest. First time in years he had slept like that. Maybe ever in his life really.

The fucking room was cold—that was the trouble. The singer turned on the bedside lamp and got out of bed and went to his suitcase for a sweatshirt and a pair of socks. Always better to have your feet warm when you're trying to doze off. His address book was also in his suitcase. He opened it now at the M and gazed at the 212 number that he had written down over a year ago by now. He put the book down with the page open and went for his Kools, lit one, and came back to stare at the number. Maybe it was finally time to know. Probably all he had to do was say who he was and she'd start doing the talking. Women liked to talk and they liked to ask questions. He'd answer all her questions and then he would finally be able to ask the ones that had been burning in his heart all these years: "You were there, you must have been there because she was. Why else would you be there? The one white person at that sit-in who wasn't a cop? You knew Lavina. Why, you spent more time with her than I ever did. Tell me, why did my mother die like that? What made her do it?

LAUNDRY ROOM

❧

The VCR was on when I returned to my father's bedroom sometime later. The light from it flickered on his face; the rest of the huge room was in shadow. Even so, I could see his black silk pajama shirt was hiked up and entangled in the sheets. There was a syringe in his hand.

I watched him drop the thing down on the cluttered bedside table as casually as though he was dropping loose change. He flicked off the VCR and flashed me his yellow smile.

"Don't mind me daughter, I'm just a dyin' Dilaudid addict."

"That's morphine, isn't it?"

"Would you like to try some?"

"I think I'll pass."

He laughed. "Darlin, my late wife Margaret was very fond of Dilaudid. The last months of her life she'd lie here in this bed and say, 'Jack, give me de lordy.' That was her name for Dilaudid. She grew so fond of her injections, why, the doctor and I had to limit her. It's a shame you never met Margaret; she was a fine woman."

"And does the doctor limit yours?"

"Men don't suffer from addiction like women do, Mary Jacob. Our pain threshold is higher, understand. No, my doctor knows I will not abuse my privileges. And if I do, well, I'm gonna die soon anyway. You know your papa's dyin', don't you Mary Jacob?"

I didn't say anything, I just looked at him. He patted the bed. His voice was suddenly hearty and cheerful. "Hop back up, Mary Jacob. Did you have your supper? Good! I want to hear all about what you're doing in New York City. Come on child, don't be shy, I'm your father, not the big bad wolf!"

The big bad wolf. As soon as he said that, I cringed, thinking of the wolf in the Granny's cap, the menace of the teeth and the jaw. Not wanting him to know I was scared, I took my time kicking off my shoes, and sat as far away from him as I could on the huge four-poster bed.

He was smoking peacefully, exhaling a long stream and a couple of artful smoke rings up into the air.

"You're dyin' for a cigarette, aren't you child?"

"Yes."

"But you're not going to take one, are you?"

"Not if I can help it."

He laughed happily. "You were a stubborn little girl and now I see you've become a stubborn woman. I admire that, Mary Jacob, yes I do."

"How come you didn't then?"

I asked him this softly, but he answered me in a hearty tone. I wondered if he had rehearsed his response ahead of time.

"That's a good question, one I've given a lot of thought to, especially lately. It wasn't that I didn't like you, but the situation was difficult. Your mother was too ill to attend to you, and I didn't know what to do with you—you were stubborn and difficult, and you were dangerous."

"Dangerous?"

He was looking right at me. "It was a sad and terrible business, daughter, but it couldn't have been helped. I sent you away to school after that. I thought under the circumstances it was best for all of us. Especially since you blamed me for something that wasn't my fault. You know now it wasn't my fault, don't you, darlin'?"

He paused to look at my face. I knew he was right. That I had always blamed him for my mother's death. In fact, now I could remember calling him murderer.

My father was smiling at me, saying happily, "And I must have done the right thing, for look at you, child. Why, you're a fine upstanding woman up there in New York City with a son and a husband. You don't smoke and you don't drink much."

"I have a daughter too. She's my stepdaughter, but we're very close."

"That's right, I can't remember her name. Margaret always kept track of the names."

There were others things I wanted to say, "And I'm a writer too, Father. A well-known children's book writer who makes a decent living and I did it all myself with no help from you."

But I didn't say anything like that. How could I when he was looking at me like he was actually proud of me. As if he cared about me. As if we belonged together.

"Like I said, Mary Jacob, you're a fine upstanding woman married to some smart hebola. And you're a good mothah. I seem to remember that your husband's a deal older than you. Do you love him?"

"A lot of the time I wish I didn't."

He laughed at that. Then he looked at me sternly.

"Why didn't you name your son after me?"

"Hebolas don't name their children after the living."

His stern look was gone. I watched him take a long satisfied puff off his cigarette and smile.

"You were christened at Christ's Episcopal Church. You were named for my father. The Jewish race is conducted on the matrilineal line, therefore if you are not a Jew your son cannot be."

"The Jews are not a race. And our son's a Jew; he's studying for his Bar Mitzvah."

"I've heard of that. Margaret had a friend in college, a lovely Jewess, who visited us once, though of course, they weren't sorority sistahs."

"No, perish the thought."

"Now, now, Mary Jacob, I'll have no sarcasm in my room. I think it's perfectly understandable that you converted and that you now defend your religion. Tell me, I'm interested to know, did they anoint you with blood on the day of your conversion? In the old days, it was the blood of Christian children. Though I've been told the Hebrews now use animal blood."

Stunned, I asked my father, "You don't believe that do you? You're teasing me. Next you'll be telling me that Jews control the banks and the media."

My father looked genuinely confused. "Of course they do, it's a fact; books have been written on the subject by scholars, Mary Jacob.

But I can see that you're offended. You shouldn't be, especially when I believe it's only right and fittin' for a wife to take on her husband's religion. Perfectly right and fittin'. Now tell me about your son, the bright Hebrew boy. What's his name? I can't seem to remember his name. I wish Margaret were here to remind me."

"His name is Joshua and he's very bright."

"Like you, with his nose buried in some book all the time?"

"He's much smarter than I am and he gets a lot more encouragement because of that than I did."

"I sent you to good schools, child."

"You did."

"Why I coulda sent you to some Christian woman's college or to finishing school where they wouldn't have appreciated your fine hebola mind. But of course you weren't a hebola back then, were you?"

"I'm not a hebola now. I never converted."

There wasn't any reason to tell my father that I had wanted to convert, but Peter always laughed when I brought it up and told me that converts don't count; that anyway, there's no such thing as a Jew from Murpheysfield, Louisiana. "Besides," he always told me, "I like being married to a shiksa." We celebrated Jewish holidays at his mother's house, under her strict supervision. The Jews, I'd come to learn, were just as exclusionary as the Gentiles. I'd been informed, that next year at Joshua's Bar Mitzvah, I wouldn't be allowed to stand up next to him at the altar and say the Jewish prayers because I'm not a member of the tribe. But, why tell Jack Long that?

"You didn't pay enough attention to me to care where I went, if I remember properly. As for the hebola issue, it's tacky to make fun of someone else's religion, and you don't want me to think you tacky?"

Once again my father let out his deep, rich wonderful laugh like he really appreciated me, and the peculiar thing was, he really seemed to. And the stupid anti-Semitic slurs were just a way of teasing me. He felt comfortable enough to have a little fun with me. And that was hitting me too. That he was perfectly natural and easy with me. I was the one who was uptight, false, on the defensive.

"It wasn't that I didn't care for you, Mary Jacob. At the time, I was, how shall I say, young and prey to my earthly longings. Most women wouldn't understand what I'm talkin' about but somethin' tells me you do. You do understand, don't you darlin'?"

"Maybe."

He was looking straight at me and his delivery was polished and perfect. "'Thou hast committed fornication, but that was in another country and anyway the wench is dead. Yes that wench is dead and I shall miss her till the day I die.' Christopher Marlow, I believe."

My father was quoting Marlow in Van's honor. Somehow I knew Coco wasn't the object of this quotation. All these years later, if I remembered so little of most things, I could remember the two of them dancing in the big front room after dinner. I used to think they looked like a king and queen.

He sat up, reached for my hand, and squeezed it between both of his. His touch was already familiar. And felt good. Don't trust him, I told myself.

"You're nothin' like Kathryn," he was telling me softly. "Nothin' like your mothah. Still, I think there's somethin' of me in you."

"And what's that?"

"You know very well what that is, child."

"I don't unless you tell me."

He laughed. "You're a hard woman, Mary Jacob."

Why tell him I wasn't hard, I was scared.

"Yes, well, maybe that's what we have in common."

Jack Long laughed again. Then he let go of my hands to reach for his pack of cigarettes. I had to control myself from grabbing the hand back. Instead I reached for his cigarettes and the lighter beside it. I quickly lit it up and took a pull from the cigarette.

"You're turning green like a thirteen-year-old truant, Mary Jacob. Kindly use my bathroom if you need to throw up."

"This damn thing doesn't taste very good, I can tell you that."

"The next one will or the one after that."

He was staring at me again with his bright doped-up eyes.

"You're a good woman, Mary Jacob, a virtuous woman. I was thinking earlier this afternoon when you walked in here that my younger daughter is the only good woman I'm kin to. My mothah was a good woman, but you never knew her. It's a shame you never met your Grandmothah Long."

"I never met either one of my grandmothers. Can I change my mind and take you up on that drink you offered me before?"

"Certainly. Certainly. Will my whiskey do or would you prefer something else? We've got a whole cabinet of whiskey downstairs in the butlery. Your sistah thinks she's hidden the key from me, but I've got my own private key right here in this drawer. I'd get up and make you one myself, darlin', but de lord won't let me, understand. De lord won't let me."

"Your whiskey will be fine."

"Good. You know where my secret stash is. Careful pretty girl, don't shake the bed too much, de lordy don't like it when you shake the bed."

I was on my feet then, making my way toward the back of the room, to the bookcases where he kept his liquor. There, on the bottom shelf, something caught my eye: a large brown binding with faded gold letters. I got down on my hands and knees on the thick patterned carpet and reached for it.

I was holding in my hands *Mrs. Beeton's Book of Household Management,* smelling its musty book smell. It felt familiar, like an old friend, as many books do, though I had not held it or thought about it since childhood. I didn't need to close my eyes to see my small frail mother, beautiful even in her last days, lying ill in the bed where my father lay now. And me reading to her from the book I held in my hands, remembering her laughing in delight at the descriptions of the servants and their duties, the uniforms they wore and the elaborate entertaining they made possible. I had read to her so often we had called her Mrs. B. Or dear Mrs. B. My mother had loved to read. And she had passed that love of reading on to me. My reading led to writing and my career, and I could thank my long dead mother for that. I rested the book against my heart, happy to have a real memory, grateful to my mother. I was glad I made the trip down here—for this reason alone.

I crossed the room, set the book down on the end of the bed, and then went to my father's side. He reached out and then leaned into me, holding on. I thought of all the years we'd been apart. Those years seemed harsh—Michael, the marital therpist was right— the situation between us was sad. I had not been able to know my mother, but now at least, I could know him. We were different, but for better or worse, at least we could now be in each other's lives. He was my father, and I might even be able to call him that out loud.

He seemed to be thinking on the same lines.

"I knew you'd come child. I told myself, my daughter Mary Jacob will not forsake me."

"That book I laid down at the end of the bed, *Mrs. Beeton's Book of Household Management,* I used to read it to Mother, do you remember? Mother used to tell me her mother gave her the book, and her mother before her had done the same thing. It must date back to Victorian England."

"A family heirloom from your mothah's family, eh? That's what she told you?"

"May I have it? I'd love to have something from mother's family."

"Certainly darlin', of course take the book. There's plenty of other things you'll have as well. Your sistah plans to put me in a home, you know that don't you?"

I shook my head.

He was looking at me like a whipped dog. "I want to die here, in my own bed, where I belong. And I know I have no right to ask, but I need your help, Mary Jacob."

Our heads were close together. I could smell the sick, sour fumes of his breath. He didn't care about being my father. He wanted something from me. I wasn't surprised.

Still, I had a sense of what those words had cost him. I had the same proud blood running through my veins. Never ask for help. Never ask for love. I didn't want to say anything. For I knew when I did, they had to be the right words that could not be taken back. I owed my father that.

He was drifting in and out of consciousness; his eyes were open then shut.

"Mary Jacob, you mean what you say?"

"That I'll help you? I'm here aren't I?"

"You won't let her put me in a home? I can't live my last days out in a home, you understand that, don't you child?"

"Of course I do."

"And I have a dying wish. I'm entitled to a dying wish, aren't I?"

I nodded.

"I want you to find Van. It won't be hard. I want you to convince her to come here and let me see her. It's my last wish. It would do my old heart good to see the two of you here beside me. Then, I'll be able to go."

Tears were rolling down my cheeks, I didn't know exactly why I was crying. Because it wasn't about me? Because I didn't want him to die?

"Don't cry, pretty girl," he told me tenderly. "We'll talk tomorrow. I'm better in the mornin'. But stay here with me. Stay here with me, precious, until I fall asleep. I won't be afraid with you here with me."

I stayed there holding his hand till he fell asleep. And I stayed there staring at him long after his head went off to the side and his mouth drooped open and he no longer looked handsome.

⌇⌇⌇

At ten, I left him, dropping *Mrs. Beeton* in my room. I passed down the long upstairs hall. Though the house was dark, I didn't need to turn on the light, I could have walked inside those rooms blindfolded. Holding on to the curved banister, I made my way down the wide stairs, standing for a moment in the front hall where the light gleamed in the leaded glass fanlight above the door to the street. Off to the side of it was the huge front room and, though it too was dark and mostly in shadow, I was familiar in the dark as I made my way to stand beneath the huge Waterford chandelier: a magnificent tinkling orb as wide as the stretch of my arms. It shimmered when I moved below it. Moving on, I brushed against the tapestry chair in the corner and on through another set of doors, the ones leading to the library. I switched on a lamp. Everything was the same here too: the deep red leather couches; the glass-fronted bookshelves that stretched from floor to ceiling; the ship's bar, its row of fine crystal decanters with their delicate sterling silver collars that shined in the dim room. Everything shined in that house of beautiful things. Now I was in the corner of the room by the window, staring at the guns behind glass, four of them, knowing each one of them was different. You shoot a different kind of gun for birds, for deer, for rabbits. He even, I remembered, had an armadillo gun.

I began to feel afraid then, like on the plane only worse: a pulse throbbing in my throat, a sinking feeling in the guts, pain running up and down my arm. Sweat.

I ran from the room, as though I were running away from a shower of bullets. Through another door, along the length of the dining room and through the swinging door of the butlery to the kitchen and once again, like I had done this afternoon, to the laundry room: sanctuary.

There in the dark, simple things shined. The luminous dials on the washer and dryer and the moonlight that beamed in the window above the sink. A shaft of light ran across the maple rocker where I sat down and, without thinking, began to rock, as if the chair was waiting for me, the firm slats against my back—safe—in the one place in this house where I belonged.

DETECTIVE WORK

Reading for pleasure had been an unknown experience for Billy Ray before he moved in with Sarah and Connor. That he liked reading out loud at the end of the day, the boy sitting in his lap, turning pages, looking at words, was the pleasant discovery he had made while reading one of Mary Jacob's books. He didn't think it was just on account of the little detective being named Vina, though it did please him the detective was named for his mother, a poor ignorant colored woman who had never learned to read or to write. The little girl who loved to read was as smart as they came and always noticed everything around her. That's how she solved her mysteries. By looking around and noticing and by asking smart questions, sometimes trick questions. She was, he thought, just as smart as any grown up detective he had seen on TV.

The singer didn't know exactly what he was going to say. Though now he made a stab at a rehearsal. First would come the intro. He'd pause for a moment to let her take in his name. It wouldn't be hard. After the intro, he was sure Mary Jacob would do the rest. When he heard a young boy's voice pick up the phone in New York and say hello, he thought once more of that little girl in the books, the red bows in her dreadlocks.

"Hi, is Mary Jacob there?"

"No."

"When's she coming back?"

"Next week. Who's this?"

"I work for a newspaper in Atlanta. I wanted to interview her about her books."

"Do you want to speak to my father?"

"No need to bother him. Where did you say your mother is again?"

"Louisiana."

The kid pronounced Louisiana, not southern, but the way where you hear the Louise in it.

"Murpheysfield?"

"Yeah."

"Well then, I'll call her when she gets back, thank you." And he clicked off.

The singer sat very still, on the side of the bed with his phone in his hand. The thought that something like this would happen had never occurred to him—she had until now been at a comfortable distance. Close but not too close. This was something else entirely. What were the chances of them both ending up here in their home-town at the same time? Millions to one. He didn't like to say this meeting was meant to be. He didn't believe in the hand of fate; what happened, happened. She must be down visiting her folks. It was just a coincidence that they landed here at the same time. Her folks would be old by now, though white people didn't age as fast as black; everyone knew that. For a moment he felt that ancient rivalry that used to consume him when he was small, before he was somebody. He ought to be down here visiting his mother—and would be—if she hadn't been a colored woman born at the wrong time who just hap-pened to end up at the wrong place one day and got herself killed.

The singer continued to sit on the side of his bed at the St. James; he was dressed and ready to rehearse. He had done his stretches; he'd taken a decent shit. Best of all, he'd slept unexpectedly well last night—and he'd done all this clean. A good thing too, because wired, coming down, he wouldn't have been able to handle this news.

Still, he didn't feel entirely firm on his feet as he went first for his glasses and then for the desk off to the side of the TV. Before he opened the drawer he steadied himself, then he took out the phone book. Some names you never forget and Jack Long was one of them. He couldn't remember the name of Jack Long's wife. It was always *that Jack* who his mother had worked for. Jack Long who wrote her checks. Jack Long she had feared. Jack Long, in fact, who had gotten Billy Ray the only job he'd had other than being a singer. He hadn't thought about his brief career as a caddy in years.

No, the singer had never met the man whose name was seared in his memory. But all his life he had hated him. In his raggedy ass comedown room at the St. James all these years later, the hate was still inside him. Love didn't live. The singer could not remember his mother's love, though he knew his mother had loved him. Love didn't stay with you. Only hate did. He could feel it throbbing in his temples, in the ropey muscles of his arms, hatred was alive and pumping through his body like his blood.

The girl who had saved his life and had loved his mother was there with Jack Long now, maybe even at that same house where his mother had scrubbed toilets and worked on her miserable swollen knees. A place where, had she just lived past that summer, he could have taken her away from. That's what always hurt the most. How much she had missed. How much he could have given her.

It didn't take him long to discover that it was in fact the same house on Fairfield Street. Rich whites knew how to hang on to their money. All these years later and everything was the same.

He'd been little when his mother went to work there full time. Little enough to have to leave him with the neighbor for the first few years. One summer morning when he was eight and old enough to stay by himself, he had convinced her to let him ride the bus with her to work.

"Sugar, they is not that kind of house; she tole me that the first day I come to work there."

"I'm not comin' in, I just wanna see where you goin' every day. I'll go back home just like I come."

And so instead of watching her set off down their dusty street with her wig on, carrying her pocketbook, sometimes with an umbrella to keep off the heat, he had gone with her to the bus stop. And he had been thrilled, sitting with her and all her friends in the bright cotton dresses they wore to work. Colored women changed into their uniforms once they reached work; on the bus they still looked like colored women, not just like colored maids. Her friend Noog had been on the bus. And he had been little enough that summer to still enjoy sitting on Noog's lap with the hot summer breeze on his face, down King's Highway, which he knew, then along streets that he had never seen, and finally to where the white people lived.

Noog was almost the first one out. Then, one by one, the other women from his neighborhood waved goodbye and left. They were all alone on the bus, when it come time for his mother's stop. She had tried to get him to stay on the bus and ride back home. But he had insisted on seeing where she worked. They walked off the bus and down the deep green street, where the houses were bigger and grander than anything he could have imagined. One after another they passed the places where white people lived, houses that seemed glorious enough to house the angels. Finally, at the driveway of the biggest whitest house, she stopped, took him by the shoulders, shook him a little, and told him in a harsher voice than he was used to that now he had to go home. Before he did, he took in the gleaming place where the windows shined and the huge trees shaded the lawn and the grass looked soft enough to sleep on. He had been amazed that this is where she went everyday and more than a little envious.

The singer consciously brought himself back to the present. You learn that before you go on stage. Before you do an interview. You learn to check in with your body. You learn to breathe. You learn to see the audience at a distance but be one with it.

Today he'd go there. It had to be today. He would have to call her first. Tomorrow they were headed early for New Orleans. In an hour or so, they'd pile in the station wagon and head for the Riverhouse where local musicians were scheduled to meet them and rehearse. Often the local backup guys were good. Everyone big and small had gotten their start that way. He'd see how it went, take them through their first few sets, then he'd drive over and see her. The singer told himself that the real thing was a having a good show in Murpheysfield. Murpheysfield would be practice for N.O., when it would really count. But he also knew he was faking himself out. The real thing was seeing her. And putting all them years behind them.

The Riverhouse, where the gig was, had not been in Murpheysfield in his day. He'd only played one club; after that everything had gone so fast. It was only now, since life had slowed down, could he see how fast the years had gone. Though he couldn't remember the name of the club where he'd had his first live appearance, he could see it plain as day: the ugly little shanty on the lake, no more than just a lean-to on pontoons. Funny word, "pontoon," sounded like "poontang."

The singer played with the word "poontang" for a moment. It didn't work with anything—it was a stupid word. No song he would ever write would ever have "poontang" in it.

He was back on the bed, staring at a long zigzag crack on the ceiling that had some ugly, rusty brown stain around it. He took a long, satisfying swig of water. He'd have to go stock up on Evian today. They wouldn't have it at the colored stores; he'd have to venture out to the white neighborhood. It was a better friend than drugs and he was faithful to it. Back in his day, he had been a vigilant addict. As the lines got fatter and fatter, them plus the Quaaludes and Demerol to balance them, he'd always measured what he took in. How many hits off a joint or how many downs it took to sing him to sleep. Made himself eat a little too. Not the way Sarah fed him, though he'd never been like them who never ate and let their gums bleed; the ones who'd hoover their way through bags and bags, never measuring how much they took in. Or how much booze or pills they swallowed. He'd always gauged his dose. Used a little bottle or a clean straw, never the dirty hundred-dollar bills the stupid show offs liked to use. Even at the height, he'd been careful. Increased scientifically. Took less when he went below a hundred and fifty. A tich more when he got past one fifty-four. Never did crack. Or freebased. His fear of fire wouldn't let him do that.

He punched the numbers for Jack Long's house.

A white woman's voice answered.

Even from the first "hello" he knew she wasn't who he wanted. The voice was harsh and very southern. Not a woman he'd want anything to do with. He hoped he wouldn't have to deal with her when he went there. A voice told you everything. That voice did not belong to the girl who had saved his life.

"I'd like to speak to Mary Jacob, please." He was using a rich white voice—anything connected with sound was easy for him—and it worked like a charm.

"Why Mary Jacob cain't come to the phone. Who may I say called?"

"A friend from out of town. I'll call back later, ma'am."

"Are you sure you don't want to leave your name?"

"No ma'am, I'll call back. Thank you very much, ma'am."

"Why certainly, toodle loo!"

A FRIEND OF YOURS CALLED

~

Kathryn was looking me up and down, frowning.

"Where have you been, for God's sake, Mary Jacob? We went lookin' for you this morning. What in the world are you doin' runnin' around town like that?" My sister was smoking at the kitchen table. I could feel the effects of my two cigarettes from the night before when I ran this morning. Still, I was tempted to grab her pack and lose more lung capacity.

"What do you mean?"

"Those short shorts with your mannish legs."

"My, my, do you think people will say I'm tacky or in trade or I advertise in the phone book?"

Kathryn's eyes widened. "Who said anythin' about advertsin' in the phone book? Daddy's a devil. He has no right criticizing my fiancé. Why Jack Long couldn't even make a living. He ran through all mother's capital."

My sister was fuming, the smoke coming out of her wasn't just cigarettes. She was still looking me up and down, giving me the evil eye. In spite of standing up to her, I was shaking inside, aware of my sweaty T-shirt with the baboon on it, of my muscled legs I was proud of, everywhere but here. In front of her I felt ugly and funny looking.

"Daddy's in his walker now in the upstairs hall. He won't like the way you look either and will be ashamed you went out in public like that. What do you think of him, by the way?"

"I feel sorry for him."

Kathryn laughed contemptuously.

"Sorry for him? Daddy's the last person I'd ever feel sorry for."

"He's pretty sick, Kathryn, and he's taking an awful lot of drugs and booze. Doesn't the doctor tell him all that boozing and drugging is bad for him?"

"For God's sake, Mary Jacob, the drinkin's the least of it. Besides, he's been takin' those shots for years. He and poor Margaret used to stay up there in that room high as—"

I pointed my finger at my sister. "Don't, Kathryn, I'm warning you."

My sister's hands were tiny, little claw hands, feminine versions of our father's hands, with bright red tips. She was drumming them like castanets against the wood of the table top. She was mouthing, "n-nnnnn."

We stared at one another practically hissing. Then the moment passed. Perhaps Kathryn thought better of it. She blew a smoke ring. As I was heading toward the swinging door, she called out in a casual voice,

"A friend of yours called a few minutes ago."

I turned around.

"Vincent?"

"No. He didn't leave a name."

"It was probably Peter."

"I'm quite sure it wasn't your husband. Doesn't he have a Yankee accent?"

Peter's voice is as New York as a bagel and cream cheese. I always try and sound like he does, but it's never any good; no matter how hard I try, my cornbread background always comes back to haunt me.

"No, this was a southern gentleman. He said he was from out of town."

I felt my sister studying my face. "Yes, as a matter of fact, he said he met you on the airplane. That y'all chatted at the Hertz counter. Why are you staring at me like that, Mary Jacob? if I didn't know better, I'd think you were scared. Are you scared of some southern gentleman you met at the airport?"

I shook my head lamely.

"Well I could swear you were." Kathryn laughed. "Anyway, he told me to tell you he'll call you back real soon. Anytime now."

I stood there saying nothing, picturing the big red lush at the airport. *Bye bye Mary Jacob, toodle loo.*

"Before I forget, when I went in your room lookin' for you this morning, I saw Mrs. *Beeton* in there. I have fond memories of her. Don't plan on takin' that book back with you to New York. I was with Mama when she bought it at Caine's Antiques. We got it the same day as we bought our Clementines that are now worth a fortune; I have mine in storage."

"What are you talking about? That book belonged to mother's mother, and to her mother before that. It's a family heirloom. You got the jewelry; all I want is that book!"

"That's my book, Mary Jacob. Mama and I got it together at Caine's Antiques. It was the last time I remember going out with her before she got sick. Take any old book you want; there's more than you can count in the library. But that's my book. I won't let you steal it."

Well see about that, I thought melodramatically, and high tailed it out of the kitchen, through the butlery, the front hallway, and up the stairs, taking them two at a time. Toward the end of the long second-floor hall, I saw the tall frail figure of my father in a dressing gown holding on to his walker. One of his quivering hands held a cigarette.

I was glad to see him. He felt like an ally. It didn't even feel strange that he seemed glad to see me too.

"My, my, if it isn't the goddess Diana herself. Darlin' you look like one of those exercise girls on the television set in the morning. Your stepmother Margaret and I used to watch them. But I swear I never thought to meet one in my own upstairs hall. Take off those dark glasses and let me see your face, pretty girl."

I did what he asked, smiling at him. "Good morning."

He cast aside his metal walker and held on to my arm. I could tell by the way he held on to me, that he felt close to me. He was leaning on me, drawing strength from me. I wanted to spill the beans about the man at the Hertz counter. I told myself this battered old sinner would understand and be simpatico. I wanted to tell him about the book too. Hadn't he said he wanted me to have it?

"Have you had your breakfast, darlin'? No? There's some of those tacky frozen waffles without any sugar in them, but what you ought to have is some chicken eggs. Some chicken eggs with a rasher of crisp bacon. If you help me down the stairs, I'll make you breakfast myself."

"You don't have to make me breakfast. I need to take a shower and call my son and see how he's doing. But thank you anyway."

By now we were passing through the door of his bedroom.

"Well, Mary Jacob, when you call him, do it from my room. I'd like to say hello to my grandson, even if you didn't name him after me."

I was touched he wanted to speak to Joshua, even if he was twelve years too late. Still, it mattered to me. We had reached his bed by then. I was helping him to stretch out on the high four-poster.

Kathryn's shrill voice sounded from behind me.

"I see sister's takin' very good care of you, Daddy."

"She is."

Kathryn was by the bed now, flicking her ash into one of the full ashtrays on the bedside table.

She was telling our father as though it were the most natural thing in the world, "Sister made a friend on the airplane and he called her this morning to say hey."

Once again I was afraid to look at her face. I reached for one of my father's cigarettes; with so much secondhand smoke, how much worse would it be to actually smoke myself? I needed something to do with my hands. And to calm myself. It wasn't hard to imagine the man from the airport, smiling as he picked up the phone, asking for me. I could see the distorted Asian face he made yesterday from the doorway of the rent-a-car place. I wondered if he was a real psycho or just a practical joker. But a practical joker wouldn't call the house of a total stranger. A mere practical joker wouldn't carry the joke this far. It was just my luck, I thought, to have the one indescretion of my married life witnessed by a maniac.

My father was saying, "Mary Jacob hasn't had her breakfast. Since Annie's off today, offer her some nourishment, won't you?"

Kathryn squashed out her cigarette and, with her free hand, began twiddling a lock of her yellow hair.

"There's waffles in the freezer. I've got to take a shower now and lie down for a while. I'll bring you up your tray at lunch, unless of course you'd rather have Mary Jacob do that."

"Mary Jacob will do no such thing. I'll make my own lunch, Kathryn. Go have yourself a rest and make yourself pretty for that beau of yours. Has he asked you to marry him yet? Or are you two just gonna shack up here after you put me away in that home?"

"We're not gonna stay here, you know that, soon as we sell the house, we're all movin' to Atlanta like I told you."

"Have you told your sister what you have planned for me?"

My father was looking at me now like a whipped dog.

"Last week when I awakened from my afternoon rest, I saw a stranger in my room, one of those real estate vulture women peering around, snoopin' here and there. Why your mother and I bought this house together right after the war."

I looked at my sister who was standing apart, manifestly bored.

I heard a drawer rattling open and then a determined click. When I turned to look again at my father, he was holding a small gun in his hand.

"A man should not be torn from his home. It would be kinder to shoot me like some old horse." He gestured to Kathryn. "Here sister, why don't you shoot me?"

"Stop this!" I shouted. "Put that gun away this instant."

Kathryn said dully, "It isn't loaded, he's just trying to get our attention."

"I don't care if it's loaded or not, I won't be in the room with it."

Kathryn said, "Daddy, you heard what she said. Put that gun away."

My father looked at Kathryn then back at me. He leaned over and put the thing back in his bedside table.

"Now if you two lovely ladies will excuse me, I've got to talk to de lord right now. I'm takin' my injection in my groin so I need a little privacy, ladies."

⁓⁓

"Why should he sell the house? Why can't he stay here?"

"This doesn't concern you; this is between Daddy and I."

I didn't say "Daddy and me." Bad grammar was the least of my sister Kathryn's sins. I stood off by the side of her dressing table and watched Kathryn strip off her dress and drop it over a chair.

My sister had on the same fancy push-up bra and half slip from the day before. There was a large purple hickey on her left shoulder. She was heading toward the closet now, unhooking her bra and tossing it over another chair. She turned around as if she wanted me to see. Repelled but fascinated all the same, I took in my sister's new breasts. There was another large hickey near the nipple. Still Kathryn was obviously proud of the breasts, as if they were a pair of rare vases acquired at considerable expense. I wondered how much they had cost.

"Daddy's broke."

I nodded my head.

Kathryn's voice rose, gaining momentum, "That's why I'm sellin' the house. It has to be sold. The nursing home I've found for him makes you put down a perfectly huge sum of money. And it's got to come from somewhere. He's gone through mother's money. What Van and Coco didn't steal. He's gone through what Margaret left him. But I'm not gonna let him go through what little I have left. John's not a wealthy man and I'm not about to plop myself down in some tacky ranch house where my furniture won't fit while he's livin' here like a king. I've got to keep my capital and I have to live besides.

I kept nodding my head.

Kathryn began to shriek.

"And quit lookin' at me, you in your cheap clothes. Don't you understand everything has to be sold? All Mother's beautiful things. You can have *Mrs. Beeton*; I've reconsidered. I was just upset seein' her in your room without my permission. But you have to help me get him in the home."

"And what if he doesn't want to go to a home?"

"It's not up to him; it's up to me."

"If that's why you sent for me, to back you up, then you can count me out. I'm not going to put him in a home if he doesn't want to go to one."

Her hands on her hips, my sister stared at me scornfully. "Why would I send for you—you're of no earthly use to me. Daddy's been asking for you night and day for months. After that last coma of his, I called you from the hospital and you could've said no and stayed away like you have all these years. But you didn't. You're here. But that doesn't give you any right to go tellin' me what I should or shouldn't be doin' with my father."

"He's my father too."

"Fine then," she shrieked. "You take him. Take dear Daddy back with you to New York City or stay here with him and pay the air conditioning bills. Believe me, little sister, I'll be glad to have the whole thing off my back. And John will too."

"Don't get involved," Peter had warned me. "You're such a sucker for a hard luck story; the old man probably wants something. You'll come back and start screaming in your sleep again. You've been quiet for a while."

"You scream in your sleep too," I reminded him.

"Yeah, but I was conceived in a displaced person's camp. What's your excuse?" My husband hated my father, whom he had never met, and before I had left kept repeating over and over in front of Joshua about when we first knew each other, I was walking around with a big hole in my back tooth because I was young, didn't have a permanent job or insurance—or, more to the point, a father who I could turn to, even though he was rich.

Joshua had finally put his hands over his ears and cried out, "I'm sick of the tooth!" Still Peter kept seizing on it. "Your father never helped you out; you weren't much older than Lizzie when I met you."

I realized now, perhaps my father would have if I'd asked him.

My sister was pulling off the half slip. Underneath she had on a black garter belt and stockings attached to them. She unhooked them and pulled off the garter belt, tossing it down casually. Naked people are supposed to look vulnerable. Not Kathryn. She looked perfectly secure and happy and pleased with herself as she moved languidly toward her big high four-poster bed and stretched herself out luxuriously.

"Kathryn, do you know how I can find Van? He wants me to find Van."

My sister and her big boobs sat up.

"What are you talkin' about, he wants you to find Van?"

"He asked me last night. He wants to see her before he dies."

"Good Lord, Van! Just what we need! He'll give her all the furniture and there'll be nothin' to sell. Don't you dare call her, you hear?"

Kathryn lay back down. I couldn't help but notice that though she was flat on her back, her big boobs stuck straight up.

"I'm not gonna think about Van right now; I'm having a rest. Draw my curtains for me, won't you? Thank you so much. Pull the door closed in my sittin' room too please. And for heaven sakes sister, take yourself a shower. You smell like the locker room at half time."

BRENDA AND MARY JACOB

꩜

A place called the Riverhouse, he thought, ought to be somewhere with big windows looking out over boats with outside tables. But most places don't look like their name. A
lot of the time, the bigger, the fancier the name of the place, the
smaller and more raggedy-ass it turns out to be. The Riverhouse in
Murpheysfield was just a tan-colored brick building off a long tar
road in the middle of nowhere but pine trees. The sign above the
door had his name, Billy Ray. But no point in looking for a crowd
waiting there. This weren't the old days.

The three of them were leaving the van. He felt the chilly cool-
ness in the air that was blowing through the pine trees. The sky was
getting dark too. He watched Floyd and Steve lugging in the equipment, hoping no thunderstorm were gonna mess with the performance. Though in the old days, of course, all hell could be coming
down from the sky and the fans would be there soaked to the bone,
waiting for him.

The club was dark the way nightclubs always are during the day.
Still, he could see a good size dance floor and a raised stage with a
quality Japanese piano and new looking mikes. A decent bar always
classed things up and the place had this too.

Pimpy looking dude with short legs, too much curly hair, and
pointy-toe shoes nodded at him from the bar. The singer decided
he must be the manager. He didn't look like no owner. You could
always tell the difference. Sitting a few seats down from him was an
old light-skinned colored lady with her hands folded in her lap who
must be the maid. Still, the maid ain't supposed to sit at the bar, and
for a moment he was confused. The pimp guy was smiling and wav-

ing. The singer held up his hand to tell him to wait. He wanted to do his checking before he talked to the management.

In all the important ways, the Riverhouse passed his inspection. It wasn't some low down beer joint. There'd be a decent cover charge, though they'd cheat him. They always did. But a high enough cover brought in the right sort of crowd. Billy Ray went into the bathroom and checked it out. It also passed his test. When they put those mothballs in the urinal, it was a bad sign. The Riverhouse was small but respectable. He guessed it was the racetrack outside of town Floyd told him about that made a place like this possible. Probably it all had to do with the mob. The mob run Louisiana in the old days. The mob would front the money for a black nightclub in exchange for whatever they wanted out of the deal. No one else would.

Growing up, you almost never heard of a Murpheysfield black having money. Preachers had houses and decent wheels. But no real money. If you were a man, the best you could do is be some cook at some restaurant. Or a Tom at one of their private clubs. A head cook could make some money. They liked a black man, covered from head to toe in sparkling white clothes, holding a big metal spoon, smiling and stirring in the red pepper sauce. A funeral parlor could make money too. That's where the major money was made.

Once again he thought of the boy's question, much as he wished he could forget it. If Sarah got killed where the fuck *would* the little dude go? Before he split, he better get that straight with Sarah. He supposed it would be with one of her girlfriends. Though he didn't really like the thought of that. Sarah had cut herself off from her family when she left Connor's father. They had never come after her either. She hadn't said that her shacking up with a dark man had anything to do with it, but the singer knew it must. He guessed he'd keep Connor for a while. He wouldn't just throw him out, though what would he do when he went out on the road? The boy had never been to one of his performances. He had all the tapes and the singer had bought him a CD player a while ago, but he never had seen him live on stage doing his stuff. In the old days they used to let kids in clubs in Louisiana. Rule used to be if you were tall enough for your head to be above the bar, they'd serve you.

He was back in the nightclub area now. The Riverhouse was a black club. Whites could cross the line, but blacks would still have trouble. Even in 1993, black and white in Murpheysfield. New Orleans was different, it had always been different, at least if you were a performer. N.O. wasn't what you thought of as a real American town. First time he'd been there, he was fifteen years old. He'd gone straight from the sit-in to the bus for N.O. Had to put Murpheysfield behind him in a hurry. They had paid him five hundred dollars, which was a fortune. Back then his head was so full of music he thought it was gonna bust sometime. Years went by like that. Head filled with sound, body high or strung out. Being a star was great. The power it gave you. All you had to do was stand there and do what you wanted to do anyway. The money had been even better. Knowing you could look at something and it would be yours just by pointing your finger and telling the manager to go fetch it. His first manager made a fortune out of him. His second and third had too. Probably they all had the first dime they made off him. And the one who made it all possible, where was he? Living in some ordinary house in the middle of nowhere, with a two-slot carport. Still making payments on the car too. Jail had wiped him out. He'd been headed toward it. No use lying and saying he weren't headed toward it. Drugs started it, but jail finished him off.

He knew the only way out was a hit. His last song hadn't even gotten close. And the one before that hadn't either. Neither of them had come easy. Not like it was in the old days when the whole number would take shape faster than he could move his fingers. He'd had his share of arrangers, but he was the one who come up with the original song. A song starts in the brain. The brain tells the voice what to do. The fingers follow. Some line of communication had broken down. Something was always off these days. Billy Ray had been doing it for some many years that a lot of the time he could fake it. But you can fake yourself out only so long. When you've had your whole soul humming, no way you can tell yourself that it's the genuine thing when it ain't. And you can't fake them forever either. They liked the old songs, but they wanted new ones too. And if the new ones weren't as good as the old ones, they nailed you. Said you'd lost your touch. It wasn't your touch, it was your hum. But they don't know that.

He watched Floyd and Steve up on the stage setting up the equipment. The local backup guys were coming after lunch. He went to the bar and sat down. A few stools down, the maid was still sitting there, waiting for someone to pay her. Out of the corner of his eye, he saw her get to her feet. It came to him then this colored lady was old enough to have been someone who knew his mother. She looked in a way a lot like his mother used to. With a wig and some tired old cotton dress that stretched open around the buttons.

Now she was standing in front of him, smiling at him. He was glad about his nose not really working much. If it did, he knew he'd be smelling bacon grease and sweat.

"Billy Ray," she was saying in a soft voice, one that was softer and younger than what she looked like. "Billy Ray, I'm Brenda. You remember me, don't you?"

He shook his head. She probably was one of his mother's old friends. This wasn't Noog. Noog, he would remember.

"I was your first girl," the old lady was saying. "You took me to Shreveport."

He shook his head at her. "I never took nobody to Shreveport. You got me mixed up with somebody else, woman."

He dug in his pocket to hunt up his wallet. Probably the old woman wanted cash. He couldn't deal with why else she'd be here. Women, they say, aged a whole lot faster than men, but not this fast. It couldn't be possible that this old woman was the same age as he was.

She kept on standing there in front him smiling sweetly, so sweetly it was making him angry.

"I don't want your money, baby, I just want to say I wish I'd never run off from you in Shreveport."

He stood up. And offered her a twenty. The woman smiled and shook her head. Something about the smile reminded him of his mother. Something sweet and sad and worn out. If this old woman didn't want money, what did she want? In the old days, girls threw themselves at his feet. Hundreds had thrown their bodies at him: naked bodies, fine bodies, young bodies. This was the first time somebody old had made a play for him, which meant that she was probably speaking the truth, this Brenda. And that meant that he was old too. Small-town hookers and million-year-old women. Without the hum it had come down to one or the other.

The singer offered her the twenty again. When she refused he upped it to forty. But old Brenda just shook her tired wigged head and smiled. And pretty soon, she turned and headed toward the door.

When enough time passed, where he wouldn't have to see her in the parking lot, he headed for the van.

According to the map he'd consulted downstairs at the St. James, he didn't have all that far to go. This wasn't like Atlanta where one huge suburb ran into the other, going on forever. Murpheysfield was still just a one-horse Louisiana town.

He was passing a diner, a dry cleaner, an old-fashioned looking Italian restaurant, beer joints and places that served po' boys. He'd forgotten po' boys, a specialty of Louisiana. Po' Boys and crawdads. Special kind of doughnuts too. Connor would love it all. He made a left turn and soon he was out of the business district and into the residential area. The trees were getting older and bigger. So were the houses. In no time at all he was turning into Fairfield Street.

He stopped the van in front of the house next door to the big white house but he kept his eyes on it. All these years later it was downright dingy and sort of like the St. James in a way, a place that had seen better days. The wide front lawn was more dirt than grass. And it had needed a paint job years ago. He turned off the engine. The neighborhood was so quiet and peaceful he could hear the sound of his own breathing. With his eye on the maroon economy car parked in the driveway, he waited behind the wheel.

He didn't have to wait long. In less than a quarter of an hour, he saw her coming out the back door, headed for the maroon sedan. She had dark hair like the picture of her on her books, and though the sun wasn't out she had on her shades. She was slim. Nothing all that special about her appearance. She walked fast. She dressed like a city chick. Her looking like that somehow reassured him.

When she turned out of the driveway, he waited for a moment, then stayed a little behind her in the quiet suburban streets. It would be better, he knew, to run into her, make it look like it just happened, that it was the most natural thing in the world.

When they reached the shopping center, less than a mile away, he turned in and parked a few slots behind her. It couldn't have been better if he had planned it.

OUT IN MURPHEYSFIELD

K athryn and my father were both asleep; it might as well
have been the middle of the night. I had that creepy mid-
dle-of-the-night feeling too, being alone in the huge house
on the quiet street. Outside the sky was turning dark. Stepping out
the kitchen door, I could smell rain in the air. I went back in the
kitchen and called Vincent from the wall phone. I wanted to tell him
my idea for a book called *The Secret in the Broom Closet.*

"So, what do you think?" I said at last. Vincent was quiet. I could
tell he was turning my idea over in his mind.

"I don't know darling, I think I'd rather do the secret in the butler's
pantry. It would be more fun to draw. I assume there's a butler's pantry."

"Yes," I laughed, "of course."

"My mother's was huge. She didn't have a butler though, just
some tired old black man named Wilbur who drank her good scotch
Does Big Daddy have a butler?"

"No. The woman who works here is some darling old thing who
calls me Miz Mary Jacob like it's fucking *Gone with the Wind.* I'm
sending the NAACP a donation as soon as I get home."

"How is Big Daddy?"

"I sort of like him."

"Really? That's a switch but I think it's cool honey. Tell me about
him; what's he like?"

"Colorful, intense, he's an old degenerate. But we like each other.
I can't tell you how bizarrely wonderful it is to have a straight man
other than Joshua approve of me."

"You don't have long with Joshua, I hate to tell you. He's already
got a little mustache; pretty soon he'll start acting like Peter. Probably

right after the Bar Mitzvah. Maybe that's what all the Hebrew is, instructions on how to torture women."

"Vincent, don't say that!"

"I'll always love you, Mary Jacob."

"I love you too, Vinnie. There's something else too . . . I was sort of fooling around with this guy on the airplane. And some weirdo was spying on us and now he's calling here looking for me."

"You were *what?*"

"This gorgeous man was sitting next to me. We started talking, you know what they say, one thing led to another . . ."

"You joined the Mile Hile Club! I always knew you had some gay male in you."

"No Mile High Club, honey, we just messed around. Quit embarrassing me!"

"What did he look like?"

"Gorgeous! Slim, Asian, coal-black hair like silk, one earring. Younger than we are."

Vincent was chortling on the other end. "Mary Jacob, I'm proud of you. It's time someone other than Peter had a little fun. That's why you did it, you know. To get even. Did you exchange numbers?"

"No."

"I can't get over it. You being wild. You're always such a good girl."

"Well, I'm not cut out for this." I explained to Vincent in detail what had happened at the counter and then the guy calling on the phone and speaking to Kathryn.

Vincent sighed.

"You didn't talk to the guy when he called the house. Just your sister?"

"Yeah."

"How's she?"

"A royal bitch. And that's putting it mildly."

"It's probably nothing, just a redneck weirdo, but be careful, Mary Jacob."

We were both quiet for a moment.

"My father's given me a dying wish too."

"What's that?"

"He wants me to find his second wife, you know the one I liked, the beautiful girl Van?"

"The one who bought you clothes."

"Yes."

"Are you going to do it?"

"Why not? Kathryn mentioned she owns a store in Dallas. She probably won't be hard to find."

We talked a while more then hung up. I called our apartment in New York and left a message on the answering machine. Then, I left the house and drove to where I remembered was the main shopping place.

∽∽

Remarkably some of the stores were the same—the stationery store and the hardware store and a shop called Southern Gifts. And I was in luck. Not only was there a big chain grocery store, the strip even had a bookstore. I went to it first.

"Where's your children's literature section, please?"

I asked this of the nice-looking woman behind the counter who was very fashionably dressed in a beautiful blouse.

"Follow me and I'll show you." She came around the counter. I saw she had a well-cut black skirt and nice leather shoes with her pretty blouse. This was no small-town outfit. She would be right at home in New York, I thought. She left me to peruse the children's books. I did so, seeing the standard fairytales, picture books, and an unusual amount of biblical themed books. I carefully checked. I wasn't represented. If they had carried me, would I have taken one home to my father?

I went back to the counter.

"Have you ever heard of a young reader series by Mary Jacob with illustrations by Marino?"

"No ma'am. I don't recall seeing that author. You say it's a series? Would you like me to look it up?"

"Sure," I replied.

"Here it is," she said presently. "There are several titles in the series. Do you have a particular one in mind? I can get it in, say, in two weeks or so."

"No, I'll be gone by then."

I turned to leave. Halfway to the door, I had an idea. And turned back around.

"It's obvious you care about your clothes. When I used to live here, a long time ago, all the fashion-conscious ladies used to drive to Dallas to shop at Neiman Marcus. Is it still the same now?"

The woman behind the counter touched her blouse.

She smiled. "We still drive to Dallas, but these days we all go to a store that's called "The Collection"—in fact a former girl from Murpheysfield owns it, Van Long."

"The Collection?"

"That's right."

Next stop, the grocery store. I wasn't used to big suburban grocery chains with wide aisles. Back home I shopped at a small green market, I had a butcher, a fish store, a bakery where I bought bread and desserts, and I took the bus uptown when I needed cheese and coffee. Here, there was just the one grocery store where everyone shopped.

I was standing with my cart in front of the salt-free foods reading labels when I felt someone behind me. I turned around.

A few feet away from me stood a very handsome African American man, someone around my age, I guessed. He was carefully, expensively dressed and he was staring at me as if he knew me. Our eyes met. I studied his face a moment, but although he seemed familiar, I couldn't recall how I knew him. His cart was filled full of Evian water and fruit. He must have had more than a dozen liter bottles.

I was about to say something, when he shook his head, turned, and quickly wheeled his cart away. I told myself I must have met him at a book signing. He had brought his son or daughter to one of them. We've been all over the country. As far south as Atlanta. He didn't look like a Murpheysfield native. That had to be the explanation. Like me, he was in from out of town; like me, he was visiting a sick relative or a friend. What kind of relative wanted a shopping cart full of Evian water? I couldn't think of an answer to that one.

∽∽

I don't remember checking out or driving home. Next thing I was aware of was being back at my father's house in the kitchen. All the groceries were spread out on the table and I was at the sink submerging a bunch of not very fresh rosebuds I had bought at the grocery store, about to weight it down with one of the big cast iron pans. I had read about this last night in Mrs. *Beeton* and I was wondering if it would work.

Letting the flowers soak, I ran upstairs to check on my father, but from the doorway I could tell he was sleeping. Afterwards, I made myself a strong cup of tea and sat with the *Murpheysfield Times* at the old wooden table in the kitchen. Turning the pages, I came on it, in the entertainment section. It was a picture of the man in the grocery store. He had looked familiar because he was famous. He was the singer Billy Ray. By then, I was starting to shake. My tea cup rattled. My knees were shaking too.

I tried to calm myself by closing the paper and folding it neatly. I checked my hands for ink. I checked them over and over. Practically everyone in America of a certain age knew Billy Ray. When you like someone's work that person feels familiar to you, even close. But Billy Ray had seemed to know me, and that connection was what I was trying to explain to myself. All my books have a picture of me on the inside back cover, though I am by no means famous. Still, when I arrive in town for a book signing, that picture runs in the paper. But it was the dream I was thinking about. The dream that's been with me forever, though I am sometimes young in the dream and sometimes the same age I am when I'm dreaming. In the dream, Billy Ray and I are passionately kissing. And that was what was making me shake, how the dream was so much a part of me, as integral as the color of my eyes or my desire to write.

෴

When the phone rang, I jumped.

"Hi Mom."

"Joshua! Joshy! I'm so glad it's you,"

Joshua was breathing heavily into the phone. I knew right away something was wrong. My son almost never calls me mom. Like Lizzie, he calls me Mary Jacob. When he calls me "mom" he's sick or someone has hurt his feelings. Lizzie calls me "mom" then too.

I listened to my son's breathing, comforted by the sound of it.

"Talk to me, Joshy!"

"I miss you," he said. It sounded like I hate you. But I knew my son didn't hate me. Just hated missing me.

"I miss you too. And I love you a million."

There's no such thing as love. Only evidence of love. Cocteau? He wasn't saying he loved me back. Why should he when I wasn't there to love? I heard the familiar computer music that was a background to my life at home. Joshua didn't watch much TV. But my son was hooked on his computer. It worried me. Staring at the small screen had to be bad for the eyes and his eyes were bad already, like mine. His current favorite was some kinky S&M game called *The Prince of Persia*. Peter had set up a soundboard for Josh that piped the electronic music all over the apartment. I listened to it now. It sounded like some low down strip show was going on in his room. In no time at all, Josh would be bringing girls back to his room. I wondered how he'd treat them. Like his father? The hootchie kootchie music droned on.

Things were better at home, though last year Peter had been lying and cheating and not even bothering to cover his tracks. I had gotten so used to it I was still, as they say, holding my breath. But Vincent was right; of course that's why I got even and messed around with a stranger on the airplane. It was pure revenge. Revenge with a soupcon of lust, of course. And maybe as much as that, the pleasant little interlude gave me something to do with all my feelings. Wasn't I entitled to have feelings? Everyone else seemed to have them in abundance, why not me for a change?

Peter's affair seemed to be over and the midlife crisis under control. He had broken down and confessed the whole thing to me, not that I had been surprised, not that I hadn't known just by the way he smelled. For a while, my husband wasn't coming home; a couple of times he stayed out all night. If that hadn't been enough to tip me off, he acted guilty and once or twice his girlfriend actually called our apartment. Peter claimed he didn't want to leave us, it was all a mistake; he went crazy. He wasn't cheating anymore, I could tell he wasn't. But now he was having trouble with Josh. They fought all the time. Some of the fighting had to do with the fact that Josh was growing up and wasn't so easy and yielding anymore. It had been the same with Lizzie. Peter picked on Josh as he picked on Lizzie.

And every time my husband and I fought about it, I waited for him to cheat to get even.

Maybe because Peter's ten years older than I am, he's always had the upper hand in the relationship. Though now that I'm older myself, and have a little money of my own, I'm better at not letting him get away with his power trips. I moved in with him when I was twenty-two. We both worked in advertising: I wrote ad copy; Peter directed commercials. He still does. Lizzie was little when I moved in. Her mother had gone back to Sweden a couple of years before that. She and I fell for one another big time. After I was able to quit advertising and start writing books, I thought I had the perfect life. Vincent and I worked, went on occasional book readings. There was plenty of time to raise Lizzie and make a home for everybody. If I needed extra money, I taught a course on how to write children's books. I didn't mind staying home with Lizzie. I'd fallen in love with her as much as with Peter. I wanted to be the mother she and I both never had. And I succeeded. We adore each other and still talk all the time. We had Josh when I turned thirty and Peter turned forty. A few years later, Peter's father died and that's when it really hit the fan at our house. Oddly enough, Peter had never been close to his father, a refugee who had lost most of his family in the camps. But his death brought on a serious depression, a gun license, three firearms, and an affair—the affair and the guns have always seemed connected—the banging I suppose. By the time the whole thing came to a head, our marriage was almost over. These days, there's marital therapy and trying to patch things up. Peter says he wants to, but I don't know if I do anymore and have told him that. My not knowing has made my husband interested. He's on his toes now; sometimes he even brings home flowers and will ask how my work is going. My playing hard to get may save my marriage. Love and understanding—something I used to give him in abundance— apparently wasn't that much of a turn on. If I stop the game, though, will he stop being interested?

The hoochie kootchie music droned on. Josh was still breathing heavily.

"Honey, talk to me."

"I'm in the middle of a game."

I could see the princess with her big firm boobs and the hour-glass throwing down grains.

"Joshy, turn down the music, honey."

"I just died and I haven't gotten to the third level."

"What's the third level?"

"The third level has the pointy things sticking up. If you die on the third level, the moochers stab you in the stomach."

"What if you live?"

"It's never happened. I've never gotten that far. It's the hardest game I have. I wish it weren't so hard."

"I do too. May I speak to your father?"

"He's not here."

"Who's there with you, Joshy?"

"No one."

"What do you mean, no one?"

The line at the other end was silent except for breathing. Finally my son said, "We had a fight and he said I had to stay here because he didn't want to run errands with me."

"When's he coming back?"

"I don't know. We're supposed to go to Brooklyn, but he might change his mind. He told me that."

"Are you okay?"

"Yeah, sort of."

"How long have you been there alone?"

"For a while."

"I'll talk to you until he gets back."

"Okay."

"What's the weather like?"

"Cold. I wish I could get a hat that doesn't itch. I'm going to order pizza if he doesn't come back. I have twenty dollars in quarters. Plus the money you left me."

"He'll come back, sweetie."

"He said he might not."

"That was wrong and he won't do that. He was just trying to scare you."

"I know," Josh said, and he sighed. I heard some noise in the background. Then my son said, "He's home." I could hear Peter's voice in the background.

Josh turned up the music. Then I heard Peter.

"Hi, how's your father?"

"Never mind my father. How come you left Josh alone?"

"Just a second, I'm going in the bedroom. I can't hear over this fucking computer game."

The rain outside the kitchen window was still coming down in sheets. I stared at it wondering how long it was going to last. Feeling guilty also, that I'd left my son with his immature, out-of-control father who took his shit out on him.

Peter said, "Are you there?"

"I'm here."

"So how are you holding up?"

"I'm fine. But Josh was scared."

"Josh's not a baby, Mary Jacob. When I was his age I stayed by myself. Besides, he was impossible."

I knew very well who was impossible, but it wasn't any use pointing fingers over the phone, especially when he would just take it out on our son.

"So how are you holding up? You sound weird."

"I'm not weird, Peter."

"So what else is new?"

"Jesus Christ, can't you just behave for one day?"

"Quit busting my chops. We were having a fine time and then he went completely berserk at the hardware store. I brought him back here, went back to the hardware store for half an hour and now I'm home again. What do you want out of my life?"

The same thing I want from my father: love.

But I didn't say that. Instead, I stared out the window at the rain.

"My father's broke and Kathryn's going to put him in a nursing home. He doesn't want to go to a nursing home."

"Don't tell me your thinking of bringing him here?"

"Somebody's got to look after him."

"Is he really broke? Don't give him any money."

"I didn't say I was. But I'm worried about him, Peter. He sits up there in my mother's huge old bed injecting himself with morphine."

"It sounds charming, Mary Jacob. Like a Tennessee Williams play. Don't do anything you'll regret, okay? You owe him nothing. Remember that. Promise me!"

"I kind of like him, Peter."

"What do you mean you kind of like him? You've hated his guts your entire life. You haven't seen him in twenty years."

"Maybe I was wrong. Maybe I should have at least called him. We kind of get along now. It's strange."

"It doesn't sound strange to me. It sounds like he wants something. And you're playing right into his hands."

"Could it be possible he likes me. Just for me? Or is that too unlikely a scenario?"

"You're twisting around what I said. Look, why shouldn't he like you? You know the answer to that better than I do. Why hasn't he called all these years? Ask him."

"You think I'm crazy don't you?"

"Certifiably mad. But seriously, I want to say something and I want you to listen."

"Okay."

"Don't trust him. He fucked you out of a childhood. When I first met you, you were living on Avenue A—"

"I'm over Avenue A."

"Even so, why should you trust him?"

"I don't trust him. That doesn't mean I might not help him."

My husband sighed.

"We've got to get to my mother's house. You know how she is if I'm five minutes late. Too bad your old man's not a Jew. We could hook him up with my mother. What do you think honey? We'll buy him a fake nose and a glue on an Auschwitz tattoo."

I tried not to laugh.

"Come on, I hate going over there without you. I need you there to protect me."

"Your mother worships the ground you walk on."

"What's so good about that?"

"That's why you married me, isn't it? To have a Gentile to protect you from your mother?"

Peter was laughing. It was reassuring to hear him laugh—it reminded me of better times.

"I never liked nice Jewish girls."

I refrained from asking him, "Then why did you cheat on me with one?" Yes, that had come out too. His girlfriend was a wild Jewish girl who worked for another ad agency. Not his type really; he didn't really like her.

"Listen, did Josh tell you someone called here looking for you?"

"No."

"A journalist said he wanted to do an interview. I thought Alba handled that for you."

"She does usually."

"Well she didn't this time."

Oh," I replied. Peter didn't know Alba was in Europe. And if she had arranged an interview, would have told me beforehand. She would never give out my number. Was it the man from the airport again? If so, he knew a lot about me. Why was he doing this and when was he going to stop?

Peter was saying, "Well have fun, I gotta go to Brooklyn. "Take care of yourself, honey chile," he added in a fake southern accent. And then added "I love you," in his normal voice.

"I love you too," I replied. "And be nice to Josh."

⁓⁓

Mrs. Beeton was right. Thanks to her, I now knew how to revive rosebuds. I was walking back upstairs to my father's room with them gleaming in a vase, imagining her advice to me on my current dilemma. Impropriety. Should you be ill bred enough to commit an indiscretion in public and there is a witness, do not let the witness intimidate you. If he confronts you, stand your ground, and with a firm voice declare, "How dare you call my house. Kindly desist or I shall inform the authorities!"

But was I in danger? I am listed in the New York phone book under Mary Jacob Ascher, but how did he know I was from New York unless he'd gone back and questioned the woman at the Hertz counter and somehow obtained my number from her? I still couldn't figure out what this creep wanted out of me. It felt like a practical joke. But a practical joker wouldn't call the house of a total stranger.

A practical joker wouldn't carry the joke this far. I decided I'd call Vincent again as soon as I had the chance and discuss what to do.

Before I even got to the long upstairs hall, I heard the same strange music as before coming from my father's room. I knew now what it was even without hearing him laughing, "Take it off, that's a girl," as I entered the doorway. He was sitting up in his four-poster, too enthralled in his dirty video to notice I was in the room with him. Is this what I wanted on my hands?

"It's time to turn off the peep show."

He flicked off the switch and flashed me his yellow grin.

"Darlin' I beg your pardon. I've developed deplorable taste in my decrepitude. You'll forgive me, won't you? Are those flowers for me?"

"Yes."

I set the vase down. Deplorable taste in my decrepitude. How could I resist that?

"What are we going to do with you?"

He was looking up at me, still smiling. I saw that his pupils were completely dilated.

"I've been ruminating about the same thing myself, but there's one thing I have decided, I'm not going through with that kidney machine business."

"It won't be so bad. I'll go with you. It takes several hours, but I'll stay there with you."

I didn't say "and hold your hand." But I didn't need to; he had already reached for mine.

"I'm deeply touched, Mary Jacob, but you have your life up there with your husband and your son. Kidney poisoning is a kind death. Now that I've seen you again, I don't mind meetin' my maker. Bring Van to me. And seeing the two of you, I'll die happy."

"Promise me you'll go for the first treatment. We'll go together. The two of us. I'll drive you there and when it's over I'll bring you back here. Don't worry about the bills right now. Kathryn and I will work it out. Concentrate your energy on getting well, you hear?"

"Sister, you're gettin' your southern accent back. A few more days down here and those Yankee kinfolk of yours won't be able to understand a word you say. Why you'll be a genuine pariah."

I laughed. "But you'll do what I ask, won't you? If it's Atlanta you're worried about, don't. We can work something out, we really can."

"What do you have in mind? Some well-run Yankee nursing home up there in New York City?"

"I don't know what I have in mind, but it isn't that."

He was squeezing my hand. Nuzzling it.

"Like I've been tellin' you, Mary Jacob, you're a kind woman, a virtuous woman. But that doesn't surprise me. You were always championing the underdog. Still, I'm not really sure I want to let you do that. Better you say goodbye and remember me the way I want to be remembered."

"Maybe I don't want to say goodbye."

"I'll think about it, darlin'."

I headed toward the heavy curtains and threw them open. The rain had stopped. "Maybe we can take a walk outside. The fresh air will do you good."

He was laughing and it was a happy laugh.

"Yes ma'am," he called back. "Yes indeed, Miz Nightingale, lady executive, there's nothin' your patient would like more than a walk in the garden with you."

෴

It took me one phone call to Dallas information to find the number of Van's store. And she answered the phone herself. I had no trouble remembering her voice. Here was friend, not foe.

"Van, this is Mary Jacob."

"My word!" Her soft, low voice on the other end of the phone hesitated for a moment.

"My goodness, Mary Jacob, you've given me a start. How in the world are you?"

"I guess you could say I'm in shock," I replied honestly. "I'm here in Murpheysfield for the first time in twenty-something years. How could I be?"

Van laughed her soft, sweet laugh that was very appealing. I wondered if she was still beautiful.

"Just a second, Mary Jacob, I'm in front of the store; I've got to go in back and get a cigarette."

There was the noise of the phone being put down. And now taken up again.

"Do you remember when I taught you to smoke?" I could hear Van blowing out smoke. "I hope you've had better luck quitting than I have."

"I've started again since I'm back here. I don't remember your teaching me to smoke, but I remember you well. You are practically the only person I remember. You were always so nice to me."

"You were the sweetest little girl in the world. I often wonder what happened to you. Have you married?"

"Yes?"

"Children?"

"Yes, a son and a stepdaughter. She's off at college, but we're all New Yorkers. Everybody except for me was actually born in New York."

"Now that doesn't surprise me one little bit. You were always so smart. You must have a career too; you were such a smart little girl, always reading."

"I write childrens books. I even earn a living."

"Why, Mary Jacob, that's just plain wonderful. I'm so proud of you!" Van sighed. "I'm so glad you have a family. There's just Clyde and I."

"Who's Clyde?"

"Clyde's my best friend in the whole world, Mary Jacob, aren't you, Clyde? Here, Clyde, talk to Mary Jacob."

I listened for a moment or two, waiting for Clyde. Then Van got back on the line.

"Clyde is smiling, Mary Jacob, you should see his little face. Aren't you smiling, my little man?"

"Clyde's your dog, then?"

"Clyde's much more than a dog, my dear; he's smarter than most humans you meet. When we come up to New York for buying trips, you'll meet him then. They know him at the St. Regis. They let me sneak him into the dining room in my purse. We can't wait to meet everybody."

"Are you still beautiful?"

Van laughed. "Hardly beautiful at all, Mary Jacob. I'm forty-eight years old. I got my face done last year in Houston, but now I look sort of pulled, you know, I think I looked better when I just looked old."

Both of us were quiet for a second. I was already at ease with her on the phone, in a way I've never been at ease with Kathryn. It seemed perfectly natural to say after a moment,

"He's dying, Van. He's drugging and drinking and his kidneys are shot. He asked me to find you."

"Well, you've found me." She sounded almost pleased. "You know I knew his last wife? In fact, I knew the one before her too, the one who came after me. I was happy, though, when he married Margaret. I picked out her weddin' dress myself. I put the pins in her hem. She was a lovely woman and she was crazy about Jack. I was sorry when I heard she died. She was good for Jack."

"He still loves you. Will you come?"

I heard Van sigh.

"I'll drive in tomorrow morning—you can expect me before lunch. Is Kathryn there?"

"Yes, going for number five."

"She won't be happy to see me. Last time I saw her, she cut me dead."

"Her fiancé is in town; she'll probably be off with him the whole time."

"Mary Jacob, tell her I'm coming and that I'm looking forward to seeing her. You'll do that, won't you?"

"Of course."

"I can't wait to see you too, little sister!"

REDUX

~⌒~

The singer paid for his Evian and fruit and drove back toward the Riverhouse, playing the scene with Mary Jacob over and over in his mind. She had acted like she didn't know who he was. She had acted like they had nothing between them. Why had she not come up and talked to him? What was wrong with her? He was pissed at himself. That her reaction had shocked him into silence like that. Worst of all, he'd looked like a fool turning and running away. Not like someone who had been a performer all his life; used to playing for an audience of thousands. His timing had been off; he hadn't made the right moves. Probably he shouldn't have surprised her like that. He had caught her off guard, that's what went wrong. He'd fucked up by not doing the intro. If he'd started out right, then it would have gone how it should have gone. He could have said, "Thanks Mary Jacob, thanks for saving my life," found out about his mother, and put the thing to rest.

He was pissed at Mary Jacob, he was pissed at himself, and though it pained him to realize, he was most of all pissed at his mother—even all these years later.

Back at the Riverhouse, he parked the car and, on the way inside, looked up at the sky. It was dark and rumbling with thunder. Presently, the singer was sitting backwards on a wooden chair, listening to Steve and Floyd and the local backup play an arrangement of a song he'd written when he was just a kid. It was a good song, a pretty fucking great song and he'd written it before he'd turned twenty. A good song could take away your pain, but a good song could also make you feel the pain more. And it was true. At the back of everything always was the pain of losing his mother. Hadn't she robbed them both of the happiness that would have come had she lived? Good as she was, good as she'd always been to him, he could never forgive her for giving away her life like that. Only the stupidest, most ignorant trusting fool could have got herself talked into sitting down at some raggedy-ass Woolworth's counter in 1963—where she had no fucking business parking her tired old ass. Why hadn't she been thinking of him? He was just a boy back then. He had needed her. How was it that he, who had never been a father—who had gotten himself fixed years ago because he didn't want to be—knew a shitload more about being a father than she had of being a mother in the most important way? He'd never risk his life if the boy was depending on him. And Sarah shouldn't risk the boy's as she was doing either, by hooking up with someone like himself who was going away. And would break the boy's heart. Women didn't understand about boys who acted brave but were soft inside, as soft as girls, maybe more. Women, if the truth were told, didn't understand anything at all about anything other than women and women's things. That was what was wrong with them. They didn't get it.

The singer got up and walked toward the stage. He hadn't played his harmonica once on this tour, though Floyd kept setting it up as if he were going to. The boys stopped playing when he stood behind it, put his hands on it and began to breathe it to life.

As Steve played the piano and Floyd played the bass, and the new guys backed them up, the singer fell into his music. Every note was clear and distinct: the mellow glow of the sax, the driving rhythm of guitar, the sweet blast of the horn, the bright keys of the piano. They were playing as if all four of them had been playing together their whole lives. He thought then of a story he'd heard, old dude, one of the best musicians of all time, who went to a concert where they were playing his music, stone deaf. Heard every note of it too. No one but a musician could understand that hearing and playing were in your head and in your heart—sound was what happened, what the world heard. When you were a musician you were more than the music—your soul was in charge of the deal.

For the first time on the tour, the band was starting to cook. Billy Ray put his lips up to the mike and closed his eyes. They were playing "The One Who Got Away." And after that, straight into "Skin Deep," where he'd broken out of rhythm and blues and put some hard rock in. Without even thinking about it, he was putting his whole heart into the songs, hearing things in them he hadn't heard before. Somewhere in there, as though it had never left, as if it were his best friend come home after a short visit away, the hum arrived; the singer could feel it pumping through his body, in his throat, on his lips that made the harmonica sing. The boys behind him had the hum too. It was just like the old days: the whole world was humming. He looked toward the doorway, and the heavens were letting loose, rain was coming down; it seemed to him the sky itself had heard the hum.

A good song could make you forget your pain, but a good song could also make you feel the pain more. He knew all at once, he'd have to walk through brick walls of solid pain with his own unprotected body to keep the hum going. On his own he wasn't strong enough. He needed love to help him through. Drugs could numb you; for years he had walked through them walls with drugs. But drugs only worked for so long. And in the end, they chased the hum away.

He turned to the boys, nodded his head and with a sweep of his hand, told them to go on playing. He was covered in sweat, he'd soaked his shirt through. He went to stand in the doorway where it was cool. The rain was still coming down, pleasant and sweet, washing all the pine trees clean and turning the red dirt into rich black soil. He wanted to talk to Sarah. Wanted to talk to her as badly as he ever wanted to talk to anybody. He was grateful they had gotten the phones to stay in touch. Didn't know what he'd do without the phone. Best fucking investment he ever made, though he remembered now, it was her who gave him the phone.

He hit the numbers for her office. The machine with her voice picked up. But a machine couldn't cut it. Didn't sound like Sarah either. He clicked off, confused. He couldn't remember a time when she hadn't been there. All he'd have to do is hit a few keys and find her: simple. Five minutes went by. Seven minutes. How long did a pee break last? He wasn't in the habit of thinking of her as having a life apart from him. But now he could feel the distance between them. He sat for a few moments with the phone in his hands. Then he gave it one more try. He hoped the storm wouldn't mess with the fucking connection, but, no, the connection was fine, it was the person who he was trying to connect with who wasn't there. Same machine voice. No Sarah. He was stunned by his need to speak to her. Usually he didn't like that she was so easy to reach. She was too dependable and it bored him.

The boys up on stage were playing an instrumental leading off with "Diamond Buttons" and now, as if they could read his mind, a really old one, "Without You." He realized then she never called him, she knew better than to do that. Always been a one-way street with the two of them. A one-way street going one way: his way.

Fifteen minutes, twenty minutes, soon a half an hour had gone by and still no Sarah. Either something bad had happened, or maybe she didn't want him no more. His body was cool; he was starting to shiver. By now the rain had slackened off. If she threw him and his few raggedy ass things out on the street, where would he go? Who would play ball with Connor? A boy needed a man to play ball with. Women didn't get that either.

He looked out at the pine trees glistening with rain, feeling the fresh wind blowing sweet air in his face. A few cars were parked in the lot, but not fans' cars. This wasn't the old days when specially hired cops would be there directing traffic by now. Back then, the fans would line up a day ahead of time for tickets. Weren't no time to be lonely then. On the day of the performance, they'd be camped out, waiting since morning. In the old days, he'd arrive by limo at the last moment. Back then, they'd wait forever. Never did understand how patiently they'd wait there like sheep for him and his band. Used to have to sneak him in the back door to get away from the chicks who were waiting. Though guys would wait too. Keeping an eye out on their women like he should have been doing. Once they snuck him in, they'd do his hair, make up, spray his pits, zip his pants, powder his face, even hold the little amber bottle up to his nose. Didn't have to give the word—they knew when to hold it up. Back then they did everything but wipe his ass. Would have done that too, probably. All he'd have to have done is make it known that's what he wanted. All this going on, while the opening act got the crowd warmed up. Big break back then to open for Billy Ray. Lot of well known groups got a start heading off for him. He used to sit in his dressing room listening, telling himself the other group was getting them wet and excited. All he had to do is walk on stage to have them start coming like Fourth of July.

He called Sarah again. He thought of calling the daycare place and asking to speak to Connor. But he didn't know the daycare number. Sarah took care of the numbers. Sarah took care of everything.

He took the piece of paper from his pocket and then rang up the big white house again. Second time today, but he'd never called his mother, not once in all them years. To call her there would be to lay his weak body trembling on the ground for them to step on. He'd been hip enough even then to know not to be some whiny little black boy crying for his mama. She had called him sometimes in the afternoon, especially the first year she left him alone in the house to wait for her shuffling footsteps on the porch when she finally come home, tired and dark when the moon was up in the sky, after more than twelve hours and a bus ride besides. Smelling and sweating like a horse and they worked that woman like a horse or a mule. She had everything but them patches at the sides of her eyes.

This time, when the voice picked up, he knew it was the right voice.

"I'd like to speak to Mary Jacob."

"This is she . . ."

When the conversation was over and the singer clicked off, he wondered why he heard so much fear in her voice. Especially since he was the one who used to be scared of her. He could see that little picture of the girl on the shelf of his mother's room, where all the miserable treasures of her life were: the long slat of wood with the pink rusted candy box and that ugly white doll she called Pauline with the bright blue eyes and the frilly skirt. Kept her extra money hidden under Pauline's skirt. Five dollars was a fucking fortune to her. She never get on his back when he ripped off a dollar or two. That's the way she had been, always generous. Always sure her Lord were gonna see her through. Where had her Lord been that day? Or where had he ever been was more like it? There were several school pictures on that shelf of him and that one of Mary Jacob in her ugly black eyeglasses. Back then he used to wonder if the same sorry ass photographer came to both their schools. The pictures had looked so much alike, except for the skin, of course. It was always a matter of skin.

He was heading back toward the rich neighborhood. Once again he could feel the power of it coming at him, the big ass trees, the soft green front lawns, how long money had been here. No house he had ever owned come close to the ones he was seeing through the windows of the van. And he was rich years ago. No neighborhood of his had the huge trees. It was like the school pictures all over again. Things looked the same on the surface: a child's face looking posed, hands folded, eyes cast up to heaven, the ugly blue background, why all that were the same. It was the skin color that made all the difference. Always would too.

He felt that difference when he called her. And now in the van heading toward her, he was feeling the difference even more. He parked outside the big white house and waited, feeling shy like he used to feel shy before he'd walk out on the stage and blow them away. But in there, wouldn't be no harmonica to bring to his lips. What would he say? He had fucked up the first time. He did not want to fuck up again. The singer never felt comfortable shaking hands and this weren't the music business where you made a big ass show of a hug, even when you hated that person you were hugging.

He stayed behind the wheel studying the maroon economy car he had followed to the shopping center. It was there in the driveway, same as it was before, meaning Mary Jacob was home. Still he sat there, unable to make a move.

Presently, another car turned into the quiet street. The singer watched it swerve into the Longs's driveway. Tires screeched. A door opened, and a big blond man emerged. When you pull in like that and block the car that's there, that means you're a guest. The big blond man who was pulling his coat down over his big butt must be expected.

The singer sat in the van, watching him make his way to the door.

RUN BILLY RAY, RUN

⁓⁓

The smell in my father's room was worse. I could smell it from the doorway. He was on the side of the high bed, trying to get his feet on the ground. I could see the bottom of his stick legs coming out of his pajamas, the distended ankles hovering several inches above the carpet.

"I can't feel my feet, darlin'. The doctor told me the diabetes has caused the nerves to shut down in my feet."

His strong voice and elegant diction had deceived me. My own overwhelming feelings had covered over the rest. I could see now, that soon even a short journey to the bathroom would take all his strength.

Was I up to emptying bedpans?

I was heading toward him when the phone rang.

"Answer that phone darlin'. No doubt it's the grim reaper callin'."

"Hello."

The voice was clipped, matter of fact, impersonal. "Mary Jacob, this is Billy Ray. We saw each other at the grocery store."

"Yes. I saw your picture in the paper today."

"I'd like to come over and talk to you about my mother."

I studied the pattern of the rug on the floor, the blue velvet settee against the side wall.

"Your mother," I replied and then I said it again, "your mother." I was in shock I suppose. Yet, I felt—if anything—calm. His voice seemed to be coming from a long way away, as long as an ocean or a continent. He seemed so far away, I could barely hear him. I looked once again at my father who was still trying to get his useless feet to the floor.

"I could come to your house, or would you rather meet me some-place?"

"I'm here with my father; why don't you come here?"

"I'll be there soon. About half an hour." I did not ask myself how come the singer Billy Ray knew where my father lived.

I hung up the phone and looked at the man in the bed.

"And who was it? Mary Jacob, don't tell me. A finance company or a real estate vulture woman with eyes the color of money."

"Someone's coming to visit me."

My father's voice was soft, "I don't know if I can make it down-stairs, Mary Jacob, and I was so lookin' forward to that walk in the garden with you, child."

"Me too, Daddy."

I left his bedside. I didn't want him to see my face balled up like you crumple paper in your hand. Had he noticed that I said the word at last?

Little girls love their daddies. Grown up ones do too. The hatred of the other years, it was a twisted form of love; but all those years I could have loved my father. Whose absence paved the way for Peter, who had also broken my heart. Elementary psychology but now that I grasped it, I felt its immensity. The man in the bed had cast a long dark shadow. In that moment I was watching from the moon.

I went to the window and even with the barrier of glass I could see what was rising up out of the horizon like a miracle.

"Look, there's a rainbow!"

How many rainbows do you see in a lifetime? This one was a perfect arch that spanned the rooftops high above the shade trees, pulsing with life. I turned to look at his frail figure collapsed in the bed, washed in white. The light seemed to be obliterating him.

The doorbell rang: four long melodious chimes. It did not seem like half an hour. My father was collapsed against the pillows. I went to his side and when I heard him breathing I was grateful. I leaned over and kissed the top of his head. Sick as he was, he had managed to spray his hair; it was stiff and hard under my lips and there was dandruff on his shoulders. Hate, love, and now revulsion.

The huge bedroom was ablaze with sunlight pouring in the room over his face, his wasted form on the bed, his skin translucent like pearl, and the delicate blue-and-purple veins on his face and neck were shining too. I heard voices downstairs. Kathryn's high shrill one and a deeper one, laughter. I moved down the upstairs hall, past the highboy toward the picture window and the blue sky beyond it. Down the curved stairs holding on to the banister, where I leaned over, straining to hear.

"Mary Jacob, Mary Jacob! Come down here and meet my fiancé." Kathryn's voice rang out happy and filled with laughter. The grandfather clock came into view and then the open doorway and the live oaks. My hand left the banister—there was nothing to hold on to, nothing to brace the shock.

He was standing in the front hall with the door open behind him, framed by the live oaks shining with rain and sunlight: the big blond man from the airport, Kathryn's fiancé, my tormentor.

For a moment, I thought wildly that he'd come with a gun to shoot me. I kept seeing a gun and blood.

But he didn't want to shoot me; he wanted to laugh at me. His big blond head was thrown back. Kathryn was laughing too. I was the funniest thing in the world.

By then I was in the front hall with them. And I remembered, Kathryn had even told me before I got down here, her fiancé had been in New York, and we'd probably be on the same plane together if I took that Tuesday flight. And of course he had been.

"So it's you!"

"If you hadn't been so busy on the airplane with that oriental fellow, I would have introduced myself then, honey. I knew who you were; there wasn't anyone else it could've been. I knew for sure when you didn't get off in Atlanta it was Kathryn's sister, the Yankee girl. Nobody else it coulda been."

"Why have you been calling and scaring me like that?"

He wasn't smiling anymore; his face was blank, expressionless. He had no idea what I meant. I turned toward my sister who was leering nastily. Now I got it.

"He told you he'd seen me on the airplane. But it was you who decided to keep it up. This was all your idea, wasn't it?"

Kathryn was saying contemptuously. "It was just a joke, Mary Jacob. Can't you take a joke, sister? You always play it so high and mighty with me. Where are your children Kathryn, don't you miss your children? And all the while you do it with anybody you can find on an airplane."

Kathryn pushed the front door shut. The two of them moved away into the huge front room. And I heard my sister's contemptuous laughter and her words, every one of them.

"Mary Jacob, why, she never could get anybody white. She married some Jew up in New York. It's pathetic really. Why, when she was growin' up her only friend was our maid."

I stood there stunned. I was aware Kathryn was imparting valuable and vital information. I knew this the same way I knew to run from it, to shut down, do whatever I had to do to stop the kind of pain it would bring on. I've got to write that down, I thought. I was having trouble moving. When I could, I went and stood in the doorway that separated the hall from the huge front room, moving very slowly, as though I was swimming under water, not walking on a carpet. By then Kathryn and the man from the airport were standing holding hands, looking at a picture on the wall, a nymph on a swing, very romantic, and silly. It was the kind of picture where the artist spends quite a lot of time detailing the underwear, especially the lace. Their backs were turned to the doorway. I stood there listening.

"John, we'll put her in the bedroom. Mother had her since she was a little girl in Oil City. She was painted by a very famous Frenchman who used to come to Louisiana once a year to paint the children of the aristocracy. And I've loved her ever since I was little. We'll hang her above our bed. That way when I walk in our room, she'll be the first thing I see."

"Kathryn, I'd like to ask you something."

Kathryn whirled around.

"This is *my* picture!"

"I don't want the picture, I just want to know her name."

"How would I know her name? She's just a picture."

"You said when I was growing up my only friend was our maid. Who was she? What was her name?"

"What's wrong with you, Mary Jacob? She was your best friend. You lived in the kitchen with her. Mother and I used to laugh and call you her child. You even used to have kinky hair like her. Why, if you can't remember her, then there's something wrong with you."

"There is something wrong with me. That's why I'd like you to tell me."

"Lavina," Kathryn said very clearly. "Her name was Lavina. Daddy had to fire her because she was drinking his whiskey. You went out of your mind when he did and threatened him with one of his guns. That's why he sent you off to boardin' school. Van and I convinced him not to send you to the ninth Floor of Shumpert to a padded cell. We had to hide the whole thing from poor Mothah who was dyin'. Though she missed Lavina terribly. Lavina understood her ways. I always thought Daddy did the wrong thing firin' her like that, though he gave her a thousand dollars. He had money in those days."

Kathryn turned her back on me again.

The doorbell rang for the second time.

I went to open it. The trees were shining with light and the air smelled soft and sweet. Billy Ray was standing there looking just as he did at the grocery store: tall, slim, and very handsome.

"Excuse me," I heard my sister say from the direction of the front room. "Who, may I ask, are you and what are you doin' here at this door?"

"I'm here to see Mary Jacob."

"Naturally," Kathryn replied. "I don't know why I'm surprised. I shouldn't be surprised at anythin' she'd do."

I didn't feel so detached anymore. I knew I had to get the singer out of there before she said something else.

"Let's go back to the kitchen; I'll make you a cup of tea."

He was following me past the grandfather clock by the little door under the stairs where the powder room was. That's when something fluttered across my conscious mind. I didn't know what it was. I thought instead of the winter afternoon a few years ago, when a bird flew in our living room window and landed on the dining room table where the poor thing sat, quivering and terrified.

"Sit down, Billy Ray. Would you like something to eat? I could make you some lunch."

I was hoping he'd say yes, so I'd have something to do.

"No, just bring me some water. I don't guess you have any Evian water do you?"

"I could run out and get you some."

"I've got some in the van. But I can wait. Bring me a glass of plain tap water and then sit down. This isn't any easier for me than it is for you."

I did as I was told then I sat down and looked across at him. Up close he didn't look so handsome. His thin face was worn and tired looking.

"I never did understand what happened that day. I don't know why they killed my mother. You were there because she was. You saved my life. I thought maybe you'd be able to help me understand. I left you there with her on the ground and I split for New Orleans. I knew she was dead but I worried about what had happened to you too. I worried about you for years. It was a long time ago. But I want you to help me understand why they killed her."

I knew even through the elaborate games my mind was playing with me, how hard it was for Billy Ray to be here and to be asking me this. I knew he didn't normally admit so much about himself or open up like this. I could sense this the way a blind person can tell what color sweater you are wearing. Much as I wanted to respond, I had nothing to say. What I knew was this: it felt good saying her name. I felt myself smiling doing so. "Lavina, her name was Lavina." I was thinking too, by then, of my little fictional sleuth Vina. I knew who her real mother was. My little sleuth born by parthenogenesis.

Did Billy Ray think I was putting it on? How could I forget something like that? How could I not know who had killed his mother when I had been there? By then my heart was beating like a head pounding against the wall or a fist striking flesh. Images moved across the surface of my consciousness. Someone beating a child, over and over till its soft white skin broke. A clot of blood running down a leg. More blood. An enormous explosion and a mushroom cloud. The cloud was wrong. Even as I thought of it, I knew it was wrong. What was right was the face behind it: large and dark with a mole on her nose. The face I was searching for in the kitchen, the form I was sensing in the empty rocker. The homey smells when I walked in the door yesterday—bleach, pie, cleansers, the smell of starch and ironing, those all belonged to her, to Lavina. And then, all at once, I had a perfectly clear picture of myself at three. I was standing up, my arm raised. The hand in my own small white one was rough and callused.

Billy Ray was drumming his fingers on the table impatiently. I'd traveled a great distance but now I was back. I wondered how long I'd been gone. I knew I was rude to keep him waiting such a long, long time. I felt like a zombie. My voice was dead too, shut down, devoid of feeling.

"The little girl called her Vina. And when she grew up, she named her own little girl after her. She's not a real girl. She's a character in a book."

"I know about your books. I read them to my son."

"I'm glad," I said. Then added inanely, "I'd love to meet your son."

"Is that all you have to say?"

"No, please, just give me a minute. I don't remember things very well."

Billy Ray got up from the kitchen table and looked straight at me. Then in a clean swift motion, he sent one of the old wooden chairs to the ground. It splintered and broke.

"Fuck you," he said. "And fuck this kitchen. I don't give a rat's ass what happened. It's over."

He moved toward the back door and threw it open. I followed him. Trees, blue sky, but the rainbow was gone. I thought perhaps I'd been hallucinating. But, I was sure I wasn't seeing things now. Billy Ray was running away. He ran away that day too. Run, Billy Ray, run. Run as fast as your legs can carry you. He was always running. The first time I saw him, he had stolen the shoes. Tie-up shoes in a heap at the end of the counter. It was Woolworth's that day too. Woolworth's with the big red sign.

A phone began to ring. He was pulling something out of his back pocket and bringing it to his lips. Not a harmonica, but a cellular phone. Still, it's a harmonica I was seeing. He was playing and singing. "I have a dream." But that was someone else. And he died too. Died the same way Vina died.

Billy Ray was smiling now instead of scowling. Smiling, he looked so handsome, standing still under the low hanging branches of my father's live oaks. Billy Ray had reached the front yard by then. I was remembering the day he smiled for me. That day in front of Woolworth's. And kissed me. The kiss was real too. Just like Vina has always been real to me. I could hear him singing "Diamond

Buttons." And I could see absolutely clearly, the boy who stood in the sun playing for me. For me Mary Jacob.

That was in front of the store. They killed Vina in back of the store. It was Vina's wig I saw first, lying on the ground. Not on her head where it was supposed to be. That's when I knew it was Vina. I thought, if Billy Ray will just stay still, I'll be able to see everything I've forgotten. But Billy Ray was moving toward his van. He opened the door and drove away.

I stood in the driveway for a while, hoping he would come back. When it was obvious he wasn't going to, I went back in the kitchen, looked at the ruined chair, and gave it several kicks of my own. I sat down at the table and put my pounding head in my hands.

I could see that hot August day now at last, stretching before and after.

THEN
(SUMMER, 1963)

Blow the horn in Zion, sanctify a fast,
Call a solemn assembly;
Gather the people
Sanctify the congregation,
Assemble the elders,
Gather the children.
– The Book of Joel

GROWING PAINS

~~~

Mary Jacob grew four inches in that first month of the summer she turned twelve. School in Louisiana let out early in May; a throwback to the days when cotton was king. The summer holidays were four months long. Her only friend was away at camp that summer. It was just as well, for early in June her body exploded. She was relieved her friend was not around to see; she wasn't someone you could really share things with. She was a freak, just like Mary Jacob. In that logic peculiar to the outsider, the girl knew what was happening to her body was shameful; soon she could not even hide under her clothes. June passed. She was still swimming in June. By July, none of her clothes fit her anymore. Her breasts sprouted. Not in an interesting, pointed way. They were fattish, ill-shaped things: all nipple with no real breast.

She stopped going to the country club and swimming, which had always been her chief summer pleasure. She had always loved the sharp sting of chlorine. The aquamarine water. The musk smell of Coppertone oil. Since she was six, she would spend the long summer mornings, from ten on, swimming in the pool. She could swim forever. The butterfly. The backstroke. The crawl. She'd only stop when she was too ravenous to continue. Sitting still for a moment, she'd wolf down club sandwiches and potato chips. Chocolate malted milks. The afternoon was for reading under an umbrella. Her mind was the only organ in her body that seemed to function well. She could read and she could think. She could lose herself in the desperate passions of strong female characters without exactly having to understand what sex really was.

As her body started changing, she realized that the equipment for passion was not going to be given to her. She caught one of the handsome bronzed lifeguards who had always been her friend looking at her in a different way. She believed it was because she stank. When her armpit hair began to erupt in ugly, angry little tufts, she took to keeping her arms rigidly down to her sides, as though they were glued there. She was even afraid to move them in the semi-secrecy of the water. Hoping to alleviate the problem, she stole Kathryn's roll-on deodorant. The sticky stuff flattened the hair out, but the smell did not go entirely away: it was rank and earthy. Her breasts continued to grow. Not up but sideways. She feared if they kept on their wayward path, they would end up permanently facing each other on her back. At night she dreamt they were snakes with angry heads that jumped like a can of trick peanuts, out from the shelter of her blouse. She'd awaken after those dreams and bunch her breasts together with the top of her arms. If only she could make them grow right. She could press together some semblance of cleavage. But it looked nothing like what her sister and Van had on their chests without any effort. How was it that Van and Kathryn had never known an awkward moment in their physical lives? Both had been beautiful little girls and were now shining, perfectly formed teenagers. Kathryn, like Rose White, silky blond and delicate. Van, like Rose Red, dark haired, lush with white, creamy skin.

By the summer of 1963, the summer her sister and Van were seventeen and she was twelve, they were already women. Mary Jacob was nothing. A poor, half-formed creature: a demi girl. Without warning, her stomach swelled up. Then, to her horror, more dark hairs appeared below her belly button in a straight line headed down to a nest of them. Mary Jacob feared the hair would soon cover her body like an ape. She stole her sister Kathryn's tweezers and yanked the hairs up so viciously, she pulled up hunks of skin. As precocious as she was intellectually, she was as ignorant as a six year old in the basic facts of life. Paranoid fantasies beset her waking hours. Would the tweezing make the hair grow in thicker? She had heard all her life if you pull out a gray hair, three will grow in its place. Was it true for this other kind of hair for which she had no name?

When the scabs were starting to heal below her belly button, a thin brownish stain that smelled even worse than her armpits appeared one morning inside of her pajamas. Mary Jacob was forced to ask her sister Kathryn what to do. But she bungled the operation, missing the fact that the napkin was to be placed inside the underpants. When she complained about the arrangement to Kathryn, her older sister went screaming hysterically to tell their mother, "You'll never believe what she did this time. She put the Kotex on the *outside* of her pants!" Their laughter echoed down the long, upstairs hall, but they did not ask her to share in it.

That event took place sometime after July fourth. It was the last time she ever raced in the annual swim meet held each year at the country club, and the last time she ever confided in her sister. The girl easily won the crawl and the butterfly, though she refused to enter the backstroke, fearing that people might gape at her armpits. After that, for the rest of the summer, Mary Jacob exiled herself to home.

When she ran out of books, she biked slowly to the library in the streets that smelled of mown grass and heat. Other than that, she hardly moved. She had read in a book at the library, the same dark smelly thing was to happen to her every month until she was an old woman. She could not comprehend such an awesome sentence with no reprieve. She awaited its second coming like the doomed man awaits the signal to pull the trapped door from under his feet.

She ate her breakfast and lunch at the kitchen table with Lavina. Dinner was a silent affair, with her father at the head of the table, and Kathryn at the other end, playing with her food. Only when Van was present was there laughter.

Kathryn took small white pills that kept her awake and killed her appetite for Lavina's wonderful meals. They looked exactly like the pills her mother took all day to help her rest. This represented another arcane mystery to the girl: Why would you want to swallow a pill that made you unable to eat golden fried chicken, beaten biscuits, okra stewed with onions, tomatoes and corn, and especially baked white grits bubbly with cheddar cheese? Along with books, food became Mary Jacob's solace. She could not get enough to fill the sad emptiness inside her.

Without all the swimming, she gained weight. She saw that her father avoided looking at her. But it had been the same before she became a freak. She could hardly blame him, particularly now. For in his absolutely mannish way, Jack Lynam Long Jr. was as beautiful as Kathryn and Van. As handsome, surely, as the heroes in the books she devoured. Kathryn smirked at her. Van sometimes took pity on her and would roll up her hair. She even bought the girl one of those little calorie counting books. She promised Mary Jacob, "One day you'll be pretty. It'll just happen; you'll see!" But Van could never be counted on for long, even to help her count her calories. Her attention always wandered.

Lavina was the only person who did not look at her strangely or with whom she did not feel like a freak. Still, she could not ask Lavina how to get a desired female shape without somehow pointing out that Lavina lacked the equipment as well. She did not want to hurt her feelings. For she had always known somehow, in spite of her serene good humor, the older woman's feelings could easily be hurt. Nor could she discuss her period. She had more than once caught Lavina in the laundry room, muttering over a pair of Kathryn's stained underwear as she moved them up and down the old slate washboard. Mary Jacob emphatically did not want her own stained underwear revealed—still less—remedied. Instead of throwing them in the laundry hamper, she threw them out. At night, when Kathryn was out on her dates, she stole hers. But soon they were too tight.

Mary Jacob visited with her mother on the days when her mother was feeling well enough—some days she wouldn't see Mary Jacob at all. She'd read to her from *Mrs. Beeton's Book of Household Management*, when her mother felt up to Mrs. B. The big old heavy book that had been written in England that her mother loved better than any book in the world, was the way they measured good days from bad. On bad days, her mother would sigh, "I think Mrs. B is going to have to wait, Mary Jacob." And she'd hold out her weak little hands for Mary Jacob to rub with her own sturdy ones that were usually grubby.

In March of that year, her mother's remaining breast had been removed. The year before that, her womb had been removed. Mary Jacob wasn't exactly sure what a womb was, but knew it was linked somehow to her own shameful bleeding. Lillian had been ill for most of Mary Jacob's life. "After you were born," was the refrain Mary Jacob had heard as long as she could remember. "After you were born, I never really recovered my strength." "After you were born, I started bleeding for months and months." "After you were born, I took to my bed for six months." "After you were born, poor Daddy had to move to his own room, I kept him awake with my moaning. I tried to keep quiet, but I was disturbing his sleep." "After you were born . . ."

When Mary Jacob was not wishing for the miracle of a perfect body, she wished for an act of mutilation to occur. It seemed only proper that she should give away her own breasts to her mother. Her mother's beautiful life had ended with her own. The pictures on the bedroom wall testified to the beauty and grace that her own arrival on earth had ended. Would not the gift of her own unwanted breasts be the fitting sacrifice for all her mother had endured? And when she did not dream of snakes popping out of her shirt, Mary Jacob dreamt of dolls' chests. Flat and plain as a sheet of thank-you-note paper. For that's how she imagined her mother's chest looked, beneath the dainty dimity nightgowns and robes she always wore.

While her mother lay in her bed, with no breasts, her sister and Van were preening around the upstairs rooms at their end of the hall in shiny white cotton underpants and their even shinier white bras—like pedigree cats, continually grooming themselves. Both girls were going steady that summer. That meant they went out every night. They awakened at noon or later. They breakfasted long after Mary Jacob and Lavina had finished their lunch. The two of them spent their days entirely inside, in the cool, air conditioned second-floor rooms at the end of the hall: "the girls' wing," their mother called it.

Mary Jacob's room was officially in the girls' wing. Her side bedroom door opened on the shared dressing room. But she was always an outsider in the pretty wallpapered and mirrored sanctuary, as she was an outsider everywhere else. They would summon her when they wanted something. She'd walk in and their toes would be stuffed with tissue. The harsh, pleasant smell of fingernail polish would mingle with the smell of Marlboroughs burning. They'd send her downstairs to make them Cokes. Or on her bike to the drug store for movie magazines. But she was not a part of them. Mary Jacob showered at night when Kathryn and Van were out. And took to using the powder room toilet when they were at home.

It never occurred to her to question why Van, who was not really an official member of the family, enjoyed all the privileges of the household denied to her. Van's dead father had been Jack Long's best friend. Van's mother worked, which was a terrible thing for a white woman, even more so for her daughter. Van had been with them forever. And anyway, Van was her nice sister. For, other than Lavina, she was the only person who had ever been consistently kind to her. Mary Jacob thought Van the most beautiful person who had ever walked the face of the earth. And she was not entirely wrong.

POVERTY

✧✧

He was an ugly runt with a mean little face. Smiling came hard to him. Maybe he was disagreeable by nature. Maybe he was simply hungry all the time. When success came to him, almost overnight, Billy Ray grew tall and handsome. But in the beginning of the summer that it all happened, he was a pitiful sight. Without his loose button shirt, with his rib cage jutting out, his torso resembled a burnt rack of lamb. Billy Ray turned fifteen in March of 1963, but he looked no older than a small, undernourished twelve year old. His mother insisted he keep his hair shaved close to his head in the summer, and that accentuated his childlike appearance. Head lice was endemic to the black community in Murpheysfield in the summer. Head lice and pin worm. Still, in his fifteenth summer, though he let her shave his head (Billy Ray always felt the heat terribly) he refused to wear the clove of garlic on a string around his neck to ward off the pin worm. Billy Ray disliked strong smells as much as he disliked the heat. Besides, garlic was for children.

In the beginning of July, just about the time Mary Jacob left the country club, his mother's boss, Mr. Jack, got him a caddying job there. Billy Ray had never met the man his mother called *that Jack* anymore than he had met Mr. Jack's children or his wife, Miz Lil. Still, Billy Ray hated him. Hated him with a passion only equal to the passionate hatred he felt for that Jack's children. Particularly the little one his mother loved. Sometimes he wanted to throw out the picture of her in her crooked eyeglasses on the shelf and see what his mother said. But fear held him back.

Caddying was a brutal job. That Jack's children weren't toting no bags, that's for sure. He imagined the little girl with her crooked eyeglasses spending her whole day inside in the air conditioning getting waited on by his mother's gray work-worn hands. He hated that physical reality as much as he hated the almost unbearable heaviness of the golf bags he had to carry. They weighed almost as much as he did. The heat was terrible. The white hot summer days reminded him of the descriptions of hell he had heard all his life from the minister of their church. One of the reasons why he had stopped going. Hell, Billy Ray knew, could not be hotter than the Murpheysfield Country Club at high noon. Why sit then, in church, and have to listen to descriptions of hell? If you asked him, hell was in fact, the Murpheysfield Country Club at high noon. Particularly if you were a boy carrying one of their bags. The merciless sun beat him down. And the golf bags beat him down. The first one he had carried actually had mink-lined covers for the clubs. Just thinking of how they could afford mink covers for their golf clubs beat him down in a way the sun and the bags could not.

Billy Ray was a terrible caddy. It wasn't just his lack of strength, though at first, he could barely move beneath the weight of the clubs. And moving was what he was paid to do. If you called pay two quarters for four hours of work. Though he and his mother needed the two quarters. Two quarters could buy an icy cold watermelon. Two quarters could buy a gallon of three-day-old milk from the dairy annex down the road from their house. Two quarters, little though they were, could make so much difference.

The other caddies promised it would get better, but he knew it would not. He knew he lacked the persistence to turn this job into silver or green. It was not merely strength or movement. Strength and movement would come if he persisted. Young Billy Ray knew he lacked the pleasing smile. The easy, graceful bowing down to the white man the other more successful caddies had mastered. Billy Ray could not make his lips move in a smile. Could not set the bag down and run happily like a swift brown colt, the way they wanted you to, all those Jacks, into the woods full of poison ivy and snakes. *Their snakes. Their poison ivy.* Some vague, half-formed suspicion had always warned Billy Ray that to please them was to lose the songs. He did not know what the songs had to do with maintaining his distance from the white man, but he knew the two were linked.

He did not know where the songs came from. They had been playing in his brain for as long as he could remember. When he was younger, he thought the songs had come from God. Now that he was older and no longer believed in God, he still wondered about their origin. It was a mystery even deeper than the mystery of flowers and birds and sky—far more important than any he had ever heard hinted at in church. His music was beyond mere religion, which was for simple folk like his mother and the rest of them at church.

When the hum hit, earth and sky were not big enough to contain the songs. Alone on his mother's front porch, with his cheap, dime-store harmonica, Billy Ray had reached heights and descended to depths unknown to any of the people he knew. And he sensed, somehow, that to smile and pretend he was made for anything else was to give up that gift. For he always knew it was a gift. One he had to guard with every morsel of strength he could summon.

Carrying a golf bag was nothing compared with the strength it took to guard the hum, from his mother, from their neighbors; he even refused to participate in band during the school year. Why should he join some marching band and parade down the streets playing "Dixie" like the white man expected him to do?

He had a plan, though he did not know exactly what the plan was. He was waiting for it to take shape. In the meantime, he resolved to show up at the Murpheysfield Country Club like he was supposed to and carry their bags that tore at his shoulder till it was raw—though, not for a minute did Billy Ray accept this as his fate. He did it so he and his mother could eat more. That was all.

VINA

ᠬᠣᠬᠣ

S ummer I died, started out exactly like every other summer I worked for the Longs. Eleven years, five days a week from eight in the morning till eight at night. Thursdays and Sundays were off. I made good money, thirty-five dollars a week. Every day, when I goes to work, it were the same. I'd let myself in the back door and pass into the laundry room where I keeps my things. In there, was a brand new washing machine and dryer and so many cabinets both high and low, you could never count 'em. There was a linen mangle too, though never could get used to them mangles. And a big old deep laundry sink big enough to wash a pig in and an ironing board built into the wall. Under the little winder, was my maple rocker. I brought my own cushion for the rocker from home, and I can see it plain as day, a sort of pinkish thing with old blue flowers on it.

Truth is, that maple rocker weren't mine really. I started workin' for the Longs in 1952, and I saw it the first week I was there, when I was cleaning the attic. But, it took me three years to get it down to the laundry room where I could get some use out of it. Funny thing is, nobody ever even notice I took it down from the attic to my room. I just did it one morning when the girls were off at school and Miz Lil was asleep. Don' know why it took me so long to get that old rocker downstairs where I could enjoy it, but I never like to ask. Didn't have to as it turned out. No one ever come in the laundry room except Mary Jacob. It used to make me so mad that I had gone without that rocker all that time when I could have been enjoyin' it. Seems to me I were always sayin', "Girl, why in the world did you go without that rocker all them years?" A nice solid rockin' chair's the best thing in the world when your back got the misery in it. I sat there and rocked whenever I could.

I had my own little toilet in the laundry room. I know it ain't ladylike to mention toilets, but since I died because of toilets and lunch counters and other such things, I guess I can be excused. It was in a tiny little closet and I had to keep the door open so I could fit my knees in. Why, I never would have thought to lift my old skirt up in any of the other bathrooms in that house than I would in the middle of a church service. If nature called—even when I was upstairs scrubbing a toilet—I'd make my way across the hall, down them curved stairs, and past old grandad clock ticking away, for all the world like some old housecat to her box.

Mary Jacob, she were always there in the kitchen waitin' for me. The child had started cookin' that summer. At least she thought she were cookin'. When I opened the door that morning, the kitchen was filled with smoke and the smell of burnt bacon. The kitchen radio was on playing that turrible white music. Roll and rock. I couldn't take that music, much as Mary Jacob loved it. Roll Jordan Roll, was what I liked. Mary Jacob was in front of the stove, and all around her was smoke.

I said, "Lord have mercy, Mary Jacob, you gonna burn the house down or what?"

The girl turned around and smiled at me. "I'm making us bacon." Yesterday was french toast with half a bottle of Karo syrup poured over it. I ate some, not wanting to hurt the child's feelings, though it had been raw in the middle and oozed. But I knew I wasn't gonna be able to eat the bacon she was burnin'. Cooking bacon ain't easy as it looks. You have to put it in a cold pan with just a drop of water. And you have to worry over it. Chirrun just don' understand how you have to worry over bacon. Not like greens where you can go do your chores while they is cookin'.

"You ain't fixin' bacon, you burnin' it, Mary Jacob."

The child just stood there over the pan.

"Take it out, Mary Jacob, 'for it get burnt worse. Get yourself a plate and put a sack down to let it drip."

Mary Jacob, she just stand there. She ain't gonna leave that pan of bacon she'd already ruint. The trouble with chirrun cooking is they never get things ready beforehand, which is the main reason why they shouldn't cook. That and the terrible mess they always makes.

I could have told her was gonna happen, not that she'd have listen. The bacon started spittin' and one them land on Mary Jacob's arm. She scream like a whipped dog, then stamp her feet. That's when I took charge. I turned off the gas. Then I works on the switch for the kitchen fan, another thing the child had failed to do. Then I went to the ice box for butter.

I left Mary Jacob with a pat on her arm and went back to the laundry room to change my clothes and do my bidness. When I come back to the kitchen, Mary Jacob, she were eating a bowl of cereal and tapping her feet to the roll-rock music.

I went to the stove to heat up whatever coffee Mr. Jack hadn't drunk. I was in no mood for that ugly roll-rock white music and was about to ask Mary Jacob if she minded if I switched over to my own station. Then, I guess the music stopped. I weren't paying close attention. What I was thinkin' about was how much extra work she had made for me. I was gonna have to take out all the burners and soak 'em. Then wipe the whole stove down with vinegar and water. The coffee pot, I knew, would have to be soaked too, and so would the kettle. I was gonna have to teach her to take off the kettle and the coffee pot from the range so they wouldn't get themselves all covered in grease. Anyway, I missed the first part of the news report. The one that started all my troubles. White people talkin' on the radio are hard for colored to understand.

It sounded like "sick men caluding Martin Luther King stayed sick men." Then there was more fast talkin', though I managed to understand that it was a sit-in they was talkin' about. Had to be because they were saying Alabama, state troopers, and segregation, so clear even I could understand the man.

I stared at the radio, even when the screaming white music come back on. I wondered how long it would be until the next time they tells us anythin'. I was wishing I could switch it over to the colored station, but I didn't want to involve the child in colored bidness. So, I takes my cup of coffee to the kitchen table and sits down next to Mary Jacob, who was wolfing down a another bowl of Sugar Pops. Lookin at her eatin' away like there was no tomorrow, I wished, like I always did, that I could take some of the fat off Mary Jacob and give it to Billy Ray. Billy Ray was a poor eater. Nothin' seemed to please him. The boy picked at his food like he was sick all the time.

Mary Jacob, she lookin' at me and askin', "Do you know him, Lavina?"

I looked at her.

"I want to know if you know him."

"I don' know what you talkin' about, Mary Jacob."

"Martin Luther King," she says, cool as can be. "I like Martin Luther King and I hate George Wallace. George Wallace has the ugliest face in the whole world." The girl went back to eatin' on her cereal.

"Mary Jacob, you gotta hush your mouth, you know your father think George Wallace second cousin to Jesus Christ."

"Everybody's asleep," says she like it don' matter.

So I says, soft as I can, "Honey, anybody hear you, includin' that fly over there, they gonna think it's me put them ideas in your head."

"But I want to know if you know him, Vina."

"Know who, Mary Jacob?"

"Martin Luther King."

"Do you know President Kennedy and whatchacallum, Jackie Ann?"

"It's Jacqueline, Vina. 'Course I don' know them."

"Then why you thinks I knows the Reverend King?"

For some reason that made her look sad, the way she did way too much. Mary Jacob looking sad, always made me feel sad too. Nice white child with everythin' anybody could wish for ought to be happy. But, Mary Jacob were not happy. Even with her beautiful bedroom and all them books she read and a Daddy rich as any white man in Murpheysfield, she were miserable. So I reaches over and pats her chubby little arm, just below the burnt place which was red and angry looking. I was about to ask her if it still hurt when we hears the bell.

Mary Jacob, she jump up, "I'll get it," she say.

That ole bell go off again. I knew it was prolly Miz Lil too weak to get herself to the toilet. I took a last swallow of my coffee and get to my feets. I had slept poorly—the heat had been turrible the night before. It was only Tuesday. I had another long Wednesday to get through until Thursday when I could rest. I was fifty-five that summer and for a colored woman, fifty-five is old.

"I'll be right there, Mama," that sweet child was callin' into the voice place on the wall. Then, she flew out of the room through the wide front hall where Granddaddy clock ticked away and up them curved steps. It always took me by surprise the way that child could go from plug down to pert. But that's the way Mary Jacob was—never could keep your finger on her.

MRS. BEETON

∽∽

Her mother was watching the *Today* program on the big television set in her bedroom. All the shades were down and the curtains drawn. Though it was a bright, sunny morning outside, here, it was the middle of the night. The bedside lamp was on, and Mary Jacob could see her mother had not groomed herself yet for the day. Lillian looked tired and hopeless first thing in the morning. She was already smoking. The room smelled strongly of sickness and cigarettes. She liked it best on the days when her mother felt well enough for Conrad and Lorraine to come do her hair and nails. Then the room would smell pleasantly of hair spray and fingernail polish.

A Yankee woman's voice, harsh and bossy, was coming out of the TV.

"Five men, including the Reverend Martin Luther King Jr., are holding a sit-in protesting the state's segregation laws. A large crowd has gathered outside the local restaurant. Governor Wallace has ordered State Troopers to stand by."

Lillian looked up when she saw Mary Jacob. Her mother's voice was weary.

"He's going off to jail again; he reminds me of Gandhi. I only hope to God he doesn't come to Murpheysfield. I'm quite sure your father would take it upon himself to shoot the poor devil."

"Is that what he said?" It was not difficult for Mary Jacob to imagine her father taking aim, one strand of chestnut hair falling in his handsome face, sleeves rolled up, his eyes peering steadily into the tiny sights of his deer rifle. There'd be a fast *click, click,* then a deafening blast of gun fire, and the Reverend King would lie slaughtered, like a lamb in a pool of blood. What color was Negro blood? Was it bright red like white blood? She had heard all her life that Negro brains were a different size than white brains—this had always puzzled her—was it different also with their blood? What color was their blood? Dark brown like their skin?

"Reverend King is a great orator. You and I both admire him. Just don't share your feelings with anybody else. Especially not your father. Now, switch the set off; it exhausts me."

She switched off the set, then turned to face her mother.

"Did Daddy really say he'd kill him?"

She knew she shouldn't press. It was wrong to, with her mother being so sick and not exactly right in the mind from it. Still, Mary Jacob was anxious to know what plans her father had concerning the Reverend King. Her father was an important man in town. He was on the White Citizens' Council, the mayor's special committee—he even knew the governor of Louisiana.

Integration worried the life out of Mary Jacob. If it happened, she knew she would not be able to stand the way they'd shout out "nigger," and probably beat on any colored person who had the courage to show up at a white Murpheysfield school or restaurant. Thinking about it made her cower, the way nails did running down a blackboard: it was a physical loathing. Deep in her heart, she knew she lacked the courage to defend the Negro like she ought to. She wondered even, if she could summon the wherewithal to defend Lavina if she were called upon to do so. She hoped and prayed she would. And pretended how brave she'd be in the numerous fantasies she concocted in her febrile imagination. But King, she knew, had the courage to do anything. He seemed like Jesus was supposed to be. How was it that other than her mother—who was too sick to count and wouldn't admit it anyway—no other white person heard his majesty? She more than halfway suspected her own ears were different, as Negro brains were meant to be different—of a different size, a different shape perhaps—it was obvious her own ears heard differently.

Her mother was saying, "We must abide by the custom of the country. I was reading Edith Wharton last night; you're intelligent enough to read her now. Do you know she wrote all her novels in bed in the morning?"

When her mother started talking about literature and Mrs. Wharton, who wrote stories in her bed, that was a good sign.

"Mama, are you ready for Mrs. B?"

Her mother gave her a wan smile.

"If you insist, Mary Jacob."

"You'll feel better, Mama, Mrs. B will make you feel better."

Her mother sat up a little, straightening her fragile pajama top where it gaped in the middle where her breasts used to be. The gold cross her mother always wore gleamed in that fearful space Mary Jacob never wanted to see. Their father had given them all gold crosses one year for Christmas, and at the time, Mary Jacob had been thrilled to be included in the same way as her sister and her mother. But she had lost the cross as she lost or broke everything that mattered. She was as clumsy as an ox, as her father always said. It wasn't surprising that he hated her.

"Maybe just a little would be nice. But when I say I'm tired, Mary Jacob, you must stop at once."

"I'll go get her," she called out happily and ran to the corner of the room and the big bookshelf where the photograph albums and *Mrs. Beeton* were kept.

Back by her bedside, she could see her mother was improving by the minute. She was happily recounting a story Mary Jacob had heard many times. "Have I told you that my mother, your dear Grandmother, kept a perfectly beautiful house?"

"No ma'am," Mary Jacob always replied, because she knew her mother wanted to tell the story. And that the story made her sit up in her bed and her eyes shine.

Her mother was fingering her cross, as she always did when she talked about her childhood.

"When I was a little girl, she dressed for dinner and my father did too. My mother wore black with a fresh-cut flower from the garden in her hair. She was the most beautiful woman anyone had ever seen. The first time I came down to join them, I wore a white dress with a blue sash and I curtsied. Where did we leave off reading, Mary Jacob?"

Mary Jacob opened the book. On the chapter entitled, succinctly, "Servants." They had started it last week. Her mother was smiling her sad little smile and lifting her chin just a little in expectation.

Mary Jacob cleared her throat, "Section 2185. 'For dinner, the footman lays the cloth, taking care that the table is not too near the fire, if there is one, and that passage-room is kept.' What's a passage room, mama?"

"Room to walk, Mary Jacob, keep on reading, I want to close my eyes and imagine."

Mary Jacob saw her mother's delicate blue eyes with their heavy purple lids close.

"'A tablecloth should be laid without a wrinkle; and this requires two persons: over this the slips are laid, which are usually removed preparatory to placing dessert on the table. He prepares knives, forks, and glasses, with five or six plates for each person. This done, he places chairs enough for the party, distributing them equally on each side of the table, and opposite to each a napkin neatly folded, within it a piece of bread or a small roll, and a knife on the right side of each plate, a fork on the left, and a carving knife and fork at the top and bottom of the table, outside the others, with the rest opposite to them, and a gravy spoon beside the knife. The fish slice should be at the top, where the lady of the house, with the assistance of the gentleman next to her, divides the fish, and the soup ladle at the bottom: it is sometimes usual to add a dessert knife and fork; at the same time, on the right side also of each plate, put a wine glass for as many kinds of wine as it is intended to hand round, and a finger glass or glass cooler about four inches from the edge. The latter are frequently put on the table with dessert.'"

"Section 2186. 'About a half an hour before dinner, he rings the dinner bell, where that is the practice, and occupies himself with carrying up everything he is likely to require . . .'"

Mary Jacob looked up. Her poor sick mother was sleeping already. Her mouth was a little open and she was snoring softly. She marked the place with the strip of leather and, like a good mother, straightened the covers and crept softly from the room.

BAREFOOT

〜〜

It was a three-mile walk home from the Murpheysfield Country Club. In late July, it was like walking through hell; one hundred and two degrees and the sun refusing even for a second to hide behind a cloud. The boy walked along the soft turf of the shoulder, careful to avoid the thick patches of poison ivy and bull nettle that proliferated along the road. Billy Ray had removed his shoes as soon as he turned the corner off the long, tree-lined driveway that led to the country club and on to the main road south. Even his considerable pride could not force him to wear the torture boxes when no one was looking. The boy's feet were tough and calloused, though ten feet of callous would not protect him from the pinworm that could burrow in through iron and steel. The rich Louisiana earth was rife with them. They came in through your bare feet and toes. When you caught them, they lived inside you. Ate your food. Took all the flesh off you. When you caught pinworm you had to drink evil tasting stuff and be treated like a baby by your mother. Even if you didn't die from them, you'd want to after a while. The eggs hatched inside your pants. Laid eggs in your turds. It had been dry for a while. And pinworm liked the dampness. Probably all the pinworm had burned to death like he was likely to do if he walked in this heat any longer without water or shade or anything to eat.

Billy Ray shielded his face with one hand as he walked, all the while looking for patches of dewberries. Dewberries were wonderfully juicy and delicious, but unfortunately always seemed to grow near the patches of poison ivy. Even though his stomach hurt from hunger and his mouth was parched, he would not stick his hand in poison ivy to save himself from starving to death. When he was little, poison ivy never troubled him. Could stick his hand in a patch of berries surrounded by it and nothing would happen. Suddenly, last summer, the stuff took to biting on him. His first case of poison ivy had taken him so bad, he had to soak in the kitchen tub in baking powder all one day and night. Since that time, he lived in fear of exposing himself to all that misery again. Though he spied now a thick cluster of the dark purple berries, he was not tempted. Not with the way the terrible stuff spread. His mother had told him somebody went blind from rubbing the stuff near their eyes.

Billy Ray came to the turn off that led to the Morehouse Road. Cars whizzed by with the windows rolled up and the air conditioning on full blast. Black cars: Cadillacs, Chryslers, Olds, Lincolns. The cars the colored drove always overheated. Never did see no colored car with the windows rolled up, unless it was winter. Colored cars were too old to use the air conditioner if they were fortunate enough to own cars with air conditioning. Why was it, Billy Ray wondered, the rich whites always seemed to drive black cars? When he made money, he'd drive a white car. A great big white car with an air conditioner that never heated up the engine. Maybe he'd get two air conditioners. One for the big plush front. And one for the big back seat. He'd teach his mother to drive, if she was willing to learn, and get her a big white car too. If not, then he'd hire someone to drive her.

Billy Ray kept on walking. He could daydream for only so long. The sharp dry twigs, and the hot parched earth felt like razor blades on his heels and toes. It particularly hurt on his soft high instep where there were no calluses. Yesterday, Billy Ray had been lucky and been able to hitch a ride with one of the caddy's older brothers who worked construction near by. But today, it was three hot miles in the sun for two quarters. The other caddy, the smiling boy whose head was bald from worms and was skinnier even than Billy Ray was, had gotten three dollars. Billy Ray had not been surprised. The other caddies had told him the way it was going to be his first day. They all gathered before and after the games in the little caddy shack over to the side of the club. They sent over one can of Nehi each for the boys. Same flavor every day: grape. What did they think, caddies only drank grape? Probably didn't notice. Some of the boys would bring sandwiches wrapped in brown paper sacks from home and eat them with the Nehi soda. When they had seen he was new, they all gathered round and told him the way it was going to be: "If they wins, they pays; hole in one or birdie gets you up to five big ones. If they don' win, you lucky for two quarters. And if they loses real bad: prolly a dime." They had been right. Today, the tall, gray haired man with the wire glasses had won. And the red faced, fumbling turkey-faced golfer, who Billy Ray caddied for, had not. It was that simple. If they played good, they rewarded you. If they stumbled and swore, after digging up the soft green grass with their golf clubs, they did not. It would help to smile. To run after the ball fast and eager, but all that extra effort would not be worth more than a quarter.

Billy Ray heard a horn honk. Then he turned and saw an old blue De Soto pulling off the road just ahead of him. As it came to a stop on the soft shoulder of the road, it blew a great wave of hot, dry red dust all over him. He closed his eyes and coughed. When he recovered, he approached the car and saw a smiling colored woman with a glistening wet face open the door and motion for him to get in.

He hopped inside, without a word, and shut the door. The car pulled out and more of the evil red dirt blew in the car. In between them in the front seat was a brown paper sack brimming with fresh greens. They drove in silence for a while. The car smelled bad, a dead chicken smell: heavy, bloody, and sour. The woman was sweating like a pig too. Her dark purple dress had huge wet stains that spread from under her arms to where her waist was supposed to be. She wore a big curly, greasy wig like his mother always did, when she was away from the house. Another thing he was going to do when he had money. Tell her to let her hair grow. He'd pay for the beauty shop bills. For colored women like his mother never did have enough money to go to the beauty shop regularly. They cropped their heads and wore wigs. Billy Ray did not know how they stood it in the summer heat with their heads covered up like that. Particularly on Sundays with a big hat in addition to the old wig. Church didn't have air conditioning either. Still church every Sunday was filled with them women.

"Where you goin?" the fat woman asked him presently.

"Morehouse Road."

"That's good," she said and then she switched on the radio.

The breeze, hot though it was, felt good blowing on his face and neck. The boy leaned his head back and closed his eyes for a moment. He listened to the end of an Ernie K. Doe number—he could do better than Ernie K. Doe with one hand tied behind his back. Then the announcer came on.

"Crowds stood by as the Reverend Martin Luther King Jr. was led away in handcuffs by a policeman. Earlier today, the Reverend King and six others held a sit-in protesting segregation at a local restaurant."

Then the radio started playing Mahalia Jackson singing "Soon, We'll Be Done with the Troubles of the World." The fat lady reached out and turned up the radio full blast. Like his mother, she loved gospel. They all did, come to that. As Mahalia wailed and rolled on the radio, the driver kept piping in "amens" and shaking her head, setting her dark, greasy curls in motion. Gospel enraged the young musician. With all its power, all the music did was imprison you, promising a better world after death, with no rewards now, when you needed it. Gospel was church on Sunday. Women like his mother, and this one behind the wheel, who worked their fingers to the bone for a plate of mustard greens and a dead chicken. Had to be dead chicken somewhere in this car. They lived their lives fearing the devil. *Devil gonna take your soul.* Didn't they know the devil was the white man? Their reward for a life time of toil, for a life time of saying, "yes sir, no'm, thankee verah much," was what? The chance to enter heaven? Their heaven, their God? Billy Ray hated Martin Luther King for the same reason. How he stood there so passively, so gently. With all that power in his voice, and the way everybody believed in him, he chose to lie down and let them handcuff him. If Billy Ray had the power of King, he'd kick and scream and throw off their shackles. Why didn't they see that King was a trap, just like church, just like gospel? A sad, stupid white man's trap that imprisoned them all.

The woman left him off a quarter of a mile from home. When Billy Ray got out of the car, he put his tight shoes back on. His feet were swollen from the heat, so he had to squeeze them on. He dared not walk barefoot, here in his own neighborhood. For Billy Ray was convinced that if any pinworms had survived the recent drought, they'd be the ones here. The rich white neighborhoods, he was sure, were totally free of worms of any kind. The whites could afford the poison to kill them. Just as they could afford grown black men to pull up the poison ivy from their back yards. If they wanted dewberries for their jelly and cobbler, they didn't have to pick them neither. Little colored boys would comb the bayous full of water moccasins and poison ivy and happily sell the dewberries for seventy-five cents a tin quart full. As Billy Ray made his way toward home, he thought about their life of ease with air conditioned cars to carry them, black hands to pick and pull up whatever they wanted or didn't want, and the rage inside him grew until it felt almost too big to carry inside his body.

At the corner of his own street, Billy Ray stopped at an unattended wooden stand and bought two bunches of mustard greens. Half his miserable earnings for two bunches of dirty mustard greens he'd have to soak three times in water to get off the grit. If this was the way he was going to have to live the rest of his life, he would not live long. He wouldn't want to. How had his mother stood it all these years? The thought of even one more summer in this hateful, evil place with no relief from the heat made him want to beat the earth.

His street was deserted. Not even strong black children could play outside in this heat. The women were all at work. The few men who lived here were too old to work anymore and not much better than children. The younger men came and went, usually in the night. He had been a child just a few years ago on this miserable street. He knew well what summer afternoons had to offer here. Not television and air conditioning with Nehi soda in every flavor and Fritos by the bag full. Here, in the heat of the afternoon, the children hid inside the houses with the hand-me-down toys their mothers and older sisters brought home at night in brown paper sacks, idly playing with the balls and the jacks no white bastard wanted no more. By the time you turned eight, you were expected to fetch supper. Most every summer some poor child, usually a girl, burned half the skin off her body fetching supper. A few houses had burned down that way and, a couple of times that he remembered, a child actually died. If you asked him, it was better to die than to live burned like that.

Billy Ray let himself into the house and first thing put the greens on to soak in the big slate sink in the kitchen. The small, low-ceiling house offered almost no relief from the afternoon heat. He went over to the old claw-footed bathtub in the corner of the kitchen, turned on the cold tap, and stuck his head under it for a while. The cool water changed his mood for the better. When he was finished, he took off his shirt and let the cool water trickle down his back. Then he went for the icebox on legs, opened the heavy door, and peered within. Inside was a little jar of mayonnaise, a half-stick of lard, two chicken eggs, and a little cube of salt pork wrapped up in a piece of wax paper. Sometimes his mother left lemonade or ice tea, but never, it seemed, when he was truly thirsty.

Cool now, the boy returned to the sink and separated the greenish-yellow curly mustard greens. A couple of doodlebugs were attached to the inside leaves, and right near the center he found a worm. He went to the back door and let the doodlebugs crawl away. The worm he squashed and threw in the trash. He ran plenty of fresh water over the greens again and put them on to soak for the second time. He went for their huge tin cooking pot, brought it over to the bathtub, filled it halfway with water, brought it back to the stove, and put it on to boil. The small bit of salt pork he took now from the icebox was not, he knew, enough for two big bunches of greens. It was not much bigger than a healthy serving of margarine. They were out of bacon fat. And would be for a while. It took several pounds of bacon to build up a can full. He'd have to boil this miserable tidbit of salt pork to death and still there would not be enough grease to coat the leaves.

When the water came to a boil, he dropped the little tad of white pork fat in the water. Then he went to the food cupboard and withdrew the Snowdrift shortening and the bottle of hot green peppers in vinegar. A gob of the Snowdrift shortening in the water would add some grease, which was good, but the flavor would suffer. The hot green peppers would help. And so would an onion, only they didn't have one. There was some garlic left in the backyard. It kept coming up no matter that they didn't plant it. A couple of cloves of garlic would, he knew, help mask the bland greasiness of the shortening. He stirred the water with a long wooden spoon and put the lid on the pot. He left the kitchen by the back door and stepped outside in the small dirt lot in back.

In the time he had been inside, the weather had changed. Summer was like that in northern Louisiana. One minute the sky could be blue and the sun beating down, and the next minute dark clouds would fill the sky and there would be a powerful thunderstorm. Billy Ray could smell the storm coming on. It would cool things off. Not a lot. It never got really cool. But the dark clouds and the rain were better than the miserable sun. Billy Ray felt the hot wind on his bare back and he watched with pleasure the dark clouds filling up the sky. The old worn clothesline that ran alongside of what used to be the garden, swayed and shimmied in the wind. With any luck, it would rain tomorrow and the golf course would be closed. Then he could stay on the front porch and play his harmonica and watch the rain fall down.

Billy Ray gazed at the half-dozen garlic plants swaying in the wind. The tall ugly plants, like pompoms on sticks, were nearly as tall as he was. The garlic was all that was left now of what had been for years a rich summer garden. Together, they had grown big boy tomatoes, pole beans, peppers, two kinds of greens, and even watermelons one summer. During the summer months and way into fall, they had eaten the food they grew. When he was little, he had faithfully tended the garden for her. But, for the past few years, both of them had fallen lazy. She said her shoulders had the misery in them and she couldn't hoe no more. And he had not offered to do it for her. As Billy Ray looked at the leggy garlic plants that came up whether you planted them or not, he felt a sad longing deep in his gut like a fist grabbing hold of him. He wished he had hoed and tilled the soil and grown the little seedlings in the paper cups. If he had, by now the garden would be in bloom, all ready for the rain that was now starting to come down from the sky in big drips, turning the dry red soil into rich black earth.

Billy Ray stood there and let the rain beat down on him. He felt it on his bare shoulders, dripping down his back. He raised his head and opened his mouth to let the drops fall in. Soon, he forgot the neglected garden, the miserable hours on the golf course, even his rage at Martin Luther King. The hum was coming. It was building in his brain. He listened to it, trying to remember each and every little turn the music took as it played inside his head along with the rain. It was a new sound. One he had not heard before: rich and complicated. He moved the sound into his fingertips. He had discovered that if he worked his fingers when the hum hit, it didn't matter whether he held the harmonica or not. The fingers held the song in them whether the instrument was in them or not. Billy Ray did not know how to read music. He had scarcely seen written music. Other than worn out band music at school. But at times like these, he could almost see the notes dancing in his brain. Yes, it seemed to him he could probably play anything that fell in his hands. Even an old stalk of garlic.

He did not know how long he stood there. That's the way it always was when the hum hit. It took you where it took you. And when it was over, you were not the same person you were before. You had wealth, you were stronger: someone with power. The hum was like the storm passing through. But it was your storm. Your lightening. Your thunder.

It was really raining now. And huge claps of thunder were sounding closer and closer in the afternoon sky. Billy Ray suddenly remembered the pot of water with the salt pork and shortening and for a moment he was paralyzed with fear. What if at this very minute, their kitchen were burning down? What if, when he walked in the back door, the whole miserable place was covered in flames? Low down though it was, it was the only home they had. Where would they live? What would they wear? He did not even possess enough money to replace his little harmonica.

Billy Ray looked toward the house. With the rain beating down it was impossible to tell if something bad were going on inside. Still he squinted his eyes, looking for curls of smoke pouring out of the roof.

He walked toward the back door, his heart pounding. The back door was open and the rich smell of boiling fat reached his nostrils. He flung the door open and headed for the stove. The big tin pot was giving off smoke, even with the lid on. And the range was all wet and glistening. Billy Ray reached for a potholder and lifted the lid of the pot. Fragrant steam hit his face. The water had nearly boiled away. The fat was almost gone too. All that was left was a little fat glob of salt pork and nothing else. Billy Ray knew he should be grateful he had not set the kitchen on fire, but he wasn't grateful. He was angry and hungry. He had boiled away their dinner. He could still cook the greens, but they wouldn't be the same. Without the pork, they would be just boiled green leaves with no taste. All he had was a quarter left. And even if he could get to the store before it closed, what would he pay with? They already owed the place five dollars. After five dollars, you had to pay.

Billy Ray stared at the pot. The fragrant fat water made his stomach growl just smelling it. He had eaten nothing since midday. And that had only been a MoonPie and a couple of peanut butter crackers. He went to the pantry for a cup and brought it back to the stove. He carefully lifted the pot with two potholders doubled over. Burnt fingers were the worst thing for playing. He carefully poured the pot liquid in a little blue-and-white cup with the handle missing. He took the cup between his two hands and sipped it. When he got to the little bit of fat, he let it rest between his teeth for a minute. It was slimy and greasy: delicious.

VINA

~~~

The Longs, well, they was the richest people I ever work for. And the fanciest. Though Miz Lil almost never come down for supper since they cut off her other bosom, I always fix things her way. Like corn. We don' serve it on the cob at the Longs. We cuts it off so the corn milk stay with it, then we puts it in a black pan with plenty of butter and a dab of cream. Tastes better that way, though it take extra work is all. Watermelon, you has to seed it first, then fetch that little thing that look like a baby-size ice cream scoop and shape it into little balls. You serves it in a cut crystal bowl. Looks right pretty it do in that bowl, though you has to be very careful. If you put it in the icebox you gotta let it warm down 'for you wash it. Otherwise it crack. Happened to me my first year at the Longs. I was washin it after supper, and the bowl, why it fall apart in my hand. Had to say, "Miz Lil I done broke your bowl." Felt terrible having to tell her, though I remember it weren't as bad as I thought it might be. It weren't her best one. Though she did say, real serious, "Why Lavina, you broke my Wafard bowl."

That afternoon, when all my troubles started, I was out the back door, shuckin' white corn into a brown paper sack. I heard a big clap of thunder and when I looks up, the sky is grey and the clouds they is moving fast, fast. I was outside settin' on the back step on account of the fact that shucking corn is a messy job, and you don' do it at the kitchen sink 'cause it clog up the garbage disposal; even one little thread be enough to have to call the plumber. I watched the rain for a spell, under the back door, so I wasn't gettin wet or anythin'. I loved watchin' rain. One of my favorite things was watchin' the rain fall down. Sittin' for a few minutes was good too. I was wishin' I could stay with the rain and not have to go inside and score that corn into the wooden bowl. Perry knife was what I used for mowing them rows of corn. It took a while. It always do. After that, I cut up a fair size watermelon. Another messy job, if you want to *know the truth, all that juice from the melon can't help but get everywhere. It was raining cats and dogs and was dark, dark out, by the time I finishes with that melon. After that, I set to peeling potatoes. But that didn't take long, luckily. 'Cause I was runnin' a little behind, what with watching the rain for too long. Earlier that day, when the sky had been all blue and the sun high, I had seared the pot roast we was havin' for supper in bacon fat and seasoned it with onion and garlic powder. It was bubblin' in the oven and giving off a fine smell. The doors were shut in the kitchen and the fan was on. Miz Lil, though she hardly ever came downstairs, like I said, hated cooking smells getting past the butlery. By this time, it was coming on six o'clock and all I had left was to make the biscuits, which was nothin really, boil the potatoes, mash them, then put them in the top of the double boiler with plenty of butter to stay warm, cook that white corn in the big black skillet, fix a salad, set the table in the dining room, and wait for the family to sit down at six thirty. I had made the ice tea that morning and a dewberry cobbler after lunch. My day was nearly over 'cept for serving them their supper, washing the dishes, and getting myself to the bus stop, thank the Lord.*

I'd kept the kitchen radio on all day. The station had been playin' my favorite gospels and it weren't even gospel afternoon. Every so often, there'd be another report tellin' all about the troubles of poor Reverend King. Mary Jacob had been up in her room readin' all afternoon, hadn't even come down for a snack. When she's in the kitchen, we is always fussin 'bout radio stations. She wants roll-rock and I naturally votes for Roll Jordan Roll. Still, it was awfully quiet in the kitchen without the child, though I was thankful, at least, that she weren't wantin' to help me fix supper.

I enjoyed the gospel music much more than I did hearin' about the bidness with the Reverend King. Fine godly educated man like the Reverend King shouldn't be in no jail with common murderers and thieves. What's the good of a college education and the deepest, soul-stirring preaching voice, if jail's all it get you? I was thinkin' too, if they could lock up a man like the Reverend King, who shook hands with the President of the United States, why just think of what they could do to the rest of the poor ignorant colored people like me and my own.

Anyway, a little after six, Mr. Jack come in the back door like he always do, swingin' his big brown briefcase. He set his wet umbrella in the corner near the back door and don' bother to wipe his feet. Why should he, when he never have to wipe up the mess his wet shoes makes? Colored men generally remember about wipin' feet. They mothers made them. And if you learn when you is young, it become a habit. As usual, he say "Evenin' Lavina." And as usual, I says, "Evenin' Mr. Jack. Your ice is laid out in the butlery." Then he say, "You've heard, I suppose, that your King's in jail."

I didn't look up from the bowl of potatoes I was mashin'. "That's what I hears," I said.

Mr. Jack just stand there, swingin' his briefcase. "He's gone too far this time, Lavina. The man's simply gone too far. The liberal ministers can't even defend his actions anymore."

I just kept on with my mashin'. Finally, after some time I say, "No sir, I reckon they ain't gonna do that." You have to understand, I was proud of myself for that "ain't gonna do that." I was no good with words, but just the same, I had given Mr. Jack an answer without giving away what was really in my heart. Trouble with white folk like that Jack Long, is they can't be happy with runnin' the world and havin' things their way. They want you to tell 'em their way is right. Just like babies, they are.

Mr. Jack he say, "I'm glad you agree with me." Then, like he always do, he pushed the swinging door that led to the butlery and left me to my mashin'. I could hear through the door, that sound of ice cubes droppin' in his crystal tumbler. Mr. Jack's wet shoes, they has left a trail across the black-and-white linoleum floor. You could see the mud marks on the white squares but not on the black ones. I looked down at the floor and wondered if the good Lord made us dark so we wouldn't show all the dirt we is always cleanin' up.

It was drizzlin' at eight o'clock, when I lets myself out the kitchen door and head down the driveway. The air outside that summer night was thick and steamy. Patches of fog rested on that pretty street filled with trees, looked like little grey puffs, it did. Street lights go on about eight thirty in the summer, but when it's fog and steam you can't see them clearly. I was hopin' I would catch the bus that suppose to pass the corner of Fairfield at eight fifteen. The bus ain't reliable. Sometimes it come at eight fifteen, other times as late as eight forty-five. If I missed it, I'd have to wait until at least quarter past nine to get another one. That would put me two blocks from home in the pitch black night. With this thick fog and mist, I'd be no better than a blind dog tryin' to find my way home.

It were good to be outside. The big yards looked so green and nice after the rain, I started to feel right nice. It was the beautiful green yards that did it. For to me, there was nothing prettier, more satisfying to look at, than deep green grass and matchin' shade trees. Green growin' things calmed my spirit. I forgot to mention why my spirit needed calming. I'd seen something at dinner that upset me. And it heped being out of the house, so I could think about it without havin' to worry if it showed on my face. When I seen it, I nearly dropped the china platter of pot roast and mashed potatoes I was servin'. Now, thinking it over, all the while admiring the dark, velvety green yards glistening with rain, I told myself, why Lavina, you should have known all along. It was a shame. A terrible shame but not a surprise. Why, the same sort of thing happened in my own neighborhood all the time. Human nature's the same no matter what color your skin happens to be. Jack Long didn't think so. And his wife and their friends didn't neither. By that point I was right cheerful, smilin' to myself, remembering the way I had answered Jack Long when he come in the door with his swinging brown briefcase. "No sir, they ain't gonna do that." Is that what I said? It didn't matter exactly what the words were, I had tricked him. Made him think I agreed with him when I hadn't and better yet, hadn't lied either. All them, why, they is only too happy to think white human nature is different than colored human nature. And they were always tryin' to make you believe it were different and better. What was different, I knew, was the places where they did what their natures bid them to do. Yes, white human nature is about the same. About the same. It don' matter where you live—in a great big old house on Fairfield Street with a bright green lawn, or a run-down shack on the Morehouse Road with soil so poor even zinnias won't grow—sin is still the same in the eyes of God.

I reached my own street at nine o'clock. A soft curtain of rain was fallin' when I gets off the bus. I had my pink umbrella with me. It weren't ample enough to cover me. Like I tole you, I was a large woman. But at least it kept my wig dry. My wig were made of artificial hair, but it acted like real hair, lost its set when the wetness got to it. Usually on summer nights chirrun would be playin' when I gets to my street. None of us had the air conditioning and we all stayed outside in the summer. Couldn't sleep outside unless you had a screened-in porch, but I don' think there were a one on that street. What I'm trying to get at is that in the summer, late into the night, peoples were out on the street. Chirrun played and their elders sat; we all visited. But that night, on account of the rain, the street was all quiet. The rain shined on the black tar road and on the dozen or so white shacks that looked all the same really. We were all so poor and every single house was in a sorry state. It was almost dark. I looked down the street to get a look at my crepe myrtle tree. It were way above the houses. The light was so dim in the sky that I could barely see its color. Crepe myrtle, it's a deep, deep purple color, and the flowers look very much like grapes. Puddles of water stood on the shiny tar road that was filled with cracks and holes. When it rained hard, the front of every house flooded and the mosqui-toes breeded in them. The rain was a blessing—it had been dry for at least two weeks—except that it brought the bugs out more.

I stepped over a big puddle, then stood still for a moment and listened. I remember thinkin' it was just like Billy Ray to play and sing when it rainin' and nobody be outside to listen. Why, if Billy Ray saw me, his own mama, likely or not he would stop. That's why I stood there, 'cause I want to hear this song. Soft and sweet it were. Put chill bumps on my arm. Usually Billy Ray's songs weren't so soft and sweet. More like roll-rock they were. Everybody on the street listened to Billy Ray's songs, whether he knew it or not. Though, folks knew better than to get close to him when he was playing. Or to say anythin' to him about them songs of his. Specially if he happened to be singing. Billy Ray was even more private about people hearin' his voice than he was about his harmonica playing.

Pretty soon, the soft sweet music just drifted off. I moved down the street toward my house. The sky was almost all dark now. And the lights were comin' on in the winders of the houses, one after another. My neighbors were dirt-poor people who did not turn on lights until the very last minute of daylight. Dirt poor was the right name for it. Dirt poor meant you could not afford a thick velvety lawn like the Longs and their neighbors had. Dirt poor meant you had dirt in the front of your house that turned to mud every time the rain fell. Not well tended, green growin' all together on a smooth soft carpet.

I wasn't in the habit of thinkin' about the meaning of words but that night, I was suddenly doing what I never had before. Made me feel right good. Tonight I had tricked Jack Long with words, and now I understood dirt poor, somethin' I'd been sayin' for years without ever thinkin' about why. You need to understand I could just read and write. Just. Not nearly as good as Billy Ray who were fifteen and Mary Jacob who was twelve. Anyway, by this time I is in front of my own little broken-down gate that was set in between the two front bushes. I walked up our two rickety-rack steps, pushed open the screen door, and called out, "Billy, Billy Ray, I'm home."

HAIR

∽∾∽

Up in her room that night, Mary Jacob lay belly down across her four-poster bed, studying the latest issue of *Teen Magazine*. At dinner, she had eaten three helpings of mashed potatoes with gravy in addition to the wonderfully juicy pot roast; Lavina's deep golden biscuits, her green salad, watermelon, and several large servings of dewberry cobbler. Her stomach was hurt and swollen from so much food, yet she craved more cobbler. Van and her sister Kathryn had eaten none of the sweet deep-dish purple pie, though her father, who usually avoided sweets, always made an exception for Lavina's dewberry cobbler. Usually he laughed and said he liked to drink his sweets, which Mary Jacob knew meant whiskey. Though she could never comprehend how bitter brown whiskey qualified as sweets. If her mother ate at all, it would only be a thimble or so. Lavina had made two glass dishes full, so there was bound to be a substantial amount left, even after what Mary Jacob had eaten.

Lavina always made two dishes and brought the second one, wrapped carefully in tin foil, home to Billy Ray. She would never take roast home the first night, not even pot roast. If food was still in the ice box after the second night, she'd always carry the rest of it home in a brown paper sack. Chicken was different. Nobody at the Longs' house ate the back or the neck. So Lavina would carry home both backs and necks from the two chickens she cooked for them. She wouldn't even put it on to crisp in the same place as their chicken. It was painfully clear to Mary Jacob, always had been, that Lavina and Billy Ray's food—like everything else connected to their darkness—must be what everyone else didn't want. The happy exception to this rule was dessert. Lavina would nearly always bring it home for Billy Ray the first night she made it. In fact, Mary Jacob strongly suspected that Lavina made Billy Ray's favorite desserts with him in mind, not them. Why else would Lavina consistently fix banana pudding with vanilla wafers when no one, not even piggish Mary Jacob, ever took a mouthful of it?

She was flipping through more pages of *Teen,* glancing at the pictures of the pretty, carefree models in their handsome pleated skirts and brightly colored fall sweaters and coats, for it was the August back to school issue. Kathryn had given her the subscription to the magazine as a Christmas present the previous year, but that's not why Mary Jacob studied each issue so conscientiously, diligently studying clothes, hairdos, wardrobe, customs, even the facial expressions of the models who lived their beautiful lives within the pages of the magazine. They lived in a culture she very much wanted to understand. Mary Jacob had an exaggerated respect for the printed word. To read something even once, was to call it her own, for she possessed a photographic memory for print. She had halfway convinced herself that if she carefully read each issue of *Teen* she would, by the end of the year, miraculously be able to comprehend the secret to teenage success.

Presently, Mary Jacob came upon a two-page article on straightening hair. "How to say no when he wants a kiss," was not remotely in her frame of reference. How could it be? If she wasn't the absolute ugliest girl in her class, she was certainly second. No one could be uglier than Beverly Smith, who not only had a glandular problem, but acne as well. Still, Mary Jacob's hair was a perpetual source of discontent, not just to her mother, to whom she pretended not to care, but to herself. Her full head of thick, uncontrollable hair shamed her. It lay down so nice and flat when it was wet, yet balled and frizzed like an SOS soap pad the minute it was dry. If she could change her hair, she was convinced everything else would fall into place. She didn't hope to be pretty or stylish, but she wanted from the depths of her soul to be normal looking. It was such a small thing to ask, not be a white girl with Negro hair. Mary Jacob could not understand how God who was meant to be so good, or Jesus Christ who was less stern and therefore, to her mind, better, both refused to grant her this small wish. Their failure to do so was turning her into an atheist.

The article suggested wrapping the hair tightly around the head, then securing it with metal clips. According to the article, the longer the hair stayed wrapped, the straighter it would be. Mary Jacob wondered if she kept her hair wrapped while she read, stayed in the kitchen with Lavina, and slept, whether it would turn permanently straight by the time school started in September. She carefully studied the diagram, but could not figure out where the wrapping started. The arrows confused her, but she had to try.

Mary Jacob rolled off the bed, took up the magazine, and headed for the side door that led to the dressing room and to her sister's top drawer where she kept her rollers, bobby pins, and hair clips.

The pretty wallpapered room smelled of hairspray and Shalimar talcum powder. One of Kathryn's pale blue monogrammed bath towels was on the floor. Mary Jacob did not have any monogrammed towels. Mary Jacob picked the thick, sweet-smelling thing up, held it up to her nose briefly, then took it over to the laundry shoot. Then she opened her sister's roller drawer and stared inside with admiration. It was wonderfully well organized, with its different rollers arranged according to size in neat exacting rows. There were hard brush rollers for after shampooing and soft, spongy pink rollers for sleeping. There was a pretty box for bobby pins, another for small clips. A separate one for barrettes. Coiled in tight little rolls were dozens of hair ribbons, some patterned, some solid, some edged in lace. Unlike her own messy drawers, her sister's were wonderfully dainty. For as messy as Kathryn was about her room, she never cared if her bed was rumpled, or if the magazines spilled over, or the ashtrays were heaped with cigarettes. Certain things, her purse, her shoes, her makeup, her jewelry, were always arranged in a queenly manner. Lavina never needed to straighten Kathryn's drawers, she did it herself. The long silver clips, arrayed in a white cardboard box from one of the downtown stores, were all shiny and clean, as bright as sterling silver. Mary Jacob was reaching for the box when she heard a door click, then she smelled smoke, more Shalimar and hair lacquer. Looking up, she saw Kathryn, who she was sure had already left for her date, entering the dressing room. Her sister's smooth helmet of light blond hair fell in a straight line to her shoulders.

Kathryn's hair was so straight and smooth, she had to roll it on tiny little rollers to achieve even the slightest curl. She had on a pretty white blouse and a full pleated skirt. Her unbelievably tiny waist was cinched in black leather. She was, as Mary Jacob knew all too well, far more beautiful than any of the models in the magazine.

"What do you think you're doing you scruffy little dog?"

Mary Jacob put the box of clips back.

"Is this what you do every time I leave the house? I'm going to tell Mama that you're stealing my things."

Mary Jacob shook her head. "I'm sorry, Kathryn. I just wanted to borrow some clips to wrap my hair, like it says here. Look here, it's that *Teen* magazine you got me last Christmas. Please don't tell Mama."

Kathryn took a deep pull on her cigarette and blew it directly into Mary Jacob's face.

"The hair you oughta be worried about is the hair on your legs, Mary Jacob."

"Kathryn, you know I promised Mama I wouldn't shave my legs until the end of summer."

"If it were me, I wouldn't wait six minutes to stop looking like King Kong."

"But I promised Mama," Mary Jacob replied mournfully. What she did not say was that she had also promised God and Jesus Christ that she would not shave her legs until September. This was part of her general scheme with the higher powers. If she made her mother happy and kept her promises, then, perhaps they would award her with a normal looking appearance. Not going out in public, except to the library where no one ever went, wasn't that hard. Half the summer was over already.

Kathryn looked bored. "I seriously doubt she'll notice, Mary Jacob."

"Of course she'll notice," Mary Jacob replied.

"What's she gonna do? Get up out of her sick bed and make you glue it back on?"

The point was not what their mother would do, which was probably nothing, Kathryn was right, but what God and Jesus Christ would do if she broke her promise to Them. Mary Jacob did not fear death, ordeal by fire, or that the devil would snatch her soul. She feared the punishment of more unruly hair on her head and on her body. Her legs were particularly disgraceful. Other than wearing high white socks, she could not conceal the fact that she was without doubt the hairiest girl in Murpheysfield. She wasn't Kathryn Calhoun Long's younger sister. Anybody with half an eye could she was the sister to that huge dark gorilla on the screen.

"You can use my clips on one condition."

Mary Jacob looked up. Kathryn's beautiful lips were curled in a bright pink snarl.

"Ok."

"Shave your legs tonight."

"But Mama says it grows in worse once you start doing it."

"Mary Jacob, it couldn't be any worse. You'll just have to shave everyday like Daddy does."

A lump formed in her throat as she digested this information. Mentally coating her legs in shaving cream, she supposed she'd have to acquire one of those shaving brushes and maybe a little china cup like Jack had. Surely this was a punishment even the devil himself would be satisfied with. For the rest of her life she was going to have to shave like a man.

Mary Jacob looked at her smooth, beautiful sister, who looked as though she were spun of gold and silk.

"And you won't tell Mama? You swear on a stack of Bibles you won't tell Mama?"

"I'm telling you Mary Jacob, she's not going to notice. She never notices anythin' you do."

"That's not true," Mary Jacob replied, not knowing who she was defending, herself or her mother.

"Now I'm gonna scoot, Foster's waiting, but I expect when I wake up tomorrow to see those legs shaved, you hear? Otherwise you're going to be in awful trouble."

VINA

◡◡◡

I was sittin' there at the kitchen table after supper with the radio on. Hundreds of colored folk were gathered outside that jail where they was holding the Reverend King. I hears a knock at our door. Billy Ray, he never answer the door, but I was hoping, just this once he would change his ways and let my ole swollen legs stay where they was. When I sees that he weren't gonna do that, I went and took me a look outside. There on my porch is Houston Moseley, a bent old colored man who claimed to be a hundred years old. When I say Houston standing, I weren't really telling the truth. Cain't remember the name of his condition, what makes that man shake. I weren't surprised to see him. He's a vistin' man. In fact, once a month or so he generally ask me to marry him. Houston don' just bestow this honor on me, Lavina Davis. Asked nearly all the other women on our little street often as he asked me. That's on account of the fact that Houston live with his daughter who is older than me and has a temper. Houston was continually trying to better his living arrangements. Not one of us blamed Houston, but we don' take him serious. Why, the last thing any hard working women wants is an old husband without no front teeth, who couldn't chew right and soon would be wetting his bed like a baby. Still, I weres fond of Houston, who had a kind heart and a pension from the government that he was free with if anybody was in real trouble, which was the main reason his daughter was nearly always fussing at him.

"Lavina," he say to me, "Lavina, go get your pocketbook, girl."

I looked at Houston, who had never in all the years I known him, ask me for a nickle in return. Once in a while he do ask for you know what, he like to play is all. Anyway, I was thinking he had finally found hisself a wife. And now he was going to get after me for all that money I owes him. "Go fetch your pocketbook, girl. Ain't you heard, M.L.'s in jail? We taking up a collection for the defense fund."

Lord have mercy, I were relieved. Know I shouldn't have been since it was on account of the Reverend King's troubles. But I was. It were around ten thirty by now. Rain stopped some time ago. But, the air was thick. I took myself a look out in the street and what I sees are people. Lights were on in all the houses and the chirrun of the block were dancin' and playin' like chirrun always do when their elders ain't payin' them much mind. I helped Houston down our two front steps, told him to watch them puddles, then stood for a moment looking before I goes back inside.

My bedroom didn't have much in it, and the ceiling were low, not much higher than I am with my Sunday shoes on. Most of my room was bed that was covered with an ole soft pink spread—loved that ole soft spread. There's a winder and a shelf with all my nice, pretty things. It were here I was going on account of the fact that on that shelf, alongside my red wig, were Pauline. Pauline was my Mama's. Don' know how she got her name, but long as I can remember she were called Pauline. Under her skirt is where I keeps money for special times. I was lifting Pauline's skirt, when I hears Billy Ray thumping in the room. I straighten Pauline's skirt. Smooth it down some. It were a heavy fabric, stood up by itself. The money was in my hand. And that boy of mine was standing there looking at me with a plug-ug look on his face.

"What you lookin' at boy?"

He say real sassy, "I'm lookin' at you throwing away our money to your boyfriend M.L."

"Oh, Billy, Billy Ray, giving's nothing. I'm too old and too tired to sit down in front of no bus. All my life I've been saying yes'm and no sir. But, for them that's received the word, why this house can spare some money."

He pointing his finger, "The gas bill's coming due and so's the electricity. How come you ain't received the word to pay for them?"

"God and Jesus they is watchin' over us Billy Ray. They always do."

"Only watchin' they doin' is over your friend, M.L."

"Reverend King, he's doin' for all us. That's why we gots to pay back. Everybody give just a little and that add up to what he need to get out."

Billy Ray's face right on my face, "He prolly get more meat in jail than we do around here."

Then he turns around and thump out. I was so shook up, I felt like a hurricane had come and gone, destroying everything we had.

I closes my eyes for a minute. When I opens them, I reaches out for my black wig that was resting on its little head and put it on. Then I looks at my bright red wig, trying to remember the last time I'd worn it. Must have been a wedding. I wouldn't have worn my bright one to a funeral. But I couldn't remember the last wedding I'd been to.

Part of me knew Billy Ray was right. But part of him were wrong too. Billy Ray just a baby, a selfish baby what think only of hisself. Way I figured it, it were too late in the day for me and my kind. But it weren't too late for him. Why, the boy, he were only fifteen years old that summer. So, I lifts up Pauline's skirt and put her back some money. Tucked three back under her skirt, put two in the pocket of my dress, and heads out to the street. The storm had passed. And our little house was still standing. Truth was, of course, that this little storm was nothin' compared to what happened later. But I'll get to that.

MEAT MONEY

⌒⌒

Billy Ray listened to his mother's heavy footsteps leaving the house; the house was so rickety-rackety that each one of her footsteps could be heard distinctly. It was only a matter of time before the place was going to fold up like the piece of worn-out junk wood it was. The house leaked when it rained, shook when the wind blew, and smelled of poverty and cooking fat. She knew it. Just as she knew they would be near to starving without the leftovers she brought home. Yet she carried on like everything was just fine. Like they had more than enough to share with Martin Luther King or any other dressed up preacher man who had nothing better to do than rob less fortunate colored women of the few dollar bills they had managed to save.

Billy Ray turned off the front porch light and walked out. He wanted to see what was going on, but did not want anyone to see him. If that happened, his mother's friend Noog would call out, "Billy Ray, get yourself down here, boy, and bring your harmonica." Noog wasn't shy about asking for his music. The rest of them were, especially his mother, who knew better than to ask. Sometimes Billy Ray sat on his front porch at the end of the day, hidden by the hedges, and let them hear. He knew they were listening. He liked them knowing it was something special they were listening to. Something not given away so easily. Tonight was King's night. The boy wasn't about to sing for the glory of Martin Luther King. When he played, it was going to be for Billy Ray.

The street was filling up with people. Some of them were carrying lamps. A few were carrying flash lights. Black faces looked grey next to fire light. He had never noticed that before. More people than lived on this block were here. Why couldn't they do their robbing and stealing on some other block he'd like to know. For there must be forty, maybe even fifty people, gathered outside now on the wet tar road. Cars were pulling up. A broken down De Soto, an old Ford pick up. He did not recognize the women who were coming out of the cars, either. Billy Ray scanned the crowd for his mother. She was easy to spot on account of her height. Someone was holding a kerosene lamp just underneath her and the thing was lighting up her face. She was laughing and talking with her friend Noog, a fat lady like herself with a nearly identical wig. The only difference between them was that his mother was tall and fat and Noog was short and fat. Years of hard work and poverty made them all look similar. Colored women usually got fat when they got old. Either that or they stayed rail thin and dried up looking. They all bought their clothes at the same low down discount store downtown. No colored woman could afford clothes from anywhere else. They all wore the same kind of fluffy, greasy wigs and most of them had bad teeth. They thought the same way too. That throwing away their money was going to send them to heaven. Probably every single one of them out on the street were giving away their last dollar bills.

Men didn't give away money easy like women did. That, Billy Ray realized, was the trouble with their lives. The women were too soft and forgiving. Billy Ray did not often think about the lack of proper husbands on his street. He had lived here all his life and was accustomed to its ways. But looking at all the women out there, and the few old men, the thought struck him now. There weren't enough men. Real men that is. Old men were always around. They came home to live with their daughters when their wives threw them out, but they were worthless really. There were plenty of boys. Grown ones too, who couldn't hold down a job. Like himself, they lived with their mothers. Ran out on their mothers, too, taking the money with them. Billy Ray feared to the depths of his soul, that fate befalling him and her. He would never be a grown man living off her. When he left he was going to leave her with money. Lots of it.

Billy Ray didn't often think of his father. The man had left so long ago it was hard to remember him. There were no pictures of him in the house, though his mother had told him once he took after his father. Still, over the years, a picture of his father had taken shape in Billy Ray's mind. He dreamed of him sometimes and he always looked the same: like Billy Ray himself, only bigger, stronger. He wore a clean pressed shirt and respectable looking trousers. He was very clean and he didn't talk much or slap his knee or cut up or engage in colored gabble. Billy Ray longed for him now. Part of him accepted the fact he was longing for someone who had never walked the face of the earth. For Billy Ray had always somehow known the difference between what the imagination is capable of creating and what really exists in reality. His music had taught him that. Still, living with his mother was hard. He worried about her and what was worse, knew all along she was the stronger one of the two. He wanted to save her. But he needed help. Someone strong. Someone who could share the burden. Someone who could bring home some money so they wouldn't have to be so poor.

But it wasn't going to happen.

Now they were singing on the street. "Good Lord, I done, done." And Billy Ray could make out that a hat was being passed. "I done, done what you told me to do; I prayed and prayed till I come through." That was the trouble. Gospel made them into sheep, let them sing their troubles away without fighting. The music was rich and the melodies, he knew, were in his soul much as they were in theirs. Maybe more. But they were suffering songs of endurance that made them throw away their money every Sunday morning at church. Now too. Twice this week when they couldn't afford even once. He'd been raised on these songs. Their beauty and strength were in his bones. But he had never been like the children who he saw now, standing on the fringe of the group, dancing and carrying on, clapping their hands. He'd always known the difference. Long as he could remember, he knew the songs were lies. Now, as the rich voices of the women rose up in the humid night air, "I done, done what you told me to do," Billy Ray wanted to shout at them to stop. Shout at them to save their money. But he knew if he did they would not listen.

He stood there for a little while longer till his rage died down. Then he went back inside the house, turned on the front porch light so she wouldn't fall down and break her stupid neck, and then went back into his own little room off the kitchen. He took up his harmonica, lay down on his bed, and began to play. He played the song he had heard this afternoon outside in the rain. The notes traveled from his brain to his fingertips, and in no time his whole body was humming with it. No one was listening so he was free to sing and play. Let them obey the white Lord and throw away their money to Martin Luther King. He had the hum and no one could take it away. None of them. Not his father. Not his mother. Not Martin Luther King neither.

THE VOICE

⌇⌇

The rain started up again in the middle of the night. The little window of her mother's dressing room was all fogged over. Mary Jacob had positioned herself outside the door where her mother was bathing, sitting perfectly still, something that was always hard for her to do. The pretty chintz swivel stool creaked every time she moved and might break any moment, under her weight. Every couple of minutes, Mary Jacob would call out, "Mama, is everything all right?" "Yes, Mary Jacob," would come the inevitable weary reply from the other side of the sliding door. Lillian had fallen last spring and had lain on the bathroom floor for an hour before Lavina found her, which is why someone now had to be within hearing reach when she was in the tub. Lillian never let anyone, not even Lavina, see her naked. But Mary Jacob knew if something happened, all that would change. What was there, on her chest? When the doctor had cut off her bosoms did the nipples remain? Were there just two red dots with the tiny gold cross gleaming in between them? If her mother cried out, she would be brave, matter of fact, like a doctor. But part of her knew it would take all her willpower not to scream.

"You all right, Mama?"

"I'm fine, Mary Jacob. Go fetch Lavina and tell her I'm ready to get dressed."

She and Lavina were taking her mother to the doctor this morning. A long, complicated business that would take the rest of the morning and some of the afternoon, depending on how many women were waiting in the doctor's office. The rain made things worse. They would have to dress her in her raincoat and hold the umbrella as they slid her into the back seat of Smith's enormous black Cadillac. Smith was an old colored man who used to be a driver and houseman, who now earned his money driving ladies around. Getting out of the car once they reached the doctor's would be a little harder. There was no porte cochere in front of the doctor's office. They'd have to lead her under an umbrella to the door. If she was feeling weak, Smith would have to carry her. Poor old Smith who was older than Lavina and a lot less strong. Mary Jacob felt as bad for Smith on these occasions as she did for her mother. When he lifted her, his deep eyes bulged and the veins on his forehead stood out. Lavina was always talking about the blind leading the lame. Surely Smith carrying Lillian was a no less pitiful sight.

"Lavina," Mary Jacob called out, as she rounded the staircase, sliding into the kitchen. "Vina, Mama wants you."

Lavina was unpacking the week's groceries that had arrived in a dozen wet cardboard cartons a short while ago. Half the big kitchen was literally overflowing with groceries: bags and bags of fresh produce—melons and cooshaw squash; okra, tomatoes, and ears of sweet white corn. There were packages wrapped in crisp white butcher paper; cleansers, paper towels, and tin foil. Lavina was at the sink with the tap on full blast, washing lettuces.

"Vina," Mary Jacob called out again. "Vina, Mama wants you."

Lavina turned off the tap and moved around to face her. Vina's face was all wet, glistening like the kitchen window covered in raindrops. The big mole halfway down her nose had a single drop of water clinging to it. To Mary Jacob, it looked as though the mole was crying. Lavina dried her big brown hands on her apron, blotted her face with a sheet of paper towel, and headed out of the room and up the stairs.

The girl knew they would have to lead Lillian through the kitchen to the porte cochere, and she wouldn't like it if her kitchen wasn't perfect. Everything was always supposed to look perfect. "Lavina, why is the kitchen in such disarray?" Lillian had no idea how hard Lavina worked. None of them did, for that matter. Mary Jacob knew Lavina hardly ever sat down and if she did, it was nearly always with some kind of work in her hands, like sock rolling or button sewing. When Lavina wasn't cooking or ironing or cleaning, or helping Lillian to sit up or get dressed or button or unbutton her peignoir, she was polishing or folding or dusting. Once a month or so, an enormous colored man named Carver came to help Lavina with the chandeliers and floors, but Carver was lazy and for what he saved Lavina in cleaning work, he more than made up for in cooking. Carver always got a hot meal for lunch and never cleared his plate anymore than he put away the cleaning supplies, the tall step-ladder, or his work cloths. Lavina had complained to Mary Jacob on numerous occasions that she "would rather take down that ole Wafard chandelier piece by piece myself than have Big Carver to cook and clean up for."

Mary Jacob set to work now, sliding around the kitchen in her high white socks. First, she put away the canned goods in the food pantry. Then she opened the refrigerator and began to shove white paper packages of meat in. In the process, she overturned the glass casserole full of pot roast left over from the night before. She watched the gravy ooze down from the top shelf and drip on top of everything below it. She closed the door of the refrigerator and went for the paper towels to clean up the mess and then decided to do it after she put away the rest of the groceries. She emptied the remaining cartons, arranged the vegetables in a neat pile off to the side of the sink, wrapped the washed lettuces in clean white cloths like Lavina always did, and finally stacked the cardboard boxes in the corner near the door.

By the time Mary Jacob heard them coming down the stairs, the kitchen was presentable. She went to the table and sat down. When Lavina and her mother entered the room, she stood up like she'd been taught to do. Children always stand up when their elders enter the room, even if it's five times in one hour. Lavina held her mother's skinny little arm and the two of them stood there near the doorway between the kitchen and the butlery.

Her mother was all dressed in a navy blue suit and jacket with her make up and pearls on. She had her white cotton gloves clutched in one hand. Her small patent leather purse was in the other hand. It seemed to drag her down like a heavy suitcase. She wore high heeled shoes, which made her skinny legs look even skinnier. Her stockings bagged at the ankles. Mary Jacob had not seen her mother dressed or out of her room in several weeks. Having her in the kitchen felt strange. She looked odd, out of place. She did not belong here.

Lavina led her to the kitchen table and fussed over her, helping her to sit down. Lillian put her gloves down on the table, opened her handbag, and withdrew her leather cigarette case and lighter. "Get me an ashtray, Mary Jacob. And Lavina, you better change into your black uniform before Smith gets here."

When Mary Jacob returned from the butlery with the ashtray, she set it down gently in front of her mother, but she did not want to sit down again. If she did, her mother would see her close up. Her legs would be hidden under the table, but her face and hair would be in plain view.

But her mother was not looking at her. Her eyes were fixed on something in the corner of the room. She took a puff of her cigarette and called out, "Lavina, Lavina, what in the world is the matter with the icebox?"

Lavina entered the room, buttoning up the bodice of her black nylon uniform. Her curly black wig was on, and she was wearing her huge white nurse shoes. They squeaked as she walked across the floor.

"Yes'm?"

Lillian gestured to the icebox.

Mary Jacob stared at the thin stream of brown trailing down the base of the ice box onto the floor and her heart started pounding in her chest. Lavina and her mother were both staring at the icebox.

Then her mother did something completely unexpected. She smiled. It was a radiant smile, young and happy. "Why, if I didn't know any better I'd think some canine had done his business on my ice box." Then she laughed and took a deep pull on her cigarette.

"Lavina, is there some canine in my icebox?"

Lavina smiled. Then she walked over, opened the door, and saw the dinner she was planning to take home tonight all over the shelves.

"It's the pot roast, Miz Lil, I guess it turned itself over when I put the meat from the butcher shop in."

"Well hurry up and clean it up, Lavina, Smith will be here in a minute. And Mary Jacob, get your shoes on and comb your hair. I refuse to be seen with a messy waif. Now run, scoot, child."

Mary Jacob and Lavina made their way through the wet streets of downtown Murpheysfield. Luckily, the rain had stopped when they were on their way to the doctor's office. Now, the sun was beginning to peek through the clouds, though some of the people around them were still walking with their umbrellas out.

Out on the street, Lavina was a different person. The opposite of the way she was at home. She didn't talk and joke, for one. She kept her rich, strong voice low and moved differently. Nothing like the easy way she moved through the rooms of their house confidently from task to task. When Mary Jacob was younger, she thought the difference was due to Lavina's fancy dress-up uniform and shoes, and of course the wig. For Mary Jacob knew she herself acted differently when she was all dressed up with her hair combed and brushed. She did not know exactly when she started realizing Lavina's change of behavior had little to do with her change of clothes. But she had known it now for quite some time. She had grown used to Lavina's public persona, enough so to expect it, though it always alarmed her. Would there come a time when Lavina turned into that other self forever?

When Mary Jacob and Lavina entered the downtown Woolworth's, the familiar smell of cooking fat hit her in the face. Woolworth's always smelled of grease. You could even smell it when you were smelling their perfume. It was one of the biggest stores in Murpheysfield, occupying half a city block. Today, no doubt on account of the rain, the long aisles crowded with merchandise were nearly empty. Lavina headed for the back of the store and Mary Jacob stayed at the front to look at the lipsticks and face powder. Another of Lavina's rules for public behavior—they were not allowed to peruse the aisles together. It was not long before Mary Jacob grew bored with the lipsticks and face powder and moved toward the back of the store to look for Lavina. On her way there, she passed a little colored boy with a nearly bald head. He was thrusting his bare feet into a pair of navy canvas tie-up shoes. The shoes were marked two dollars. Mary Jacob had been told all her life that you didn't try on shoes without your socks on. No one ever said why; it was like wearing clean underwear. Was it different for colored children? Why didn't their mothers tell them the same thing?

Mary Jacob saw Lavina toward the back of the store. It was easy to spot her because she was so tall. Lavina's big black pocketbook was hanging from her wrist and she was rummaging through a pile of brightly colored scarves. Lavina had a pleased expression on her face as she held up a bright pink one with some kind of pattern on it. Mary Jacob pushed her eyeglasses up her nose a bit so she could stare better. Lavina looked so peaceful and happy, messing with the scarves. Mary Jacob knew that if she went to her, Lavina would stop with her messing and patiently pay attention to her. Lavina had to. Just like she had to change who she was on the street.

Just then, the little bald colored boy brushed by her. He was a delicate little boy, so frail it wasn't like a real person brushing by her. He was whistling a light, happy tune that didn't match his bald head and his grim little face. She turned and watched him move with the grace of a cat toward the front of the store, humming his little tune confidently, light on his little feet that were wearing the canvas tie-up shoes with no socks. It was the first time in Mary Jacob's privileged life she had ever seen anyone steal from a store, though Mary Jacob was an accomplished thief of a different sort; she'd been stealing dollar bills from her father's dresser for years and sneaking them into Lavina's big black purse. But, this Mary Jacob knew, was a far graver matter. Still, the little boy was so grace-ful, she wasn't afraid for him. He was gliding out of the store now, right past a cashier in her turquoise smock, whistling his little tune. When he reached the big glass double doors, he pushed one open and turned into a shadow as he disappeared into the street that was bathed in sunlight. She had a sudden urge to follow his example and steal a scarf for Lavina.

As Mary Jacob moved toward the back of the store, she felt the same electric charge of energy that came with her own successfully accomplished thefts. She understood the feeling had to do with the little boy and though she knew she should be ashamed, it was wrong to steal from a store, still, she could not stop it. Lavina was still smiling, messing with the scarves. Then, without warning, every-thing started to go wrong. Mary Jacob saw a carrot-haired woman in a turquoise smock striding toward Lavina, who did not notice right away. Then the woman was upon her, grabbing the scarf out of Lavina's hand. She saw Lavina shaking her head, and the quick change of expression from happy to terrified. Mary Jacob felt her own stomach sinking.

The carrot-haired woman had a harsh, trashy twang, "Open up yo' pocketbook girl." From where Mary Jacob stood, the woman seemed on top of Lavina, and though the woman was small and skinny compared to Lavina, she loomed over her like a huge, evil spirit from hell.

Mary Jacob moved slowly toward Lavina then went and stood by her side. She stood right next to her so that their arms were touching. She could feel Lavina's ample arm trembling. Mary Jacob wanted to pray, but it came to her in a flash of horror that God and Jesus Christ were at last exacting revenge.

It was then she found her courage. From the depths of her came an unfamiliar voice, though she knew at once it had been hiding inside her all along. It was harsh, grown up, and wonderfully fierce. "Leave her alone," she told the clerk. "This lady works for my family and she wouldn't steal anything from your ugly store."

The clerk turned her furious face on her. Mary Jacob grabbed hold of Lavina's warm fat arm that was trembling. She wasn't going to let the woman open Lavina's purse. For she knew if she did, a long bright scarf, like the serpent in the garden, would fly out at them.

Praying just after you sinned was cheating. Still Mary Jacob was whispering, *"our father who art in heaven . . ."* but it didn't do any good, because the woman was reaching out for Lavina's bag. Things were falling everywhere: a pack of tissues; a huge, worn purple wallet with bits of paper falling out; a yellow-green rabbit foot with keys that jangled when they fell to the floor; a bottle of aspirin, one of those plastic rain hats that folded up like an accordion, and pennies. Pennies everywhere, rolling under the counter, down the aisle, twirling and spinning and dancing like freed spirits.

It took Mary Jacob a minute to realize that no scarf had fallen to the floor. The woman was still savagely digging in Lavina's bag. But it was no use. There was no scarf to be found.

Once again, Mary Jacob found that harsh, ugly voice that seemed as much a part of her now as her feet and hands. She liked the voice. It went along with the boy stealing the shoes and the dollar bills she slipped out of Jack's wallet. The voice commanded the clerk to leave them alone. And this time, it worked. She dropped the big black bag, turned, and then slunk away.

The two of them stood there for a moment, like statues in the statue game. Lavina was a big dark statue, and she Mary Jacob was a smaller squat one. Neither of them were pretty statues. Mary Jacob wondered why she even thought about pretty now. What mattered was getting to her knees and picking up Lavina's things, though anyone could see the stuff on the floor was no better than trash.

Lavina said, "Well, sugar, I guess the angels was watchin' ovah us today. Scared that one away." They both smiled, but Mary Jacob knew Lavina's smile was as false as her own. They were ugly statues with false smiles, but that didn't matter either. Mary Jacob got to her knees. Not to pray. She would never pray again, not to God. Or to Jesus Christ. No one was looking out for them. It was she, Mary Jacob, who had to look after Lavina now. Mary Jacob counted the pennies as she picked them up. Twelve, thirteen, fourteen. Lavina was patting her head, but the large hand that was patting wasn't Lavina's calm, comforting hand. It was some nervous thing that scuttled over her hair like a spider.

VINA

∿∿

Sun were shining hot, hot on the street. Mary Jacob, she want to hold my arm, and I am taking her arm away, real gentle-like. But it weren't no good. She kept puttin' it back. I was thinking 'bout that fifty-cent pink scarf with the blue roses on it. Was gonna buy that pretty thing before they accused me wrongly. Thought about that scarf that night and some of the next. Ain't that always the way it is when you gets your heart all set on something and you don' get it?

By now we is to the corner of Milam and Marshall streets, on the side of the courthouse where the bus stop. My first thought when I sees him standing there in the sunshine was, shame on you, boy, playing hookie from that job Mr. Jack got you. Then, I remember it were raining that morning. Nobody playing golf when it rain. Still, I were kinda nervous about seeing him there. Longs weren't the kind let you bring chirrun to work. No, they tole me the very first day. Miz Lil asks me how many chirrun I has and when I says just one, she look relieved and she say, "Well, that's good. But you can't be bringing him here to work. We is not that kind of house, Lavina." Well, I could have told her I knew that just by looking at her, but I just said, "yes'm," like she wanted me to do 'cause I need that job.

My boy Billy Ray, he is standin' there whistling in the sunshine. His back were turned to me and I guess he could feel my eyes on his back. Now he turning round and givin' me a look. I raises up my arm and gives him a little wave and smile. Billy Ray, he staring at Mary Jacob. And Mary Jacob, she staring at Billy Ray. Then the bus pull up. Billy Ray runs up them steps, my boy, he was always real light like on his feet and I watches him make his way to the back of the bus.

Mary Jacob say, "Vina, who's that boy? Do you know him?"

I says, "Well I reckon I do. That's my baby. Billy Ray."

Mary Jacob look all shook up. "That Billy Ray?" she say.

"What you act so surprised for. I been tellin' you about Billy Ray your whole life." Mary Jacob, she say, dull like, "Oh I don' know. I just thought he would look different. I thought he would look like you."

"He look like his father," I tole the child, which was the truth. Billy Ray do favor his father.

Then Mary Jacob say, "Vina, how come he didn't speak to you or anythin'?"

And then I says like I sometimes have to, "Don' ask me them kind of questions, Mary Jacob."

We start walking again. And the child, she kept her hand on my arm tighter than before. Didn't worry her any about it. Don't know why. Then I start for some reason thinkin' about the baby girl I lost when I were just sixteen years old. Weren't Billy Ray's father's. She were what they used to call a love chile. And I loved that man and his baby, though he left and she passed. Something happen to her in her little crib. They say it happen sometime. And that's the truth—it happen to someone else I knew—her baby girl died like that one night when she ain't even sick. My baby girl, her name was Mary too. Mary Louise. I thought to myself, why if Mary Louise hadn't passed, she'd be a grown woman with chirrun of her own. Couldn't figure out how old she'd be; my figurin' weren't no better than my reading. Then, Mary Jacob and I, we gets to the door of the doctor's office. I remember it were there 'cause we open the door and a great big old blast of cold air hit our face. Mary Jacob, she say, "Were you glad to see him? I mean you don't get to see him all day long." I was back with Mary Louise at the time, and I didn't know who we was talkin' 'bout right away. Mary Jacob, she say, "Billy Ray, were you glad to see Billy Ray?"

"'Course I was glad to see him, Billy Ray's my baby boy." Then we goes up in the elevator. We don' say nothin' 'cause they people in that elevator. But when we gets to the office and sit down to wait for Miz Lil, she start up again.

"Vina," she say, "Vina, when the summer's over and I go back to school, do you miss seeing me when I'm gone?"

I laugh a little and say, "'Course I do. You're my baby too. Why I tell everybody at the church you is the sweetest white chile in Louisiana." And that's the truth. She were.

RUMINATIONS

∽∾∽

On the bus ride home and long into the hot sticky after-noon, Billy Ray could not stop thinking about Mary Jacob. He did not name her—he called her the "ugly one." It had shocked him to see her walking so close to his mother. Had he seen it wrong or had her ugly white hand been holding his mother's deep brown arm like she belonged to her? He knew that couldn't be true. His mother was their slave. For thirty-five dollars a week they owned her five days a week from the time she woke up till she dragged herself home on the bus every night to take off her shoes. That fat white arm holding her like that did not go along with the picture he had painted in such intricate detail over the years. During all those afternoons and evenings when he was young and she paid the neighbor lady fifty cents a week to look after him. When he was old enough to stay alone, the picture had not changed. It had grown, enlarged. And the ugly one was at the center of the canvas: a spoiled white child with everything she wanted ordering his mother around. What were they doing at the Woolworth's? He always pic-tured his mother at their big white house, ironing, cooking, cleaning toilets, never out on the street. Never away from there. When he was little, she had sometimes called him late in the afternoon to tell him she'd be late or just to say hello. He never thought of her as being anywhere but there in that big white house on Fairfield Street. After he saw the place when he was eight, when he was very lonesome, he'd steal coins from her purse until he had enough for bus fare. He'd ride out to Fairfield on the bus, get off, and stand in front of the house, knowing she was near. One summer afternoon, a police car stopped and ordered him to the car.

"What you doin' nigger boy? You're too young to be working the yard. You up to no good, nigger boy? What you doin' in this neighborhood?"

"My mother work here," he had told the policeman, and the policeman had let him go.

The encounter with the police had kept the boy from ever riding out there on the bus again. In those years, he had grown used to his loneliness. And forgotten the house that was her palace and her prison. Still, it knocked his world upside down to see his mother out in the world, walking down the street with that little girl.

Where had his mother been when he was snitching the shoes? The boy hadn't seen her—was she there at the Woolworth's too? If so, why hadn't he seen her? She was always so easy to see on account of her height. But, mostly the girl worried him. All day long the thought of her ate at him, and on his free day too, away from that hateful caddying. When he just wanted to lie on his bed and play his songs, all he could see was her with her black eyeglasses. Billy Ray knew her face from the little picture his mother had on the shelf in her bedroom, but he had never once seen her in person. She was so big. Somehow he had always pictured her as an ugly brat with eyeglasses and a fancy white child dress that cost more than any black person made in a week. The girl he had seen today was wearing clothes not much better than his. How come she wore clothes too small for her when all she had to do was hold out her fat white hand and have green money pouring into it?

He had worried about her at the Woolworth's, before he even knew who she was. Worried about her opening her mouth on him. She was white, wasn't she? Luckily for him, she had kept her mouth closed. But now, since she knew who he was, she would certainly tell. His mother wouldn't do nothing. Nothing she could do really. Just look sad and worried. Double up on her prayers. She prayed for him every night on her knees next to her bed. Her big hands on the bed tight together, her little head with no real hair bent over. The walls were thin as cardboard; had to be stone deaf not to hear the floor creek and her voice soft and pleading with the Lord.

Didn't she have plenty enough of her hands and knees at that job without getting down on them again at night next to her bed in her big white nightgown? She wouldn't tell him to his face, but she'd tell the Lord. She'd say, "Jesus, forgive my Billy Ray for stealing." "Lord, I don' want my Billy Ray in jail." Then, likely as not, she'd go ask old Houston for money for new shoes. Billy Ray hated that. Hated to think what that old man, who thought nothing of walking around their street with his zipper undone, would demand back in payment. The loans from Houston had worried him for years. Didn't matter if it didn't work no more, still it was there. He'd seen it often enough flip-flopping on the street, seen it his whole life. If she went to Houston and came back with money, he knew what he'd say, "If you hadn't given your boyfriend M.L. all our money, I wouldn't have done it." Either that or he'd simply say that big ugly girl had lied. Who was she going to believe, that white girl or him, her own son with skin the same color as hers?

TABASCO

⌀⌀

S
he found out about Van and her father on the day she also found out once and for all that she and Kathryn were never going to be sisters. Her re-education began in the afternoon. Van and Kathryn were in the dressing room. Mary Jacob was lying on her bed, having put aside the book she was reading to eavesdrop on the older girls. They had been in there for a good while, though she had not heard anything until now that excited her curiosity.

"Foster and me and Jane and Bill are goin' to the cub. How come you're not goin' out with Beau?"

"I gave him back his bracelet. I hope I didn't hurt him, Beau's sweet and all, but I don't want to lead him on."

"Well he does have more pimples on his face than Carter's does pills, Van. I never did know how you could stand kissing him with all that Clearasil flaking off. It's absolutely disgustin'."

"Beau's a very nice boy, Kathryn. He can't help all those pimples, poor thing!"

"You know what they say pimples come from? Sexual frustration!"

"Kathryn Calhoun Long, you leave poor Beau alone, you hear? He's unhappy enough as it is with me breaking up with him. I hope he starts going steady with someone else real soon."

Van was always so nice about everything; the only way you could tell she was being serious was when she used Kathryn's full and proper name. Mary Jacob had never heard an unkind word issue forth from Van's beautiful red lips. She often wondered how someone as mean as Kathryn would have a friend as kind as Van, or vice versa, but they were friends, they'd been friends their whole lives. If only Mary Jacob could have such a friend herself: someone who was beautiful and kind and also popular. Because everyone loved Van, she had twice been voted most popular girl at the high school.

Mary Jacob pulled down her long white socks and admired her hairless legs. She crossed the uncut leg over the cut leg, pleased with the result. She was thinking about showing Van her long, smooth legs. Kathryn hadn't even bothered to check on them. Mary Jacob was hoping if she showed Van her legs, the older girl would be sufficiently impressed with her maturity to drive her downtown and show her about getting a brassiere. Mary Jacob rubbed her hands up and down her chest that had two soft bumps on it with hard little nipples. Her poor mother would be the last person she'd ask about a bra. And she certainly wasn't going to ask Kathryn. Van was her only hope.

She was saying, "Y'all have any Midol? I'm supposed to get my period tomorrow and my cramps are always worse if I don't do anything about them beforehand."

"Take one of these," she heard her sister say. "They'll take away your cramps. And you never get hungry either. If poor Mama would take these instead of those damn sleeping pills, she'd be scooting around like she used to."

There was silence for a while. Mary Jacob had not experienced cramps. She'd only gotten her period once. Kathryn was forever complaining about her cramps and was home in bed at least one day a month. Mary Jacob believed her lack of pain during the monthly cycle was just another example of her not being a proper girl. She had nothing in common with her sister or Van or any other beautiful female—not even pain while menstruating.

She was about to pick up her book once again when she heard Kathryn say in her nastiest voice, "Gawd, will you ever in your life forget how Mary Jacob put the Kotex on over her underpants? I swear that was the only time I heard Mama laugh since her last operation."

Her sister's unrelenting meanness did not surprise her. The only time in her life Kathryn had ever been kind to her had been the night they both learned their mother's remaining bosom had been removed. Their father had summoned them to the library and related in a matter-of-fact way that their mother was very ill, what had transpired that morning, and that they were to be particularly careful to be cheerful to her when he took them to see her in the hospital. And that above all else, they must never, ever make the mistake of mentioning the subject to her. The two of them had returned to their room upstairs, not mentioning the taboo subject between them or even when they returned that evening from the hospital visit. But that night, Mary Jacob had gone into Kathryn's room and asked to sleep there. And miraculously Kathryn had let her slip in beside her. That night the two of them had been sisters. Mary Jacob had crept out the next morning afraid to awaken and annoy Kathryn, and neither one of them had mentioned the incident since then. But Mary Jacob had taught herself to hope after that night. Not for a constant comforting friend, but a ray of kindness once in a while. Now all at once, Mary Jacob understood—a hard ball of pain was always going to be between her sister and herself. Their mother was as likely to grow another bosom as her sister would be to grow fond of her and treat her well. Mary Jacob put it to herself exactly that way.

She grabbed up her teddy bear and rolled off the bed and went for the sliding door and opened it furiously. She hurled the teddy bear at her sister. It missed the mark, landing instead on the top of the dressing table where all Kathryn's perfumes were arrayed on a long silver tray. There was a satisfying smashing of bottles and a sudden powerful smell of perfume in the air.

"You are the meanest person in the whole world. And I hate you!" she hollered, not caring at all that she sounded like a two year old.

Van floated over. Beautiful Van in her high lacy brassiere and her hair all pretty, up in curls on top of her head. "Don't feel bad, Mary Jacob. First time I used a tampon, I left the cardboard in. That's much sillier than what you did."

Van was an angel. A beautiful angel in her lacy brassiere and her glistening white skin. But her sister was a devil from hell and she hated her.

Mary Jacob smiled at Van. "You did, you really did?"

"I certainly did, Mary Jacob. Now, if you run downstairs and fix me a Coke I'll tell you all about it."

Kathryn blew out a long stream of smoke and said in a bored voice, "Fix me one too and put a little bourbon in both of them."

Mary Jacob glared at her sister. "Daddy keeps the whiskey locked up. You know that."

"Mary Jacob you don't know anythin'. Look in the middle drawer of the butlery. The key's underneath the cocktail napkins."

She turned and left the pretty wallpapered dressing room. She passed through her own room and stood inside a moment, her face burning, close to tears. "Mary Jacob, you don't know anythin'." It was one of her sister's favorite phrases, and the trouble was it was true. She didn't know about Kotex, brassieres, babies, kissing, why, she was even too much of a baby herself to know where Daddy hid the key to the whiskey. Van was saying, "Kathryn, do you mind if I spend the night here tonight? Mother's having her bridge game and you know how it is when she has her bridge games."

"I'm spending the night with Victoria, but you can stay. Nobody will notice except Mary Jacob. But if you see her touching any of my things, you let me know. You hear? Oh God! She's broken my Shalimar atomizer."

Mary Jacob did not wait to hear what Van said or if she was going to spy on her. She halfway suspected Van would turn on her. Why wouldn't she? Everyone else except Lavina did so on a regular basis. She made her way down the long upstairs hall, past her mother's room, where the door was shut. She stopped and rested her cheek against the highboy. All her life she had hated to cry. The one name her sister had never called her was crybaby. She was good at stopping them. Though now, her self-control was gone. Terrible swift tears were spilling from her eyes, running down her cheeks. She had a lump in her throat and her body was heaving. She forced herself to walk down the stairs, but she had to hold on to the banister. What she wanted to do was curl up in a ball and howl.

By the time she reached the butlery, she wasn't crying anymore. She went to the drawer where her mother's cocktail napkins were kept. There were dozens of them divided by wooden insets: heavy beige damask, snowy see through ones with flowers. In the back part of the drawer, the holiday cocktail napkins were kept, the ones with holly, turkeys, and even bunny rabbits. Like Kathryn's drawers, it was perfectly organized. She found the key underneath the damask ones. The liquor cabinet had a double door. When you unlocked it, you had to reach inside and unlatch the other side. She knew how to do this because her father, in one of his rare good moods, had shown her how.

The drawer of the whiskey cabinet was on rollers. Mary Jacob pulled the heavy drawer toward her and stared with admiration. It was just like the cocktail napkin drawer, only much more important. Jack Long's whiskey bottles were housed in perfectly proportioned little niches. Every tall, shiny bottle, every short squat one had its place, even the little bottles of bitters and hot pepper sauce and cocktail onions. She, Mary Jacob, was the only one in this beautiful house without a place. She had known it all her life, but the thought had never articulated itself to her in this way.

She took out the big bottle of bourbon and the little bottle of pepper sauce. She went to another cabinet where the bottles of Coke were kept. She passed through the swinging door that led into the kitchen and went for the icebox. She could hear Lavina humming to herself from the laundry room. But she did not call out to her as she normally would. She took an ice tray from the freezer and brought it back with her to the butlery. In one glass she measured a careful jigger of bourbon then filled it with ice and Coke. She set it off on her right side. Then she banged the little jar of pepper sauce so hard the cap chipped. But that made it easier to get the tiny grooved cap off. In the other glass she poured the entire small bottle of pepper sauce; it took quite a while because the fiery red sauce came out in little drops. Then she filled it with ice and Coke. She took out a pretty silver tray from another cabinet, one lined with silver cloth and fitted just for trays. Then she went back to the cocktail napkin drawer and took out two napkins. She put the prettiest one, the one with the turquoise initials and pink flowers, under the pepper sauce drink. She put everything away, threw the empty pepper sauce bottle in the trash, locked up the liquor cabinet, and replaced the key.

Now, just a few minutes later, she was laughing, flying down the curved stairs, taking them three at a time. Familiar things whirled by her: the Grandfather clock, the door of the powder room under the stairs, the big kitchen with the black-and-white floor. Laughing was like flying really. Lavina whirled by, Lavina who was calling after her, but it was hard to hear her over Kathryn's screaming. Screaming like she had never heard in her whole life. The house was shaking with it. On her bicycle, racing down the driveway, she could still hear it. Her sister, Kathryn, screaming and screaming. But Mary Jacob was flying away from them forever and she told herself she'd never come home.

VINA

〜〜

Funny thing is, if Mary Jacob hadn't made her sister swallow that pepper sauce, I never would have got myself in so much trouble. No, I wouldn't been there on the late bus to sit next to my friend Noog, who was always late on Friday night on account of them Jewish folks who have their Lord's Day on the wrong day.

Kathyrn, she screamin' and screamin'. Why, you never heard nothin' like that day in that house. I thought somebody had set herself on fire. Made me freeze right up. I was downstairs, rockin' on my chair, rollin' socks when I hears it. Knew right away it weren't poor Miz Lil who don' have the strength to make such a fuss. I thought it were Mary Jacob. And that's the truth. And I couldn't stand it, anything happenin' to my baby girl. So I unfroze myself, got up, and went into the kitchen where the noise were even stronger. Lord have mercy, I didn't know what to do, thought of calling the fire department.

Mary Jacob, she come flyin' in the kitchen with a look on her face I'll never forget. She were smiling, her head throwd back, galloping like a horse gone wild out the door, left it wide open. Then I sees her out the kitchen winder, hotfootin' it to the garage, going fast, fast down that long driveway on her bicycle.

Screamin', it were dyin' down. Didn't know whether that were good or bad. So I says a little prayer as I goes past that old Grandad clock. He say it were three o'clock. Three bells, they goes off when it's three o'clock. One go off when it three thirty. I goes up them curved stairs, then down that long hall, and takes a little look into Miz Lil's room. She weren't in her big old bed, and everything's as quiet as a mouse now. That put the fear into me too. I went back to check to see if she were in her bathroom. But she weren't there neither. Whatever was happenin' was happenin' in the girls' part of the house. Mary Jacob's the first room in the girls' part of the house. Dressin' room's in between, then there's Kathryn's room. Like I said, I'd already seen Mary Jacob galloping wild out the backdoor. So I knew not to look for her in her room. Still, I stayed there little bit. Don' know why really. I straighten her bed. Then, I goes in the dressin' room. And like I tole Noog later when I sees her on the bus that night, "Honey, that room look like the wrath of God had come to call." There was a big old glass, look like of coke all smashed and coke running everywhere, so much it were dripping off the counter onto the carpet. One of Miz Lil's silver serving trays were on the floor. And one of her best cocktail napkins were all soaked through. Kathryn's perfume bottles, they mostly fallen over. And in the middle of them spilt bottles, why there were Mary Jacob's teddy bear. Don' know how that bear got there with them spilt bottles. I sponged him off before I put him back where he supposed to be on Mary Jacob's bed. But that poor teddy smell like he spent all Saturday night in a cat house.

I hears talking comin' from Kathryn's room. Before you gets to her bedroom, there's a little room, so I couldn't hear talkin' real clear. Prettiest room in that house if you ask me, with a velvet chair and violet plants and pitchers of old-fashioned white chirrun with gold hair. I stands there in the door and sees Kathryn, who is curled up like a baby with her head in Miz Lil's lap. Miz Lil, why she lookin' alive for the first time in a long time. Didn't surprise me none—she needs to pay some mind other than to herself. She pettin' Kathryn on the head. Van is sittin' next to them on the bed too. That girl, she were wearin nothin' but her brassiere and her panties, which I thought weren't real respectful. Though she was a pretty sight with those high bosoms of hers and them soft, silky underpants. See right through them underpants and that lace brassiere of hers. Trouble is with pretty girls like Van, they is always flaunting themselves. Cain't help it.

Then Miz Lil say, "Lavina, go fetch Mary Jacob." Then that Kathryn, why she start moaning and curl up even tighter on her mother's lap. What you call those silky puppies? Golden ones with long hair, she put me in mind of one of them. Pretty to look at, but very nervous. So I say, "Why, Mary Jacob she gone."

"What do you mean, Mary Jacob's gone?"

I nods my head and says, "Mary Jacob gone on her bicycle. Prolly went to the library. You know how she read."

Then Miz Lil, she look at me real stern like and she say, "Lavina, do you know anything about what happen this afternoon?"

I say, "No'm," which was the truth.

Well, if you ask me, what they done to that poor girl was much worse than what she done to her sister, though it must have stung, that pepper sauce.

Sister's always be fighting. That's nature's way. And now that those girls were growd up, they should have let them settle their differences between them. Kathryn, she call Mr. Jack downtown at his office to let him know about the pepper sauce. I'm cleaning up their dressin' room now and I could hear every word of what she said, though I knew the story by then.

Kathryn, looking pained and pale. But I knew she weren't hurt any. She got herself dressed and started packing up her little suitcase on account of the fact that she was staying over with her friend Victoria that night. Then Miz Lil say, "Lavina, get me back to bed." Pretty Van, she say no, she'll do it. Van got herself a robe on by this time—think it were one of Kathryn's robes—a long pretty thing like everythin' that girl has. Well, Van, she take Miz Lil back to her room and Kathryn go off in her blue car. Mr. Jack, he give her her own car when she turn fifteen. Brand new car. Then I finishes cleanin' up the dressing room, and when I goes past Miz Lil's room on the way downstairs, I sees Van fussing over her, petting her head, givin' her them terrible pills. She ain't suppose to take more than one at a time, but she don' listen to a word no one says. She take three, I seen her take four.

Sure enough, Miz Lil, she were fast asleep when I look in on her right before dinner. It's them pills cause her to sleep like that. When Mr. Jack come home, he want to know right away. "Lavina, where's Mary Jacob?" I was fixin' supper fast, on account of I was late with all the goings on upstairs, and I tole him, "I don' know, Mr. Jack."

It were then that poor child, she walk in the back door lookin' dragged down, I can tell you. That Jack, he still in the kitchen. Mary Jacob, she is standing by the back door froze like. He smile real ugly. Then he set his briefcase down, take off his belt, and still she just stand there not making a peep.

If you ask me, if a father gonna whip his child, he oughta do it in private. But that Jack, he done in right in front of me. What he do is say, "Mary Jacob, get over here this instant." She walk to him then he has her kneel over the kitchen table. "You too big and fat," he says to her, real ugly like. Then he pull her pants and he starts whipping her with that that belt of his. Felt like he was whipping us both. Every time that belt of his come down on her, it come down on me. Thought it would never be over with. Kind of whipping only bad boys suppose to get. Then he orders her to her room. Tell her to stay there until he say she can come out, puts his belt back on, cool as can be. And that child, why she don' let out a peep the whole time. Don' know how she stood it.

Well, that weren't the end of the day of the pepper sauce. Though it were calmed down considerably at the Longs' after that whipping Mary Jacob, why she weren't allowed to have no supper, so there were only the two of them to serve that night.

Well, it were almost quarter to nine by the time I got out of that house. They was whispering and giggling and drinkin' wine and more wine and I thought that dinner would never end. Shame on them. I was tired. Dead tired by the time the bus pull up. Weren't nobody on the bus except my friend Noog. When she sees me, she start waving her arms.

And before I could boo, Noog say, "Lavina, they sprung M.L."

"Praise the Lord," I says, "that's the first good news I heard today."

It were dark by this time. Looking at the winder of the bus, I couldn't get my mind away from that chile up in her room alone after that whipping. Don't matter if you have the prettiest room a girl could ever ask for, it don't help much after a whipping like that.

I was fixin' to tell Noog about it when she say, "I wonder what they gonna do when he come here?"

"What you talkin' 'bout, comin' here?

Then Noog, she look at me with her great big smile. I can see it now—she had a gold tooth like mine, only hers in a different place off to the side

"Why Lavina, I'm telling you he's comin'. Before the summer's over, M.L. be here."

Well, you could have knocked all two hundred pounds of me over with a feather when I hear that. I say, "you don' mean?" Noog, she look all stuck up. She love to be the first one in town to know the news. She say, "Where you been girl? There's a meeting at the church on Tuesday night. M.L. gonna be there. He comin' to Murpheysfield!"

DISASSOCIATION

~~~

She had been upstairs in her room for hours before she became aware of the passing of time. It was dark in her room now. And before it had been light. She was used to losing days of her life happily in books, but this was different. Several hours of her life had passed and she had not been there to notice. It was as though she had been swimming under water for a long time. Where she had gone was somewhere like that. A place without sound where there were no people. She got up off her bed now, for she had to use the bathroom, badly. She told herself it would hurt when she sat down, but in an odd way she did not feel the hurt; she would not let herself. It took a long time using the toilet. And there was something plugging up her insides. It wasn't painful, just odd. When she was finished, she passed through the dressing room and flicked on the light and looked at her face up close in the full-length mirror on the front of the bathroom door. Her whole face was patterned with big red marks. Popcorn marks, like she often got on her thighs when she read too long on her stomach. She pulled down her shorts, turned her backside to the mirror and even without her glasses she could see that there were red marks there. The bedspread had not caused those marks. She knew what he had done, but like the hours that had passed, she could not connect the experience to herself. It had happened, but she had no feeling about it.

She went back into her bedroom now and went to the window and stared at the twisted shapes of the live oak trees and the quick flash of lights from the occasional passing car from the front of the house. Now that she was back, she remembered Lavina, who had come to the door and brought her a biscuit wrapped in a paper napkin. She had gotten up off the bed opened the door and seen Lavina. Her room had still been light then. She had not wanted the biscuit. Lavina had gone away. She had shut the door, put her face down on the bed again. And the late summer day had passed into night.

She had run away that afternoon. Though that too was cloudy. She had not gotten far. First, she went to the library and read for a while. But the library closed at five. She rode around for a while, then killed some more time at the drug store looking at magazines. She rode around a subdivision of new houses all close together with no real trees in front. She remembered the bank, but it was closed when she got there. She was hours too late to make them give her the sixty-three dollars she had there. It was then that she had thought of her jewelry. But her jewelry was home in her jewelry box. She had read books where women pawned jewelry, but she knew she would not get much. She had a garnet ring, an aquamarine heart on a gold chain, and sixty-three dollars she could not get to. Kathryn had a pretty diamond ring, a sapphire lavaliere, and nearly a whole string of pearls on her add-a-pearl necklace. But she didn't want to steal Kathryn's jewelry. She didn't want anything of Kathryn's. Not her lipsticks or her eyebrow pencils—she never wanted to touch anything that belonged to her ever again.

Mary Jacob had come home for two reasons: because she could not think of anywhere else to go and because there was blood on the bicycle seat. Now Mary Jacob understood what that stuffed feeling inside her was. She reached inside her pants and felt it: the damp soft thing that was plugging up her insides. When she was still running away, the thought had crossed her mind that she might bicycle out to the country club and charge dinner to her father's account. For at the end of her three-hour absence, though hot and dead tired, she had been horribly hungry. She'd been in the little park then, the one near to the house resting under a tree from the heat. She was so hot and sweaty, she had not noticed the dampness between her legs. She didn't put it together until she'd gotten off her bike and saw the blood on the leather seat. She'd touched it with her finger. It was warm and dark. Just like the goop that came down her leg. She had gone to the bathroom in the park and rubbed it off her leg with a brown paper towel. The bathroom stank. It was funny how you could not recall a smell exactly, but the memory of it could make you cringe just the same. The bathroom stank even worse than she did. It was then she had known that she had to go home. It was either home or someplace that stank. She did not have far to go; all the same it took some time walking her bike home.

After her father had whipped her she had come upstairs. She had gone straight for the cabinet under the sink and taken out Kathryn's box of Tampax. She read the directions, made sure she did not leave the cardboard in; then finally she had come back here in her room and put herself down on the bed.

The house was quiet. It must be very late. That's why she was so hungry. Mary Jacob hoped Lavina had made pie. She didn't want real food. She wanted something sweet. Pie or cake with milk. She listened to the sound of the air conditioning groaning on. Then the clock downstairs began to chime. She strained her ears to listen and count. Eleven times, she was sure it chimed eleven times. Her mother would have been asleep for hours. She had nothing to fear from her. And her father usually went upstairs to watch the news in his room at ten. She remembered now that Kathryn was gone. She could sneak down to the kitchen, bring what she found back to her room and nobody would even notice. After she ate, she'd rinse her dishes in the bathroom sink, put on her nightgown, and go to sleep. The heaviness in her body must mean she was tired. But it was hard to feel anything else except this awful hollow hunger that gnawed at her insides.

There were no lights on in the upstairs hall. That was a good sign. He always turned off the upstairs hall light before he went to sleep. Mary Jacob crept down the hall, past the huge black highboy that loomed like a giant monster in the dark. The door to her mother's room was closed. She opened it carefully and, even though the room was huge and her bed way in the back by the windows, she could hear her mother's snoring. The door to his room, at the far end of the hall, was closed too. Better yet, there was no slit of light beneath the door. She was so hungry, her empty belly was throbbing. Even if he beat her again, she had to have some food.

She was by the tall clock now in the front hall. It was after twelve. She had missed one of the chimes. All the lights downstairs were off too. The only way she could see was by the light that came through the fanlight at the top of the front door. The pretty glass fanlight made rainbows on the rug in the front hall when the morning sun shined through. A different range of colors shined around the fan-light at night. She had never noticed that before.

She was in the kitchen doorway when she heard something. A mewing sort of sound. The air conditioning was off now. It went off and on all night. The house was absolutely quiet except for the faint buzzing of the icebox and this soft mewing sound. Kathryn and her mother were both allergic to cats. But Mary Jacob and Lavina some-times gave the neighbor's cat a saucer of milk outside the kitchen door. Mary Jacob crept through the kitchen, went to the back door, and quietly as possible, opened it, looking hopefully for the cat. It would be nice to see the cat, run her fingers through the warm, silky fur. But, there was no cat there. Why then could she still hear the faint mewing sounds? Once before, the cat had gotten in the house and her mother had sneezed and gotten pink eye. If someone caught her down here and out of her room, Mary Jacob could say she was looking for the cat. He wouldn't beat her then.

She crept back to the front hall. The mewing sounds were louder here. She rounded the corner and followed them. Now she was inside the enormous front room where no one ever sat. Her eyes had grown used to the dark, but it wasn't really black. The enormous Waterford chandelier that hung from the center of the ceiling gave off light just like the fanlight above the front door.

She was about to enter the library, for by now she understood the mewing sounds were coming from there. It was lighter toward the library; her father had forgotten to draw the curtains before he went to bed and moonlight was shining through. Something else was shining too. She squinted through her eyeglasses at the long shining thing glistening in the moonlight. It was white and long and shining and all over the red leather couch. Long dark silky stuff was streaming down the side of the long glistening thing, spilling down the side of the couch on to the rug on the floor. Now her father was coming into view and he was walking toward it. He too was long, glistening, and shining white. His back was turned to Mary Jacob and she saw, for the first time, how a man's back curved in; the lovely way the round smooth buttocks joined his long, graceful legs. He had a drink in his hand. He put it down on the table in front of the red leather sofa and then he put all of himself down on Van. That's what the mewing sounds were. He was squashing her as he moved slowly, up and down, up and down.

Mary Jacob knew she should not be watching. She knew if he found her, what he had done to her this afternoon would be nothing to what he'd do to her now. Still she stood there, fascinated. She wondered how something so terrible, so awful, could be beautiful too. For it was something beautiful to see, the shiny whiteness of them, as though they were made of stars, moving up and down in the moonlit room. Van was mewing like a cat does when it's contented, and then she was wrapping her silky paws around him. He was lapping at her now with his tongue. He wasn't squashing her. Mary Jacob knew now he wasn't squashing her. He was filling up her whole being with some terrible sweetness and they belonged to each other as no two people had ever belonged to each other before.

When the air conditioning groaned back on, she turned and crept away. She could hear them as she made her way through the dark front room, underneath the glistening chandelier that shimmered when she passed below it, and even in the dark front hall. As she climbed up the long curved stairway and down the hall to her room, she knew she could not hear them anymore. Still, it seemed to her the sight and sound of them would stay with her forever. She paused at the door of her mother's room and it was all she could do not to cry out. She felt fiercely protective of the pale, thin woman who didn't have a womb and therefore couldn't do what Van did. When she reached her own room, she climbed on her bed and sat rocking there in the dark, clutching her bear. But there was something wrong with it. There was something wrong with everything now. The bear that always smelled the same was different. It was damp and smelled powerfully of perfume. Some terrible, strong perfume had seeped inside his old, soft fur and he would never be the same again either.

FIRED

⌒⌒

The caddies at the Murpheysfield Country Club were expected to arrive by five forty-five. The golfers liked to tee off early, particularly in the summer when the temperature could be as hot as ninety-five by ten in the morning. If the game started promptly at six, they could play the front nine holes by eight, take a break in the cool clubhouse and refresh themselves with a second breakfast until ten, then play the back nine holes and return in time for drinks and lunch somewhere past noon. Few golfers attempted to play in the afternoon during the brutal months of July and August. Though, some golfers preferred to tee off in the late afternoon or early evening and end the game with dinner at the club instead of lunch.

Some of the caddies showed up before five a.m. and stayed until nine at night. But that was a special privilege given only to the favorites. Those who did could make as much as ten dollars a day, if they were the boys who caddied for the winning golfers.

While the golfers rested and refreshed themselves in the cool air conditioned rooms of the big white club, the boys stayed in the little caddy shack, on the side of the pro shop, lying on the floor, eating the sandwiches they brought from home, or the MoonPies they bought on the way to work at the convenience store a half a mile down the road from the entrance to country club. Twice a day one of the waiters from the club would take off his starched white coat and lug an ice chest filled with grape Nehi soda to the caddy shack; the first one at ten o'clock; the second at seven at night. There was no fan in the low-ceilinged caddy shack, and other than a few wooden benches, nowhere to sit. The boys stretched out on the dirt floor and slept between games with their faces resting on their arms. All of them carried salt in their pockets and licked it all day long; for without salt, you got too weak to carry the bags. The salt the boys brought from home and the hose outside the caddy shack were the two things that kept the boys from passing out from the heat.

Billy Ray was new that summer and so was only allowed to caddy for the first part of the day. It was dark when he got up; to be there on time, he had to leave the house no later than four forty-five. No bus line linked his house to the country club. He tried to be as quiet as possible in the mornings so as not to wake his mother. He'd sleep in his clothes, get out of bed, sneak into the kitchen, and eat whatever she had left for him; usually some dessert she'd brought home from the night before. If there was enough time, he'd wrap something up to eat in a brown paper sack before heading out the front door when the moon was still shining.

The Saturday they fired him, he was late getting up. Either the alarm hadn't gone off or he hadn't heard it. By the time he got himself out the door, without breakfast, the sky was starting to turn pink and he was already supposed to be there. His own little street was empty and, other than Houston Moseley's rooster making noise, still and quiet as the middle of the night. Because it was Saturday, it would be an hour before the women of the block were up and another three quarters of an hour before they came out of their houses with their street dresses and wigs on, making their slow way to the bus stop two blocks away.

It was six forty-five before he turned down the long tree-lined entrance to the country club. The big old-fashioned building with its graceful pillars shined fresh and white in the morning sun. The parking lot, he could see, was already filling up with their big black Cadillacs, Lincolns, and Oldsmobiles. Saturday was the busiest day of the week. He saw three white women in ugly bright plaid shorts and bright men's shirts, heading up the big front steps where an old colored man in a white coat was there to greet them. Some of the women were good golfers, better even then the men. He had caddied for a few of them ugly women with red faces and big shoulders and he hated them even more than he hated the men.

Billy Ray had been unable to hitch a ride. Three dark beat-up cars with old men had passed him on his way to the country club, but no one had offered him a lift. It was well after seven before he appeared at the front nine holes. He was an hour and fifteen minutes late and the group he was supposed to caddy for was probably half-way through the course.

A group of three men and their caddies stood at the top of the hill on the first hole. Billy Ray watched as a tall handsome blond man whacked the ball with the wood club, sending it high in the air. The second man teed off. He too was blond and tall and he sent the hateful little white ball high up in the air and straight into the little pond way off in the distance. The blond man swore and threw his club down. Though he could see the other golfers exchange a look and smile when this happened, the black faces were solemn. Caddies were not allowed to show emotion, except if the white man made a good hit. Then, and only then, were they allowed to smile and move. When the white man hit the ball good, they liked an audience. Billy Ray watched one of the caddies, a boy about the same age as himself, hand the man another club, then fall to his knees and smooth over the patch of soft green grass the white man had dug up. Seeing the boy fall to his knees, then smooth what the white man had tore up gnawed fiercely within Billy Ray's own empty stomach. He turned and headed for the caddy shack.

He had never seen the place empty like it was now. Usually when he come here, dragged down with heat and hunger, he hardly noticed anything more than the floor, or the can of purple soda when it came. But now he realized the room was no better than Houston Moseley's chicken coop.

Billy Ray went into the tiny cubicle where the toilet was and did his business. There was a sign that said "clean up after yourselves," a toilet brush, and a tin jar of cleanser in the room. There was always the cleanser and the brush and the sign, but often as not, no paper. And you had to wash your hands outside with the hose. The room was clean though. He knew right away he was one of the only ones who never cleaned up. The toilet was too clean for more than one or two of them to go against the rules.

Billy Ray sat down on one of the long wooden benches. It was wobbly. One side of it dug lower in the dirt floor than the other. It was miserably hot. The only thing missing was the smell of chicken shit; though the room didn't smell any too good. Billy Ray didn't know what to do with himself. He did not want to present himself late at the pro shop. Probably, in a while, someone would come in looking for a caddy, and then he would get himself up and carry the bag. He closed his eyes and as soon as he did, the room started spinning. He swore to himself, remembering that he had forgotten his salt. It wasn't even seven thirty and already he was worn out and badly needed his salt. The next thing he remembered was looking up and seeing some red-faced white man shaking his shoulder, telling him to *go on, scat*, like he was some miserable dog. It was eight by then. Billy Ray took himself home, ending his brief career as a caddy.

It was going on ten when he walked up the rickety front stairs of his mother's house and unlocked the door. First thing, he took a cold bath, then turned the fan on in the kitchen and sat under it with his wet skin till his dark flesh was goose pimpled and pleasantly chilly. Then he tied a white rag they used for drying dishes around himself. He fixed eggs and toasted some Wonder Bread over the gas pilot on the range. His mother had gone shopping and there was sweet grape jelly to spread on the bread. He thought briefly of the sweet grape drink he would be having at the country club about now, and the jelly did not taste so sweet and satisfying suddenly. He decided he would never as long as he live ever eat sweet grape anything.

When Billy Ray finished with his meal, he did not get up right away and rinse his dishes. Instead he sat there, stretching his legs out under the table, and his arms over his head. A delicious relaxation filled his small frail body. The extra few hours of sleep and the fact that he had not sweated his day away toting bags for the white man's pleasure made him feel a sense of wonderful well-being. His body was his own and didn't have to tote no bags. The overhead fan was cool, his belly was full, and the house was quiet except for the drip from the bathtub off in the corner and the occasional chicken call from Houston Moseley's yard.

Presently, he got up, went into his little room, got him his other pair of shorts, reached for his harmonica, and spent the rest of the day playing it in his mother's kitchen under the fan, nearly oblivious to the heat or to the hours that passed. Around one, a group of small neighborhood children gathered outside his house and started to dance, but he was unaware of them too. For the first time in his life, Billy Ray did not care who heard him. And he realized now, that it was not shyness that had prevented him from performing up to now, nor was it fear. He simply had not been ready to share his music. He was finished with secrecy now. The time had come for him to take himself and his harmonica to some place away from home.

It never crossed Billy Ray's mind that day he would not succeed. Though it did that night when he went to the club. One thought, and one thought only, ran through his mind that Saturday they fired him from his caddying job. *I'm gonna do it or I'm gonna kill myself.* He was not ready, he knew, for the thick rope he would tie around his neck if he did not go up on a stage with his harmonica and play what had been inside him for so long. The rope was neatly coiled in the little closet where the broom was in the kitchen, had been there as long as he could remember. He would take the rope and go somewhere and hang himself from a tree.

Murpheysfield was not a major music city like New Orleans, or a well-known stop like Shreveport, where black musicians regularly came to play. But Billy Ray had known for as long as he could remember, about the existence of several nightclubs outside of town. Local legend had it that Ernie K. Doe had made his start in Murpheysfield. Groups like Little Anthony and the Imperials came to Murpheysfield several times a year. James Brown and Otis Redding had played the big auditoriums in neighboring cities. Kids at school had gone to see James Brown and come back with fantastic stories about how the performer had made a crippled man walk. Sounded like church to Billy Ray; still he was impressed.

Billy Ray had never before seen a live music performance, except in school when the band played. Or in church, before he stopped going. But he listened to the radio whenever he was at home. And by the time he was thirteen had become a rather discerning critic. Listening to what other musicians did taught him what he could and would do, and also what he would not do. He had never been to a recording studio and knew nothing about sound engineering, but he knew instinctively what he was going to do when the time came, what instruments would back him up and what kind of vocal accompaniment he would require.

Before their television set broke, Billy Ray had watched *The Ed Sullivan Show* and seen Elvis Presley and the way the audience went wild when he shook his hips in his fancy clothes and threw his long black hair back. Billy Ray had no hair or clothes other than the rag-gety stuff he wore everyday. He did not know what he was going to do with his body when he played and that was what he set out to teach himself now.

During the long hot hours of that Saturday, as Billy Ray played in his mother's kitchen, he set his body free to move with the music. He had never done that before. For he knew he could not just stand there. His performance would mean as much as the music he played. If you were a real performer, people would claim you could heal the crippled. You could get them to their feet, have them crying and shaking if you did it right. Billy Ray didn't need a mirror. Even if they had one big enough to see his whole body, he didn't need it. He could feel the movements were right as he sang and played and danced around his mother's kitchen that day. He played and sang for hours and hours, stopping only to rest his voice and his body. He drank water, he licked salt just as he had at the country club. He sprinkled it on white saltine crackers, and when he was revived he played on.

Billy Ray played every single note he had ever heard humming in his brain. And every word he had put to the hum. He had not realized he'd made so many songs inside his head. Never played them all in a row like he was doing now. Never moved much either. Simply stood there and let the hum just happen. By the middle of the afternoon, his consciousness had altered. He did not call it that. But he noticed funny things had begun to happen in his brain. As his fingers traveled across the harmonica and his voice rang out with words and moans and cries, his life seemed to pass before him, as clearly as if it were a picture show.

One particular day kept flashing before him. He had been lit-tle, practically a baby then, so small that his father had to put him on his shoulders to see. His mother and his father had taken him downtown to see the marching bands. And he could see them now, as though they were marching through his mother's kitchen. First there had been the endless procession of the dull white bands with their beautiful, bright uniforms, playing songs like "Dixie" and "You

Are My Sunshine." The white bands did nothing for him. But you had to get through them to get to his own. When they come at last, the boys and girls did not really march neat and dull in strict rows like the white marching bands. Some of the boys didn't have uniforms, a lot of them didn't even have instruments, but that made no real difference. They danced and threw what few batons they had up in the air. Their movements were free and wild. Girls did cartwheels and the splits. Boys jumped up in the air. Drums beat, symbols clashed, brass instruments hooted and screeched. They played some of the same songs the white bands played but even if the words were the same, the songs came from another world. A world of sound and motion and joy.

He had been just three years old that day, when Billy Ray realized for the first time that music was something as basic to him as the food his mother cooked and the watered down canned milk with chocolate syrup she gave him to drink. He had not put that notion in words exactly—it was more of a feeling. As he sat on his father's shoulders, his little legs wrapped about the big man, feeling his strong body sway and looking down, saw his mother's sudden bright smile, Billy Ray had felt, as surely as he could feel his father's strength beneath him, the even greater strength of the crowd. The rhythm of the music held them together, made them into something more important than a family. Something stronger, better. The music made them throw their arms out and move; it changed their sad set faces into joy and rightness. Billy Ray knew that day he belonged to the music just as he belonged to the man whose shoulders his little legs were wrapped around. When his father left, not long after that day, the music had not left with him, but the happiness had. Somehow, this day, it had miraculously returned. Billy Ray did not stop to wonder why.

At the end of the day, Billy Ray called up the radio station he always listened to. He knew the telephone number by heart. People were always calling in and they repeated the number of the station every hour at least. Calling up the radio station was nothing now; it was as easy as moving with his own music. One day, he knew, his name would be on the radio. Billy Ray. Wouldn't use his last name. His songs that he had locked up so tight inside him would be humming in the kitchens of people he knew and people he had never dreamed of. But until that happened, it was best to lie. When the woman from the station answered the phone, Billy Ray said he was from out of town and needed directions to the place where the best music was played. He made his voice sound old, grown up. It was not hard to do. Anything connected with sound was easy for him. The woman he talked to told him the name of the club and how to get there if he didn't have a car. Soon, he was pulling on his one pair of long pants, then placing his feet in the new canvas tie-up shoes, and buttoning his best shirt. Right before he walked out the door, with his little harmonica case in the pocket of his trousers, he took a look at himself in his mother's little mirror. The smiling stranger whose face he saw assured him.

When he walked through the door of the nightclub, after his bus ride and long walk down the lonely country road, he was anything but assured. He was young and his clothes were old and tattered. The handsome people who were sitting in the club drinking had shiny clothes and a sophistication Billy Ray had never seen in people with skin the same color as his. There were no live bands playing when Billy Ray walked through the door, though he knew it was local talent night. Tonight and Wednesday night too.

Music was coming through the speakers on the wall. It was the usual stuff he heard on the radio. Otis Redding, B.B. King, Little Anthony and the Imperials, Bobby Blue Bland. Irma Thomas. He knew he could do it too, all by himself with his harmonica, just as good as any of the singers blasting from the speakers on the wall.

But the audience awed him. Little tables were set up where handsome men and beautiful women were talking and drinking. When the slow numbers came on, some got up and danced, cleaving to each other though the room was hot. When the fast dances came on, Billy Ray saw how much he had to learn. For their dancing was skillful and practiced. These were no church-on-Sunday people.

Billy Ray had supposed that his own sorry movements would awe anyone who stood before him. Now he knew his terrible limitations. He needed clothes, he needed shine. When the lights went on the stage, he needed to stand before them like someone. He learned this all in the first twenty minutes of his arrival. He watched from the back of the room near the bar. Billy Ray did not attempt to order a drink. He had two dollars in his pocket, but he knew not to pretend he could stand here and drink. They would laugh at him if he ordered a beer. Just as they would laugh at him if he stood up before them as he was.

What saved him from going home and hanging himself was the local talent who performed there that night.

The first performer was a boy even younger than he was—a fat little boy with a white doll in his lap. The boy's lips moved as the white doll said any number of stupid things. But the audience laughed. And didn't appear to think the act was stupid. Even give the boy a decent round of applause when his sorry act was finally over. Three teenage girls got up after this. They each had on bright sequined dresses and they danced all right. But their voices were weak and the tired old song they sang wasn't even what he'd call music. They did not know how to sing with backup. The musicians who backed them up blasted them out. It was just as well. Billy Ray reached inside his pocket and felt for his harmonica as he watched the girls. He wanted to play. He wanted to march right up on that stage and show them who he was. He wanted to kiss the pretty one too. The one in the middle. He wanted to lay his lips on her lips and feel her high round breasts against his chest. But he knew, just as he knew he would not get up tonight, that if he approached her as he was, she would be right to laugh at him.

He stood there until their act was over. And joined in the applause that followed it. He was not clapping for the music, but for the girl, the pretty one. When the hi-fi system starting playing again, he took himself backstage to watch what went on there. On Wednesday night, he wanted to know exactly where to go. What to do. No one noticed when he left the club with his harmonica in his back pocket and walked the long miles home. It was the last time he ever had to.

LISTENING AT THE WINDOW

‿◌‿

She was sitting on her mother's bed reading her an Agatha Christie mystery. Along with *Mrs. Beeton*, it was a sign that her mother was feeling well and could be amused. It was nice before he came in. Just her and her mother, alone in the quiet house on Saturday night. Her mother loved the funny little Detective with his huge mustache. Tonight she said, as she sometimes did, "When I'm better, Mary Jacob, your father and I will visit England. He's promised to take me when I get well. I've been an anglophile my entire life!"

"You'll have a wonderful time there, Mama. And you'll get your picture taken in front of Big Ben. You and Daddy both!" She was saying what she always said to her mother, but tonight, she didn't dare meet the older woman's eyes. Because even if she halfway knew before they'd never go to England, she knew now for sure. Her mother and father would never go anywhere since her father loved Van and not her mother anymore.

The light was fading outside the windows when they heard the noise from downstairs. Her mother shot up with as much energy as her pitiful body could muster. Mary Jacob wanted to keep on reading, but it was no use. The safe world of the funny little detective had come to an end: they were both of them scared. Her mother's hand went first to her hair, then to her golden cross. She asked Mary Jacob for her silver mirror, her powder, and her lipstick.

When Jack strode in the room a few minutes later with a drink in his hand and a slightly red face, the very air already belonged to him. When he came in a room, everything stopped. Yet her mother loved her father through and through. The only time she ever seemed really alive was when Jack Long was in the room.

Mary Jacob got off the bed and headed toward the door. When she was past the blue velvet settee, he called out to her.

"Just a minute, Mary Jacob, I want to speak to you."

"Yes sir."

"I want you to stay upstairs tonight."

She could not believe her father was saying these words in front of her mother. It did not seem possible—even for him.

"A few of the men from the council are coming here at nine, and if you want to watch the television, you can watch it in my room—you understand, missy?"

"Yes sir."

It was the first time she had seen him face to face since he had taken off his belt and beat her with it. He did not seem to remember. And her mother never mentioned it either. She still had belt marks on her backside, but that wasn't important enough for either of them to say it happened.

She left the two of them in her mother's room and walked down the hall to her own room.

Shortly after the clock struck nine times, Mary Jacob returned to her mother's room and quietly opened the door. The lights were off. The only light was the dim one from the dressing room they always kept on, in case she needed to get up in the middle of the night. Mary Jacob went to stand by her mother's bed. The light illuminated the pretty silver tray that was always next to her bed. The one with her pills. And her bottles of perfume and the silver mirror, brush, and comb. The room smelled bad. It was always worse at night. Her mother was sleeping, her tiny little head sideways on the pillow like a little girl in a story book. She heard a car door shut and Mary Jacob supposed Van would soon be coming in. She'd been coming and going here her whole life. It was her house, more than it had ever been Mary Jacob's house. He would lead her through their kitchen, through the butlery where they'd stand for a moment making drinks. They'd take their drinks into the library and soon there would just be the moon and them.

Another car door shut, then another. She did not understand. Mary Jacob crept out of her mother's room and down the hall to the big window that looked out over the side of the house. A big black Cadillac was parked in the driveway and in back of it, a tan sedan. A third car was now turning in the driveway. Soon a big fat man was working his way out of the car, then making his heavy way toward the front door. Mary Jacob crept down the first part of the long curved stairs. She could hear men's voices coming from downstairs. Then the clock struck the half hour and the voices disappeared.

The front room was dark now as usual. No one had ever used the room in her memory, though Kathryn had said her mother used to give parties there before she got sick. The library door was shut. But she could see the slit of light at the bottom of the heavy paneled door. Men were in the room, not Van. She could not hear their voices over the groaning of the air conditioning, but she could smell the rich cigar aroma drifting in from there. It was a funny thing about cigars, sometimes they smelled almost good, though most of the time they were stale and bad.

Mary Jacob went to the kitchen, found a glass, and let herself out the back door. She rounded the corner of the house and stood below the windows of the library. The curtains were drawn. That was good. No one would see her. Mary Jacob put the glass up to the window, the drinking side right on the glass. It was a trick she had learned from a book, and though she had never tried it, she understood at once that it was working. She could hear them plain as day.

"And God looked down from heaven, and said, 'I hate niggers.'" There was a sudden burst of heavy male laughter. Someone was coughing and wheezing. Then she heard her father's unmistakable voice say, "Now that we've had our laugh, we better get down to business."

The room was quiet for a moment. She took the glass away and held it in her hand. There was a small opening in the heavy library curtains, if she shut one eye she could make out the fat man sitting on the couch with a cigar stuck in his lip and next to him the policeman in uniform. Her father was standing, drink in hand, in front of the gun case. She could hear them murmuring, but nothing like the way it was with the glass.

Once more she laid the glass on the window and then put her ear against the solid end. The glass that had been cool was warm now, and damp, like her skin was getting outside in the hot humid air. It really was magic. Although she could not see and hear at the same time, she knew it was her father's voice. Her father had been reared in Virginia and no one in Murpheysfield talked like he did.

"Now we don't know for sure whether we'll have the honor of having King himself here in Murpheysfield or whether it's gonna be one or two of his nigger errand boys. But we do know there's a sit-in planned. Likely as not, it'll be the downtown Woolworth's lunch counter."

There was a pause and her father continued. "Now we all know the way King operates. What they'll do is walk in and act like they have the perfect right to sit there next to white people. In fact, likely or not, they'll import some white niggers from up north to come with them. The Jews are in on this, you can guarantee, and there will be some of them, likely as not. They'll sit down and order just like they have the God given right to do just that. It's blasphemous!"

Another man was speaking now. "Jack, why don't we just find out where they're going to have their sit-in and simply close the place for the day?"

Her father's voice was fierce and angry. "Roy, we can't keep closing down our places of business every time a few unruly niggers and Jews from up north try and bully us. Our own niggers know how to behave. We've taught them to, and my friend Armand Murov, who goes to the Temple, wouldn't sit down to dinner with the likes of those coming to Murpheysfield even if they do worship the same God. It's the outside agitators we have to worry about, not our own."

Someone else was talking now. He had a trashy voice, so unlike the cool elegant way her father spoke. "Last year when King landed in Shreveport, their police commissioner, who's a friend of mine, met him at the airport, put him in a squad car, and drove him around handcuffed to a police dog."

Her father sounded angry, his careful Virginia drawl was growing harsh and loud. He seldom raised his voice. He did not need to. "We've got to set an example," he was proclaiming. "We've got to show them that Murpheysfield is a town where white people still have rights. Otherwise they're gonna take over. The next thing you know, they'll be trying to get into the schools. For God's sake, we've got our daughters to think of."

Mary Jacob took the glass away. She had to look at him. *Our daughters.* He was still standing in front of the gun cases. His beautiful chestnut hair was falling in his eyes. She watched him take a long pull from his whiskey glass. She was not his daughter. Never had been.

The big fat red-faced man stood up. And Mary Jacob could make out that now he was talking. She put the glass to the window.

"Shoot King," she heard. Then, "Hell, we could shoot the whole pack of them. No court of law in Louisiana would indict a white man for shooting a nigger who sat next to him in a restaurant."

Then her father said, "Roy, do you want to shoot Martin Luther King?"

"Hell yeah."

Now everybody in the room was laughing. The window seemed to shake with their terrible laughter. Then her father said, "The niggers think he's Jesus Christ. He eats dinner with that cheap son of an Irish bootlegger who calls himself our president. Do you really want to go down in history as the John Wilkes Booth of Murpheysfield?"

The man who wanted to shoot Reverend King said, "We could call it an accident."

Then the trashy voice said, "He ain't armed. He's never armed. That's where he's clever. He makes it seem he can't fight back. There's legal implications."

"Precisely," Jack said. "But that doesn't mean we can't fight back. We can and we will."

It was past eleven now, and the meeting had been over for some time. Mary Jacob had come in the kitchen door and crept up the stairway when the meeting was breaking up. The men had not made any real plans. They could not make real plans because they did not know as yet what was going to happen. She wondered how it was that they had learned about King coming in the first place. Who had told them? She wanted very much to know.

She was following their movements as best she could. She'd positioned herself now in her sister's bedroom, so she could monitor what they said in the driveway. She was hot and dragged down from her time outside peering in the window of the library. And her stomach hurt. She was having cramps. She understood that the pains in her stomach were caused by her period. But now, the knowledge did not interest her much. The house was cold. And she felt clammy after her time outside in the humid air. She was crouched on the velvet cushion of Kathryn's window seat, peering down at her father and the policeman outside in the driveway. The other men were gone now. And for the first time tonight she could see and hear at the same time.

The two men's backs were turned to the house. Her father's long, elegant back with his narrow hips and his long legs and the policeman's thick back, with the wide leather belt and the gun worn low. Her father was talking; her father had been doing most of the talking tonight. It had not taken her long to understand that he was the leader in all this. Mary Jacob was not surprised.

"Tom, I want you to do me a favor, keep an eye out for my daughter Kathryn. She's been carrying on with young Foster Reeves. If you see his car parked at the end of some lonely road—why you give 'em a scare."

The policeman nodded his head. "Certainly. I'll tell my men to do the same."

"Much obliged, Tom. She's got a friend too. Beautiful young thing, Van Morley. Her father, Bob Morley, passed on when she was just a child. Bob was a fraternity brother of mine at the University of Virginia. I'm very fond of Van."

"You want her followed, Jack?"

"No. Nothing like that. But she used to go about with some young rascal. Find out how far it's gone. If he goes to her house, if you see 'em at a drive-in movie, well you let me know, hear? I owe it to her father. Besides, Van's like a daughter to me."

"Certainly, Jack."

Then she saw her father shake the policeman's hand. After the handshake, the policeman nodded, then put what her father had given him in the pocket of his pants, down near his knees. The tan sedan was backing out the driveway and her father was walking toward the house, whistling a little tune. The front door shut. The clock chimed the half hour. The man who was walking up the stairs was not her father. He did not own her. He had paid the policeman to watch his other daughters: his real daughters. She, Mary Jacob, was not important enough to pay for. But it was better that way. Better that he did not own her.

SUNDAY

∽⌒∽

Luckily on Sunday it was still raining. So Billy Ray did not have to explain to his mother why he was at home instead of at his job. It seemed right that it was raining, that the weather was cooperating with his plans.

He lay in his bed, feeling the wonderful luxury of time on his hands. His feet were almost at the point of dangling off the bed and were getting numb, but that vague discomfort didn't bother him either. He put his hand between his legs and quietly satisfied himself. Then with a sigh, he lay back again, feeling happy and safe.

Usually on Sunday his mother would go to church for most of the day. But when it rained, she let herself stay home and rest. This Sunday, with the rain pouring down and the tin cans they used for drips set in each of the four small rooms, their house was peaceful. They ate peach pie and pork chops for breakfast. And she brewed a big pot of coffee and chicory in the old drip pot. The pork chops were thick and tender. And the stuffing inside tasted spicy and delicious. The sweet pie and bitter coffee afterwards filled him with a pleasant glow. Billy Ray knew she had carried the food home from work. The pork chops they could occasionally buy themselves were always thin and hard. But today, he did not care so much that the food he was eating had been served first to them. He needed strength for the coming days ahead and he did not care where it come from.

He helped her with the breakfast dishes, and afterwards they both went in their rooms. Breakfast had been silent but satisfying. They had fallen out of the habit of conversing with each other years ago. She had not dressed for breakfast and now, still in her big white nightgown, she headed back to her bedroom and her rickety old bed to listen to the church service on the radio. Billy Ray did not mind that his mother was here, though he knew if it were just a week ago, he would have wished her far away. Nothing could interfere with his plans now. Her smile would not pain him. He would not even mind if she mentioned his playing. Maybe he even wanted her to.

It was after nine now, when Billy Ray went into his little room off the kitchen, lay down on his narrow bed, and for the first time in his life, consciously brought the hum inside the house. Always before, Billy Ray had waited for the hum, waited for it like it was a special guest. It took him by surprise; it had a life of its own, at least he thought it had. The hum had always been something apart from him: something bigger, stronger, like the earth or the sky. He had known for quite some time that the hum was connected to him, in the same way he knew he walked the earth and stared up at the sky in wonder at the stars. But Sunday morning, with his belly full and the rain beating down in the room that was cool now from all the rain, he understood something else. And it filled him with joy. He was very young then and did not need to hope for inspiration or to struggle for it. He did not need to wait. He hadn't even heard of getting high then. The gift was right inside him waiting to come out, bursting to come out. And with this wonderful knowledge came another great secret, one he would spend his whole life trying to understand. No one but Billy Ray could ever take the hum away.

VINA

∽∽

When I goes to work on Monday, why things at the Longs' house, they were lookin' up. Didn't last long, but while it were happening we was all smilin'. Mary Jacob, she waiting for me in the kitchen. Had me a cup of coffee cool the way I likes it, and creamy with Pet milk. "Vina, we gonna get Mama out of bed today and we're gonna bring her down tonight for supper."

I say, "Honey, I think that's mighty sweet, but you know your mama ain't come down for supper since before March." But Mary Jacob she ain't listening to word I say. Monday fancy man come and wash Miz Lil's hair and set it for her. Don' know why white women don't wear wigs. Much easier, if you ask me, puttin' a wig on than worrying yourself sick every week with the hair dryer.

Anyway, Mary Jacob, she say, "Lavina, you just wait, you gonna see Mama at the dinner table!"

Mary Jacob, she stay up with her mother nearly all day. She stay when fancy man Conrad come to do her hair, and afterwards, when he leave, she don' go away from that woman's side. And when I go up there to take Miz Lil's lunch tray, why, she is lookin' downright cheerful. I didn't know then that Mary Jacob gone and switched them little white pills Miz Lil takes to help her sleep with the ones Kathryn take to keep her from eatin'—pep pills they call 'em. Mary Jacob told me later what she done, 'cause she felt turrible. Blamed herself for what happen to Miz Lil. Though it weren't her fault—she just tryin' to better things around that house. Friend a mine at the church, her doctor put her on them pep pills to lose weight, and honey, I tell you she said them pills put so much pep in you, they could make the lame pick up their heels and dance.

And that's the truth, 'cause Miz Lil, she be up and walkin' that day. Her eyes is bright, bright and when that big old bunch of flowers come to the front door after lunch in that shiny white box, why, she come downstairs herself in her robe and slippers and arrange them just like she used to do. Found out later that Mary Jacob sent them flowers too, but I didn't know that then. All I knew was Miz Lil, she were lookin' good. And when Kathryn come in and see her mother walking around, why, she even join in. "Mama," she say, "you look so pretty and who sent you the roses?" Miz Lil, she say, "Darlin', I only got one beau," and that's the truth, there was only one ribbon on that box of flowers. First time I saw the three of them acting like family for as long as I can remember. The girls, why, they didn't even fight. They just stay up there in Miz Lil's room talkin' and gigglin' and they lays her out a dress, and after I cleans the house, I gets to work and I starts fixin' us a fine dinner. Fried chicken, grits casserole, pole beans, and I does the watermelon in them tiny little balls and puts them in the cut crystal bowl.

Six o'clock come. That Jack, he walk in, sets his brown case down, head for the kitchen table, and puts one of them melon balls in his mouth. Then he into the butlery like he always do, make hisself a whiskey drink and then he come back in and ask me who that extra place for at the table tonight. I reckon he thinkin' Van, but I say, with a big smile on my face, "Why Mr. Jack, Miz Lil, she comin' down to supper." That Jack, he stand there lookin' at me, and he pop another melon ball. Then he leave the room for his whiskey.

Mary Jacob, she come in the kitchen right then. "Wait till you see her, Lavina, Mama look so pretty and she happy too!" Then Mary Jacob, she run out the door again and I thought that was that.

But the door open again and Jack come back. "Sit down Lavina," he say. And then he sit down too.

I thought he were gonna get on me about Miz Lil because I seen the look on his face when I tole him who the place is for. But it weren't that. He take a drink from his whiskey and put the tumbler down on the kitchen table.

"Lavina, that caddying job I got your boy at the country club, why, I'm sorry to say, the club dismissed him. I thought you'd want to know."

Couldn't find my words for a moment, tryin' to get my face back, but it jumping all over the place, my lip is quivering, and my eyes is fillin' up with tears. I is tryin' to hide all this from Jack, who I don't want seeing me all sick in my face.

"I appreciate your telling me, Mr. Jack."

"Why, it's a real shame it didn't work out. Some of 'em, why, they can make as much as five dollars on a good day. That's mighty fine pay."

"Yes sir."

"I know it's just the two of you, and I wanted to help you out, but the boy was dismissed for insubordination. There's no way I can intervene in a case of insubordination. Do you know what that means, Lavina?"

My throat is tight so that my voice is coming out funny. Sound like some old bull frog.

"I reckon I do, sir."

Mr. Jack, he look at me and he say, "Well, since you do, keep that in mind, you hear?"

"Yes sir."

"I'll have no insubordination in my house either, Lavina."

We both know he is speaking about Van. And Miz Lil comin' down for supper. And him telling me not to get in the way of that. Though for the life of me I cain't figure out how what he is doin' with pretty Van have anything to do with why Billy Ray was dismissed. Except that he is telling me to be sure and keep my old mouth shut.

After he leave, I sit there, tryin' to remember the big old word he use. Mary Jacob would tell me what it all mean. But I can't get it in my head. I keep seeing Billy Ray settin' out light on his feet when the stars are in the sky, headin' toward that country club to carry the bags. And the look on his face when he put down the dollars he earned there or pointed to the milk or the greens. It always been worse for the boys and men then it were for us. We always knows there's a place for us in some white lady's house. We can earn our money if we cooks and irons and cleans. Not too many places for our men. They don' like colored men in their houses and very few use drivers no more. Not since the war. Feelin' bad, bad for my boy and scared for us both because we need the money. How we gonna get by if we don' have them dollars? Felt sick in my face, I can tell you.

I got on with our supper, there weren't nothin' else I can do. Close to six thirty by now and the girls, they come down. Mr. Jack, he sits down. Then they rings me in the kitchen. I goes in with the platter of chicken and Mr. Jack, he say, "Lavina, run up and see if Miz Lil's gonna join us or not." Mary Jacob, she say, "I'll go." But that Jack, he say, "You'll do no such thing." Then Kathryn, she say, "Mama's coming; you know how long it take her to get herself up." I'm out of the dining room by now, going past old Grandad and climbing up them curved stairs. That's when I sees her, Miz Lil. Why, the poor woman, she were lyin' with her skinny legs sticking out of her pretty long skirt, look like bird's legs. She were spread out there on the first part of the stairs where the landing is.

At first I thought, sweet Jesus, Miz Lil done broke her neck. She dead. But she weren't dead. She look up at me with her big eyes. Her lips are red, red and her face dead white and them streaks of black coming down from her eyes like wet soot. "Lavina," she say in a little bitty voice, "Look what I done. I fell."

HUMMING

◦◠◦

He was up on stage, playing his harmonica. The room was filled with men and women in bright shiny clothes, sparkling with light. But their faces were turned away from him. When Billy Ray looked down, he knew what it was that had made them turn away. It wasn't because of his music. His music was rich and powerful. The hum was all around him, but when he looked down he was buck naked. Naked as a baby, though he didn't look like no baby with his thick old thing pointing out. He was playing a new song he had never heard. Billy Ray knew even within the dream that the song was another gift—he was accustomed to such gifts. He thought the hum was bottomless then.

He awakened to the sun pouring in his window. Billy Ray drew the sheet over his body to cover him, though he longed to feel what little air there was on his bare skin. His mother was in the kitchen clattering pots and pans, so it must still be early for his new life. Less than a week ago, he would have already put in half a day of work by now. Billy Ray lay there on his little bed with the lump in the middle, listening to her messing about. His mattress was of horse hair and was old now and getting less comfortable each night. The sun was not so harsh yet, though if he were out on the golf course he would have been half dead by now from the heat.

Today was Monday and he wondered how long it would be before his mother found out the truth. She would not be ugly. She weren't ever really ugly, but he knew the disappointed look her face would take on once she knew. She had worn that disappointed look the whole year after his father walked out the door. It was a look, he knew somehow, only her men could bring her.

Then the song he had heard in his dream started playing in his brain, exactly as the songs played on the radio. His mother's disappointed look flew out the window where the sun was pouring through. Gone was the sense of shame he had felt in his dream too. The shame from the dream and the nagging guilty voice inside him when he thought about her in the kitchen was not as strong as the need to remember the song.

It did not take Billy Ray long to put the song inside his brain—that was the wonder of the hum. The hum did not let you forget. Each note was connected to a finger and the pattern was clear once the hum took over, never forgotten neither. He did not think in notes; he thought of song as movements in his fingers. Each little set of moves was a means to an end—though the end was always there waiting too—all you had to do was get there. The words generally came later, though Billy Ray had begun to realize lately that the words were always there too, just waiting for him. There were even times when the words came right along with the sounds and the movements. Soon, how long he did not know, the whole wonderful being of the song was safe in his brain. And the words were falling into their place nice and neat—they always fit in, didn't know how, just happened that way. Once it was in there, safe inside his brain, no one could steal it or take it from him. There was no door to lock, no key to lose. No payments to make. You did not have to go without supper or electricity. No one to take it over because you could not buy the hum. It being free but better than money was something he had known as long as he had known about the gift of the hum. It was what had always got him through.

Billy Ray continued to lay there, peaceful and happy after the hum had come. It was like a record player: you could take the needle off the record and let the machine stay on. When you put the needle back on, the song was there waiting for you—any place you happened to want to be in the song was as easy as setting the needle where you wanted it. By then his mother was gone. He had heard her footsteps and the front door shut. Billy Ray sat up in bed. He was starving. Never in his life had he ever been so hungry. He came out of his little room off the kitchen and went for the icebox.

Food had meant very little to him before. Just something to put between your teeth and chew when the hollowness gnawed inside you. Hunger was something connected to anger and pain. There had always been just enough in their house to ease the pain. Once in a while she carried home more than usual, but before Billy Ray's pride never let him grow too attached to fullness or plenty. Now, as he ate the leftover pie his mother had carried home Saturday night, the taste and feel of it in his mouth was deeply pleasurable. The crust weren't crisp now. It didn't stay crisp after a few days, but the soft mushy dough was satisfying too, with the ooze of the sugary peaches she'd spiced with nutmeg and cinnamon. After he ate up the pie, Billy Ray fried three eggs and drank what was left in the coffee pot. There was very little food left in the house now. She shopped on Thursday and he was usually the one who brought the greens and eggs home with the money from his job. Their supply of eggs was gone now. He'd eaten three days worth just now as though they were nothing. Why, if they had a whole wonderful dozen, he would have cracked and cooked them with pleasure.

He drank a big glass of water. Water helped after a meal. Fooled your stomach into thinking there was more in it. Helped in between too. The hum was coming back in his brain. Different from the one that had come in his sleep. He sat there at the kitchen table playing with his fork, letting the hum in. Now, as the words and sounds were pouring in, Billy Ray did not stop to put them in his hum place. Instead he sang out loud and fast, as fast as the music was throbbing in his veins, filling up his whole being as his pure sweet voice was filling up the miserable kitchen with joy. There was no stopping now. No time at all between the hum and the song itself. Billy Ray and the music were one.

Later that morning, empty and famished, opening their last can of tuna fish, smelling the oily fish smell with pleasure, there came to him, a vision of himself up on the stage. He laughed at it with pleasure as he spooned the fish into his mouth. No time to enjoy the taste. He was seeing himself as he would be, as close as if the bowl with the tuna fish inside was a mirror to admire himself. He could see himself up on stage, wearing his mother's wig, the red puffy one, and a pair of dark glasses. It would work. Billy Ray knew it would work. No black, greasy lady wig. He'd wear the bright one. The red one.

NURSE

ᔆᔆ

ary Jacob had never hated the way she hated the nurse.
Not even her father or her sister or even her own hateful life. First the doctor had come. He pronounced her
mother well enough not to go to the hospital but in shock. Then the
doctor picked up the phone and within an hour the nurse was with
them—though Mary Jacob did not know it then—for the rest of her
mother's life. Though her father had appeared solemn, even tender
when he lifted Lillian in his arms and carried her upstairs and laid
her on the bed, Mary Jacob knew beneath the smooth sorrowful
mask he wore on his handsome face, he was pleased. And from the
moment the nurse appeared at the front door, with her ugly green
suitcase and her bag of trashy magazines, the two of them were in
silent but perfect collusion.

Mary Jacob came to understand that the nurse would be his
weapon. The nurse would act on his behalf. He would pay her just
as he paid the policeman to watch his daughters, his real daughters.
The nurse would be paid to sit by her side, forever reading magazines. Paid to keep the curtains drawn, paid to carry the bedpan
back and forth, paid to lift her mother's nightgown and thrust the
long needle deep inside her so she would sleep even more than she
did before.

Mary Jacob knew it was her own fault that the nurse had come.
And she would have gladly accepted punishment for what she had
done. Accepting the punishment herself would have been nothing.
She would have welcomed a beating. She would have stayed locked
in her room. She would have taken anything he cared to mete out
to her as just punishment for what she had done. But Mary Jacob's

punishment was far worse. She had to stand helplessly by and watch the nurse take what little bit of life her mother had left in her away.

"Don't worry your mother; your mother needs her rest," she told Mary Jacob the next morning, and every morning after that. Mary Jacob wanted to scream at the nurse, "she doesn't need rest. She needs sunlight and roses, she needs love." But the curtains stayed drawn, the pills by the bedside table soon had a bigger silver tray to house them. Her mother's lipsticks, scent bottles, silver comb, brush, and mirror were put away like unused toys are put away in a child's room. But there were no new toys to take their place. Just darkness, drawn curtains, and drugs. With her pitiful girlish vanities gone, her mother became an old woman virtually overnight.

The nurse's presence was everywhere. She changed the rules of the house that had once run so smoothly under Lavina's gentle hand. It was like having her father home all the time—but worse. Her father at least was a known enemy. She had learned what to expect. But the nurse was the unknown. Her every act held the power to shock and horrify.

She lumbered in the kitchen at noon on her first day while Mary Jacob and Lavina were eating their lunch.

"I'm ready for my dinner, girl," she said. Lavina did not look at her, but said mildly, "The Longs eat their dinner at supper time. "I'll fix you a sandwich just as soon as I finish my own."

"I don't want no sandwich. I told Mr. Long I get a hot meal noontime. Everywhere I work, I get a hot meal noontime. Mr. Long says if I run into any trouble around here, all I have to do is pick up the telephone and call him at his office."

Mary Jacob looked at Lavina, then she looked at the nurse. "Why don't you sit down. Lavina'll fix you something to eat after we finish."

Still the nurse stood there, staring at Lavina. "I'll eat in that room back yonder, you hear?"

"I hear you," Lavina said softly. "I heard you the first time I saw you."

The nurse turned and lumbered out.

Being the outsiders of the house, Mary Jacob and Lavina were both excellent mimics. Mary Jacob was, however, the better of the two. Though she could not look at Lavina, she managed to imitate the nurse's trashy twang quite accurately. "Everywhere I work, I always get a hot meal midday."

"One too many, honey, by the look of her."

"Vina, think she'd like one of my special hot meals with a cup of Tabasco sauce?"

"Sugar, don't be pulling any of your tricks, you hear? It'll just make things worse around here."

"Things couldn't get any worse around here. Besides, I hate her."

Their eyes met. Mary Jacob saw a look on Lavina's face she had never seen before—a look that was a thousand years old.

"Don' do no good hatin' her, darlin'. It won't change change things any."

Mary Jacob wanted to shout, "but they have to change." Instead she looked down at their plates. They both loved tuna fish sandwiches with sweet pickle relish and slices of raw onion. And when they had tuna sandwiches they always had them with Fritos. A whole big bag between the two of them. She and Lavina had hardly started eating their favorite lunch when the nurse had walked in the room ruining everything. Now, the smell of fresh cut onion was rank and unpleasant. The toasted white bread oozing with mayonnaise made Mary Jacob want to gag. The Fritos that she had gleefully dumped on their plates looked disgusting. Food had always been a bond between Lavina and her. But not any longer. She had ruined everything by switching the pills. The whole world had changed.

Mary Jacob got to her feet and cleared away her lunch dish. She scraped her plate into the trash and watched the golden Fritoes fall like dead leaves into the garbage.

Lavina was on her feet beside her. She looked down in the garbage can then back up at Mary Jacob.

"You need to be with chirrun your own age, Mary Jacob. Call up Ruthie Wilkins. I like Ruthie Wilkins. We ain't seen nothin' of that girl this summer. Can't be much fun around here with your mother the way she is and now Miz Hot Lunch."

Mary Jacob wanted to hurl herself into Lavina's strong dark arms. But she felt shy suddenly. Lavina had been shamed in front of her, and the shame could not be scared away, like the Woolworth's lady had been scared away. It had arrived by the front door last night, suitcase in hand. "You're fun, Lavina, you're always fun," she insisted. But Mary Jacob knew she was lying. Lavina wasn't fun. Lavina was a dark, shameful figure of tragedy, and her face was a thousand years old.

As if she could read Mary Jacob's mind she said, "Sugar, I'm just a tired old colored lady with one more hot meal to fix. Now I 'spect Miz Van will be comin' for supper. Go on and call that nice chile Ruthie Wilkins. We're having roast so you don' need to worry about us having enough."

"I hate Van," Mary Jacob heard herself saying, "I hate Van even more than I hate the nurse. Van's a whore. That's what she is."

Lavina grabbed hold of her arm. Lavina had never grabbed hold of her arm like this. Not even when she was little and misbehaved.

"Mary Jacob Long, you oughta be ashamed of yourself callin' that nice girl filthy names. Now go on, get out of my kitchen for I wash your mouth out with Ivory Liquid."

In all her life, Lavina had never spoken this way to her. And this was the greatest shock of all. She glared at Lavina then turned and left the kitchen. Everything was lost.

And her father had won. She stared at him now. It was evening and they were seated all around him, Kathryn, Van, and herself. He was at the head of the table carving the bloody hunk of meat. One strand of chestnut hair falling over his eye. Van was sitting on his right and Kathryn was at the place where her mother used to sit. In the next room, the little morning room, the nurse was eating her supper. When the door opened with Lavina carrying platters, Mary Jacob caught a glimpse of her shiny white uniform and her thick white legs planted firmly on the floor like she belonged.

Her father was pouring wine, his handsome face flushed red, like the roast beef. Then he started carving. Jack loved to carve, and always made an elaborate ritual of sharpening the blade before supper. Other than polishing his guns, it was the only hand work she ever saw him do. Blood was oozing off the meat now as his knife tore through the hunk of flesh, which seemed to Mary Jacob alive and trembling. Slice after slice lay now in a circle of blood. Mary Jacob used to love roast beef, though how she did not know. She looked down and the same blood was oozing off the meat onto her plate, spreading into her squash, her potatoes, and her beans. It was the same color as the wine he was pouring again in their glasses.

He was even pouring wine in her glass. Her father had never let her drink wine before and once Mary Jacob would have been pleased to be included. But the wine, she saw now, was the same color as the meat. The same color as blood. They were eating and drinking blood like vampires.

Her father held his glass in the air and smiled. His full curved lips were stained red with blood and wine. "To wine," he told them, "beautiful women," and then he looked at Van with a little laugh. "And what else is there, I ask you?"

Kathryn laughed. Van threw her beautiful silky black hair back and Mary Jacob stared at her soft white throat with the pulse trembling in it, the white throat and the dead meat made her sick. They all emptied their glasses and Jack poured more. Mary Jacob mumbled, "excuse me," but none of them paid her any mind. From the other room she heard the nurse say, "bring me more of them potatoes, girl."

Mary Jacob left the dining room, passed through the front hall, then let herself quietly out the front door. It was still light outside and blessedly hot, for she was cold and trembling. She sat down on the front step of the house and she stayed there watching the sky lose its light, listening to the birds' song die out and the night crickets begin. The gracious green street with its wide curved front yards was very quiet and peaceful. Presently, she heard the sound of an engine and saw Foster's car turn with a screech in the driveway. Mary Jacob quickly got up and hid on the side of the house until Foster and her sister left arm and arm.

Music was coming from the living room now. Johnny Mathas. Kathryn called it "make out music." Mary Jacob walked to one of the tall front windows and peered inside. Her father and Van were dancing with their arms around each other in the beautiful front room where no one ever sat. Where no one had ever danced, not that she remembered. It was nearly dark and the crickets were loud and screeching but still the same record came on again and again.

Mary Jacob turned away from the window and sat in the shelter of the wide front door. She watched a large mosquito alight on the underside of her arm and the small pimple of blood that appeared as it drank. She was wiping the blood on her shorts when she heard the back door shut. Now Lavina was heading down the driveway in her street dress and wig. Mary Jacob wondered what Lavina would do if she flung herself on her in the driveway and said "Take me home with you, on the bus." Lavina would say, "Go on, sugar, back upstairs to that beautiful room you got and let this tired colored lady go home." And so, Mary Jacob sat there and let her.

VINA

W

ell, I'd forgotten all about the meetin' at the church on Tuesday night. But Noog, she call me up and reminds me we was gonna meet on the bus and goes together.

Folks she works for, they lets Noog use the telephone. In fact, she has one all to herself in the kitchen. Longs weren't like that. Not even when Miz Lil weren't sick and the nurse come and took us over. Not that it were what a house ought to be 'for she come. It were always a sad house. Knew it moment I come in the screen door all them years ago. Sadness is somethin' you can smell when you first walks in a place. By the time that old white nurse come marching in our door with those fat white legs, the sadness, it be so big and strong you could feel it even downstairs when she were upstairs by Miz Lil's bed reading them magazines.

Not one of us wanted her. Not even pretty Van who start takin' over the downstairs just like old thick white nurse woman taken over the upstairs. Rich white people don' like no trash, wouldn't sit next to her eating, though the girls always eat with me. We all knew she were trash, that old white nurse. And the girls, like I said, didn't take no better to her than I did. 'Specially Mary Jacob—old thick white made that chile so sick she couldn't eat. I hated to see that 'cause eatin' is part of life. And Mary Jacob love to eat. Funny thing is, just about the time Mary Jacob stopped eating, my Billy Ray, he gets his appetite up. He eatin' everything don' eat him first. Started carrying home everything Mary Jacob didn't eat. There were always food, food at the Longs' house, though when she come, I started havin' to order more from the grocery 'cause that nurse, she eat. Whole plate of mashed potatoes in gravy and two helpings of roast weren't nothing to her. That only be enough to get her started.

Church, it were full of people by the time we got ourselves in the door that night. We went directly from the little front room into the church. Everybody was standing, the pews, they were full of colored folk old and young. Look like Easter Sunday except that none of us is wearing our hats and our Sunday clothes. I were a tall woman, close to six foot, so I stands on my tip toes tryin' to see what were going on below the altar where it all seemed to be. Noog, she were sayin', "Lavina, I can hear him. He sound just like he do on the radio." Understand, all of us knew Reverend King and his fine preaching voice, and for a moment I could hear it myself, the deep soul way he say his words, better than any preacher ever said his words. We were standing halfway down the aisle and I gets a little bird flutter in my chest, 'cause I knows any second there he'll be, M.L. in Murpheysfield.

Noog, who is short, way below my shoulder, she say, "Lavina, you sees him yet? Tell me girl!" But all I sees is black folks taking their places. But, there's still a crowd down there so I can't really tell. That's when I sees my neighbor. Old Houston is looking no good. He shaking his head, and it don't seem like it's coming from his condition. Lookin' sick in his face, I can tell you, because I know Houston, he's a man whose face I know. Houston, he pointing to somewhere in back of where we is.

"Noog," I say, "Noog, turn around." Soon as we do, here come our minister walking with a tall skinny white boy with eye glasses and a beard. Then our minister, he start wavin' his hands down like he do on Sunday, telling us to sit ourselves down. Noog, she ain't sayin' nothing when we sits ourselves down and nobody around us is sayin' nothing—the room is so quiet, like you could hear a pin drop or a mouse squeak. I were shocked. And I could see the faces around me showing the same shock look on their faces. Understand, we weren't no better than white folks wondering what the wrong color skin was doin' showing up at a place where we come together.

Now that tall skinny white boy, he is heading straight for the stairs and the altar.

"Ladies and Gentlemen," he say, "I'm Matthew so and so." Right away, I took to the boy on account of the fact that he said Ladies and Gentlemen. I thought that was very polite of him. Anyway, he say, "I'm here tonight on behalf of Dr. Martin Luther King Jr., who can't come tonight because of legal problems."

Then somebody in the front say, "Thought they sprung M.L." And that Matthew, he look confused, I can tell you. Then that somebody say, "He ain't still in jail, is he?" "No," Matthew say. But he can't leave Alabama on account of some legal whatchacallum and then somebody else said, "We all heard M.L. gonna be here. We gave our money to the defense fund." Then that Matthew, he smile at us all and say, "Dr. King has asked me to thank each and every one of you." He said it better than that and talked about the Reverend King's heart being full and how Murpheysfield done raised five hundred dollars for the defense fund. Everybody smilin' by the time he say this, some of us said "Amen," 'cause it were a very pretty way he had with words, that Matthew.

I don' remember very much of what the boy said. If you want to know the truth I could hardly understand a word he say. Don' think the rest of us did neither and it weren't just on account of the fact that he talk that Yankee talk fast, fast using all sorts of words none of us ever heard before that day or since. What he do is start telling us about some ray-she-oh which he say mean nothing more than what we all knew: that there were more colored than white in Murpheysfield. Then he starts tellin' us we is oh-pressed and when he do that, Noog, she start laughing and shaking in her seat and she say out loud in that big voice of hers, "You don' mean you drove all the way down here to Murpheysfield from New York City to tell us that?" Everybody start laughing then, and that Matthew, he look like a boy whose mother forgot his birthday. Dragged down, I can tell you.

We stopped laughin' when he started talkin' about the vote. And how Murpheysfield had the worst colored voting record in the South. What he do is look at us and say, "How many of you voted in the last election?" Well someone up front she say, "They gone and closed the polls 'for I could cast my vote. Lady I worked for had a party that night." Then Houston Moseley, he tell it like it really is. He stand up and point his finger at that Matthew and he say, "I flunked the test." Heard somebody say they gives the colored a votin' test no white college teacher could understand. Then that Matthew, he say, "Well, it's time things change around here." But nobody said amen. 'Cause we all knew things around Murpheysfield be hard to change.

Guess it were then that he started talking 'bout the sit-in. He say Dr. King and him and two other folks from up North were comin' to Murpheysfield on August 17 to sit-in at the Woolworth's lunch counter and he was here tonight to ask two of us to sit down with them. That hit all us right in our faces because we all knew what a sit-in would mean. We all knew the police commissioner in Murpheysfield be the meanest white man in the South worse, worse than that old George Wallace or Bull Connor. Somebody up front told that Matthew, "Why, if we sat down at the Woolworth's counter, they'd call out the dogs. The Klan'd burn the place down."

That Matthew, he look at us and say, "They can't. We go in unarmed. The whole country will be watching."

Then somebody else, she say, "No colored ever sat down at no white lunch counter in Murpheysfield." Matthew look stern, stern and say, "No black person has ever tried to sit down at a white lunch counter." Then Houston, he starts tellin' Matthew about what happened to a friend a his over to Monroe and how they hung him from his own front porch for looking at a white woman the wrong way. He say that were only five year ago and that things hadn't changed any in five year, which we all knew was the truth.

Matthew looking even sterner and he starts talkin' about how nothing changing around Murpheysfield since Harriet Be Sure Store. Noog turn to me and say, "Lavina, you ever been to Harriet's Be Sure Store?" I never been there. But I just shook my head. I figured that Matthew gone got us mixed up with some other town 'cause I never heard of no Harriet Be Sure Store and far as I know none of the rest of us had either.

Then nobody said anything for a while. This big sad quiet come down on us. Then Matthew tell us, we need two people to sit down. We need two people from Murpheysfield and he look around. He look and he look. Then he pleading with us, he is saying, "The worst that can happen is y'all have to spend the night in jail. Our group will bail you out in the morning." Then he say real proud like, "I spent three nights in jail myself." That old devil Houston, he call out, "The white jail or the colored jail?" and when he do that, Matthew, he hem haw and tell us he asked to be questered with the black men but they put him in the white jail anyway.

Lord only knows what made me do it, 'cause it was shortly thereafter that I stood up myself.

Another big sadness had come in the room and maybe I was taken by the sadness of us all sittin' in our church like we always do, hoping for a better life, hoping we can make it through. I remember right before I did it, a little girl, couldn't have been more than five years, running down the aisle clapping her hands with a smile wide and fine on her little face. She run lickety split down the aisle and up them stairs to where Matthew is and she is callin' out, the way chirrun do, itty bitty voice that pierce right through you,

"Reverend King," she say, "Reverend King, I want you to bring me a diamond ring for Christmas." Matthew, he bend over and take her hand and he say, "I'm not Dr. King." Then he send her down and she is ballin', tears runnin' down her cheeks and I was hoping whoever's chile this was wasn't gonna give her a whipping for what she done, 'cause she didn't know no better thinking this white boy was the Reverend King. That's when it come over me, a feelin' I never had before or since. I thought to myself, why that chile, she don' know *black from white but when she do, why it gonna change that little face a hers. I felt the wrongness of it. The wrongness of it for her. The rest of us, we were used to the way things were, and I sat there tryin' to remember if I ever in my whole life go run free and happy like that chile in her pink dress who didn't know the difference of black and white. Well, I don' think I ever didn't remember. Seemed to me I knew it since the day I were born into this world.*

By this time, that sweet chile was gettin' led by her mama up the aisle. She were cryin', wailing on account of the fact that the white boy weren't the Reverend King or Santa Claus or whoever she wanted. Everything still and quiet in the church. I hear myself, but though it sound like me, it don' feel like my own feets standing in my old worn down shoes. "I'll do it!" I says.

Everybody in the church turn round and look at me. Matthew, he come down the stairs and up the aisle heading toward me and he is smilin' and everybody singin' "Lord Laid His Hand on Me" and Noog, why she is clapping her hands and people are smiling and singing and I'm in the middle of the biggest party our church ever seen. Lord, we were happy. Though that bluebird of happiness, it didn't last long. Fact near as soon as I say it, second it fly out of my mouth, I know I is making the biggest mistake of my life and I'm going to have to do everything to keep Billy Ray from finding out what I done. But it were too late now to jump up and say, "I don' mean it, I take it back!"

DIAMOND BUTTONS

꽃

Tuesday morning Billy Ray went downtown determined to steal the clothes he needed for tomorrow night. But he went home empty handed. He'd seen a shiny blue shirt with ruffles down the front, with buttons that looked like diamonds. But something told him not to take the shirt, though he wanted it almost as much as he wanted something to eat. Since he'd left the country club the hunger for food was growing stronger and stronger. He was beginning to understand that he needed food in the same way growing things needed watering.

Billy Ray had four dollars in his pocket. Two he had saved from his caddying. And two he'd taken from underneath his mother's doll. The shirt cost twenty dollars—not that the price put him off. He'd been stealing the things he needed since he was twelve—sometimes things that cost twenty dollars.

What changed his mind was the hum. It come right over him when he walked in the door of the store where the pimps bought their clothes. Words with it too. "Diamond Buttons." Somehow having a song given to you was as good as getting to wear the shirt—maybe even better. He took the bus home, for he was too weak to walk and the shoes he had stolen were already starting to feel tight. He spent the rest of his money on food. Now, as he set off early in the evening on Wednesday, he wore his old long pants and a short sleeve shirt, couldn't wear no socks for the shoes were even tighter. Couldn't understand how his feet could grow so fast; his skinny legs ached from growing too. Billy Ray carried his mother's red wig and a pair of ten-cent dark glasses in a brown paper sack. His harmonica was in his back pocket of his pants and the song "Diamond Buttons" was going to be the first song he'd give them tonight.

After a lift and a long painful walk down the dark country road, with just the sliver of the moon and the early evening stars to light his way, Billy Ray arrived at last at the club. The parking lot was already full and songs he knew from the radio were pouring out into the parking lot. The club was by the lake he used to go fishing in with his father. He had forgotten about that. But now as he smelled the strong lake smell, not as heavy as the bayou smell, but similar, mingling with the pine tree smell, he remembered the day he had caught his first—and only—catfish.

His father had caught four that day and the two of them had taken them home for supper. They had sat on the end of a pier. Couldn't afford no boat to take them out, though his father had promised one day they would. Couldn't remember how they got home that day, though it seemed to him if he stood smelling the good pine tree smell, he could remember everything he needed an answer for.

Billy Ray stood in a thicket and watched the cars pull up and the people heading toward the blue light from the open doorway. Billy Ray put on the dark glasses so he could grow accustomed to the strange way the night world looked, rose colored with the dark glasses on. When it was time, Billy Ray reached inside his sack and drew out his mother's red wig and when it felt right, he crumbled up the brown paper and threw it down on the ground. He walked slowly toward the back entrance of the club, where he'd seen the entertainers come from on his previous visit. He told himself he was one of them now. As he neared the doorway, Billy Ray reached in his back pocket and took out his harmonica and started playing "Diamond Buttons." He was playing "Diamond Buttons" when he walked inside the doorway in the red wig and dark glasses. And just like in a dream, everyone stopped and stared.

They thought he was blind. He had not figured on that. The dark glasses were just something he thought of that was cheap enough to do. While he was playing and singing "Diamond Buttons," Billy Ray let them go on believing that he was a blind boy standing in that doorway. It gave him a delicious sense of power, seeing their faces, seeing their mouths drop and their eyes start popping. Hands started clapping. Then a boy with a pair of drumsticks in his hands started accompanying him on an old wood table. A girl began to dance. Then the host he had seen the other night walked through the door in back of the stage wearing a shirt just like the one he hadn't stolen the other day. A blue shiny shirt with ruffles down the front and a row of diamond buttons. Rays of light bounced off the diamond buttons on his shirt.

Billy Ray was standing on a chair now; didn't know how he got up there from the doorway. Flew maybe. They were down below him staring up. The whole little room was clapping and moving and shining and smiling. And he could see it all: the wonder of the hum was lighting up their eyes, wetting their lips, causing their hips to shake. When "Diamond Buttons" was over, he did not play another song. He wanted it to stay with them. He wanted them to feel his power. And it was there. Still on their faces. Still in their bodies. And he was standing there in the little backstage room that was quiet now and hushed. Billy Ray stood very still and felt himself take possession of the room with his being. Just as he had taken possession of them with the hum. It was easy. The easiest thing he'd ever done in his whole life. Though he weren't doing nothing now. Just standing there on his chair with his harmonica in his hand. No one moved. They were his. He had them in his pocket, nice and neat the way his harmonica always stayed in his pocket when he wasn't using it. Now Billy Ray ripped his dark glasses off and let his eyes laugh at them. Then they were laughing with him with their eyes at his eyes. Laughing because the hum had got them laughing.

Then, as if it were nothing, he got down off the chair, walked toward the host—right up to him, tapped him on the shoulder. He didn't have to say it loud. They were still in his pocket. But he said it loud enough so that everybody in the room could hear. "You got the shirt man, but I got something better than the blues."

Everything moved so fast after that, he could not recall what had come when. He wanted to remember every detail, because for the first time in his life he had something to remember. He had memories to play in his brain, same way the hum had always played there. The whiskey Billy Ray knew, had come to his lips backstage before he walked through a little hall and stood up before them. Then his lips were on the microphone. The microphone was candy—

and he'd been worried about the microphone. Didn't know what he was going to do with it before it was there under his lips. But his lips knew what to do. Just like they always knew what to do on the harmonica. The whiskey was throbbing in his veins. An older man with a little electric piano was on one side of him. And another man with drums and percussion was on the other side. Billy Ray played "Diamond Buttons" with his dark glasses on. And when it was over he ripped them off threw his head back and laughed.

The room was filled with men and women and they weren't really dancing. Not dancing in their own world like he'd seen before. The women, beautiful in their bright dresses, stood in front. And their men stood behind them, hands on their shoulders, and they were waving their arms and moving their hips and every move they made was for him. The songs he sang were part of them—the crowd just sucked them in—he could feel that right away. Now, Billy Ray belonged to them and he to them. His music made them one.

Billy Ray played and sang for forty-five minutes straight that first night. And the men beside him backed him up—didn't know how they knew what to do, but they did. They could read his mind. When he walked off stage, he was dripping wet, his mother's red wig was soaked through like it had been under a shower. Someone threw a jacket around him. Whiskey met his lips again. He felt the warmth of the whiskey coursing through his veins. The crowd was shouting, "bring back the harmonica player." And they kept on shouting, "harmonica player, harmonica player," and stomping their feet till he went on again at midnight. And this time he was wearing the shirt with the diamond buttons. Someone had taken off his wet one and put it right on him, though it was big. Person who put it on buttoned it too. Called him "harmonica player," like the crowd was shouting "harmonica player," louder, louder, "harmonica player, harmonica player." Pinned the shirt in back so it wouldn't be so full. All seven diamond buttons. He played till two in the morning, only stopping once for whiskey and a small rest behind the stage.

He would never be alone and afraid again. He would not have to steal. When his feet grew, soft shoes would be his. He could satisfy his hunger—all he'd have to do is open up his mouth and food would be his. Billy Ray understood all this right away, the power that was his now. Then the women were climbing on stage and their hands were reaching out to him. He shrugged them away when he saw the girl from the other night, the pretty one in the same spangled dress. Then her arms were all around him and her hair was silky and smooth, not nappy like his own. She smelled of sweat and perfume. Her soft round breasts were up against the diamond buttons of his shirt and her soft pink tongue was teaching him what he already knew—didn't need no rehearsal with this either.

Billy Ray Davis was fifteen years old—and now the world was his.

His backup guys drove him home and by the time they got there, it was four thirty in the morning. In a quarter of an hour the sky would start to turn light. But Billy Ray did not stop to remember that a little more than a week ago, he would be heading out that door by now, heading for drudgery and pain. All that was behind him now. The past was gone. He had twenty dollars in his pocket and a date to play on Saturday night. He had a date to rehearse at four o'clock this very day and he wouldn't have to walk there in shoes that pinched his toes neither. His walking days were over. That was the only concession to his past he allowed himself to make. Billy Ray took the key to his house out of his front pocket and inserted it into the loose front door lock. He heard somewhere in his head, like he was in a dream, his mother's voice. She was calling out in her sleepy voice, "Billy Ray? Better carry yourself some pie to work, boy." Then the voice died out. He was standing in the dark front room of his mother's house, the only house he had ever known. But he didn't know this house anymore. It was just someplace that felt familiar, not home really, just a place whose smell he knew. His mother was back asleep. Billy Ray could hear her snoring in her wobbly pink bed. He tiptoed in her room and stared at her big form snoring on the bed. Her red wig was on his head. He took it off, tiptoed around her little shelf, put it back on the chipped white head where it lived; then he went to his own little place off the kitchen, lay down on his bed, and fell asleep.

VINA

I were just plain spooked, walking 'round like I was in some kind of dream. Had so much on my mind, what with Billy Ray, then that thick white and poor Mary Jacob, that chile, she look like she was losing her mind. Trouble with chirrun is they thinks every bad thing that happen is gonna stay that way forever. By the time you get yourself grown, it come to you that there is the good times and the bad times. Got to hold on to them good times and keep them close when the bad times rolls along. But Mary Jacob, she be too young to know that.

I didn't know then that Billy Ray he were havin' the first good times of his life. I thought he gone and taken himself up with the devil's own. I come in from work and he weren't there and understand, Billy Ray, he were always there. Always ate our supper together—nobody make collards better than my boy. Then that morning when I wakes up and sees him lying passed on his bed, room smelling like whiskey, face covered in lipstick. Boy hadn't even gotten his clothes off. He were wearin' some blue shirt with shiny buttons. Why, I thought, Lavina, your nerves ain't gonna be able to take another dose of that medicine.

Love of whiskey and the devil's way is something you is born with. But I never saw it in my boy—thought he were takin' after me, not his father's side. But I knew that morning, with the whiskey smell and that red lipstick all on his face and that fancy shirt the boy wearing to sleep, that all them years, I were just fooling myself. Either that or the devil, he be foolin' me into thinkin' I could outsmart him. Part of me wanting to shake that boy of mine out of his whiskey sleep. Another part of me be remembering when I opens up my mouth, that's when that handsome father of his left us for good. Thought my heart were gonna break in my chest, day he walked out that door, though it didn't. It were just a bad time that passed. It took a while was all. Took considerable time.

Same day as I seen Billy Ray passed out in his whiskey sleep was when I goes to work and the fat's in the fire there too. I was giving Kathryn and Van their breakfast— them lazy girls, eat their pancakes and french toast in their robes though it be the middle of the day. Mary Jacob was with me in the kitchen when Van say, "Mary Jacob, you come right over here and sit next to me." Then she look at me at the stove and say, like it were her house, "Lavina, there any more pancakes for Miz Mary?" Well Mary Jacob, she glare at Van and stomp her feet and say, "I ain't Miz Mary and I already ate my breakfast."

Pretty Van go on eatin' her pancakes and Mary Jacob, she come stand next to me at the stove where I is drinking my coffee. I reckon that would have been that, but just then, old Thick White come marching in and she stand there lookin' the way she always look.

"Girl!" she say to me, in that ugly way of hers, "Girl, I'm ready for my dinner." Kathryn look at her and say, "Lavina's givin' us our breakfast." Then Mary Jacob, she say, "Lavina's drinking her coffee." They both is talking at the same time but then they stop and we all just is there quiet, quiet in that kitchen. Mary Jacob, she reach out and hold onto my arm, real protective like, and Kathryn, she light up one of her cigarettes and start looking bored, like she ain't there. Pretty Van, she get up and come over to where we is by the stove. She say to Thick White, "Why don' you sit down and I'll pour you a cup of coffee. Then, Lavina will fix you your dinner."

But Thick White, she just keep on standing there with that look on her face. Van pour her a cup of coffee and sets it down on the table. "I take my lunch in that room yonder." Then she move her head in the direction of the breakfast room. Then, like we didn't know already what's on her mind, she say, "I don' eat with colored."

Pretty Van, she keep on smiling, then she come over to where we is and put her arm round my waist. Always smell nice, Van did, though she weren't up to no good with that Jack, I can tell you.

"Now isn't that funny that you don' wanna sit down with Lavina, 'cause Lavina, she feel exactly the same way you do, only she has such nice manners, she wouldn't say it to your face." Then she say it again, she say, "Lavina doesn't want to eat with you neither."

Well, Mary Jacob, she start laughin' her head off. Hadn't seen that chile laugh that way in a long time. Kathryn, she start laughing too. Pretty Van looking like the cat what ate the mouse. Thick White, she glare at Van. Then she march out through that swinging door and soon I hears her chair at the breakfast room table. The girls, they keeps on laughing, but I ain't laughing

I can tell you. All I is thinkin' is how downright peculiar life is sometime. For pretty Van, she were speaking the truth. I didn't want to sit down next to that Thick White no more than I wanted to sit down next to one of her kind at the Woolworth's. And I wondered what in the world had gotten into me, telling that Yankee white boy and them at the church that I were only too happy to risk my life doing just that.

WIG ON A BROOMSTICK

ᨆ

One day changed everything. He came home and found her dressed up in Lavina's clothes.

If her father had walked in and found her in one of her mother's fancy dresses and high-heeled shoes, he would have smiled maybe—though she never had felt the faintest urge to dress up like her mother—even in those other times when her mother did dress. Or if he had found her in a pair of his trousers and one of his neck ties, holding a gun, he would no doubt have called her a regular tomboy. But walking in and finding her dressed in Lavina's wig and apron, sweeping the floor, was something he would never find a way of forgiving. Yet her whole life had prepared Mary Jacob for that day. She had not needed the wig and the apron; Lavina had always been inside her. The one reliable source of love and comfort: her real mother.

Thursdays and Sundays, when she was very little, were the bad days when Lavina went somewhere else to rest. That was all she ever told Mary Jacob about her mysterious absences. On those days, someone else came in the back door in the mornings, gave her supper in the kitchen and afterwards a bath and put her to sleep. When she was old enough to communicate with other children, Mary Jacob learned that on Thursdays and Sundays their mothers did not mysteriously disappear to sleep. Kathryn's certainly never did. Her mother lived upstairs and slept all the time, and sometimes disappeared to sleep and rest in another place. Lavina had a separate magical existence—a secret life that Mary Jacob knew not to question her about. Though sometimes Mary Jacob asked her, "Vina, did you have a good rest?" when she ran to greet her at the door on Friday and Monday mornings. Lavina would pick her up in her strong, soft arms and smile, "I had a fine rest, Mary Jacob, and I hope you did too, honey." That Lavina needed her rest only on Thursdays and Sundays while Kathryn's mother needed her sleep all the time came to be a source of great satisfaction to the very young Mary Jacob— it proved the innate superiority of her own mother over Kathryn's. Mary Jacob even learned to feel sorry for the beautiful girl whose mother slept all the time. In Mary Jacob's mind, this accounted for her sister's chronic ill temper and her nasty pinching ways.

Sometime after her third birthday, Mary Jacob overheard Lavina who was standing by her mother's bedside asking her for extra money to fix the roof of her house. "Of course I'll give you the money to fix your roof, Lavina, but don't tell Mr. Jack, you hear me?"

Mary Jacob ran up to her room and hid under her big four-poster bed with her teddy bear. That Lavina had her own house wasn't the problem. Children slept in the same house as their parents and she could not comprehend why this simple thing was denied her. Worrying about it kept her awake at night, long after Lavina left her room. Finally, when she could no longer bear the mystery, she grabbed hold of Lavina's hand and asked, "You're my real Mama, aren't you?"

Instead of saying what she was supposed to, Lavina let go of her hand and stared at her with round terrified eyes. "Lord have mercy, Mary Jacob, you better hush your mouth. I'm your mother's maid, darlin'," and hurried out of her room that night, without even kissing her goodnight.

For a time after that, Mary Jacob concluded that Lavina was really like Cinderella, who also had to scrub the floor and do all the work around the house. But as the months passed and soon the years, Mary Jacob lost her illusions about royalty disguised as scullery maids and began to face the grim reality of the life Lavina lived during the day; though it took her many years more to acknowledge to herself that the life Lavina lived at night and on Thursdays and Sundays was not enough of a life left for anyone. The dollar bills she stole from her father helped a little with that. But not near enough.

Where Billy Ray fitted in was more problematic, Mary Jacob knew it was wrong, but she hated him.

Seeing Billy Ray steal the shoes had changed some of those feel-ings, at least uncomplicated them. The shoes made him a thief, like herself. And now that everything at the house had changed, and Lavina had been stripped of all her authority, Mary Jacob needed Billy Ray. She wanted to give him fifty of the sixty-three dollars she had taken out of the bank and now had in her room, hidden in her new library book.

Billy Ray, clever thief that he was, would know how to give his mother the money—of that she was sure.

Mary Jacob scribbled Lavina's telephone number now, in the corner of the puzzle page from the morning paper. She knew the number by heart, though she had never called it. Her father had already read the morning paper—no one in the house was interested in the papers except her and Jack, though he always got it first. Still, it was something they had between them, this silent sharing of the newspapers. He brought in the morning paper, for he awakened even earlier than she did. Mary Jacob brought in the evening paper and put it in the library for him to read with his whiskey after work. When he finished he'd leave out the puzzle page for her on the red leather ottoman in the library. They never talked about this sharing of the newspapers; nor did he ever forget to leave it out for her, even on the day not long ago when he had beaten her. It was there the next day when she finally left her room.

Mary Jacob was in the habit of working on the puzzle page here at the kitchen table while Lavina fixed dinner late in the afternoon. It was always the nicest time of day in the house—even now when the nurse was upstairs. But something was wrong this afternoon. Lavina, who always went about her cooking efficiently and qui-etly was not herself. A fury seemed to have descended upon her. She was banging iron pans. Slamming down canisters with bread-crumbs and flour. She was making such an awful racket Mary Jacob couldn't concentrate on her puzzle. She looked up at Lavina's pad-ded, stoop-shouldered back. As usual, her small nappy head looked way too small for the rest of her. Lavina was muttering to herself as she dropped the raw chicken pieces into the grocery sack with flour.

When Lavina left tonight, she'd sneak into Kathryn's room and use the telephone to call Billy Ray. She did not know what she'd say, but she'd say something. They'd meet and she'd give him the money.

She smiled to herself thinking of the fifty extra dollars Lavina would have. Enough money for food and shoes and scarves, maybe a new wig too. Lavina only had that dark greasy one she always took off in the morning at the same time she took off her street dress and shoes.

She was done at last with the scramble word, but the crossword was not going well. She liked to call out hints to Lavina; it was a game they had been playing for as long as Mary Jacob had been doing word puzzles at the kitchen table. Lavina always pretended that she knew, but could not remember. "That's got to be, now let me see, it's on the tip of my tongue, Mary Jacob." Then when Mary Jacob would supply the word, Lavina would beam and say, "I knew it. I was just 'bout to say that very word and that's the truth, honey. You just beat me to it."

Another pot clattered. And Lavina muttered "Lord!" like it was a curse word. Mary Jacob did not look up from her puzzle. Still, she asked, hopefully, "Vina, what's a three letter word for vacation place? There's a "P" in the middle, but that's all I know."

Now Lavina was coming toward her, holding the bag with raw chicken pieces, her gentle eyes yellow and sick looking. The bag with the chicken was quivering like a bird was inside. Mary Jacob thought of something Lavina once told her that when you kill a chicken you have to wring its neck. Even after it died, the chicken moved. Lavina was looming over her. Mary Jacob hunched her shoulders together and looked down. She feared her father but she knew him. She feared her sister but she knew her. She did not know this dark angry stranger with her bag full of quivering chickens who was yelling at her for the first time in her life.

"Why you goin' and asking me them kind of questions? I don' know no three letter word. My readin' so bad I cain't even read no recipe book. I have to keep it in my head. Half a cup of this, a soup spoon of that."

Mary Jacob kept her face down on the newspaper that smelled bad this close up.

"Close them eyes if you want, Mary Jacob, but remember girl, by the time I were your age, I was out a school pickin' cotton in them fields near the airport. Don't go asking me them kind of questions ever again girl. Don't you think I feels bad enough the way things is?"

Mary Jacob kept her head down. She could hear Lavina moving away across the floor in the loose shoes she always wore when she wasn't serving dinner. She lifted her head from the newspaper and looked toward the sink. Lavina's back was facing her. That was good. She did not want her to see the tears that were falling from her eyes, rolling in her mouth, salty and bitter. She wanted to scream out, "If you start being mean to me, I won't be able to stand it."

She got to her feet. Lavina was turning around. Tears were running down her cheeks too. She'd never seen Lavina cry in all her life. And this was the most shocking thing of all.

Like in a dream, she moved across the room toward Lavina and put her arms around her. "Don't cry, Vina," she said, just like Lavina used to comfort her when she was little, "the angels like it better when you smile."

She and Lavina were hugging. They had not hugged each other in so long. Mary Jacob put her head under Lavina's chin, against the soft pillowy shelf of her breasts and let her wide soft arms envelope her. She knew she must protect Lavina, but all she could think of was that she felt blessedly safe rocking back and forth in Lavina's arms.

Abruptly, Lavina let go and she felt herself falling against the hard tile of the counter tops. Mary Jacob's head struck something. Clouds of flour were everywhere, pouring down from the counter top onto the floor in a torrent. Fascinated, Mary Jacob stared at the red top spinning like a charmed thing across the kitchen floor till at last it collapsed with a clang near the chair where she'd been sitting. Flour was everywhere: in mounds, in little trails and puffs. The kitchen floor was covered in it. "On no, Lavina, look what I've done."

It was Lavina speaking now. Not that terrible stranger she had imagined. It was Lavina's soft, everyday voice. "Don't worry yourself, none, sugar, I'll clean this ole flour up. Go on back to your game."

"No, Vina, I'm gonna clean it up," Mary Jacob insisted, then headed for the broom closet. She had never used the broom, not once in her whole life. She now felt the shame of it. Lavina was saying, "and get that dustpan too, darlin', your father comin' home soon so we gots to clean this up."

Mary Jacob moved across the room toward the long closet doors. When she opened them, she let out a scream. Lavina's wig was sitting on top of the broom like a head without a horse. She touched it. It was soft and greasy and the whole closet smelled like Lavina. It was in her hands, and without knowing how or why, now it was on her head, the little fringe of hair, tickling her forehead. She reached for the broom and from behind it on a nail, one of Lavina's extra kitchen aprons, which she wound around her. Lavina's whole being was her being now. She was Lavina carrying the broom and handing herself the dustpan. She was Lavina heading toward herself, saying, "Go on, Mary Jacob, go on and take hold of that ole dustpan while I sweeps it into the pan."

The other Lavina had her mouth open wide and Mary Jacob could see the bright gold tooth glittering in her smile. Mary Jacob smiled back and replied. "You gots to hold it steady darlin' otherwise the flour gonna get spread everywhere. I got 'nuff work round here without this here spilt flour messin' up my kitchen."

Lavina was laughing her deep laugh. And Mary Jacob was laughing her deep laugh. It was the best kind of laughing in the whole world. Both of them laughing, together and apart.

Then the door shut. And there was no more laughter left anywhere in the world. She saw his shoes first. The black tie-up shoes covered in a fine coat of white flour. She was frozen to the broom handle, waiting for the shoe to come up and kick her in the face.

"Lavina, what's the meaning of this?"

Mary Jacob got to her feet and looked at him. He was shorter somehow. And queer looking. Not handsome anymore, just a red-faced white man looking mean and angry. She did not know whether she was looking at him. Or Lavina was looking at him. He did not matter anymore. She did not belong to him.

"Is my ice laid out, Lavina?"

Lavina was scurrying to the top of the icebox and she heard a crunch, but Mary Jacob could not take her eyes off him. She wanted to take the broom and scat him out of the room—but if she did that, he'd punish the other Lavina. She could not let him do that.

"You missy. Take that thing off your head and go to your room. I'll speak with you later. And Lavina, after you fill my ice bucket, get yourself upstairs and tell Miss Kathryn I want to see her in the library."

"Miz Van's in there with her, sir."

"Good, send them both down."

Lavina moved past them through the door to the butlery and now she was gone. But still Mary Jacob stood there. He was looking at her for the first time ever and saying with vicious sincerity, "I said, get that nigger wig off your head, girl, before I use that broom on you."

She handed him the broom. Shoved it right in his ugly white face and watched him grip the handle, his knuckles turning white. Then the broom dropped, but still she stood there until he said, "I'd pull it off myself, but I can't bring myself to touch that filthy thing."

Alone, up in her room, Mary Jacob waited for him to come up and beat her. Just as she waited for the faint sweet smell of Lavina's wig to fade where it had rested for so brief a time, greasy and sweet on top of her own head of hair. She'd left the kitchen wearing Lavina's apron. When she got to her room, she took it off, for she did not want him to come find her in it. A faint Lavina-like smell clung to the apron, though it was more starch and bleach than Lavina's wig smell. Mary Jacob put the apron under her pillow, once in a while taking it out to hold it in her hands.

She did not come down for supper. When she knew they were eating, she took the fifty dollars from her library book, wrapped a piece of notebook paper around it, addressed and stamped it, and put it with the apron under her pillow. She waited for much of the night, long after she heard Van singing "Heavenly" in her low, off-key voice in the dressing room while the tap ran, the toilet flushed and the horizontal slat of light disappeared from under the door. After Kathryn came home and went to bed, Mary Jacob crept out of her room with the envelope in her hand. She stood outside her father's door and listened to his rhythmic snoring. Satisfied that she was safe, she crept down the stairs past the Grandfather clock and into the kitchen. She considered food briefly, and though she was vaguely hungry, she could not think of a single thing she'd like to eat. For a while now, Mary Jacob had grown used to the hollow feeling inside her. Sometimes it ached and her stomach often growled, but the hollowness suited her.

Out of the kitchen now, she passed through the dark butlery and on to the dining room and through the great double doors with the graceful curved moldings that led to the huge front salon where her father and Van danced after dinner now beneath the shimmering chandelier. They carried on now, nearly every night after Kathryn left with Foster. She was by now accustomed to the music from the records drifting upstairs to her room when the air conditioner went off. Her mother never left her bed now, not even to use the bathroom, and the nurse sat next to her, making sure she did not get up. At night, the nurse slept in her mother's dressing room. They were inseparable, the nurse and her mother; the only time the nurse left her was when she came down for meals to bully poor Lavina. The house, Mary Jacob knew, belonged to Van and her father now, and though she felt no sense of her own dispossession, she felt a sense of shame for her mother and fear for Lavina.

She was in the library, their room: Van's and her father's. It smelled, when they left it, of cigarettes and whiskey and something else too, something that reminded Mary Jacob of the smell of pork roast; something rank and salty. She had formed the habit of coming here after they left. As always, their whiskey glasses were on the table and the deep red cushions of the leather couch had dent marks and wrinkles in them. It was Van, Mary Jacob knew now, and the absolute power of her presence, that had saved her from another beating today. Why should he dirty his smooth hands on her, Mary Jacob, when there was the black silk of Van's hair and the ivory of her finer skin to touch? He could not keep his eyes off Van. He looked at her in the same deeply pleasurable way he always brought the glass of whiskey to his lips. But it was more than that. Once in a while he stopped drinking his whiskey for a few weeks. But the girl could not imagine him stopping Van, who intoxicated him.

The clock was striking the half hour after one when she made her way through the dark dining room shining with silver on the sideboard, and on through the pitch black butlery and into the kitchen, where it was lighter.

She let herself out the back door and into the hot, still night alive with crickets' chirping. Mary Jacob had never been out so late before. And it thrilled her, the hugeness of the night, the glittering stars. She walked down the driveway, light on her bare feet, making no sound at all.

At the end of her block was a mailbox. When she reached it, she opened and closed it carefully so as not to disturb the calm and beauty of the night. Then she ran home on her bare feet and at last to sleep.

POWER

◡◠◡

The backup guys were honking outside the door. Though he longed to run out the door to the night that was coming and the music he would play, skipping light on his feet, Billy Ray sat under the kitchen fan and waited. He studied the miserable little kitchen that was the bathroom too, and listened to the horn blasts, knowing soon it was all gonna change. Knowing their life was changing was connected to making them wait out there in that hot black car for him. Same way he knew exactly when to pause when he played. There is power in making them wait.

The backup guys were older than Billy Ray by years and years. Were old maybe as his father had been the day he walked out that door. But it was different now; nobody was ever gonna walk out on him again. Billy Ray had the power now. That was the beauty, the wonder of it. They needed him. Didn't matter that they had the wheels. No more than it mattered that they had played the clubs for years, earning twenty dollars on a good night, five dollars when the cut from the drink profit was small. Money and wheels were well within the touch of his own fingertips. Billy Ray knew that now as he had never known anything solid and real before. Wouldn't take no time at all. And better wheels, real money, not pocket money.

Yesterday they had taken him to supper at a restaurant outside the city limits of Murpheysfield; a little shack stuck somewhere in a pine thicket, where the faces were black and the food was rich and plentiful. Owner himself came out in his tall white hat and his shiny white apron. Backup guys, they introduced him as "harmonica player." The harmonica player. Owner smiled at him, set down a huge plate of food and a napkin so big it covered all his lap. The huge plate of food had awed Billy Ray. Ribs, slaw, slabs of soft white bread spread with butter and garlic, and bright yellow corn on the cob. Greens were good too, smoky with more than enough salt pork; more than they ever got at home. Pleasantly bitter and spicy with drops from the bottle of pepper vinegar.

Billy Ray's first thought when he saw all the food was how he was gonna carry some home for his mother. And though he wanted to share this wonderful food with her, he soon decided not to show that the food meant anything to him. Billy Ray had never even known colored had their own restaurants. All his life he thought anybody with dark skin had to eat at home or at church suppers where everybody brought a foil dish. Didn't show them his ignorance, though. Acted like it was what he had been used to, only not as good. It was easy acting high and mighty. Acted like they were his caddies. As good as the food was, the cold bottle of Dixie Beer that came with the steaming plate was even better. The bitterness of it and the pleasant glow it set off inside him was something he was growing easily acquainted with, just as he was learning the fine feeling of a full belly, a belly stuffed with food that satisfied him in every way. The backup guys paid for him, just as they picked him up and took him places, lent him clothes, slapped him on the back, and let him sit up in the front seat of the car. They knew Billy Ray was their ticket out of there.

He was heading out the door when the phone rang. It was going on seven thirty and his mother would be home in an hour or so. Might even be her on the phone. Billy Ray had not told her about his new life—he was not ready for that yet. For all she knew, he was still caddying at the country club and that was fine with him. He turned back, went to the shelf behind the kitchen table where the phone was, picked it up, and said, "yeah."

"Billy Ray, this is Mary Jacob."

The boy nodded his head and repeated the yeah once again.

"Your mother is in trouble. And I want to make sure she has some money. I'm sending you fifty dollars. I want you to get it to her. Do you understand?"

The boy continued to hold the old black phone in his hand, feeling the weight of it. What he really wanted to say was, "Keep your money, white girl, I've got the money for her." But fifty dollars could mean a lot.

"Did you hear what I said, I want to help your mother. She's in trouble. My father's mad at her."

The horn meanwhile kept blasting outside.

He said at last, "You want to give her your money, why, that's fine with me. She work hard enough for it. It ain't like she didn't earn it."

The girl said, "good." The girl said, "thank you." And told him she had sent it in the mail. "Be sure she gets it, you hear?"

And the boy hung up the phone, grabbed his sack with the red wig and glasses, reached for his harmonica in his back pocket and started playing as he walked out the door, down the steps, and into the street. It didn't matter that his mother was in trouble. His mother didn't need them anymore. His mother had him. The fifty dollars would help with that, though he wasn't awed by that heretofore vast sum of money. It was gravy, was all. That it come from her, well he'd forget about that.

But in fact, he always remembered.

VINA

～✺～

Billy Ray weren't home when I got there. Knew right away soon as I turns my key in the lock, my house were empty like it been all week without my boy there waiting for me. Only time I sees him is passed out in the morning, sometimes with them fancy clothes on before I go to work. Whiskey smell, it taken over his little room. And something kept tellin' me, "Lavina, any time now, your boy gonna walk out that door and you is never gonna see his face again." The feeling were strong that particular night on account of the fact that I were spooked what from that taking down old Jack given me. I walk in Billy Ray's room and it were neat, way it always be, but way too neat, nothin' out of place; seemed the spirit of my boy done gone and left our house. I even goes to his little cupboard, opens it up and sure enough I is expecting to see the little cupboard empty, just the way his father's cupboard were empty after that man left. Even took his bottle of whatchacallum, no more than just a drop or two left in the bottle he took with him. Thought about that old bottle long after he left. He were a man who were careful of his smell. My heart were pounding in my chest when I opens Billy Ray's little cupboard, expecting to see nothing. But thank the Lord, Billy Ray's things still be there. I took it as a sign. I say to myself, "Lavina, your Billy Ray, he ain't gone yet. And you got to stay right where you are and protect him and it gonna take all your strenth wrest him away from the devil." Said to myself too, that I had no bidness taking on no cares of the world when my own boy be in serious trouble. Here I was acting all high and mighty like I were gonna save all the colored folk in Murpheysfield sittin' in at the Woolworth's. Pride, like our minister says, always comes before the fall. It weren't fall yet, still high summer, so I says to myself, "why, you still have time girl." Didn't feel none too proud that night after ole Jack done gone and threatened to fire me without my references. Took me down a peg or two, I can tell you.

So what I do is go back in my room, take my wig out of my big ole black purse. Didn't feel much like wearing it after what happened with Mary Jacob, poor thing. Anyways, I looks across my little shelf and I sees that my red wig is gone. Her head, where it sit, is bald as a baby. Gave me the queerest feeling seeing her head all bald with just her face Billy Ray done painted when he were little, colored it dark brown like a colored lady's face. Something tole me my wig being gone had to do with Billy Ray being gone. Lord's truth, I thought he had taken up with fancy women and here he was givin' his mama's wig away to one of them. Whiskey can destroy your soul—it eat into your goodness—saw what it done to my husband, seeing now what it was doing to Billy Ray who were not the kind of boy what would give away his mama's best wig to some fancy girl. So I stands there awhile and stares at that bald head where her wig used to be. Seemed to me I were finished with wigs; decided right then and there my own nappy head were gonna have to do.

I go to Pauline, my mama's doll, on account of under Pauline's skirt is where I put that white boy's number up in New York City. What I sees then, spooks me even more than my good red wig gone. Understand, there's money under her skirt. Pauline, she got twenty dollars, ten ones, and two fives. All crisp and new. Why, it seems to me I could smell the brimstone in them new, crisp bills.

So what I do is I takes the little piece of paper that New York boy given me, gets out my reading glasses, and goes into the kitchen and sit down at the kitchen table. Never made no long distance call before that night. Some white lady done answered the phone and we leaves my name and number. I sits there at my kitchen table and I prays. I prays and I prays. Then I fixes myself some scrambled eggs and some Vienna sausage and after I eats, I prays again. Finally, I just falls asleep at the kitchen table with my face on the phone. Half asleep I were, when the phone rings with that Matthew pleadin' with me, sayin' the whole country gonna be watchin' and I owes it to my people. I says, "I'm sorry to go back on my word, very sorry, but the whole country gonna have to watch somebody else." When he sees he ain't gonna get me to change my mind, he lets me off the phone, but it weren't right away. That Matthew be a boy who want his way.

Still, I were relieved. Mightily relieved I'd gone and got that sit-in off my back. Part of me were sad too. Kept thinking about that little girl in her pink dress at the church meeting that night. Could see her little face plain as if it were sitting there staring at me in my own kitchen. I thought about my daughter Mary Louise, too. Saw her sweet little face mornin' I found her with the breath gone out of her. Part of me still wanting to sit in for them. But most of me knowing I had no bidness riskin' everything I had for somethin' I wasn't gonna get anyway. Didn't throw away the little wad of paper, though I was sorely tempted to get it out of my life. Went back to my room and stuck it back under Pauline with all that money. Don' know what made me do it. If I hadn't, why, sure enough I'd be somewhere else today instead of where I is.

Next morning when I wakes up, I knows that our little house were still empty. Second I open my eyes I can feel it. The sad emptiness of the place, the way it feel now that my boy were gone. Outside my house, Houston Moseley's rooster be cock-a-doodle-doing, though it were way past the time he normally makes up his mind to wake up the whole street. Everything quiet, quiet. Clock next to my bed say almost six o'clock, so what I do is pray for a while, lays my hand on the Bible next to the clock on my bedside table. I is still prayin' when I creeps out my room, through the kitchen, then to the little door of Billy Ray's room. Still praying when I gives it a little shove and weren't nobody in there. Room just be neat. Little bed of Billy Ray's with that old patchwork quilt my husband's sister make, still bright, them colors.

I were buzzard lonely, I can tell you, standing there in my empty house, house that always had Billy Ray and me in there. Different from what it felt when my husband gone and run away from us. I were a young woman then. And when you're young, you have the strenth and the hope that start to leave you when you're older. Seems to me that morning, this were worse than some old bad times that rolled along. This were like some tractor with big old wheels heading toward me, gonna crush the life outta me with the sadness of it all. Part of me feeling like just laying down on the floor and letting it come over me. Wishing there were someone strong gonna come and save me from the sadness. Wasn't any particular someone I was hoping for. Never had nobody to save me; couldn't even make a picture in my mind, like you can do when you is a young woman. And funny thing is, that knowing there's nothing to hope for sometimes give you all the strenth you needs to shake yourself and say, "Girl, get yourself out of this condition 'cause you is too old and too fat to be hopin' for Santa Claus."

Minute I starts thinkin' about Santa Claus, I starts to giggle, remembering how when I were a chile, my mama tole me that ole white Santa Claus who come to the farm where we lives in the little house way in back, were really Mr. Stevens. And that old big belly he got under the red suit is a bed pillow. Just thinkin' 'bout that skinny white man what worked us all to the bone dressing up in some foolish red costume to visit the colored he got there workin' his fields put my mind in a new direction like.

So I turns around. I take a bath, fix me some breakfast, turn on the radio, and Mahalia, she be singing my favorite hymn. "Soon We'll Be Done With the Troubles of the World." When she gets to that part of the hymn where she sing, "I wanna see my mama," the sadness come upon me again. Loved my Mama and I missed her every day I walked the earth after she passed. That's the trouble when you let the sadness come in the door—it don't want to be goin' away any too soon.

By now it were time for me to gets to work, and I'm buttoning up my dress and getting my money ready for the bus when what do you know, the key turn in the lock and there is my boy. He is standing there in the sunshine of the doorway looking so golden brown and handsome, what with his skin shinin' and his eyes all bright. Even though I knows he been out all night with the devil, I can't think of anything but for how long and lean and golden brown shinin' he look. That old runt of mine, he lookin' like a fine, fine man. What I want to do is shake him like I used to do when he were being bad but I can't. You can't shake a grown man what look so shinin' bright even if he wearing fancy clothes and have his shirt unbuttoned showing his chest like some so and so.

I says, "Good morning to you and what you think you done with my good red wig, boy?"

Well, Billy Ray stand there smilin' in the sunshine. And he say, "Mama, you gonna have so many wigs you only be sorry you have one head."

I look at my boy and shakes my finger.

"Billy Ray, I ain't gonna be listenin' to a word you say."

Billy Ray, he say, "Don' you point your finger at me, girl." And then we is laughing, both of us there, seven fifteen in the morning laughing and shaking in the kitchen of our house. Lord, I were glad to see him.

Then I says, "I gots to get myself to work Billy Ray, and when I come home tonight I 'spect to see you right here stirring the greens when I comes home." Then I proceeds to walk out the kitchen.

Billy Ray, he say, "Mama, I ain't gonna be here stirrin' them greens, and pretty soon, you ain't gonna be doin' no green stirrin' yourself."

I turns myself around when he say this, 'cause I want to look at his face. But Billy Ray, he is in his own room by now. Still I thought about that handsome face of his and what it gone and said to me. Part of me saying, "That's not your Billy Ray, girl, that's the devil speaking to you through the lips of the one you love best on earth." Another part of me remembering, though I told myself not to, that as long as I knows Billy Ray, he's a boy what tole the truth. Devil never give you nothin' you can count on. That father of his, when the devil take him over, why he done gone and lied till I swear his face all but turned itself blue. All mixed up I were between the two of them.

Get hold of yourself girl, I says. Boy ain't gonna be there when you get home and that's something. At least he ain't started giving you all sorts of things to make your head spin. But it were spinning. Wondering what I was gonna do if the devil done took him and was doin' his best to take me too. Still, I felt better. Considerably better than when old Houston Moseley's rooster gone and cock-a-doodle-doos. At least Billy Ray come home. At least he come home.

MIZ MARY

~~~

N ow, when Mary Jacob came down the stairs in the morning, a new sight greeted her. Soon it would be familiar to
her, in the same way the nurse sitting next to her mother's bed had become: the fixtures of her new life. Her father, who
should have left for the office long ago, was in his cream-colored
suit in the dining room with the morning paper spread out before
him. Sitting next to him, in a filmy turquoise robe, was Van, like
they were married. Van with her gleaming black hair spilling down
her back, holding the silver pot from the sideboard that no one ever
used, like she was playing being married too. But Mary Jacob knew
right away, neither one of them were pretending. They were real,
like the coffee pouring out of the little silver spout; the bittersweet
smell of it reaching Mary Jacob, even a room away. Filtered sunshine
came softly through the lacy underskirt of the dining room curtains,
bathing them in a soft glow. They looked less like husband and wife
than king and queen, Van caught sight of her and flashed a smile.
"Sit down and have your breakfast, Mary Jacob," she called out gaily,
like there was some kind of party going on instead of breakfast.
Mary Jacob watched her put the coffee pot down and motion to the
chair next to her. Her father looked up briefly, then back down at
his newspaper. Van smiled again, urging her with her beautiful eyes.

Mary Jacob moved past them, not speaking, and went into the
kitchen. Lavina was at the sink with her large round back turned
to her. She wanted to go over and hug the single thing that seemed
real, but instead, she went to the pantry for a box of cereal and on
to the icebox for milk. She took the bowl to the kitchen table and
sat there, waiting for Lavina to say something. But Lavina kept her

back turned. Though, when the swinging door flew open and Van floated in, she finally spoke.

"Miz Mary," Lavina said, in the soft emotionless voice she always used when she spoke to the rest of them, but never her, "You'll be having your breakfast in the dining room now." Then Van was by her side, the soft floating robe was brushing up against her arm and she was patting Mary Jacob's head in a kindly sort of way.

Mary Jacob sat there, staring at the familiar grain of wood on the kitchen table. "I'm not Miz Mary," she started to say when her father's voice, harsh and insistent from the other room, stopped her.

"Mary Jacob, Mary Jacob, come in here this instant."

She rose slowly to her feet and followed Van out of the kitchen where Lavina was still at the sink. Lavina was not allowed to look at her. But her father could. He said, "You'll eat breakfast from now on in here, like a lady." Though she knew he did not want her presence in this pretty game he was playing with Van, in a room where they both knew Mary Jacob didn't belong.

He was on his feet now, and she looked at them, the shiny brown shoes that glowed from so much polishing. He ordered his shoes specially made from England. His feet were small and narrow for a man. Just as his hands were dainty and narrow and elegant. He had never worn a wedding ring, but he always wore the heavy gold signet ring that had belonged to his great grandfather. His hands weren't any bigger than her own. Why then should she fear them? The smooth white girlish hands with the carefully tended nails.

It came to Mary Jacob then, a stunning realization, the knowledge that he was a sissy, a sissy playing at being a man. She had no other word for what she was feeling. It was the word boys used at school for pretty boys who didn't play football. But the word, she knew, fit him the same way his light cream did and his special shoes. What he was, was a sissy. A sissy with a face that would be pretty if it weren't so mean.

His voice, however, was deep and powerful. He had been born and educated in Virginia and he spoke differently—more elegantly—than anyone in Murpheysfield. Her mother was always proud of that—the fact that he came from Virginia. His coming from Virginia made up for the fact that their money came from her side of the family. And he just managed it for her.

"Look at yourself, Mary Jacob, you're nothing less than a disgrace. A genuine eye sore. Your clothes are hanging off you like a ragamuffin. I know it's not entirely your fault. Your mother has been too ill to attend to her duties, but Van is going to tend to you now, and when I come home tonight, I expect to see a young lady. Not a common street urchin."

He was gone now. The back door had shut and just the lemony smell of his aftershave was in the room, mingling with the smell of coffee. Van was smiling at her with her beautiful red lips. "Come on, Mary Jacob, we'll have us a ball. We'll go on down to the Palais Royal and get your hair done and buy you some precious new clothes. Your father says we can buy out the store."

They drove downtown in Van's mother's car and parked it at the garage near her father's office, the one he always used. Van said her father's name and two old colored men whisked open the doors and took the car away.

After breakfast, Van had changed into a tight black skirt and a soft white blouse. Her face was very white and her beautiful lips stained dark red. On the street downtown, she pulled out a pair of jeweled dark glasses with pretty upturned ends. Around her neck was a string of pearls that shined like her black hair. Van had taken lately to dressing less like a girl and more like a lady. She no longer wore black suede loafers with neatly folded white socks. She wore real shoes—ladies high-heeled shoes and stockings. Jewels shined on her ears, dangled from her wrist, and she wore rings now. Mary Jacob did not question where the new glittering jewelry came from— it seemed so much a part of the new Van, the one who sat next to him at breakfast and danced in his arms after dinner. She knew too, without putting a name to it, that it wasn't a game. Van, who used to be so eager to please, gave the orders now. Mary Jacob could not put in words the power this new role gave Van, though she felt it. She could not help but feel it. The power made Van even more beautiful, that much she knew.

Van knew exactly where to go. What to do. She walked through the doors of the store the same way she waltzed in her father's arms after dinner. It was something her beauty had taught her to do. First she led Mary Jacob to the top floor, where they made an appointment for both of them at the beauty shop. Then they proceeded methodically from department to department, floor to floor. Van would point and say, "that one," to the elderly sales lady who attached herself to them, and carried whatever Van pointed at while Van led them on for more. When her arms could no longer carry the load, the sales lady would disappear and when she reappeared with empty arms, hold them out for more. It was, as Mary Jacob discovered, the easiest thing in the world, this pointing at this at that. And it wasn't dolls, it was real. "This one," she heard herself say, somewhere in that morning, "I like this one." Van smiled, and that meant yes, or made a little pout with her mouth to let her know she had made the wrong choice.

She had always known there was money, though Mary Jacob had never known what the power of money really meant. It had never really affected her in any kind of meaningful way. Today she was beginning to understand that the power of money meant it was unnecessary to look at the dangling price tags. Beginning to understand that if she pointed at the right thing, Van would nod her head and it would be hers. She did not stop to consider then that Van had the power of this money—and she, Mary Jacob, never had. Then there was so much else to think about. Lacy brassieres and underpants. Blue, pink, and yellow panty girdles. Whole and half slips edged in lace. There were blouses and skirts and purses and so much more, all here in one room, all the wonderful things that were hers now.

She and Van arrived at last in a huge dressing room on the third floor. Van sat in a chair, peacefully smoking and drinking a Coke, stretching her long legs out in front of her, admiring first one, then the other of the many pairs of high-heeled shoes she had selected for herself. Mary Jacob was standing in front of a three-way mirror on a pedestal, trying on outfit after outfit. Once again, when Van nodded her head, the outfit would be hers. And when Van shook her head to mean no, she would hand it to the saleslady to hang up. Mary Jacob said, "Thank you ma'am" to the lady in the black dress each time she handed her the outfit. It seemed to her she said "thank you ma'am" a thousand times in those strange hours she spent becoming someone else. She said "thank you," because she'd been taught to say "thank you." But she knew she was also saying "thank you" because the ugly clothes were gone. And best of all, most miraculous of all, it wasn't like dolls, it was real.

Mary Jacob was curiously light now and unfettered, with her ugliness gone. In the strange hours she and Van spent in the store—hours that weren't like any hours she had ever spent before, hours devoted exclusively to her—Mary Jacob knew another being had mysteriously taken over her body and her spirit. The girl she was seeing now in the mirror was a new girl, a girl with clothes that fit and suited her, in every way. She could not believe this proper-looking girl. She couldn't take her eyes off her in the three-way mirror in her pretty tailored blouses and dark plaid skirts.

But she could not help but wonder what had happened to the girl who had turned so easily into Lavina yesterday. Where was her reflection? Was it hiding behind the mirror, wrapped in an apron smelling of bleach and whose head was covered in the sweet greasy wig? All of today was wonderful, except when she thought of Lavina. When she thought of her, it hurt, like a fresh bruise hurts—even when you touch it just a little.

Sometime later, after they washed then cut and rolled up her hair, Mary Jacob knew the wig was wrong. And the thought of Lavina hurt less—yesterday was fading away. Her own dark hair was shiny with glints of red, not black and greasy, shiny and almost as silky as Van's. It did not lay down smooth and silky like Van's—it poofed and curled around her face, but it was beautiful hair. Even the hairdresser told her, "Hon, you've got beautiful hair." In her whole life, no one had ever used the word "beautiful" about anything concerning her. She liked it more than she could ever say.

Now, as they headed out of the beauty shop—where they had eaten grilled cheese sandwiches with chocolate milkshakes under the hair dryer—and were heading downstairs for their last stop, the makeup and perfume, Van held out her hand and said, "Mary Jacob, you just have to stop wearing your glasses. I'm blind as a bat myself, but you get used to it after a while." They were on the escalator, going down, when Mary Jacob handed Van her glasses and the world suddenly looked altogether different—and her own transformation was complete. The world looked rosy and soft. When they got off the escalator, Van took her hand and led her to some faraway place. Up close, Mary Jacob could see the lipstick shades and the careful way they blended her face powder with mauve, green, and yellow. She could admire the smooth way her skin looked with the wonderful bottle of foundation stuff that smelled like cream and roses. Up close in the mirror, her lashes were thick and her eyes shined blue beneath them, blue and dancing with light.

MARINE BAND HARMONICA
∽∽

For the first time in his life, that same afternoon, Billy Ray took the bus downtown with money in his pocket. Not just hoarded money to pay the gas or phone bill, the kind you carefully counted before you handed it over to the sour-faced white person making faces at you behind the window. Usually on the very last day before they'd send the truck and cut everything off. They'd had their electricity stopped more times than he wanted to remember. You could do without electricity. All you needed was a big bag of ice and a chest for the food. And when times were hard, it was the lights they let go first. Their stove was gas, and so was the water heater, and gas didn't cost much.

Had to use the electricity money to pay Mr. Delton Campbell— that or he would take the house away. He'd seen it happen, how he threw two families and everything they owned out on the street. Even after a whole lifetime of paying. Moved two new ones in the next day. Mr. Delton Campbell owned nearly every house in their part of town. And his name, just the sound of it, was enough to make you see everything you owned—your bed, your broken television set, even your worn out pots and pans—spread out on your front patch of land like the wrath of God had come to call.

There were jokes about Campbell, but no joke was ever free and easy. Billy Ray had figured out, when he was just a child, that the slumlord had more power than God. Another reason for his lack of faith. Had God ever saved a one of them from Delton Campbell's Sunday morning visits? Even the year when Christmas come on a Sunday, Delton Campbell was there, before church. Parked his shiny red Cadillac in the street he owned and, in his church suit and bright red vest with reindeer on them, hopped cheerfully up and down the front steps, from door to door, collecting the miserable dollar bills they went without food for. He smiled and wished all the children handing over their money, "Merry Christmas!" "Happy Easter!" every Easter Sunday too, hip hopping like the Easter fox. Their mothers were all at work. Every colored woman had to work Christmas and Easter mornings. No colored he ever knew ever had no Christmas or Easter morning off.

That was all behind him today. Billy Ray paid their bills—a crisp five dollar bill for the payment of the house—no counting out the ones carefully, hands shaking, thinking there were only four. It wasn't near as much as he wanted, but Billy Ray felt, for the first time in his fifteen years on earth, free from immediate worry and want.

Billy Ray thought from time to time about the fifty dollars Mary Jacob had promised on the phone. He didn't quite believe in it. But he didn't not believe it either. With fifty extra dollars, he could be farther along.

It was good to be out today. Even if the pavement was hot and the sun burning bright in his eyes. Except for sleep and the few hours he spent waking up with his head throbbing from whiskey and beer, it had been weeks since Billy Ray had time on his hands alone. He had not always liked it, but he was realizing now, as he walked the hot streets of downtown Murpheysfield, years of being alone was in his blood. Alone with his music in his mother's house. Never made friends too easy and he hated school. The rules, the dull reading and writing, though he made himself learn to read and write. Always known not to be like his mother, who could barely read the gas bill. Wondered sometime what they did before he learned to read and write. His father hadn't learned reading or writing no more than his mother had. Just him and his music, all those years. It had been a lonely life, way too much alone for a child. But he had grown used to it. The hum had always filled up the silence.

There was a small dark store, no bigger really than a room in an ordinary house, that sold musical instruments off the main street of downtown Murpheysfield. And it was here that Billy Ray went after he paid their bills. Even without the promised money on the phone he had just enough to buy the bigger Marine Band harmonica he'd been thinking about for how long now? At least a year or two. Didn't even know, for most of his life, a bigger one existed, though he had been in the habit of thinking for years now, how much more he could do if the harmonica was longer.

A few days ago, Billy Ray had actually had his hands on a piano. He knew learning it, big though it was, were gonna be like fresh whipped cream on top of summer berries. A piano cost at least a hundred dollars and that would not buy a good one. But, the hum would come with it too. Knowing the hum would come with his hands on a piano made Billy Ray feel like he had the pocket full of five-dollar bills he needed to own one.

He was holding in his hands now, the decorated case with the long silver Marine Band harmonica inside that cost ten dollars, walking out of the store with it paid for, like it was nothing. The new harmonica didn't fit in his pocket like his old one. Billy Ray felt pleasantly self-conscious with it in his hand. Many people had seen him perform by now. He was growing used to standing up in front of the crowd with his mother's red wig and the dark glasses. No one would recognize this ordinary colored boy in old shorts and a shirt with a long skinny case in his hand. But knowing he was someone they called, *the harmonica player*, gave Billy Ray a wonderful feeling of power and motion. He passed two well-dressed black men, years older than he was. Maybe they had seen him these past weeks up on stage.

The boy loved it up there. The height it gave him and the distance. And for a moment out in the street he had a wild desire to make the fiery pavement into a stage. He saw himself taking out his brand new Marine Band Harmonica and playing it in the hot mid-afternoon sun.

He turned his thoughts to Saturday night, just a couple of days away. It was the busiest night at the club and Billy Ray had been informed that an important club owner from Shreveport was going to be there to hear him play. If the club owner liked the sound, he would book them for a date. In Shreveport they paid, not like they paid in New Orleans, but a hundred dollars for a Saturday night was not unusual in Shreveport. And if you did well in Shreveport, N.O. was just a bus ride away.

He was thinking too, that he might let his mother come on Saturday. That look on her face—part love, part fear—this morning when he come in the door was still with him. He had spent what had remained of the night before with Brenda, the girl who had kissed him the first night he gone up there and played. It had been Brenda's idea. And the wonder of those hours, different than the hum, but like it too, filled Billy Ray with a sense of reverence and awe not only to her and her slim beauty and grace, but to his fat, worn out mother too. Somehow the two of them were connected.

Yes, he wanted to see his mother happy. Wanted to see the smile that would light up her face when he stood on the stage looking down at her. He'd say, *Mama this one's for you.* And he wanted it Saturday night. Even though something inside him said Saturday night was way too soon, Saturday night was wrong. Still, he decided if Mary Jacob's promised fifty dollars came before Saturday night, he'd take it as a sign and tell his mother. And if not, why he'd just let her worry and let it ride. Billy Ray had reached the bus stop now. When it pulled up a few minutes later, he stepped on happily, glad to have a plan. In the meantime, he had a brand new Marine Band harmonica at least a foot long. When Billy Ray took his seat in back by a window, he stared out and felt the hot air coming through. The hum was coming on too and he called it "Gonna Come True."

MISTAKE

❧❧

The curtains were drawn against the late day sun. Mary Jacob stood in the double doorway between the front room and the dining room and took in the unlit chandelier, the gleam of silver on the sideboard, the lacey mats on the long dark table, and of course her father at the head, a glass of whiskey in his hand. The table was set for two; she could not ever remember it being just the two of them for dinner here in the wonderful room where she belonged now for the first time. She could feel the belonging way down deep inside her. Mary Jacob didn't need to look down at herself; she had stared in the mirror so much she had memorized every inch of the crisp white shirt tucked inside the trim plaid skirt. She had shaved her legs again before dinner; the white socks and the brand new black suede loafers were perfect too. She loved the soft way they moved against the thick Persian carpet beneath her. As she went to take her place beside him, she imagined him standing up to help with her chair the way he did for Van. When he didn't, she told herself he was looking at her as she used to be. And anytime now, he would notice.

In the quiet beautiful room, the only sound was his soft jabbing at his salad with his fork. She studied the setting sun coming in the window and she waited.

Lavina was in the room now, clearing away the salad. She kept her head down. For as much as she was waiting for her father to see her and acknowledge the change—she was hoping Lavina would not notice. Not before she could find a way to tell her she was still Mary Jacob on the inside.

Kathryn had noticed the second she walked in the dressing room wearing the pretty skirt and blouse. She had even smiled in pleasure. "Why, your hair looks good; you're much better without your glasses. The outfit is real cute too." She wasn't wearing her glasses now, but still, her father had not noticed.

Dinner was nearly over now. And yet he had not spoken a word. She could not remember what Lavina had given them, though she had watched him eat it all, and every time he put his fork down, she thought he would say something. Now, the pretty ruffled crystal bowl of cobbler was under her nose. The fine fluted silver pitcher was in his hand; he was pouring heavy clotted cream on his. The delicious smell of crust and warm berries floated around the table, rich and sweet. She lifted the heavy round spoon, just like the one he was using for his cobbler. She was pretty now, and they both loved dewberry cobbler.

Finally, he did look up. Mary Jacob could see that he was taking her in. He was nodding his head, looking at her. She lifted her chin expectantly.

"I'm going upstairs to have a visit with your mother. When I come back down we'll talk about your sudden transformation, child." Then he smiled at Mary Jacob. She watched him carefully wipe his mouth with the damask napkin and throw it down. "While I'm upstairs, get the ice bucket from the butlery and fill it with ice. Then bring in six of the small crystal tumblers and set them on the tray. I'll be down shortly."

She was very excited and much relieved. Her father had noticed and they were going to talk about it. He was finally going to say she was pretty. Mary Jacob was too excited to eat her cobbler. He wasn't downstairs, so she could clear the dining room table. She wasn't allowed to do that in front of him because he said that's what he paid Lavina to do.

With her hands full, she used her knee to push open the swinging door between the dining room and butler's pantry. Now she was passing through the breakfast room. The overhead light was on, and the nurse stolid and thick in her starched white uniform was reading her trashy magazine and smacking her lips, waiting to be served.

In the kitchen, Lavina was at the sink. Kathryn had warned her this afternoon, "Stay out of the kitchen, little one. Why, when Daddy caught you in that nigger wig, I swear, he nearly called out the klan to tar and feather poor Lavina."

She had wanted to punch Kathryn in the face when she said that. Instead she had whined, "Don't call Lavina that, Kathryn, she takes care of us. She always has."

"For Gawd's sake, you sound like a Yankee. You know I love Lavina and I wouldn't call her nigger to her face. Still, she is a nigger and don't forget that."

Lavina turned off the tap and now she was wiping her hands on her apron. She did this for a long time. When she turned around and saw Mary Jacob, a shy smile lit up her dark face for a moment. It was then Mary Jacob understood what had changed. It wasn't her face or her hair or the new clothes. She and Lavina had changed. It would never be the same between them again.

Lavina was whispering, "Honey, you got yourself looking verah verah nice. I always knew you were gonna turn into one fine young lady. And now you have."

"Vina," the girl said softly, and both of them turned away.

Still, she was aware that some of her was tired of the kitchen; some of her wanted to grow up. With Van's help, she had entered a new world. Mary Jacob filled the ice bucket then went to set out the tumblers. Now, she was waiting for her father; sitting on the big wing chair in the library. When the Grandfather clock struck eight, he appeared in the doorway with a fresh shirt on and a stack of crystal ashtrays in his hand. He set them down on the table and walked over to her.

"So you went shopping," he was saying casually. "And after you went shopping you put away your eye glasses."

She smiled at him. "Yes sir."

"You cut off your hair, got your nails polished, and ran up a big bill at the Palais Royal."

"Yes sir. That's what you told me to do."

"Look at me, child, let me see your face."

Mary Jacob raised her chin. He was smiling at her and shaking his head. Then he reached over and patted her on top of the head, in a kindly sort of a way.

He sat down, put his feet up, and lit a cigarette.

"I made a mistake, Mary Jacob," he said, smoke pouring out of his mouth. "I was wrong. You're never gonna be a beauty. Not like your sister or your mother was. You look respectable and neat. But that's all you can hope for, child. Still, it's not the worst thing in the world. You've got other assets."

Mary Jacob could feel her eyes burning and she bowed her head. Still he kept on, in his soft elegant voice, talking and smoking as if to himself, not her. Never her.

"Before you were born, I was counting on you to be a boy. It wasn't so bad with Kathryn, I figured your mother and I had all the time in the world to bring sons into the world. But, as it turned out, your mother couldn't have any more children after you."

She knew the story. Knew every single word of the story, but she sat there. For the way he was telling it made her know he was sharing with her some long bottled up disappointment. He meant her to be sorry for him. And in some peculiar way, she was.

"Like I said," he went on, as though he were talking about someone neither one of them knew. "I made a mistake. I'm not going to ask you to dress up. It doesn't suit you. You know it doesn't suit you, don't you missy?"

She bowed her head and told herself not to cry. She was grateful she could at least stop the tears. She wasn't going to admit to him she had wanted the clothes to suit her. She had wanted to change. She had wanted to belong.

"But Mary Jacob," he was saying now in a different voice, a soft, kind voice he almost never used when he spoke to her.

"You have brains, Mary Jacob. Beautiful girls like your sister grow up and one day their beauty fades. Brains are something else. In a few years, I'm going to send you to a school in Virginia. I'm going to educate you just as if you were my son. I'm going to teach you to shoot; I'm going to take you hunting. Maybe we'll buy us an airplane and if that happens, why I'll expect you to learn how to fly."

He squashed out his cigarette, got up and fixed himself a drink. He took a long deep swallow and looked at her expectantly, and she knew she was supposed to say, "thank you sir," but she didn't. She wasn't going to ever try and say anything ever again in her whole life to please him.

Then the doorbell rang.

"Run get that door, child," he was telling her, "and send whoever it is in. Why, in a few years, Mary Jacob, maybe when you're sixteen, I'll let you listen in on one of our meetings."

VINA
〜〜

They was watching us. That Thick White and pretty Van— they both be watching. Van, why she even say "Lavina, you got to let me tend to Miz Mary now. She be too old to be sitting here in the kitchen which you. She spose to be a lady now."

That Van, she say it nice like. Not that I didn't already know what is going on in that pretty head. Got it considerably before she sat me down and tole me.

She had her shining green cat eyes all set on that Jack and all the man could give her. Don' matter that Miz Lil were upstairs or he be old enough to be her father. And that was why she was taking Mary Jacob. He tole her to. That or she thought it up all on her own. Them catching Mary Jacob in my wig and apron got them thinking, yes it did. Happens all the time. White women, they give the colored their chirrun when they is young and is way too much trouble, what with their tantrums and their wetting their beds and never wanting to go there to begin with. White women don' have the quiet inside them that colored women do. But when the chirrun grow up, why, they expect them to get them-selves out of the kitchen and start acting white. I'd seen it happen ever since I could remember. When I were a young girl on Mr. Stevens' farm, his chirrun they plays with us. And they treats my mama like their mama. They wants to hug her and love her just like we do. All of us black and white used to fight over Mama's lap.

But there come a time when they no longer want their chirrun associa-tin' with the colored and they take them back. And most of them, why they go running home, only too glad their mama and their papa wants them at last. I don't blames them at all. But Mary Jacob, why, she were different. By the time they call her back, it were too late. They done gone and missed the boat with that one.

I were thinking about just that when I is walking down the Longs' pretty green driveway that night on my way home to the bus stop. Worryin', I was, about Mary Jacob, wondering who that chile were gonna turn to when she needed to turn to someone. 'Cause I could see it in her face, even with that lipstick and face paint on, she look right pretty all gussied up. But we both knew she were meant to stay away from me. And it were sad for both of us. We had spent all her life together. And we miss each other. We just plain miss each other. We were in the habit, understand, of being in each other's company. It weren't natural for us to to be apart. She were my friend. I loved that chile. I guess, since I'm trying to tell it like it really were, that worrying about Mary Jacob took my mind off worrying about Billy Ray. 'Cause my mind, it were tired from worry, worry 'bout Billy Ray and his whiskey breath.

It were a Friday evening I'm talking 'bout, and by the time I gets myself to the bus stop it be past eight thirty. Didn't get my Thursday off that week. That Jack, he tole me, Lavina, I needs you to work. I were bone tired that night. Every night lately, matter of fact. Couldn't get out of that house on time no more, what with the nurse and her thick white self to feed.

My friend Noog, she be waving to me when I gets on the bus.

"Where you been girl?" she say. "Everybody, they is talkin' 'bout you. Why you is the Queen a Sheba."

I can't look Noog in her face. For even if I deserved to be Queen for the Day that night at church, I didn't deserve it no more after I done gone and back out of that sit-in. But Noog, she don' know I backed myself out, and nobody at the church know it either. Good thing Noog love to talk and carry on 'cause the embarrassment of my position was occurring to me, sitting there on the bus with the wind from the street blowing in my face. Felt right nice without my wig on, it did.

She say, "Lavina, well, you ever heard of the Tie-Tan-Nick?" I is shaking my head and she is tellin' me about this great big old boat long time ago, a big old boat like Noah's Ark filled with rich white sinners. The way she told it, this Tie-Tan-Nick hit some chunk of ice and split itself apart, and when that happen all these white sinners, they start rushing to save themselves, pushing away chirrun.

And the men, why, they is even pushing away their wives tryin' to save their own white skins. The way Noog describe it sounded like a turrible place that Tie-Tan-Nick.

Anyways, when she gets hersef to the end of the story, when the boat go down she say, "Now Lavina, I was thinking about you girl, all through that sermon and I says to myself, why Noog, if Lavina had been on that Tie-Tan-Nick she would have dived in the ocean and said, 'Lord take me!'" The way Noog describe it, there are them that the Lord chooses and them that just volunteers on their own because they is good. I felt two inches tall when I hears my old friend say this about me. Because it just weren't true. At least not no more.

So we sits there for a while. Noog had to get her breath after that long story' bout that Tie-Tan-Nick. When we're nearing the place where you turn for the Morehouse Road, Noog say real soft like, "Did you hear the word Lavina? I mean some axtual voice?"

I'm sittin' back on my seat trying with all my strenth to remember what I was thinkin' that night at the church. Wondering what come over me. Well, I tole her, I says, "It weren't an axtual voice."

Noog, she look at me and she say "hmmm" in that way of hers. "Honey, that's what I thought, that's what I thought." Noog like to say everything twice, like a lot of people I know. Then she look at me long and hard and she say, "Lavina, you is one of the volunteers. And that's the truth. I knew it. I knew even before you gone and tole me. Standing up to volunteer, why, that take real faith."

Well, two feet tall don' even get close to how I felt then. It were dark out by now. And the lights were dim inside our bus, that funny yellow-green like color the bus always get at night. Downright peculiar looking color—even make colored faces look all washed out. Noog look at me, and l look right back at her. We're at my stop now. Noog is the next stop after mine. I is getting' up, gathering my black purse and my brown paper sack with supper.

Then Noog, she lay her head on one side. She say, "Lavina, where your wig girl?"

And I says, "Well, Noog, the heat, why, it put me off it." What I don' say is what I am thinking about. Thinking about long and hard. They done gone and tried to take the spirit out of me, that Jack with his ugly mouth gettin' me so sick inside I be too scared to wear my wig. It weren't right, no it weren't. And I were sick of him and his bully ways, beating that poor chile, beating the spirit out of me, and tempting pretty Van with all the devil's bag of tricks. All of them chirrun. . . and him suppose to be a grown man looking after them instead of taking advantage of 'em. Shame on him!

I am getting off the bus now. The back door is just a few steps away from where I is sitting. Before I steps out into that dark night, can't barely see, what with them never puttin' no street lights outside for the colored. Noog, she is saying, "Well, Lavina, I hope it cool off soon. You don' look like yoursef without your wig, honey." Amen, I thought to myself, I reckon I don'.

Only whatchacallum of having the house all to myself, was getting to sit around in my shimmy without my hot old brassiere and panties on. Closed the shades and turned on the kitchen fan, and let it blow on my skin. Felt like some bad woman, I did, sittin' at my kitchen table eating my supper with nothing more than my shimmy on. Felt right nice it did, though it were August and it don' cool off much at night in August. I'd carried home some pork roast and collard greens and the end of the dewberry cobbler, and if I do say so myself, it were a fine tasting supper, though Mary Jacob didn't eat a bite.

All the winders in my house were open, even though the shades were down and I could hear out on the street the chirrun still carrying on. In summer, the chirrun they is playing outside, sometimes till ten thirty at night. Wished I could turn back the hands of time when Billy Ray were one of them, so at least I knows where he is keeping. Even though I was sad, I was still enjoying just sitting in my shimmy, listening to the happy sound of chirrun outside with the summer crickets. Most of them be eaten up with worms and nits on their little heads but they is happy—you can tell they is happy, God bless 'em. I were fixin' to run myself a cool bath when I hears the front door pounding. I gets myself back to my room, puts on my wrapper, and proceeds to the door. Just like the last time, it were Houston Moseley, and when I hears his voice I say to myself, why, I wish all the colored folk would just settle themselves down and stop upsetting everybody. I were sure that's what the old man were pounding about.

"Lavina," he say, "Lavina, open this door, girl. I gots to talk to you this verah minute." Houston, he is standing there in his undershirt and a pair of torn off pants, looked like a baby with his old skinny legs and his ribs poking out of his shirt. Houston weren't shaking though; I guess his condition were letting him stand still this evening. I says, come on in Houston, and we proceeds back to the kitchen where I was gonna have my bath. Houston, he is setting himself down and I is pouring him a glass of ice tea, and when I is about to set myself down again, why, the old man, he say, "Lavina, I is moving in here, yes I am."

I says, "You can't move yourself in here. I got my own boy to raise. Don' need no other boy to raise, Houston." Then I smile at Houston, 'cause I don' want to go and hurt old Houston's feelings by saying what is really in my mind.

"Your boy is gone, Lavina," he say. "And that's why I'm here to take care a you. You is gonna need a man take care of you now Billy Ray be gone."

"Billy Ray ain't gone," I say, though I don' really believe it in my heart. I know the boy be gone. But I ain't gonna tell the whole world 'bout my troubles.

They'd seen enough of my troubles with my husband and his whiskey ways all them years ago when he gone and left us. Yelling and screaming at me with whiskey in his veins when he gone, had to take me to the Confederate Charity Hospital after he got through with me. Don' even like to think about that time. Woke the whole neighborhood up—liked to die of shame that turrible time when he left us.

I is leaning against the stove and Houston, he is looking at me, looking at me with a look I ain't seen on a man's face for close to ten years now. Then Lord help me, I is starting to cry, big old tears running down my cheeks, so as I can taste the saltiness of them. I am good as blind and that's why I don' see Houston getting up and coming over to where I is. Houston be a bitty man, just a short bag a bones, but a man enough to lead me back to my bedroom and set me down on the bed. Don' know what come over me that night. And I said just that when I sent Houston home a little later on. It were the first time I'd been with a man as a woman since Billy Ray's father be gone. And I could feel the rightness of it in the woman part of me that still lived inside this old fat plow horse I'd got myself to be. I needed a man, even if his arms what felt like chicken wings. And I guess the Lord saw fit to send me one.

Night weren't over yet for me. Though usually nothing much happened after work, 'cept for tired feet and the radio. I'd gotten myself in a deep sleep, the love sleep, we used to call it. I were dreaming. Funny dream it were; can't remember much about it 'cept that I was in church and the pews, why, they is turned the wrong way, other way from the altar. There's a scratching at the door. Don' know at the time whether it's the dream scratching, or my own front door scratching, I is half in the other world but part of me is where I always is at this time a night.

Then the kitchen light goes on and I sees a shadow coming my way on the wall outside my room. Lord have mercy I were shaking in my bed 'cause the shadow is standing at my door wearing somethin on top of its head what look like my red wig Billy Ray gone and give to some fancy woman. Then I hears music. Music I knows, but don' knows, if you understand my meaning. Haints don't play harmonica music. Not ones I ever heard of. But it weren't no haint. It Billy Ray wearin' my red wig and that shirt with diamond buttons coming down the front. He's got some great big ole harmonica in his hands—biggest harmonica I ever see in my life, which confuse me too, make me think I is still in my dream. Billy Ray's harmonica be small enough to fit in your hand between your thumb and your baby finger. This one be the size of a gumbo spoon. And it were making the sweetest sound you ever heard. Billy Ray, he is walkin' toward me, playing and rolling his fingers up and down that gumbo spoon harmonica, rich and sweet. I is saying to myself, "Lavina, thank the good Lord you sent that ole buzzard away."

Billy Ray, he is smiling. Look even handsomer than he look this morning though he be dark tonight, midnight dark with his golden brown skin and his white teeth flashing, and now he is pouring money all over my bed. Greenbacks, they is falling, falling on the bed like leaves from the trees what lose their leaves come fall. Money all over the bed, like I were some fancy woman lying there with the sheets wrapped around to cover my shame. But I ain't ashamed, I is not ashamed, though Lord help me, I would have died of shame if Billy Ray done catch me carrying on with that ole buzzard. I don' know what to say, so I says the first thing that comes to my mind, I say, "Boy, what you doing with my red wig on?"

Billy Ray, he singing, "Be there Mama without your red wig on." I is shaking my head, listening to Billy Ray singing his little song with the bed covered in greenbacks, fifty dollars in greenbacks—counted them the next morning, yes I did. And like I tole Noog on the way over to the lake to hear Billy Ray play Saturday night, "Noog, Billy Ray done gone and hit the jackpot and nothing is ever gonna be the same again."

THE STAR

W ord of Billy Ray, the red-wigged harmonica player, was spreading through Murpheysfield. It started with the regular club goers. The young men and women who had few children and therefore enough money for the cover charge and drinks. Murpheysfield was a small town and there were only two black clubs where live music was played. By his third week as a performing artist, he was already a celebrity among the black community. Some of them called him Billy Ray and some Billy Red on account of the red wig he always wore. There was no doubt the audience loved the outrageousness of the wig. For in 1963, for a male performer to wear a woman's wig was "something else" as Billy Ray had known it would be. They loved the boy who dared to wear it too. Loved it like they loved his music.

A star was being born in Murpheysfield. For anybody who heard Billy Ray — even on his very first night on stage—knew he was going to be a star. The club owner knew it, though he never let on to Billy Ray, just told him casually to keep on coming—upping the money just a little—hoping in this way to keep him longer. Billy Ray's backup guys knew it too, though they too had a stake in keeping Billy Ray in Murpheysfield. The longer Billy Ray stayed, the more twenty-dollar bills they'd collect. For they knew Billy Ray would go on to the world and they would stay in Murpheysfield. Best any of them could hope for was New Orleans on a weeknight in a club that only served beer.

By that Saturday in August, the night of Billy Ray's final club date in Murpheysfield, the D.J. on the black radio station was talking about the performance every hour or so. By Saturday afternoon, the town's cooks, maids, drivers, undertakers, and day laborers, as well as the small percentage of white-collar workers: the insurance brokers, the doctors, the store owners, all of whom listened to the radio, were being told that something very important was going to take place that night, right in their own home town. Easy Al Thomas, the richest, black club owner in Northern Louisiana, was on his way in his grey Fleetwood to Murpheysfield with an offer for Billy Ray, if he liked what he saw. Word had even reached a certain segment of the white population, the older boys who liked to take their girlfriends to dance at the black nightclubs. Murpheysfield was a small insular white town, more like Texas than Louisiana. Even with money and the right color skin, there was very little to do other than go to the movies or the occasional country club dance. Being white and sneaking into a black nightclub where they did not card you at the door, as they did at the white nightclubs, was something of a local custom for white boys and girls.

By the time Lavina, Noog, and Houston Moseley reached the club that night (Noog's older daughter and her husband gave them a ride), the parking lot at the little club had long since been filled. A teenage boy with a flashlight was directing traffic, and cars were parked for half a mile on either side down the dark country road.

Inside the club, Billy Ray was unaware of the commotion that was going on that night. He had spent the first part of that day rehearsing "Gonna Come True" with the backup guys. And, the remaining time before he went to the club, in bed with Brenda. Early evening on the way to the club, one of the backup guys stuck a joint between Billy Ray's lips. And though he coughed and nearly threw up from the first smoke he'd ever ingested in his lungs, he was, by eight forty-five, stoned out of his mind. And rapturously happy.

Later, Billy Ray would learn to use more drugs—harder drugs—mixed with booze, they made him forget. He learned never to play without them, for without the drugs he was empty. He was nothing. But that first night, when the drug was new like his body was young and his life was just starting, the grass was the best gift he had ever been given. With it, the hum was everywhere: inside him, coursing through his veins, and for the first time, outside him too. The chair where he sat backstage was humming. The window of the little room was humming with the sound of crickets in the pine trees. Every word the backup guys said was funny. And the hum was in his laughter. In their laughter. In the records they were playing, that were drifting backstage from the club. Billy Ray's shirt with diamond buttons was humming. He heard the M.C. say his name and his own name was humming. His red wig vibrated on his head, and his narrow hands holding his harmonica were moving with an energy he had never known before.

On the stage, at last, when he looked down at the sea of black faces that were packed in like fish in a can, swaying from side to side, raising their arms all for him—they were humming as well.

Billy Ray could not get enough of them. Before that night he had played for himself—just himself—played out of an inner need, not to be understood, but expressed. He had learned in these past few weeks that the audience was a tool. They gave you their energy and that energy could be used to fuel the hum. But Billy Ray had always held himself apart. For the first time in his life that night, Billy Ray opened up his heart and gave it willingly. To the crowd. To his mother. To Brenda. Even to that old shaking man Houston, whom he had hated all his life. And he could see it in their faces—the love he was giving to them come back to him. It was there in their bright eyes, it was there in the motion of their upraised arms, in the sweat that was pouring from their bodies. He played long after it was time to break. He could not give them enough. He could not stop. Was afraid to stop. That would make the hum stop and the world go back to the way it had always been. Not the way he made it now, him, Billy Ray, with the hum that was his and was theirs now.

When he walked off the stage at last, a hush fell over the night-club. He found his way back to the dressing room. He was soaking wet and trembling and the veins of his arms looked like ropes. His throat felt parched and raw. He could barely see through the haze of his sweat and the tears that were falling from his eyes. The backup guys drifted in, then collapsed on chairs. A tall, well dressed black man with a pencil thin mustache was holding out his hands and nodding his head. Called himself Easy Al and said he come from Shreveport.

It all had the quality of a dream. Until the noise started. A noise like Billy Ray had never heard in his whole life. It began as a moan and then grew stronger. Something told him the people he had played for were as weary and as spent as he was. And he had never considered the audience before. Now, Billy Ray knew they were giving him their last bit of strength and pounding their feet and screaming like lost souls without him to save them. Screaming like children who had lost their mother. Screaming like dogs on mating nights. Screaming his names, Billy Red. Billy Ray.

Then the club owner was beside him draping some coat around his shoulders and the coat was gold and silky. Billy Ray could feel the sweat pouring off his body like blood, soaking into the silky gold lining. He was shivering, like a child with a fever. Glad the owner was toweling his face. And still the sweat came, pouring down his face, down the sides of his body. The club owner put his arm around Billy Ray and the arm felt good, it felt strong. He was guiding him back, back to them on stage where the noise was thundering, where they stood there waiting for him: his girl, his mother, his life—humming with love.

And so, because he could not think of what else he could do, do to prove to them his love, his gratitude—he did not have words for what he felt. There were no words for what was happening. Only sound. And motion. Billy Ray moved toward the end of the stage, feeling the force and the power of their cries. Billy Ray was one of the first entertainers to break the barrier between stage and audience. It was an instinctive move: one that went against the very grain of his nature and for that reason all the more powerful. He stood trembling on the end of the stage, like a man on a diving board though he could not swim. He opened up his arms and threw his body with a light thrust over and delivered himself to the hum.

INFANTICIDE

∽∿∽

Her father was going to shoot Martin Luther King. She had stood at the window and, when she put the drinking glass up, heard him passionately declare, "We'll stop him. If I have to do it myself, we'll stop him."

Mary Jacob had seen him shoot birds from the sky on his farm in Texas. The look on his face and the blast of his gun. The way they fell. She also remembered how he once remarked casually as he cut into his deer meat at dinner "one shot through the lung and she was down." People fell like that when you shot them; they fell to the ground with a terrible thud. It was up to her. The police would not stop him. No one could stop him. She could not let that happen to the Reverend King.

All day Sunday, she sat on the bed in her room. She considered poisoning her father with the mouse poison that was kept in the garage, a paper container with a skull on the label. But she did not play with that fantasy for long. She could no more conceive of killing him than she could imagine the earth without his presence. You could not kill God. And she recognized he was like God in his strength and his power. She then thought of hiding his guns, taking them one by one off the rack and burying them. But if she did that, he would know who was to blame. He would find her out and she would not be free to act. She knew she could not trust God, who had never answered her prayers. So she now tried Jesus, whom she beseeched to take back her hair that framed her face, to take back the new clothes and the make up. She promised not to mind being wretched and ugly for the rest of her life if only that would stop her father from killing Martin Luther King.

She worked herself up into a frenzy alone in her room, starving herself, imagining what he'd do, picturing it—the explosion—with the dead colored leader lying in a pool of blood. She prayed on her knees. And after these fevered sessions, she'd check her closets and feel her hair, hoping that her prayers had been answered. But Mary Jacob's hair curled softly about her face that was not ugly now. Even she could see it was not ugly. And when she flung open the closet doors, her new clothes were there. She had wished for the wrong thing and now no more wishes would come.

Mary Jacob even considered for a while, toyed with it like a top, spinning around, the idea that Van could stop him. Van could make him do anything. But if she told Van, fell on her knees begging the beautiful girl to stop him—all Van would do is smile maybe, pat her head, and look away. These days, Van was always looking away, lost in some kind of reverie. What she looked at was herself, if there was a mirror anywhere near; at her hands admiring her rings, or her arms sparkling with bracelets.

It was peculiar, with all the important things Mary Jacob had to think of that she'd realize finally what it was about her father and Van. It was more than her lips and skin and hair—it was much more important than her beauty. Van was the only person who was not afraid of him. When the moon came in the window, she looked at him, but not with fear in her eyes. She had seen the look many times now, on the evenings when Van danced in his arms. But if the light was right, you could see yourself in another's eyes. Your whole face in miniature was right there for you to see. That's what Van saw beneath the shimmering chandelier. And that's what he saw too. His face reflected in her face, his lips smiling back at him, in her eyes.

On Monday, Mary Jacob called the White House. When she asked to speak to President Kennedy, the woman on the phone laughed and suggested she write a letter. On Tuesday, she called the FBI, but the woman did not laugh or suggest a letter. She hung up in her face.

The sit-in was scheduled for Thursday, and by Wednesday afternoon, Mary Jacob had her plan. She would go to the sit-in and work her way near the Reverend King. She would search for her father in the crowd, and when he aimed his rifle, she'd shield the great colored leader with her own body. Wasn't her own small life nothing compared to his?

And so, as the lonely hours passed in her room, she began to see her own death as the solution to many other things as well. Lavina would not be tempted to talk to her and get in trouble; she herself could leave this hateful place; her father would be sorry and perhaps change his ways. It wasn't hard for Mary Jacob to imagine her own chest exploding with the bullet—one shot—it would be a clean death. The Reverend King would be alive to save all the poor Negroes and she would be free of worry at last. Van would look sad at her funeral, Kathryn wouldn't care at all. Only Lavina would cry. Who would look after her mother was a worry though. Other than Lavina, Mary Jacob knew no one else cared about Lillian.

It was on that same afternoon that she went to her mother's room and told the nurse, "Why don't you leave Mama with me for a while and do something else? I promise I'll call you if she needs you."

The nurse got up from her chair. She grabbed up a metal pan from underneath the bed and shoved it roughly under her mother. Mary Jacob looked away.

"Sweetheart, make your little teetee. . . . That's a good girl!"

Her mother moaned.

"Come on," the nurse prodded her. "Just tell it to come out!"

Mary Jacob heard a faint sound of water contacting steel. Her mother moaned again, then lifted her hand and the pan was withdrawn.

When the nurse returned from the bathroom where she had noisily rinsed the pan, she told Mary Jacob, "Your father should hire two nurses for the work I'm doing. But I'll be glad to have a break. I deserve one."

"I'd sit with her everyday if you'd let me. And so would Lavina, only don't expect her to if you go down there and try and bully her. You have to be polite."

"You're one little nigger lover, girl. I'm surprised y'all ain't Jewish."

Mary Jacob stared at the wide white face with its small mean mouth.

"Them Jews and niggers are planning to take over the country. Neighbor of mine told me all about it. President Kennedy lets the Jews run things up there in the White House. The banks. And the TV stations—them are all owned by Jews. President Kennedy loves niggers and Jews. He sits down next to them."

Remembering how Van had stood up to the nurse, Mary Jacob declared, "Why, we're Jewish, didn't my father tell you?" Mary Jacob had no idea why she said this to the nurse. The lie just flew out of her mouth with a life of its own.

"I ain't surprised. Could've told you that myself."

With that, the nurse lumbered out.

No time at all passed before her mother sat with her back up against the headboard, upright. It had been a while since she had seen her mother anything but lying down.

"Mary Jacob?" her mother was saying urgently.

The girl was in the nurse's accustomed seat, which was still warm from where the nurse's butt had been. She didn't like the proximity—the thought of which made her shudder.

"Yes, Mama," Mary Jacob took up her mother's hand and held it.

"Don't tell anyone," her mother told her.

"Tell anyone what, Mother?"

"That you're Jewish."

"I was just teasing her, Mama, I don't like the way she talks to Lavina. I was teasing her was all."

"I saved you from that curse. You'll never know what a curse it is, thank God. Your children won't either."

Mary Jacob did not know what her mother was talking about. Her mother wasn't right in her mind and often said peculiar things.

"Promise me, Mary Jacob. All that's over and done with and no one will ever know. And especially don't tell your father that you know. Your father doesn't know that you know, does he? He didn't tell you, did he?"

Mary Jacob knew not to pursue the subject any further. When her mother was rambling, you couldn't pay her any mind. If you did and reminded her, she'd never admit she'd said anything.

"I promise," Mary Jacob told her. And soon she could see that her mother had passed off into sleep. And she did not think of her words again.

VINA

∽∾

The good Lord, why he knew he were gonna take me, and I reckon he done gone and decide to give this colored lady a last few days to remember.

When you is young and fine things happen to you, you don' go appreciatin' them like you do when you is older. No, you don' have the wisdom that come with years of havin' days and nights of worry, worry, and work. Your body is young and your spirit, why, it keep tellin' you girl, the rest of your life gonna be jest like this. It's only when you is old and tired like I were, that the good times, why, they comes to you as a gift from above. You learns you have to do more than say "thank you, Lord." You knows you gotta pay back.

What I'm trying to get at is why I got it into my head Sunday after church to call that white boy in New York City and tell him I was back sittin' in. I didn't do it out of shame. Fact, nobody at the church said a word about my sittin' in—no everybody be too busy talkin' bout Billy Ray, how he were gonna be a whatchacallum star. Why, that boy a mine, he gone and take the town by storm. Nobody seen anythin' like it since Hurricane Ethel. And I knew, sure as I was standing there in that nightclub next to Noog and Houston, that the boy, all he ever have to do for the rest of his life is open up that mouth of his and sing.

Every mother worry about her chirrun. But the colored, why they have more reason for worry. Colored done seen way too long what tomorrow has in the way for the chirrun. Don' matter if the Reverend King promise us all that it gonna get better. Don' matter that the ministers say we is God's chirrun and is on that road to heaven. We knows what the future be like for us and our kind. We seen it too many times—what happened to our mothers and fathers and our kinfolk—and when it happen to us we know we is too poor and too tired from years of work to do anythin' more than lay down our loads at the end of the day. We know too, though we never like to say, that no matter what we do, no matter how hard we works, we can't save our chirrun. That's why when I sees Billy Ray up on stage takin' that room by storm —why it were the first time I could remember, I were free from worry.

Some of the fine feeling come from the mood Billy Ray's songs put me in; them songs, they had a way of eatin' up your worry. But it were more than that. It were bigger than that. If I could read, it would be like sayin' someone up there on that stage was holdin' up a sign, a sign that say, "Lavina Davis, your days of worry are over. The boy got hisself a future. You can lay down your load, woman, and thank the Lord." There were more than that writ on that sign up there on the stage with my boy. Sign also say, "You done your job woman. From now on, the road, why, it be clear straight through."

I can see it on Noog's face too. Her in her bright purple dress prancing 'round like a shameless woman, asking boys young enough to be her son to dance. That Noog, she love life, yes she do, though she be an old woman now. Last time I heard, she be in a rocker in the old folks' home. But you should have seen that woman go that night. Faster than the young girls in their pretty dresses.

Houston, he is even going, though it be hard to tell, what with his condition. That ole buzzard wouldn't take his arm off me that night. Every now and then, he lean over and whisper in my ear, "Are you my woman, Lavina?" Made me feel fourteen years old, that ole buzzard with his possess ways. You'd think he were a man of fifty instead of what he was, some half-dead colored man tryin' to get him to promise him more hanky panky on the way back home.

I didn't think a single thought about that sit-in at Billy Ray's show. I had got the sit-in off my back and put it somewhere where it wouldn't worry me. It wasn't until I weres in church the next day, that it come back to me. The sermon was over and we was singing our closing hymn. "Lord Laid His Hands on Me." In case you never heard "Lord Laid his Hands on Me," you ought to know that there's somethin' about that particular hymn that puts your mind in a different direction. And that's the truth. I was standin' there in my church with my friends around me, thankin' the Lord for what He done for Billy Ray and me. Then it come over me. A voice inside me that say, "Lavina Davis, you gonna have to carry through with your word. You gonna have to sit in to pay back the Lord." Soon as I hears that voice inside me, I start to hearing another voice. That old devil saying, "Lavina, don' do it. Here's the first time in your long hard life you can sit back and let others do for you." Them two voices, why, they is talking in my old head. One tellin' me to follow the Lord's way. The other one smellin' of brimstone and ashes.

The hymn, it coming to the end now, part when it say, "Lord done just what he said, healed the sick and raised the dead." Well, I took that as a sign. I said to myself, "Why girl, the Lord he never fall down on the job, he keep doing what he promise. And you gots to do it too." When I gets home from church, I go for Pauline and that little wad of paper I stuck back under her skirt. Took me some time to find that paper, what with all the money Billy Ray put under her skirt—close to seventy-five dollars. More greenbacks than Pauline or me had ever seen. And before the devil started tempting me again with his lazy ways, I calls up that boy Matthew in New York City and I tells him I has changed my mind.

That Matthew, well I can feel him smiling over the telephone. And he were real respect like, kept saying, "Mrs. Davis, I is glad you has changed your mind." Nobody ever call me Mrs. Davis. Half the time I didn't know it were me the boy talkin' to. He even say he gonna tell the Reverend King what I done, not that I done anything yet. Still, it give me a feeling being that close to the Reverend King, I can tell you.

It were past four o'clock now. And the house, it were hot, hot. I is sitting on my bed listenin' to the sound the fan make spinning 'round and 'round. Billy Ray, he weren't home last night after the show. The sad truth were, this were the last time I ever laid eyes on my boy on this earth. 'Cause it's Billy Ray at that door. Understand, I had a good idea where the boy had got himself. This last night and all the other nights he not be showing up where he always did, home in his bed.

Prolly, I would have got the pitcher soon enough, why, the writing it were on the wall for me to see; him so shinin' bright and all growd up, but the way it happens is, she come up to me and she say, "Ma'am, I'm Billy Ray's girl Brenda," and she give me a little kiss, pretty little thing with her spangled dress on. Like Noog and I were discussin' when we was riding home in the car after Billy Ray's show, that Brenda, why she had more than her share of white blood in her, Billy Ray's girl. Even though it were dark in that nightclub, you could see it in the light tan of her skin and the way her hair lies on her head. Don' know how she knew I were Billy Ray's Mama. Don' know who tole the girl, but she knew. That Brenda, she look older than my Billy Ray, not that I was holding that against her.

Truth is, I were shocked. It were all happenin' so fast. Billy Ray growing up, getting himself up that stage and finding a woman all in the same month. Why it were too much for a woman who couldn't read nor write to take in all at once. *Gave me a feeling like I never had, right in the pit of my stomach like a hunger pain. I knows inside myself somethin' is missin'.*

Billy Ray, he got on a fine set of clothes and shoes so new I swears I can hear them squeak as he is walkin' in my room.

"Billy Ray," I say. "Everybody come up to me today at the church and they smile. Everybody were so happy for me. And I is as proud as a mama ever be today."

I watches him pullin' a brand new wallet outta his trousers. The wallet, it were filled with money and he is runnin' his thumb along it like it were nothing more than a deck of playing cards. And I'm thinkin' to myself it were a real shame Billy Ray had left off his church going. Would have done the boy good to see how many friends he done got at the church. But I didn't say so, didn't seem right to. Now, if I had known this were the last half hour on earth with my boy, I would have sat him down and said a word or two about church and about anythin' else I thought he should know.

"Mama," he say, like he were a grown man, "I'll be going to Shreveport tonight. Coming back to Murpheysfield on Thursday, then I'm gone to N.O. Friday." I start smiling to myself, thinking Billy Ray never stepped one foot inside New Orleans and already he is talkin' bout N.O. like he own the place. Then Billy Ray, he take out that money he got in his wallet and he hand it to me. "You don' need to be goin' to Houston no more when you needs money," he say. "Now you'll be coming to me."

It were the first time in my life anyone tell me they is gonna be takin' care of me. Now in our honeymoonin' days, my husband, he say he were gonna do that, but the fact is the man never handed over any cash to prove to me he mean what he say. No, Billy Ray's father, when he were workin', always be takin' care of hisself and his whiskey ways. Never had more than twenty-five cents for me and Billy Ray. Don' know what put me in mind of Billy Ray's father 'cept maybe for the fact that Billy Ray favor him. But Billy Ray don' look like him on the inside and that's what count.

Billy Ray say, "Buy yourself some clothes, Mama. And find someone gonna fix this roof. And when I comes back from Shreveport, we're gonna see what else we're gonna do."

I is looking at Billy Ray and he is looking at me. I reaches out and grabs hold of Billy Ray's hand and gives it a squeeze. Then Billy Ray say, he say, "You got sixty dollars here," and then he point to Pauline. "There's money there too," he say. Then he reach over and he hug me. That were the first time my boy done reach out for me and squeeze in so long I can't remember.

Then Billy Ray, he gets up from the bed where he is sittin' and he say he be on his way to the Greyhound bus station. So I set there happy, listening to his brand new shoes squeak. Then I watches the back of my boy in his new clothes walkin' out my room.

When the screen door close and his feet go down them rickety-rack steps, I'm tellin' myself, why girl, the next time you hears Billy Ray's footsteps, they'll be coming up them steps instead of down. But I never did hear them steps again, not like I did that day in my room with the fan turnin' 'round and 'round.

BETRAYAL

⁘

The sun had set by the time the Greyhound pulled into the outskirts of Shreveport that hot Sunday evening in early August. From the bus window, the fields were the same. The trees and the color of the dirt were the same, and except for several fancy looking motels and a wider road, it might have been Murpheysfield Billy Ray was seeing. It wasn't until the bus started turning corners in the downtown city streets that Billy Ray realized what he was seeing was a real town.

Though none of Shreveport's lights were on (like the majority of southern towns, both small and large, Shreveport was governed by blue laws) still, from the high bus windows, Billy Ray could see streets and streets of shops. Not like Murpheysfield, which had only one major street for whites and behind it, a smaller one for colored. The only bright light on in downtown Shreveport was the huge neon cross on top of the United Methodist Church. Seeing how the cross shined in the darkening sky, way high above the store fronts, filled him with awe at its immensity. For other than trees, the cross was the biggest thing Billy Ray had ever seen. And for a moment, Billy Ray wished his mother was on the bus to see the giant thing shining in the twilight sky. But it wasn't his mother sleeping beside him, and Billy Ray reminded himself, he wasn't some little boy no more. It was Brenda who had her soft head on his shoulder, and he was a man—her soft sweet smelling head was proof of that, wasn't it?

Still, the bus ride—with stops—a little under three hours from Murpheysfield, was the farthest from home Billy Ray had ever been. Easy Al, the club owner from Shreveport, had made this trip sound like nothing really, with his money and his directions. Still Billy

Ray couldn't get rid of a nagging worry that something was going to go wrong. The worry, he knew, didn't have to do with the hum. He knew with his red wig and his blue spangled jacket, he could twist and turn any audience—especially with the better backup Easy Al had promised him the night before. The worry came from Brenda. He was used to operating on his own and he didn't know how to act with this beautiful girl by his side. Where would she go and what would she do? He wanted to take care of her. To show her the world that was his and hers now, because she was with him. But how? Where would they go? When she was by his side, he could hardly breathe, and forget about food and drink. With her beside him, he couldn't so much as swallow. Yet the girl had insisted on coming. Introduced herself to Easy Al behind stage like it was nothing. And to her, it weren't. With her soft skin and her beauty and grace, anything, he knew was possible.

Billy Ray's arm had fallen asleep hours ago with the weight of Brenda's head leaning against it. And he did not want to move it for fear it would wake her. Brenda, like the other riders—a couple of old men and several women who looked enough like his mother to be sisters—had fallen asleep not long after they had pulled out of the bus station in Murpheysfield. For nearly a week, Billy Ray had hardly slept—he couldn't close his eyes. There was too much to see and too much to worry about.

Trouble was, he concluded now, it had all had happened so fast. So fast, Billy Ray told himself now, he needed time and thinking to catch up with it all. Fast, like the bus was going fast. First past the fields of Murpheysfield, past the red dirt and the pine trees of his childhood. His childhood, where slow was what he had been used to. Slowness and endurance, but with everything under control. But now things were breaking loose. The hum had a life of its own. But before, the hum had been a separate thing, a private thing. Now the hum was connected to other things: to the energy of the crowd just as it was connected to new clothes, to liquor, and to the newest wonder of the harsh, smelly joints that made his throat raw and the whole world hum. Connected too, to this bus that was rolling him away, with her asleep on his shoulder. Billy Ray did not want it to stop—but it was going too fast.

Although Billy Ray did not put it into thought—his deepest thoughts, his important thoughts, came out in music—still he was aware that what he was becoming had nothing to do with who he had been all his life. He knew, too, that before he had only answered to himself. It had been a small life, a lonely life, nobody had been in that life except his mother. And she was never one he had to control. There was no fear from her, never. Now, there was so much in his life and everything was new and connected in its newness and joy to the hum: connected too to what he did with Brenda—her tight yellow body—but the connection was so easy to lose. But where the rest of him lay, somewhere in between what he had been for so long and what he had become so quickly—was where the worry lay. The worry that would not let him close his eyes or rest. Besides, even though his arm ached, it was so beautiful to look at Brenda while she slept. Brenda's sleeping self, like some long shiny yellow cat, was the proof that it all had happened.

Brenda was nineteen years old, and unlike himself, she had been places. Seen things. She had an aunt in Shreveport who she had traveled to see on these very roads. Unlike himself, Brenda had been raised with food in her belly when her belly wanted it and pretty clothes like the pale, soft dress she was wearing. Billy Ray had given her the money to buy this pale, soft dress and for the other ones in her suitcase beneath the bus. She expected the clothes. He had seen right away the clothes, and the giving of them, were far more important to him. Brenda had even been to California. Just a month ago California was as far away as the moon for how close he could get to it. She had chosen him, kissed him that first night, not because of the hum—music was not inside her, though why should it be, when she was music herself. Brenda had been past the rows of cotton fields. Seen with her own eyes the pattern the plowed fields made, like a paper fan laid out for miles as the bus flew by. Unlike him, she had left where she come from.

But now, he told himself, they were beyond the cotton fields of Murpheysfield. Beyond the red dirt and the pine trees. They were out of there, out of there for good. And in those final minutes on the cool, quiet bus, "Outta There," began to hum in his brain. Music and words took shape—he was far away from that bus, far away from Brenda, whom he feared as he loved, in the only world that ever had any real meaning for him. The next night when he played "Outta There" on his harmonica and the words rang out of the microphone and speakers and Billy Ray saw how it took the crowd in the club that was a real club—he knew what a real club was now—he understood, were it not for his mother, Billy Ray would never step foot back inside that hateful place where he had lived for the first fifteen years of his life. Billy Ray knew then that he was out of there for good—the hum knew it too. The song told him everything that had been inside him for so long.

But not what had been inside of her. Inside of Brenda. Soon as she stepped down off the bus and into the station that smelled of pee and fumes, she no longer belonged to Billy Ray. Who she belonged to, who she had come for, was not clear to him until the very last minute, though he sensed it when Easy Al kissed her hand when he strode in the station; sensed it looking at their two heads in the front seat from the back of Easy Al's shiny gray Cadillac. Though he didn't know for certain—for absolute sure—until they left him off at the motel with an empty stomach and a broken heart and drove off together.

When Easy Al picked him up the next morning and drove him to the club to rehearse, he didn't say a word. No more than Billy Ray said a word to Brenda when he saw her the next night backstage hanging onto Easy Al's arm, the same way she had leaned her head on his own arm on the bus ride to Shreveport. Billy Ray knew Brenda wasn't the reason Easy Al had brought him to Shreveport. That thought never occurred to him. Easy Al took Brenda because he could. Because he could. It had nothing to do with Billy Ray and the hum. Easy Al knew Billy Ray would play in Shreveport—play because he had to play. There was no way out of that one.

Because he could. It was a simple, brutally honest lesson and Billy Ray learned it well at fifteen years of age at the start of it all. And he never hated Easy Al for having taught him. Only thing missing in this lesson was love. Love didn't come to him until he had lost everything else. And by then, he was nearly too old and worn out to trust it.

VINA

‿‿

It were the last Monday of my actual life. And the only Monday I ever wakes up with money to spend. There I were, sittin' up in my bed wide awake, though it still be pitch black outside, thinking 'bout shoes and wigs and that scarf at the Woolworth's.

Understand, I were more worried over what I was gonna wear to the sit-in, than I weres about what I should have been worried about. Yes, on that Monday I were no better than some white woman carryin' on about her underpants.

When I were doing day work, something happen I'll never forget. This woman, she told me to throw out her underpants from her drawers. There weren't nothin wrong with them underpants, so I ask if she were gonna throw them out, would she mind if I carries them home?

She say, "Lavina, I ain't gonna give you them underpants 'cause what if you dies and they finds you in somebody's old worn-out underpants? It won't look right, no it won't." I sees right away, there won't be any good arguing with her, so I throws them out like she tell me to, though I were sorely tempted to carry them home when she ain't looking. Funny thing is, Miz Lil, she told me the same thing about throwing out them underpants, same thing exactly about dying with worn-out underpants on, though they weren't worn out, hers, they even has pretty lace on them.

Rich white women, they got nothing better to think about than dying with the right kind of underpants on. Colored, they don' have the time or the money to worry about their underpants. Long as they is clean and there is still some elastic, you wears them and be glad the good Lord see fit to clothe the neckid. That don' mean I didn't want to be looking my best for the sit-in and for meeting the Reverend King.

I were plannin' on wearin' my good church dress, which were pearl grey with big black buttons. Shoes were the problem. But shoes, they were always the problem. Seems to me I used to wish the good Lord only made us with one foot, 'cause shoes, they always wears out faster than you can walk in 'em. Either that or they get their sides worn down with them ole onions poking through.

Colored stores, they opens up early so we can do our shopping before work. So what I did that Monday was get myself to the bus stop before six so I'd have plenty time to look around before I catch the uptown bus to the Longs.

I remember everything about that morning. It were hot, hot even at five-thirty; it were getting so hot to make you think about what it be like to be deep fried in bacon grease or lard.

Walking down my street to the bus stop, I sees my neighbor outside watering her tomato plants. Old woman and skinny she were, with her bare feet watering them fine looking plants before the morning sun go and scorch 'em. She had little ones, tiny little cherries, which if you asks me, don' taste as good as the big boys. Too watery, them little ones. But she have big boys too. Bushes of them heavy with tomatoes and plenty of little yellow flowers ready to make more.

The bus, it pull up 'round ten minutes pass six and I put myself in, pays my money, and heads for the back. I is the only rider on the bus and it hit me like it sometime do that it is downright silly that I have to go in back when there are seats and seats in front with nothin' in 'em. We drives past the grave-yards and the sun is high by now. The graveyard look they way it always do, so pretty and green. Where I is heading is the little shoe store where I always find my shoes. My feet, they weres as big as a man's and it were hard to find Sunday ones in my size, though I never understand why they don' make enough since colored ladies my age usually haves big fat swoll feet just like mine with onions on them. And there were more colored ladies with big old swoll feet in Murpheysfield than Carters has pills. I've got twenty dollars in my purse, two fives and a ten, and I is thinking that for the first time in my life I is goin' to town with money. Usually I be looking and looking and never takin' home.

Sun be high now, big yellow egg yolk sun beating down like high noon, though it were just seven o'clock. Nobody be on the street but me and an old colored man in a white shirt opening up the door to the jewelry store, same jewelry store where I is standing, lo those many years ago lookin' in the winder with Billy Ray's father—Billy Ray be there too, though he inside me, if you catch my meaning. Seem to me, I can see the three of us standin' there, him, so golden brown and shiny, and me with skinny legs and what look like a pumpkin under my dress. We're about to spend my savings on a weddin' ring. Same ring he steal in my sleep—pried it off with Snowdrift shortening—for his whiskey ways. A tear worked its way down my cheek when I starts to think about that sad morning I woke up with a greasy finger and no ring, though maybe it were sweat. That's when I sees it. Laying on a little shiny purple pillow, sweetest thing you ever see in your life, that little gold necklace, shining in the sun. I puts my nose up to the winder to get a closer look. Understand, it's a teeny tiny harmonica I is seeing.

Then, the old man in his white shirt, he looking at me looking in the winder and he is tellig' me to come inside with his finger. The next thing I know, I is holding the thing with its little bit of funny shaped gold hanging down the end and the places Billy Ray blow into, they is all there in gold.

Well you don' have to have a high school whatchacallum to guess what I did. I took out my wallet and gave all the money inside to the man in the white shirt, though it weren't enough. I were ten dollars short. The man, he give a piece of paper like they always do. I left that jewelry store with a happy feeling in my heart. Happier, than it were that day when I come away with my wedding ring and Billy Ray under my blouse. I knew it were the man suppose to buy his wife the ring, and I felt it that day, felt the wrongness of it, but there weren't nothing I could do. I were dead set that Billy Ray, when he be born, were gonna be whatchacallum. Not like poor Mary Louise who never got to bear her father's name.

Now, I'm taking myself over to the shoe store like I come here to do. I even find me a pair of shoes with high heels and a comfortable strap in the prettiest gray leather you ever see. But, I has already blown my wad and it weren't yet eight in the morning, so I leaves that store empty handed like I always do.

It didn't bother me none, dying with them old shoes on like I did. When the Lord calls out your name, the last thing be on his mind is your shoes or the drawers up your dress. And I didn't have to die to find that out. Knew it all along, yes I did.

Sometimes I wonder what I lived for, why I walked the earth all them years. And though I still don't rightly know exactly for sure what He had in mind for me, I'm gettin' close. It ain't really words, more like a feelin' used to come over me when I were digging dirt 'round my plants and the dirt be rich enough to find a worm or two. Worms a good sign in a garden. Means the soil gonna make things grow. You can dig you up a whole can of them for fishing and that's good too. Though the worms, likely as not, give you that sick feeling crawling in your hand or hanging off the hook. Worms got nine hearts. You can cut 'em up this way and that, and still they squirms in your hand or off the line on your pole. Why, the Good Lord see fit to give them squirmy little things nine hearts, when lots a time he don't give most folks even one that be good for anything. And that's the truth. One's all you need long as you use it whenever you can without worrying it gonna break on you. Then that heart of yours ain't never gonna turn to stone.

The love you gives your chirrun is different than the love you gives your friends. I guess I is thinking now of what I left behind for ole Noog and Houston Moseley. The love I give them were easier. Don' have to work so hard with your friends. Your friends, they is an easy, satisfying meal to fix. Still you loves your chirrun. Maybe you loves your chirrun so much because you has to stretch that heart of yours so hard you think it gonna bust. But it don' bust. It never breaks itself and you can't shoot it dead. It want to live, same way flowers and trees do.

We is all living things and though what we're made for is different, we all have to love and to grow. And if we don' love and we don' grow, we end up like Miz Lil did, with chester drawers of brand new underpants and a heart what never got used. That poor woman and all her kind, why they has walked this sweet earth for nothing.

CHEST OF DRAWERS

W hen you die, you're there but no one can see you. Mary Jacob spent what she thought were the last days of her life upstairs in her room on her bed. No one could see her here either. She was in the house where she had lived her whole life. It was a big house—she had always known it was a big house—but never before had she experienced it as a place in which she could hide safely. Now, she understood, she could live within its walls, yet be safe from them. It was she who was running away from them now. Not them leaving her out. Still, it wasn't so different after all, she concluded, as Monday passed into Tuesday, and no one came. No one but Lavina, who she sent away when she knocked for her usual cleaning up before lunch. Mary Jacob tidied her own room now; it gave her something to do with the long days, making and unmaking her bed. Folding and unfolding the hospital corners, saying good-bye to her books and her things. Finally, on Tuesday afternoon, Van knocked on the door and called out over the steady noise of the air conditioning, which made her voice seem far away and indistinct. "Mary Jacob, what in the world are you doing in there?" But, after a while, Van too went away.

On Tuesday evening, she crept downstairs while they were eating their dinner and left the house for a few sweet moments, by way of the big front door. The hot, humid air felt like a velvet blanket on her clammy skin and she longed to stay there in the softness and the heat, outside where it was alive with bugs and trees and flowers and grass, so much more alive than she remembered. She felt alive too. She came back in, where the air was cold and she could hear the sound of their silverware against china as she crept back up the stairs to her bed.

Presently, Kathryn's footsteps came down the long upstairs hall. They had to be Kathryn's—Van always stayed downstairs till late at night with her father. Mary Jacob's days and nights now were passing by sounds. The after dinner sounds in the adjacent dressing room of Kathryn getting ready for her date with Foster, pushing drawers in and out, and flushing the toilet. Mary Jacob's ears were so keen, she told herself she could even hear the sound of Kathryn spraying her Shalimar before the sweetness of it traveled, in its mysterious way, under the door and up to where she lay on the bed. Smells traveled like sound, but lingered longer than sound—it would be quiet after the blast of his gun. Quiet forever.

After the Shalimar, the upstairs was silent again. Nothing until late when Kathryn and Van, each at different times, made their individual noises in the dressing room. Van sang low sad songs in her throaty, off-key voice as she washed up for bed. And Kathryn, who was always later, stumbled and swore when she knocked something over. When Mary Jacob drifted in and out of sleep, she would awaken to hear the singing or the stumbling and swearing and she'd whisper "Van" or "Kathryn."

Once, late at night, she was quite sure she heard her father in the dressing room while a bath was being run. Though why he was in the dressing room when Van was bathing in the bathroom was beyond her. But he was there with Van in the dressing room with the bath running. She heard his low laugh and hers too. Both of them, in the dressing room that was his now. His as it had never been hers, Mary Jacob's. Knowing that her father was going to kill her made him seem everywhere at once. She told herself it would be a relief when she died, if only to get away from him.

And so her death began to take shape. The fact of her not being here anymore. Van, she supposed, would glide into her room. Van, with her shining clothes and her soft, high-heeled shoes that would look as Mary Jacob's own clothes and shoes had never looked, like they belonged there, in the deep walk-in closet she herself could never keep straight—but Van would. Van's wonderful clothes would hang in perfect order on satin hangers with pomander balls and tissue paper. And her shoes on covered velvet forms, pair after pair of them, in rows according to their color. It would be like it was in the fairy tales, the right sister, the beautiful one, would take her anointed place. And the ugly one, the imposter, the one who had never belonged, would disappear without a trace. No one would punish her father for having killed her. You could not punish the ruler of the house anymore than you could punish God, the ruler of heaven and earth. And they would all live happily ever after.

On Wednesday afternoon, Lavina came to the door calling out, "Sugar, I come to put your laundry away." Mary Jacob rolled herself off the bed and went to the door to unlock it. She wanted to see Lavina this one last time—tomorrow was Lavina's day off and after that . . . but Mary Jacob would not say goodbye. When she opened the door, she saw Lavina was standing there with the familiar straw basket of laundry in her arms, laundry that smelled like it always did, of bleach and ironing and Lavina's own sweet smell, a smell she had known and loved as long as she had a memory. The girl was weak from days without really eating, and almost too dizzy to stand without support. But she smiled at Lavina.

"Lord have mercy, Mary Jacob, what you doin' to yourself, girl? Used to be you were nice and fat, but now you got yourself lookin' like some ole scarecrow. Are you sick or what?" To keep her head from spinning, Mary Jacob went back to her bed and sat there, with her feet dangling down off the end.

"I'm just resting, Vina, I'm just fine, really I am."

The room was turning 'round and 'round, as Mary Jacob watched Lavina putting away her laundry in her chest of drawers. Suddenly, she was giggling and moving her feet. Remembering how until this very minute, she had believed a chest of drawers was a chester drawer. For Lavina was saying, as she always did as she opened drawers, "Here, let me put your clothes away in this old chester drawers."

Chest of drawers. A chest with drawers in it. Not chester drawers anymore than the small knife in the kitchen was a perry knife. "When you is cuttin' up cheese or celery or little bits of carrot, what you wants, sugar, is your perry knife. Perry, he's the knife you use for them small things."

Not perry. But paring. A paring knife. Mary Jacob understood that now, as she watched Lavina putting away her clothes, somewhere off in the distance. And some part of her was sad with this new knowledge of proper names. She always set a great store by words, words of any kind, and now she would never have the chance to use these two properly. She said to the broad back that was facing her, "Vina, I can put my clothes away."

Vina sounded indignant at such an idea. She shut a drawer and said, "Go on! I been puttin' 'way your clothes for ten years. Why, you were runnin' 'round in training pants when I got here."

Looking back was something Mary Jacob almost never did. There was very little in her short life that she ever cared to revisit. But the hunger and her isolation had put her in a hyper state of awareness where time seemed to have stopped. Without any effort at all, she could see herself in this very room, a small girl. A small skinny girl with a mop of curly hair, back when she had not even needed glasses. It was peculiar too, that looking back, you never needed your glasses. Not for looking back or for hoping either.

She looked at Lavina now, who had turned around, wondering if she could see Lavina as she had been then. Lavina was standing there as Mary Jacob had seen her all her life: large, strong Lavina in her soft gray uniform and the bedroom slippers she always wore when she wasn't serving dinner, the ones with the holes cut in the sides. Something about her was different. She did not seem so tall. Had she shrunk? She had always told Mary Jacob that old folks shrunk. Had it finally happened to her? But, Lavina wasn't old. How could it be that she seemed, if not small, then so much smaller than Mary Jacob remembered? She said softly, "I miss you, Vina."

"I miss you too, sugar."

Lavina turned her back once more, putting away underwear and shorts, opening drawers and shutting them as though the world was not changing faster than anyone could see.

"Where you been, girl? You ain't been coming downstairs now for days. You sick honey?"

"I'm just resting, Lavina, that's all."

Lavina closed the last drawer. Then she walked across the room to the door and Mary Jacob could see her turn and peer down the hallway.

Walking back into the room, she picked up her empty laundry basket, then put it back down again. And when she looked at Mary Jacob, her eyes were smiling.

"Miz hot lunch got a set a eyes on her must once have belonged to a blood hound. I gots to watch that woman every second of the day."

The shadows between them were gone. And Lavina seemed large again. Large and strong and capable. Her eyes had been playing tricks on her, that was all. Lavina wasn't small. She was the same. Best of all, she and Lavina were back here where they belonged: together.

"Mary Jacob," Lavina was whispering. "Honey I got something to tell you."

The older woman was standing by the bed now. Close enough for Mary Jacob to feel the warmth of her skin and to smell the bleach and iron smell of her uniform that matched her hair. When she looked through her glasses, she could see Lavina was smaller again and her hair was mostly gray. But everything else was the same. Until she spoke again.

"Mary Jacob, I guess I never did tell you 'bout Billy Ray and his harmonica. But I'm telling you now, honey, the boy got himself one good looking future. Why, he making money now, playing them songs and singing. Never knew what the boy were gonna do, but now it look like the sun's coming through. My Billy Ray, he makin' money now playin' his harmonica. Looks like things gonna work out just fine with him."

What was Billy Ray doing here in the room with them, the room where Lavina and Mary Jacob belonged? But that was wrong. Mary Jacob knew now he had been here all along. She just hadn't seen him. Not until now. She knew now Billy Ray was Lavina's real child. The one that belonged to her. And she to him.

Lights were dancing in Lavina eyes, lights Mary Jacob had never seen before, and the lights illuminated the dark thing she'd been afraid of.

Lavina was saying, "Saturday night, Billy Ray brought home more money than I makes in a week. And he say it just gonna get better. He over to Shreveport now and they is paying him there too. And Mary Jacob, he say after this he be goin' to New Orleans and Detroit. Why, he give me money to get our roof fixed."

Our roof. Lights seemed to dance off Lavina's eyes when she said this too. Our roof. Yet Mary Jacob, who had given away her last fifty dollars had never made the lights in Lavina's eyes shine as they were shining now. Why, her smile seemed to have lights in it too: the gold in her smile gleamed. Raindrops gleamed too, but they would not gleam inside the house where Lavina and Billy Ray lived. Their house. It would be safe and dry; the rain would not come in. But Mary Jacob would be lying in the dirt with the worms; the wet black earth with worms and darkness.

And it was as black as earth and darkness and crawling with worms, this thing Mary Jacob was letting herself really feel for the first time. And it was wrong. She knew even through her misery that it was wrong. But that did not stop her from feeling it. She was jealous that Billy Ray was taking care of Lavina now. Mary Jacob wanted that caring to come from her. Things were changing too fast. And it was too late now to stop them. Besides, Billy Ray would be alive and she would be dead. But, it was more than that, much more than that. Mary Jacob understood that now too. A chester drawers was a chest of drawers and she had always been jealous of Billy Ray.

"I want you to make me a promise, Mary Jacob. Now promise me, girl. I wants you to promise me, word of honor."

"Word of honor, Lavina."

"If something happens to me, there's a jewelry store on Texas Street. It have a big 'A' and a '1' writ outside. You got to go inside and pay the man there ten dollars. He got my name and my money but not all of it. You got to pay the rest of it and then you got to find Billy Ray and give him what the man give you."

Lavina was describing the little chain and the charm and Mary Jacob was nodding her head and crossing her heart. Lavina was smiling at her, making her repeat, Texas street and A and 1. It was peculiar how Lavina knew something was going to happen. But she had it all wrong, of course. Still it was strange. And Mary Jacob found herself wanting to tell Lavina how it was really going to be. Something was going to happen. Not to Lavina. But to her, Mary Jacob. And for a moment, every raw nerve in her young body that she'd starved and taxed cried out for the comfort and warmth of Lavina's dark steady arms. The one safe place on earth.

Instead of jumping off the bed and running straight to Lavina's arms, as she had when she was little, Mary Jacob cried out, hoping that Lavina would understand. "They're not going to be able to stop me, Lavina." But Lavina didn't understand and she didn't stop her. No more than they were going to stop her tomorrow. Her back was to Mary Jacob and she was heading out the door, but then she turned, and for one last wild moment of hope, Mary Jacob thought Lavina understood.

Lavina was smiling her wide, sweet smile, the very best smile in all the world. And the wide smile wasn't for Billy Ray this time, but for her, Mary Jacob. "Baby, nobody ever gonna be able to stop you for long. Just remember that. And remember who tole you." And then Lavina was gone.

VINA

◡◠

I irons my best dress. Then I takes me a long cool bath in the kitchen, and when that done I powder myself till I'm all frosted white, like a chocolate weddin' cake. It were, I knew, gonna be hotter than the devil's kitchen at that sit-in. I put me on my harness too. I always called my tight brassiere my harness. With them dress shields that keep my dress from getting ruined, and a full slip on, I felt like some old plow horse. It were too hot to wear my wig, but I weren't gonna go meetin' the Reverend King wearin' nothin' but my nappy head. Noog, she would never let me hear the end of that.

I put on a hat Miz Lil give me, a pretty one with a wide brim, and when that's done I sits there in my kitchen and I waits. Someone comin' from the church to carry me there.

Before I know it, horn honkin' and I'm turnin' my key in the lock and myself around on my old front porch, and when I do, why, my heart start fluttering like a bird landed in my chest. Everybody in my neighborhood out there on the street dressed in their Sunday best and every single one of them is waiting for me. I know this by the way their faces look when they see me out there . . . though no one saying a word—the street be as quiet as church when church is quiet. There's Noog and Houston, and Carey and Wilbur, Lulu and Floyd, Etty Mae, Betty, Aline, the Marshall girls, and skinny, stooped over Miz Marion Jones who never have much to say to anybody. Chirrun, they is out there too and they ain't dressed for school. Everybody got their Sunday best on, everybody spick and span, carrying their Bibles. And still nobody be saying a word. Nobody be waving or smiling. They is lookin' at me and I is lookin' at them.

These are the times you tries your soul, is what I'm thinking. It was something the preacher said once on Sunday that stuck in my mind. I was trying my soul. And everybody out there, why, they was trying their soul too. We were all trying together.

My neighbor, lady who grows them juicy tomatoes, she come and pin a bright red rose on my dress. By that time I'm pass the gate in the bushes and out on the street. People, they is reaching out to touch me. Everybody be loving me and that feel very good.

Car door open, I get in and still nobody done said a word, though we all, every single one of us, knows where we is goin', me first, all dressed up with a red rose bud on my bosom, eight thirty on Thursday morning, the last day of my life.

HOME
༄༅

The Greyhound bus was taking him back to Murpheysfield Thursday morning. Not for long. Already, Billy Ray was way beyond Murpheysfield. He had lost his girl but he had gained a world with lights and a real stage and musicians who could back him up; he knew what backup was now. Before didn't count for nothing. There had been white faces in the audience in Shreveport looking at him and smiling. He did not know what to make of them. Only whites he'd ever known were enemies: Delton Campbell on his Sunday morning visits, them red-faced golfers at the country club. But never smiling white faces who raised their arms and smiled at him and his music. A world was taking shape for Billy Ray, one that had nothing to do with Murpheysfield or hunger. Though he did not know how to reconcile the presence of the white face in his new world, something told him he was in the white man's world now. But it was his world too. Billy Ray's. Tomorrow he was heading to N.O. He had heard about N.O. all his life, and now he would be playing there in the French Quarter and he already knew enough to call it the Quarter. Beside him on the empty seat inside a round polkadot box was a twenty-five-dollar platinum wig he had bought to give his mother. Hadn't she said she always wanted one of them light blond wigs? A platinum blond wig to make up for the one he had taken from her a million years ago.

Already Billy Ray was growing into somebody he hardly knew. Though what he knew was this: He was nobody like that boy who had stood up with his mother's wig and a dime store harmonica in his pocket, those millions of years ago, back when he was somebody else. And he weren't that boy who had come here, with that girl sleeping on his shoulder neither. The boy and that girl were gone. And nobody was gonna tie him down ever again.

He had thirty-five dollars left over from what they paid him in Shreveport. Thirty-five dollars after the wig and the bus ticket to New Orleans with a stop in Murpheysfield. That meant he could put more money under the doll's skirt in his mother's room. And he was going to insist now that she go downtown and get herself a bank account. It weren't safe keeping that much money under that white doll's skirt. Especially since soon everybody in town were going to know Billy Ray were supporting her now. She could have her old shaking boyfriend over to supper and Billy Ray didn't care. Long as she didn't have to ask Houston for money, long as she didn't have to ask anybody but him, Billy Ray, for what she need. And soon as he could manage it, she weren't gonna work no more neither. The ugly white girl had sent him money, but that didn't matter. She and her parents were gonna have to find somebody else to fry their chicken and clean their toilets. Somebody else and not his fat old mama. He knew that as sure as he knew that he was out of here. Out of here for good. If it weren't for his mother, he would never step back in that place again.

The fields were rolling by, the red dirt plowed in rows and rows that stretched out for miles were making his eyes do funny things. They were long past Shreveport when Billy Ray fell at last to sleep. The first sleep that had come to him in days. He was going home to give her the wig and the money—but it weren't really home. Home was something he was on his way to find.

METAMORPHASIS

～⌒～

The day of the sit-in, Mary Jacob woke up hungry. And her fear was gone. The heavy, dull feeling where nothing in the world mattered very much was gone too. She felt brave and alive. She used the bathroom upstairs. She showered and washed her hair. Dressed in one of her brand new outfits, she stood in front of the full-length mirror with her glasses on and inspected herself. Her father was right, she would never be beautiful, but what she was, this last day of her life, pleased her. Her soft fluffy hair framed her face. She was tall and she had a waist and long, graceful legs. The arms that came out of her sleeveless shirt were smooth and shiny. And with the brassiere on, the soft white blouse poked out like Kathryn's and Van's blouses. It was her last day on earth and she was ready. Or so she told herself.

She walked past her father's door in the long upstairs hall and heard the sound of him showering in the bathroom that adjoined his room. Yesterday, she would have slunk back to her room until he left the house, but now the need to do that was gone. Mary Jacob stood in the doorway of his room listening to the sound of the shower and watched how the sun was making patterns on his unmade bed, the high brass bed that had belonged to the man she was named for. His big brown briefcase was on his unmade bed and the top of it was open. Beside it, nestled in one of his soft beige face towels, with his initials on it in big squares, was a small gun, the one he always kept in the drawer next to his bed.

She stared at the gun for some moments confused. For she had supposed her father was going to use one of his rifles from the downstairs rack. And for a moment, it seemed the whole day was wrong—there had been a mistake. For she had always seen the rifle resting on his shoulder in her mind; not this smallish gun on the washcloth, that did not look anywhere near as important.

"When you see a firearm, Mary Jacob, you always assume it is loaded," he had told her years ago, on one of those rare occasions when he was being friendly. He had even let her hold it once in her hand and she remembered now the important weight of it, the feel of the smooth metal in her hand. She felt a sudden urge to go and touch it now, the smooth, cold thing resting on his face towel. But, as she moved toward it, she heard the pipes squeak and the metal sound of his shower door opening and she flew out of the room, light on her feet, down the long upstairs hall, past the smooth black highboy and on down the long curved stairs, past the Grandfather clock, and into the kitchen.

The kitchen was filled with soft sunshine and looked shiny and still. Even though Lavina wasn't here, the room, as always, seemed filled with her comforting presence. Mary Jacob went to the broom closet and stood for a moment smelling the little cupboard that smelled like Lavina's dark sweet wig. Lavina's apron was hanging from its little nail and she took it and wound its strings around her, feeling with a pride she'd never known before, how small her own waist was now. Then she set about making her breakfast. She fixed herself French toast. And never before had she ever been so competent. Suddenly, she knew what to do. First you soak the bread in the egg and milk. Then you set the black pan to cooking with a pat of salted butter in it. When you can smell the butter, you put the soggy pieces sizzling in the pan. You adjust the heat. You sprinkle them with cinnamon and sugar. And when you turn them, you sprinkle them again. Crisp on the outside, soft inside.

She was finishing at the table in the kitchen when she heard the door swing open and her father's footsteps in the room with her. He was looking regal with his best white suit on, the one with the vest and the watch chain. He was carrying his big brown briefcase and she knew what was inside, just as she knew how handsome he was. But that did not pain her either. His manliness and beauty did not strike fear in her now. No more than the gun inside his briefcase did. Mary Jacob's fear was gone now, like a long illness from which she had recovered.

She looked up from her plate of food right at him. Looking up at him was easy too. Like cooking the French toast. It was something, now, she knew how to do. She could look at him and smile. She'd be smiling when she threw her body in front of the Reverend King; she'd die with a smile on her face. At last, everything was easy.

He set his briefcase down on the floor. His white suit was glistening, like his small white teeth, teeth exactly like her own. Never before had she ever seen him smile like he was smiling now.

"You fixed yourself some French toast; I can smell it."

"Yes, sir."

"Your mama and sister couldn't make French toast if Sherman's army were pointing bayonets at them."

"I like to cook."

"Maybe one day you'll fix me some of your French toast. I'm awfully partial to French toast."

"I'll fix you some now, if you want, sir."

He was standing next to her at the table. His small hand with the soft blue veins on top was running up and down her back, she could feel the pressure of his heavy signet ring making patterns on her back. Her bra strap fell down and spilled over her bare shoulder and he was tucking it neatly back inside her shirt, and now the silky hand was on her bare arm again, running up and down her arm. She'd been waiting her whole life for him to touch her kindly. And now it had come. Now it had come.

He was talking to her kindly too, so kindly she almost could not recognize the tone. He sounded like a different person. Someone who did not know her. She looked at him, incredulous and pleased.

"I'm meeting a few of the men downtown at the Petroleum Club for breakfast. But I'll be very happy to accept your kind offer another time . . . Lil' Miz Cook."

How simple it was, now that she knew what to do. Now that she knew how to please him, just as she knew how to cook. One day you wake up and you know what to do. You know how to cook, you know how to make him finally love you. It had to be love he was feeling; she had never before seen him look at her this way. The way he looked at Kathryn. The way he looked at Van. The way he had never looked at her, Mary Jacob, until now.

"Child, your looks are coming in. It took a while. But now I see there truly is a change. You're going to be a beauty one of these days—your own kind of beauty. You'll see."

She wouldn't be alive to see, but she wasn't going to tell him that. She hoped that he'd remember after she died, that beforehand she'd been pretty. Would he be sad he had killed her since she was now no longer an eyesore? Is it harder to kill someone pretty than someone it pains you to see?

∽∽

Mary Jacob got up and brought her dishes to the sink. And like everything else this day, she rinsed them perfectly—the water did not splatter, the plate did not fall. The rough edges of her being were all smoothed out: as smooth as his hand on her arm.

And when she spun around, he was still smiling at her.

"What are your plans for the day, pretty girl?"

"I don't know, sir, not much of anything, really."

"I'd like you to stay close to home today, Mary Jacob. I've told your sister and Van the same thing. There may be some trouble downtown. Visit with your mother. Read your books, do whatever you want, long as you stay close to home, you hear?"

He was still standing there in the doorway looking at her, though she could not see his face because now the sun was in the room with them, shining on him and blinding her. He was moving across the floor and now her father was next to her.

He bent over her and lifted her chin. Now he was softly holding her face in his hands like she was something precious, and he was kissing her too, kindly, softly on both cheeks and on her forehead. And he left his gentle hands to rest on her face, as though he liked to be there, holding her face like that. No one had ever really kissed her, not like this that really meant something. For a moment it seemed, by the look on her father's face, that he was going to really, really kiss her. The way men kissed women in books. Both their mouths were open and she felt him trembling next to her. Her whole being was trembling too from something she did not understand. He smiled at her, in a way he had never smiled at her before, and then he turned away.

Mary Jacob watched the long elegant grace of his body in his white suit as he went slowly to where he put his briefcase down, the big brown briefcase with the gun in it. He turned to smile at her one more time. And then her father was gone. Soon she'd be going to meet him.

VINA

~~~

Funny thing is, the Reverend King, why he never did come to Murpheysfield. And if you want to know the Lord's truth, I were relieved he weren't there at the church when I walk in. Part of me were disappointed that I weren't gonna get to shake hands with the finest preaching man anybody ever heard, and I wouldn't get to brag to Noog and Houston all about it. But mostly I were glad they has decided it weren't safe, after what happened in Alabama, for the Reverend King to come to Murpheysfield.

They is all sittin' there, nice looking white preacher man with pretty silver hair all poof on top of his head the ways white man's hair turns when they gets on in their years. I sees Matthew too, and another boy who look enough like him to be his brother, with a beard and funny shoes with his toes sticking out. Dirty toes, the boy had. Felt like saying, "Son, didn't your mama teach you to wash your toes?" Now I am thinking, praise the Lord, they is gonna shut down the sit-in and I can go home and take my hot harness and wig off, and go back to the ways Thursdays always were for me: my one day off to rest.

The preacher of my church, why he is there too. And now I is finding out they have no intentions of shutting down the sit-in, no matter that the Reverend King weren't gonna show his handsome face. We is still gonna go through with it because it need to get done in Murpheysfield.

It be around nine in the morning by this time and even though there were a big old metal fan blowing on us, the room at the church, it already be gettin' hot. I could feel them dress shields filling up—felt like I had two sink sponges underneath my arms. The white preacher man, he is tellin' us we is gonna drive downtown and then we gonna walk through the crowd to the Woolworth's, and when he start talkin' 'bout it like it were an actual fact, it start hitting me what I got myself into.

He talkin' about the National Guard and the police. He is talking about police dogs and billy clubs and the White Citizens' Council and I had forgotten about all them things. Understand, I weren't a brave woman. Whatever fight I had in me had got all used up over the years, raising my Billy Ray and working. There weren't no extra left over for this sit-in bidness. And since I'm tellin' the Lord's truth, I didn't see what good it were gonna do sitting in at the Woolworth's. It weren't gonna change no white person's mind about the way they gonna treat the colored. All it gonna do is get their backs up. Make 'em more bunky than they already is. But I didn't say that. What I do is nods my head when the white preacher man say we is gonna walk in single file. Nods my head when he say, we hold our hands up to show the police that we ain't armed. I is still nodding my head when he say, if we gets past the door without them arresting us, what we do is, we sit down at the counter, we order our lunch, and since they ain't gonna serve us, what we'll do is bring our own lunch because we needs to eat there.

The preacher man, he keep calling me Mrs. Davis like I were a white woman on Fairfield Street, not what I am, one colored plow horse with dress shields felt like sponges and he keep asking me, "Mrs. Davis, do you have any questions?" Well, I had me questions a plenty, like, what is I gonna do if some policeman sics the dogs on me? What is I gonna do if they strip me neckid and throw me in one of them cells? Yes, and the biggest question of all is, how in the world did I get myself into this bidness? Though I weren't wondering how I were gonna get out of it. I knew by then it were too late.

Bus, it take near to half an hour with stops to get you from the church to downtown. But we ain't on the bus, we is riding in the car and it didn't take no time at all till we're there. Matthew, he park the car over by the municipal auditorium. Then he lead us in back of buildings, down the alleys in them hot streets, going in a way I never been before. Nobody's around. Why Murpheysfield, it look like it were the middle of the night instead of what it was—ten o'clock in the morning with the sun beatin' down.

Then everything starts changing, changing so fast 'cause now the courthouse is behind us and that big red Woolworth's sign is in front of my eyes. And that's where I sees there are people. People and people: more colored people than I ever seen in one place in my life—even over at the church. And every single one of them's here for the sit-in. I knows I ought to be smiling and lifting my head as I am going through this crowd. Matthew and that white reverend, they's in front of me, and the other boy, why, he's in back. And they is takin' the crowd in, shaking hands. And everywhere on the side, in front of me, is colored folks, and they is saying "Praise the Lord," and children's feet are dancing, and their elders' feet look like mine do, like they is already tired though it be just ten o'clock in the morning with the whole day to get through.

Where's Martin? Where's Martin? I keeps hearing, but I is too scared to look up and say, honey, all you got is me, fat Lavina Davis. I has never felt anything near to what I am feeling now. Like something big and powerful like God is gonna come up behind me. We is by the door now and I is thinkin' now, now they is gonna do it, grab us and lead us in chains back to jail. But they don't. We is walkin' in the place, with them bright overhead lights and the rows and rows of buttons and scarves and girdles and shoes and pearl necklaces dangling down.

I sees feet in them big black boots the policemen wears. I see his hands too, one petting his gun that laying on his side, next to his leg, and the other doing the same with a billy club. And we is turning in the direction of the lunch counter. It ain't far, but the way I am going it seem like we is crossing over the River Jordan, up to our heads in water and none of us can swim.

And then we is there. By them dark red stools stretched out in a long row and every single one of them is empty. Then the Reverend, he sit down and the two boys they sits themselves down too. There's an empty seat right next to the Reverend and I knows what I'm suppose to do, but still I is standing' there hanging my old head. My hands, they on the stool now, running up and down the seat, and the funny thing is, the stool, it were greasy. There's something sticky all over it and it need to be scrubbed down like the floor. And I am thinking if I sits down on that stool, why my dress will get itself ruint.

The Reverend, he say, real soft and gentle like, "Mrs. Davis you has got to sit down."

I makes my feet move just a little, and as soon as I move them they starts to quiverin' again. Now my hands, they is quiverin' too and I is holding on to that red seat that sure enough were gonna ruin my best dress. And it hit me, plain in the face, that the first time some colored person gonna get up the nerve to sit themselves down, the stool gonna be covered in grease.

STREETS PAVED WITH FIRE

∽∾

When he woke up, the Greyhound bus was standing in the Murpheysfield station. Still half asleep, Billy Ray stood up quickly and bumped his head hard enough to make lights go off inside. He grabbed the fancy box with his mother's wig in it and left by the back door of the bus, head still flashing inside.

Confused by his deep sleep and the blow to his head, Billy Ray did not notice when he stepped down off the bus that the station was overrun with police. There must be more than a dozen of them. Most of them had police dogs with pointed ears and long noses poised on leather leashes for attack. One of the policemen came right to him, grabbed Billy Ray by his brand new lapel and he felt the hand and smelt the dog all at once. The dog was drooling and growling quietly, which in a way was worse than loud barking: you didn't know when the thing was going to pounce. It was the policeman's tone of voice that awakened his sleeping nerves that had forgotten in these new weeks of his life about police dogs trained to smell black flesh and to rip it apart—just like the seam on his brand new jacket was now ripping apart in the policeman's hand. And for a moment, it seemed that these past weeks had been the dream and that he had come home to his real life and nothing had changed.

The policeman was saying, "What you doin' here boy?" Just like the white man had always spoken to him long as he could remember. The white men at the country club. The white men at the convenience store—every white man who walked across the same earth as Billy Ray.

The dog was growling and his coat were ruint, and still the policeman weren't through with him. He was grabbing the box now, digging through the layers of colored paper till he found the yellow-white wig. And now the soft fluffy thing he had brought home for his mother was lying on the filthy floor of the bus station and the policeman was pounding down on it with his boot—because he could.

"You one of them Yankee niggers here for the sit-in?"

Confused, Billy Ray shook his head and kept it down—he had a feeling if he looked the policeman in the face, he'd turn the dog on him. He said quietly, "I live here."

"And where's that, boy?"

"Over by the Morehouse Road."

The policeman finished pounding his mother's wig and now he was kicking it away, like it was some kind of small animal that couldn't defend itself. The policeman's dog growled louder and more menacing, and Billy Ray could feel the blood in his own veins turn to ice, imagining how the dog's teeth would feel sinking in his flesh. The policeman was laughing like it was the best joke in the world.

"You're gonna have a long walk home today, boy. They closed the city buses up half an hour ago."

When he got outside the bus station, Billy Ray opened up his little suitcase and drew out both his harmonicas. He put the long one in his back pocket and the short one that was still his favorite, in front in his left pocket, within easy reach. He did not dare draw out his wallet in his right pocket, but he patted it, making sure it was there. He could not stand the idea of wearing the jacket with its ruined lapel, even though it was a straight seam rip and easy to repair. Billy Ray took off the jacket and threw it down on the sidewalk, took up his bag again and began walking through the hot streets with the sun beating down on his head.

When he reached the bus stop, Billy Ray sat down on the bench and waited for a while in the sun. Downtown seemed still and empty. No cars passed by and, like the policeman had said, the bus didn't come, though being who he was, the white man might just have been dicking with his head. City buses were always unreliable, since nobody rode them much except the colored. Old white ladies sometimes rode the bus and once in a while white children did too. But the buses belonged to the colored. Women like his mother who rode them uptown in the morning and back toward downtown in the evening. Colored men, even the poorest of them, mostly had cars, broken down things that overheated in the summer and wouldn't start up in the winter, but were wheels just the same.

The group that was passing him now, they were bus riders. Women his mother's age and younger with bright summer dresses and umbrellas open to keep the sun off. Now another group of them was passing by. And Billy Ray wondered why they were carrying Bibles in their hands like it was Sunday instead of Thursday. Most of them couldn't read the Bibles that they carried, but they loved carrying them just the same. Billy Ray heard a siren go off as another group of large black women passed him by. There were children attached to this group, trailing along in back of their mothers, cutting up and dancing. Another smaller group passed by with men like Houston Moseley all dressed up with white shirts, suspenders and black suits on, and hats to cover up their heads.

Then it seemed all at once that the streets were filled with colored people. They were walking, not just on the sidewalk, but down the middle of the street. It looked like Easter Sunday at the big Baptist Church, an unending parade of hats and umbrella and Bible carrying women—all heading in the same direction. Some of them were singing. Another siren went off and the singing stopped, but still they were moving past him. Now a pair of policemen with their dogs were coming by, following the people that all seemed like one big group now, all heading in the same direction.

Nothing like this had ever happened in Murpheysfield, for Billy Ray knew it was happening now, just a few blocks away. Just like it had happened in Alabama all those weeks ago, back when he was nobody. The policeman's words at the bus station made sense to him now. Just as he knew now what all these people were doing in the street, looking like Easter Sunday, carrying Bibles they could not read, celebrating a world that never had existed for them. Not then, not now. Never until they stopped believing in the world run by the white God. And they were still coming, walking slowly by him in the sun, walking from somewhere, for there weren't no bus to bring them. The bus, Billy Ray knew, wasn't going to come no more than any miracle would neither.

He would have to walk home in the hot sun for miles till he got there; he'd be lucky to be home at noon. Billy Ray took up his bag and headed away from the crowd, the crowd that was coming toward him, face to face. Any second now, he expected to see his own mother and her friend Noog smiling, with their street clothes and umbrellas out, heading toward the sit-in. If it weren't for the sit-in, he'd be carrying her wig home, he was sure of that. The policeman at the bus station wouldn't have ruint the wig or his jacket if there weren't this sit-in going on.

Billy Ray felt welling up within him that terrible hate and anger he had somehow lost over these past new weeks of his life, when everything had seemed so easy. He had not felt this trembling hatred when Brenda was taken from him, but he felt it now: that old hatred flowing up from deep inside him, same place where the hum lived. He hated the policeman but stronger and deeper was his utter contempt for his own people who were as gentle as sheep and were probably all gonna end up in jail.

Billy Ray walked a block or two. The crowd had passed him by. He was glad of that. Didn't want to be caught being part of them. He wasn't part of them, he was different. The hum made him different, kept him apart. His playing would carry him away from here and on to N.O. tomorrow. And after N.O., he was out of here, out of the South for good.

It was then Billy Ray saw a skinny little yellow boy running toward him on the street, all by himself: barefoot with no shirt on either. His kinky hair was soft like white hair and light colored all in rolls on top of his head. It moved up and down as he ran. The streets were already burning hot. Billy Ray could feel the heat coming through his own shoes. But the little boy didn't seem to mind that the streets were paved with fire. He was light on his little feet with his light-colored hair bobbing up and down as he ran. The little boy had a look on his face that was happiness itself; the boy's radiant face danced with light.

Billy Ray had seen the expression before. It were the same way they looked at him, when he played, the look the hum brought on. He grabbed the little boy by his skinny arm, demanding to know where he was going in such a hurry. The little boy looked at him like Billy Ray was nothing—like he was a fool for not knowing what the whole town knew, everybody but him it seemed. "Lemme go," he squealed at Billy Ray. "You gotta lemme go. Martin Luther King's over at the Woolworth's!"

With the sound of the famous name, Billy Ray too felt an unfamiliar rush of excitement and he let the boy go. Nothing like this had ever happened in Murpheysfield. But his excitement soon gave way to more anger. Billy Ray could still feel the warmth of the boy's small arm in his hand. It was so thin and miserable; the boy was a half-starved thing, skinny and hungry as Billy Ray himself had been at his age. Like all the children were. Yet they believed in Martin Luther King. Believed in him because they had to have someone or something to believe in. Just like their parents had to. It was all any of them really had or ever would. He understood that now, because he had been spared. Still, Billy Ray stood there, following the boy's fragile yellow body heading toward the sun until it disappeared from his view. Back behind the courthouse, the whole town of ignorant fools, on their one day off, were waiting in the sun for Martin Luther King and would end up in jail or eaten up by dogs. But you could not tell them that. Still, at least he, Billy Ray, was different. He was not part of them.

Billy Ray continued to stand there in the middle of the empty street, not knowing exactly what to do. The eight-story courthouse blocked the view of Woolworth's, but the big red store front wasn't far away. No more than a few blocks or so. He turned and headed in the direction of home, but when he got a block or so, turned back again. Why? He did not know.

Billy Ray was moving toward something he did not understand, one foot in front of the other. He moved slowly at first, then gaining momentum, he began to head urgently toward the Woolworth's.

The empty streets were shaded by oak trees. He was running free now, running through downtown Murpheysfield. Never before could he have run through downtown like this.

When he got to the courthouse he stopped to catch his breath.

It was then that he saw the crowd: a vast ocean of black faces. Never had he seen so many black faces in one place before.

Billy Ray stood very still, though his legs were trembling and his heart was pounding.

He reached in his pocket, drew out his little harmonica, and moved toward the center of the crowd.

GOSPEL

∿∿

M ary Jacob pedaled through the familiar streets of her
neighborhood, then past the park and beyond where
she had only traveled by car. She was afraid to take
the quickest route, the straight street that ran from the suburbs to
downtown, so she took the back streets instead.

Murpheysfield was hot and empty. She did not see a single car.
Just streets and streets of empty-looking, shut-up houses that got
smaller and newer for a while, then older and poorer as she traveled
further downtown.

For a long stretch, uphill, there was nothing that ran along it but
small wilting crepe myrtle trees. Then she saw the fenced off graveyard and knew that soon she would be downtown.

But downtown did not come. Downtown was farther away. She
had only understood the way by car. On and on she peddled. Her
legs were tired and she was wet like she'd been showering all morning and still she pedaled uphill, past the big colored church and
the Ko Ko Mo drive-in and the Confederate Fort with the cannon
pointing toward the sky. When she heard sirens, she stopped her
bicycle and rested for a minute under a tree. The sirens were coming
from downtown, and she knew if she did not reach there soon, it
would all be over.

The road became flat again and she rode over a narrow little
bridge with rusty metal supports and now she was in downtown.
She could see the top of the courthouse, the tallest building in town.
She got off her bicycle, parked it next to the bridge, and made her
way on foot toward the Woolworth's.

The streets downtown were empty too: eerily quiet for an August morning. She had not known what she would encounter, but it wasn't this. And for a moment it seemed to Mary Jacob that she had made it all up. Not just the sit-in and the Reverend King, but herself, where she was, who she was even. She felt like the last person left on earth in this deserted street, in a town where she had lived all her life but no longer recognized. She rounded the cool shady side of the courthouse, and here too it was empty. People always sat on these benches under the enormous shade trees where fat blue pigeons grazed for food. No one was sitting under the trees today. All the people were gone.

Then she heard a sound that was faint and far away and, straining her ears now, sweet. Ever so sweet. It rippled over the still air, moving in waves like the heat, but not heavy like the heat, infinitely light and airy. Mary Jacob moved toward it now, past the empty benches where a flock of pigeons was taking flight. It seemed to her the sweetness that was in the air was lifting the fat silken birds off their little feet—though wings didn't sound like this—this was the sound of sunlight. Then, still moving, she saw it, the crowd dark, dark as night but bright too. The huge dark mass of colored faces that was everywhere, pouring off the streets, but there were not streets anymore, but an infinite crowd of bodies one after another that had become the streets, the buildings, the world itself. And the sweetness was louder now, coming from somewhere in the middle of the crowd that she was part of now, bright dresses and dark hands holding umbrellas and Bibles and children's hands. Bodies rubbed against her, women smiled. A couple of children looked scared. And the beautiful melody played on. And she was part of it, no longer straining, but knowing where the sweetness was: seeing it now at last. The tall thin beautiful boy with the harmonica in his hands, hands that seem to fly over the tiny thing as surely as though they were wings instead of hands.

White teeth, dark faces, clapping hands. Her own hands were clapping and the boy was doing a sort of bow like he was made for bowing, just like he was made for running his hands along the little harmonica, like he was made to lead this crowd—they knew it, she knew it—and she was part of it now. She was moving her own hands, together and apart as the waves of sweetness entered her and them, the sweetness he was giving them, all of them, the same way the sky gives the earth its sun, its moon, and its stars. And in the same way, a way that was so natural to him, the boy gave them this gift as proof of his power.

Mary Jacob knew right away it was Billy Ray. Billy Ray who was making the world this way. But when she looked at him—and she could not keep her eyes off him, no more than anyone else could—she saw he had changed. Changed from that boy who had stolen the shoes. Changed from her enemy into something she did not understand. No more than she had ever understood her father. Her father had been her enemy too. But now he was something more. And the strangest part of all, was that her father and Billy Ray were connected. Not to each other, but to her, Mary Jacob, in a mysterious way that gnawed at her insides and made her stomach seem as though it were dropping through her feet. In fact, she could feel both of them, in the bones of her feet, in her toes. For Billy Ray, like her father, was beauty itself, though dark where he was light.

Mary Jacob thought of many things as she stood beside the women and the children in the sun that was growing hotter. Beating down on her head and her face. She thought of the Pied Piper, that if Billy Ray said the word, all of them—herself included—would follow him anywhere where his playing was. She thought how right it was that this shining boy belonged to Lavina, who was love and goodness. Though this boy was something bigger and greater and stronger than all of them. And still he played, one after another, the songs he was born to play. So great was the power of Billy Ray's playing that Mary Jacob put aside, while she listened, the reason why she was here. She knew that Martin Luther King was coming any minute. She kept hearing his name in the crowd and turning her head to find him—but this boy, Billy Ray, in his beauty and grace, was luring her away from death and darkness. The boy was bringing her back to life, just as her father's kindness and lips on her face had brought her back to life in exactly the same way. She knew now all the fairy tales were true—a song could make you follow it to the ends of the earth just as a kiss could bring you back to life. For Mary Jacob wanted to live. And she wanted to kiss him. The boy that belonged to Lavina and to her now too.

There was a lull in his playing. Billy Ray just stood there, with his long narrow hand shielding his face from the sun. Mary Jacob kept inching her way toward him. And now she was standing right in front of him. And the boy, she could see was tired and hot with sweat streaming down his face. He had given the crowd his songs and his power, it seemed to Mary Jacob, maybe even his soul. A fat colored woman in a bright purple dress began to sing, "He's Got the Whole World in His Hands" and now the crowd was gathering around her, clapping their hands and singing. But Billy Ray did not join in and make the gospel song his own. The women kept singing and clapping their hands, but without Billy Ray, the energy was going out of the crowd. Without Billy Ray, they were nothing. But he would not play. Would not move. Just stood there in the sun looking around him.

Then she could feel Billy Ray's eyes on her. His mouth looked hard and mean. Mean as her father once had been mean, but she knew what to do now. She had changed. What she wanted to do was to reach out and touch his mouth softly with her finger so it would keep on playing and singing. But it was more than that. Much more than that. Though what it was, she did not know. Mary Jacob reached out instead and touched him on the arm. But still he would not move. Not his mouth or his hands or his heart; for a terrifying moment, Billy Ray seemed to have turned to stone.

Mary Jacob thought then, why she did not know, that now the great colored leader was going to appear in the crowd. The crowd that belonged to Billy Ray a few moments ago, but now belonged to nobody. She knew too that she was not going to die. She would live because Billy Ray lived. Because he played. And because he belonged to Lavina and to her. And she to him. And the boy seemed to understand this too because now he was flesh and blood again and was moving and playing the familiar gospel song, "He's Got the Whole World in His Hand"—fingers flying up and down his harmonica, playing for her, looking right at her, as his fingers flew like wings across the harmonica and the rich voices of the women rang out in the sun.

VINA

༄༅

The Reverend, he is looking at that red-face cook with his apron on, one standing in front of us behind the counter. "I wants a tuna fish sandwich and a lemonade," he say. Then, why he put his soft white hand on my old dark rough one and ask me what I wants to eat. He were a very kind man. I just shakes my head 'cause I can't find my voice. My voice, it done left me me at the door. Then the Reverend, he say, "And bring this lady the same thing."

Well, that red-face cook, he look at the Reverend and then he look at me. He look me straight in the eye and he say, "We don' serve no niggers here."

"Very well," the Reverend say, and then he turn to Matthew who is handing him something wrapped in tin foil. Then they hands me one too. He unwrapping it now and it look like some kind of sandwich what cuts in half but not square. Mary Jacob call them corner sandwiches. Mine's white bread with yellow mustard and some meat sticking out. Then cool as can be, he start eatin'. I is holdin' that soft white bread in my hand, but I can't bring it to my mouth. I is froze like. Then a great big ole fly, must be the queen fly, comes buzzing round and land right on my sandwich. Can't take my eyes off that fly, no more than I could swallow, not even if the Good Lord himself come down from heaven and say, "Lavina, you eat your lunch, you hear?"

I reckon the white bread be gettin' mushy now, all that time in my hot old hand and the sandwich, why, it just fall down on the counter with the queen fly still stuck to it. Then another fly, why, it join her and I watch the two of them black flies crawling over the soft white bread. Then the Reverend, he grab my hand and we starts to pray, but I can't keep my mind on my praying. I is still lookin' at that white bread with the black flies crawling over it, thinking about black and white and how you can't change the color of things no more than you can change the ways people think.

All of us, why, we is quiet for a while. Then the Reverend, why, he start to pray again. And just as soon as I hears what the prayer is, my voice, why, it come back to me.

We is saying the one I loves 'bout the Lord being my shepherd and I shall not want. And how he make it so we can lie down in them green pastures. And that Reverend, why, his voice be so sweet and rich, I starts seeing them dark green pastures of the Lord. They is the greenest, velvetiest pastures with sheeps roaming 'round. Black and white sheep, 'cause animals, they don' mind each other's color. Anyway, while I'm seeing them pastures, I'm startin' to hear something else. It's peculiar how you can be saying somethin', and be all tied up in it and still hear something else coming at you from a different direction. Funny little sound the harmonica make, don' sound like nothin' else on the face of the earth. Sad, it know how to be, but sweet, sweet at the same time it's sad. Only one person know how to make that harmonica sound the way it sounding now. And I guess I know then who out that door.

We're gettin' to the end of that prayer now, part when it say, "thou prepare rest a table for me in the presence of mine enemies and my cup runneth over." And I knew then, I knew, the Good Lord, he done filled my cup up to the very brim.

Understand, the Lord, he is tellin' me that my Billy Ray heard his word. And that's why he is playing his harmonica outside. I was wondering too, who had gone and told him I is inside, but that didn't matter near as much as knowing Billy Ray done changed. For it's gospel he is playing, the songs the Lord writ down for us. And folks out there, they is singing right along with him, just like we do every Sunday in church. That's when I knows Billy Ray done heard the word and he was sending it along to me inside this sit-in.

A feeling come over me then, a feeling so big I could feel it like some great big old warm place in my chest. We is holding hands and the Reverend, he is saying the best part of all, part when it go, "Goodness and mercy shall follow me all the days of my life and I am gonna dwell in that house of the Lord forever. Amen."

We sits there little bit more after we prays. That old red-face white cook, why, he is storming off now but that don' matter either. Those of us sitting in, we is happy holding hands. And Billy Ray, now he playing another one of them fine songs the Lord give us. "Rock of Ages crept for me. Let me hide myself in thee."

It were then that it happen. Happen all at once. Right in the middle of "Rock of Ages." Why, every single light go off in that store. I can't hear them *songs outside no more. Now I am hearing sirens, sirens. The Reverend, why, he squeeze my hand and he start saying the Lord's Prayer now. And the sirens, they is getting louder, louder. And it sound like there's screaming too.*

Then that Matthew, he say they is breaking up the sit-in. And they're probably arresting everybody they can get inside the wagons. He say this is what they did over in Mississippi and in Georgia too. Hauling every colored person off to jail. That scare me. Scare me something awful, because I is thinking about my Billy Ray getting hauled off to jail—I hated to think of something like that happening to my boy, specially since he done just heard the word. Everybody know how they treat the colored men in jail, even worse than they treats the women. And I is thinking, run, Billy Ray, get out of there 'for they throw you in the paddy wagon and haul you off to jail.

THE KISS

◡◠◡◠

hey were standing in the sun for Martin Luther King but
it was Billy Ray who they'd remember. That's what he told
himself when he walked in the crowd, drew out his harmonica, and began to play. He played like he played the first night at
that club long ago. But now he knew so much better what he could
do and without a mike or backup or speakers, just his heart and
hands, the hum leading them away from the lies they were waiting
for. Billy Ray told himself that if the colored leader walked through
the crowd, nobody would even notice him, not with Billy Ray and
the hum filling up their hearts. Not promising them things they'd
never have—giving them something they needed instead. Giving
them music and dancing and happiness. He had it in his mind
too, that if the colored leader walked through the crowd he would
keep on playing and let them choose. Choose which one of them to
believe. Him, Billy Ray, with the hum that would fill up their hearts
or Martin Luther King who filled their heads with nothing but lies
and sacrifice. Let them choose.

And so he played. And watched in their faces the power of what
he was giving them as a gift, asking nothing in return but what they
wanted to give anyway. Let them choose. He wondered if his mother
was in the crowd. And if she was, then let her choose too. And before
long, he knew it as he looked at their happy faces and their clapping
hands, that it weren't a sit-in no more, but something that belonged
to Billy Ray and to them too.

Then he saw her. It wasn't the girl he had hated as long as he
had a memory. Hated with every piece of bone in his body, every
inch of his own dark skin, hating every inch of her whiteness. He

didn't hate her and she weren't ugly no more. But tall and smiling and filled up with the power of the hum: it were written on her face, he could see it in her eyes. Nothing like that plug-ug picture in his mother's room. Nothing like that monster girl who had seen him snitch the shoes back when he was nobody and didn't have no shoes. And now that he was somebody she could see it. She was standing right in front of him, standing there staring at him with a look of a reverence. A look he had never seen on Brenda's face, and here it was on her face.

And still she stood there, clapping her hands and looking at him with love and forgiveness, forgiveness for all the years of hating her. Hating her for her strong white house and her soft white body and for having his mother when he, Billy Ray, was left with nobody. It were what they had between them, all that hate that was turning into something else now. He did not want to name it. To name it, he knew, was to take away its power.

Billy Ray played and sang with the sun beating down. Now he was playing to the girl. But the sun kept getting hotter and his throat was parched. He stopped finally, looking around for water. Second he stopped, a group of women started singing their gospel songs. And everyone around them was joining in. Every one of them but the girl who was staring at him, understanding his anger and hate.

And seeing that look, he could feel it going out of him, same way the sweat was pouring off his body, his own hate gone, unnecessary now—for he no longer needed to hate. Not her. Not the gospel songs. Not the lies they all believed in. Nothing. And then, when she moved toward him, even closer, reached out her soft white hand to touch him, Billy Ray took up his harmonica again and started playing gospel like it were the easiest thing in the world to play the songs he had heard all his life and were part of him. And her now too.

When the sirens started wailing and the fire trucks pulled up, he did not notice at first, Billy Ray was that far inside the hum. When the crowd started moving away from him, he knew something was wrong. It was bigger and stronger than the hum. It was breaking up the crowd, sending them screaming, tromping all over each other like animals instead of people, dropping Bibles and brown paper sacks full of food, moving away from him and the hum toward something they did not understand.

Everybody but the girl. The girl who had him by the hand and was dragging him away without his suitcase that was full of all his brand new clothes, but he could not go back for it now. Dragging him by the hand to the front of the store, with their backs up against the windows.

The police were too far away to get to them. Here, standing still with their backs up against the windows, they were safe from the crowd, who were becoming as dangerous as the white men with the clubs and the dogs. He and the girl could see it all: the women knocked down by fire hoses, screaming and writhing, dropping their Bibles and their umbrellas, skirts soaked with water, hats falling, flying away. And their screams were in her ears too. In the same terrified way. The long harsh screams of the women, and the lighter high-note screams of the children, children separated from their mothers, children getting stepped on. She could see too, the old men, heads bowed, walking like black sheep into the paddy wagons. The policemen on horses with their bullwhips cracking. A black face torn open by the whip and covered in blood. And whipped again when the body fell to the ground. She could see, but unlike him, she could move and act. And Billy Ray let her lead him. The girl was pulling him away, holding on to him, pulling him away from evil, saving his life.

They were by the corner of the store now, their backs no longer against glass. But rough now. Up against brick now. Turning the corner to a safe dark narrow place in between where the Woolworth's ended and another building began.

It wasn't much bigger than a standing space, this narrow passageway where they had to keep their backs up against the wall. It smelled of dirt and mold, this cool dark place where they were safe and holding hands. With his free hand, Billy Ray felt in his pocket for his harmonica. The other one, in his back pocket, he could feel, rubbing up against the wall. As they stood holding hands in the darkness, he wanted to thank her. But he could not bring the words out of his mouth. Not the words or her name, though he wanted to say her name now, to say her name and sing to her.

The yelling and the sirens were still going on, but it seemed as though all the danger was as far away as the bright place where daylight was pouring in, but she was inching them far away from that now. For a while they were inching along in total darkness, and the brick wall rubbed against his head and he could feel skin through the back of his pants. Still she held on to him, leading him away, and now Billy Ray could see that light was coming from the other end, the place where they were inching now, together, holding hands.

When the shot rang out, both of them stopped and stood close together against the brick wall. The girl whispered, "He's shot Martin Luther King." And still they stood there, until she said in the darkness, "Billy Ray, it was supposed to be me."

Then without warning, she let go of his hand and he heard her quick intake of breath, like she was about to run a race. Billy Ray knew then he was going to lose her, lose her for the rest of his life when all he wanted to do was keep her. He had no words for that, neither words nor song. So he pulled her to him. The light was coming through the open place in rays and he saw for a moment before he closed his eyes, the look of startled surprise before she closed her own eyes and opened her mouth to his. And for that long moment he never forgot, he and Mary Jacob were cleaving together, boy and girl, complete unto themselves. On that day, they were exactly the same size.

When at last she broke away, Billy Ray stood for a moment, dazed. He could hear the sound of her running and then her scream, like no scream he had ever heard in all his life, a scream that would not stop.

Billy Ray worked himself free from the building and out into the sunlight that blinded him, and still she was screaming, but at him now, screaming, "Billy Ray, get away from here! Run!"

He got down on his knees next to her and reached for her hand, afraid to touch the other thing. She held it for a moment before she pushed him away, screaming, "Run!" There was blood on her hand; there was blood everywhere. He got to his feet and when he turned around for the last time, Billy Ray saw her lift the terrible weight on the ground and cradle it in her arms like a baby.

VINA
◠◡◠

It's pitch black inside that Woolworth's and we can't see a thing. The Reverend, he is saying, "Mrs. Davis, they is trying to pull some kind of trick."

Then a voice ring out in the darkness. Ugly white voice that say, "Nothin' gonna happen if you do what we says."

Outside sound like the wrath of God done come to call. Sirens, and what sound like every fire truck in the parish, and I is thinking, at least my Billy Ray, he ain't trapped in here in the dark. The boy got quick wits and he can get himself away.

Now they is shinin' some great big old light. White, white light in our face. "Get up and put your hands on your head," is what we hears, and then they turns that bright light off again, but I'm still seeing lights in front of me, like when you goes to get your picture made and they flash that light on you.

The Reverend, he is whispering to me, "I'll go first, and you walk behind me, and Matthew and John will back you up."

Them bright lights keep going off and on, off and on, and now somebody standing next to us with a little flashlight and we is being told that we is gonna go out the back door. I took that for a good omen. 'Cause the last thing I wants to do is walk out that front door and get caught up in all them fire trucks and get myself arrested in front of everybody I knows in town.

They is shining the light on the floor and we is creepin' along, creepin' along and I feels some kind of club hitting me on the back not real hard, but ugly like. Can't see nothing really, though I can feel bodies right near me. That and their breathing.

I runs into some sharp corner of something, and I stops myself for a minute and that club, why, it get me again, harder this time, right in that sore place I always get between my shoulder blades.

Nobody be saying a word. Then they opens the back door, blinding us again with sunlight.

"No, you go," I hears behind me, but they don' mean me. Somebody's strong arm is holding me back. I'm gettin' my sight and I see out that door that two police cars are drivin' up. I'm standin' by the door lookin' and lookin' and there go Matthew and John with their hands in the air and a policeman walking behind them to a car. The car, it drive off in a huff and it's just the Reverend and me, next to the back door of the Woolworth's.

Now the Reverend, he walk out with his hands on his head, his black coat moving all around him. He got another policeman on his tail and now they is getting in that car and driving off. Now, all that's left is me.

I stands there off to the side of the door, still inside that Woolworth's. And I'm listening. I keep thinking someone in back of me, prolly with a club, but I'm too scared to turn myself around and finds out I'm right. Noise now, it seem calmed down some from the way it been. Dyin' down some in the front of the store. Seems to me, I can still hear in my ears, the sound of Billy Ray playing gospel. Never did hear no gospel on the harmonica. Remembering my boy calmed me down some, and now I am closing my eyes and asking the good Lord to see me through.

When I open up my eyes again, I don' know what I expects to see. Maybe the Lord's hand come down from heaven to lead me to freedom or maybe another police car come to carry me to jail. But nothing like that is goin' on. All I sees is an empty space and two big old metal garbage cans staring me in the face.

Still feel like someone's on my back, feel it clear down to my spine, I do. So I peeps my old head out from the back door of the Woolworth's. But the place look dead and empty. I hear them screams again from the front of the store and I says to myself, why girl, they done gone and forget all about you. Now they is doing their badness in the front of the store with Billy Ray and everybody from the church. I come out of the door now, just a step at a time, looking all around me.

I is thinking I best get myself out of here, when what do you know, that big old club come down on the back of me again, so hard, seem to burn a hole in my back. Fell right to the ground, I did, fell right in some old puddle that is soaking me right through.

I am lying there on the ground, tellin' myself I oughta get up now, for that club come down on me again. But I can't move. Can't seem to get my fat self to my feet. I knows I oughta be scared, but the funny thing is, I ain't. It seem so nice and quiet now and peaceful, like a day with nothing to do but sit on your own front porch, watching the flowers grow.

Guess maybe I dozed off then; I were weary, weary from all that worrying and carrying on, though it were funny, I can't remember what all the carrying on be for. Some time seems to have passed and though I still can't move, I can see. And what I sees, why, it's somethin' I never thought I'd see, not here in Murpheysfield, Louisiana. Maybe then I knows what happened to me,'cause I knows what I'm seeing is somethin' I'm never gonna see again. Not on this earth.

It's both of them, my Billy Ray and Mary Jacob, and they is close together on their knees like they been raised together their whole life, they were that easy in each other's company. They is breathin' on my face and kissing me, both of them, Mary Jacob and Billy Ray, they is fussing over me, like I is some kind of chile 'stead of what I am, Lavina what takes care of them.

Mary Jacob, she got her arms wrapped 'round me, and she rockin' me like a baby on her lap. I want to ask her, "Girl, what you doin' here?" And how she best get herself home before Jack find out and get at her with that belt of his, but my lips, they can't move. Sure enough, that club, it done gone and knocked the strenth from me and I'm cold, though I knows the sun were hot this morning and I can't understand why winter done come so soon to eat at my poor old bones.

Billy Ray, he is crying over me, and Mary Jacob, she crying and everybody getting wet and their clothes ruint from that puddle,'cause all of us is sitting there in that puddle hugging each other. I want to tells the both of them not to cry, the angels like it better when you smile, but I can't bring them words out. Cain't say nothin' now.

Then Billy Ray's head and Mary Jacob's head, why, they touching over mine and they is hugging each other and lovin' each other, them two children I done raised.

"Run, Billy Ray," she is sayin'. "Run quick and get away from here." He grab up my hand and he kiss it again. And then when I hears his shoes, I say to myself, well that's good.

Some other people, they is with us. But they don' matter. Mary Jacob, why she is tellin' them to leave her alone. I don't know who she talkin' about leaving alone. But she keep saying it. "Leave her alone. Leave her alone."

She wrap her arms tighter 'round me, for that sweet chile, why, she understands, I am cold. Cold like that winter in nineteen fifty-three when it snowed here in Murpheysfield and they shut the buses down and everybody got to stay home by the oven watching them snowflakes fall out the kitchen winder. It gettin' colder and colder and still Mary Jacob, she is huggin' me and lovin' me, and telling whoever is here to leave her alone.

I close my eyes now, or maybe they just closes themselves like eyes sometimes do. Them snowflakes, why, I can see them coming down from the sky. Look like little bits of wedding cake falling from heaven.

It were very nice and peaceful that day it snowed here in Murpheysfield. And that's the way it were now too.

MOREHOUSE ROAD

⌘

They took her home to her father who put her in a place she never knew existed, his bomb shelter in the basement, a secret room without windows that was cold and damp and smelled of mold. She was covered in blood when the two policemen brought her home and he met them at the door. They were at the front door on Fairfield Street and she was covered in blood, and the next thing she knew she was clean and in the room where he came to visit her and to bring her something to eat.

"Are you ready to talk?" he would ask. "Are you ready to tell me?" He would start out real gentle and kindly and then the vein would stand out in his forehead, just below the lock of hair that always fell right over his eye. Sometimes he'd scream, sometimes he'd put his arm around her as if he wanted to protect her. She never knew who he would be when he came in the door. The nice Jack Long or the wild-eyed, mean Jack Long with the bulging eyes. Both of them wanted to know one thing: "Tell, me," he'd say. "Tell me what happened." But she never would. For in fact there was nothing to tell. It was all a mistake. The wrong people were killed. It was her, Mary Jacob, who he was supposed to kill, not Martin Luther King. But he did not kill Martin Luther King either.

She could not comprehend her loss at first; she could not admit that it was Lavina. For all the time he kept her there in that room with the cot and the icebox and the rows of canned goods and the bible and the old-fashioned leather and gold book by Charles Dickens with black-and-white pictures, and the small shower and toilet in the nasty little slot that smelled bad, she tried to untangle the mystery herself. She imagined she was in there for weeks, months, years. In truth he kept her there for two nights and part of the third day. And by that time, she'd figured out that every single bit of it was a trick. He had fired Lavina. And killed somebody else, all to keep her, Mary Jacob, from finding out. Though still she did not understand why.

When he let her out and she was free to roam the house again, she kept waiting for Lavina to send her a message. She waited by the brass mail slot at the front door where the mail flew in each day. But then she remembered that Lavina could not write and she stopped waiting for the mail. When the phone rang she would lift up the receiver and wait to hear Lavina's voice. But it was always Foster for Kathryn. Or Van's mother, wanting to know if Van needed fresh clothes. For three days running, she was sure the secret to where Lavina was working now was written in the words to the jumble puzzle in the newspaper. But though she un-jumbled the words right away, they never told her where she could find Lavina. Then at last, one morning when she came down for breakfast and she saw the broad back in the starched white uniform that was turned away from her at kitchen sink, she was sure it was Lavina. But when the woman turned around to look at her, she had a skull's face and blood dripping from her mouth and Mary Jacob starting screaming and screaming and her father and the doctor took her up to her room and she didn't remember anything much for a while.

∽∽

One day, shortly before school began early in September, Mary Jacob remembered about the charm and the jewelry store, something very important that Lavina had told her. She took the bus downtown and when she found the little store she stood outside the window trembling with joy knowing finally she would find Lavina. She walked inside and just like Lavina had told her, there was an old colored man behind the counter with a white shirt and ashy gray hair.

She gave the old man Lavina's name and handed him the ten dollars she had in her pocket. To her great joy, the man nodded his head and took her money, then disappeared into the back of the jewelry store. When he came out, he was holding a little white box, but Mary Jacob did not take it. Instead she stood there in the little store waiting for the old colored man to tell her that the spell was broken. And where Lavina was. But the old man just stood there, like he didn't know what to do. So, at last, she asked him, quietly the first time, "Where is she?" And when he said nothing, she said loudly, several times, "Lavina. Tell me where Lavina is."

"Nobody know what happen. Somebody took her to the funeral home, paid for the funeral and that is all we knows. We is all sorry," the old man told her. Mary Jacob could tell he was more scared than sorry. She turned away from him and walked out the door with the little white box in her pocket. When she got home she put the charm on and she waited, still hoping for some kind of miraculous event to happen like things happened in the fairy tales she had read when she was little and believed now because she had nothing or no one left to believe in. She waited in her room for the little golden charm to suddenly speak or spell out its secret message in the air. And she kept it on, even when she knew no magic would ever happen again because it was all that was left of Lavina.

In the end, Mary Jacob had no one to turn to but her father. Her first day back at school, instead of taking herself home, she got on the bus and went to his office downtown, a place she'd never been invited to visit. She waited in the green leather chair near the place where his secretary sat typing and tried to get her words straight. Mary Jacob was sure if she said it the right way, he would tell her where Lavina was.

The secretary said she could go in. He walked toward her as she entered his office and helped her sit down. He drew up a red leather chair right near her and looked at her expectantly.

She was counting the weeks in her mind. Three weeks by now, though the summer felt a thousand years long. Something in her father's face made her see the truth at last. There were no words in any language on earth, no magical amulet or golden charm or secret puzzle to bring her back. She would never see Lavina again.

"Why did you kill her? She asked the handsome man in his tan suit who sat fiddling with his watch chain. "She never did anything mean to anyone in her whole life!"

Instead of answering, her father got up from his chair and began to pace around the room.

It was a room filled with fine gleaming furniture, similar to the library at home. There was a beautiful old rug in an intricate pattern on the floor that was so thick it felt like layers of velvet under her shoes. Like home, there was an old ship's bar, laden with crystal whiskey decanters. And a red leather sofa and chairs, dotted with metal studs on the arms and legs. His huge old roll-top desk was opened, and on it were files and a telephone and a funny looking machine that looked like a tape recorder. Wide shiny windows looked out over the main street of downtown Murpheysfield. On the wall were pictures of Kathryn and their mother, before she got sick, back when she was young and beautiful with bosoms and a low dress to show them off. There was a small oil painting of his father, one he had painted from a picture after he died. He was a stern-looking man with metal glasses and a thin mouth—but there were no pictures of her, Mary Jacob. She wondered why she even thought of that now, why it still mattered that he always left her out.

She watched him sit down right across from her and set one long thin leg over the other.

"You act as though I pulled the trigger and shot her myself, Mary Jacob. What happened was a police matter. Lavina broke the law and sat down at the Woolworth's counter. She conspired with communist agitators from up north. She resisted arrest. The police had no choice but to shoot her under those circumstances."

"And you missy, you're lucky you didn't get yourself shot or in jail. Why, I could have you sent to the state reformatory or locked you up in the Ninth Floor of Shumpert for your role in a highly illegal matter. Do you know what they do to girls on the Ninth Floor?"

When she did not answer, he said, "They shave your head. They put you in a locked room, and if you start screaming like you did that day last week, they lock you in a padded cell. As your father, I am well within my rights to have you committed. Ever heard of electro-convulsive therapy, Mary Jacob? Is that what you want to happen to you? Answer me child!"

But she would not give him the satisfaction of an answer. She sat there on the chair, perfectly still, facing him, and asked quietly again, "Why did you kill her?"

Her father's voice was loud and angry when he shot back at her, "Who told you I killed her?"

"I saw your gun that morning on the bed, and . . ." She did not finish. Did not say, *and that was the morning you were kind to me and kissed my face. And when Billy Ray kissed me too.* It was all she could see, like a picture show playing out before her, the kisses. First his, then Billy Ray's.

Her father was sitting across from her, studying her face, like he wanted to understand too. He was looking at her kindly and reaching out for her hand now and rubbing it.

"Of course, I had to bring my gun downtown, child, but that doesn't mean I used it. The police shot Lavina like they had to. Why, I never left the Petroleum Club or took my gun out of my briefcase. I brought it down with me for protection. But you, child . . ." he was asking her now, in his gentlest voice, "Were you and Lavina in collusion? Who put you up to it? Who made you come to that demonstration to humiliate me?"

Her father's hand felt good. It felt strong. And, as she let him sooth her for a moment, she wondered why she had gone there to hurt him. To humiliate him. He was not the one who killed Lavina. It wasn't his gun.

"Who told you about the sit-in, Mary Jacob? It was Lavina, wasn't it?"

"I listened in at your meetings."

"And supplied Lavina with the information?"

"No. I didn't know Lavina was gonna be there. I didn't know until . . ."

Mary Jacob could feel the empty space inside her where Lavina had always been filling up with something that was crushing the air out of her so she could not breathe. She rocked back and forth, wailing with her head between her knees, because she could not look at him anymore than she could breathe.

And through it all, her father sat there, for how long, Mary Jacob did not know. It seemed to her they were sitting there for hours. Hours when she could not breathe and hours after that when she could not lift her head to look at him. Instead, she stared at the floor, at his smallish feet, planted firmly on the wonderful old rug. His small feet looked right resting on it.

She regarded her own narrow feet in the soft suede loafers she and Van had selected that day so long ago now. She knew she belonged to him then. That because of Jack Long, she walked the earth in shoes that fit; on beautiful old rugs so thick it was like walking on velvet. Nothing could change that fact. Not even that she knew it was wrong. Had always known the wrongness of it as long as she had a memory. Still, that she knew it was wrong did not change things. That was always the trouble.

At last, Mary Jacob raised her head to look at him. He looked worried, and there were deep lines around his mouth. The lines seemed to deepen when she told him, "Lavina used to always tell me she had onions growing off the sides of her feet."

"Not onions, Mary Jacob, they're called bunions. You have a lot of growing up to do now, child. And you're gonna start by acting like you're white. Not some common negrah. And I'm going to help you. But first you have to tell me what happened."

Mary Jacob kept her head up. She had to look at him. She no longer cared that she was crying again. That she could not catch her breath; that she could not even breathe.

"Tell me child, you have to tell me."

"It was supposed to be me."

He did not seem to notice that she was choking to death in front of him. But that did not surprise her really. Jack Long never saw what he didn't want to see. Never saw dark swollen feet in cheap shoes with the sides worn down. He didn't see how much her mother loved him and needed his company and was dying up in her bed without it. Nor did he care how she, Mary Jacob, had always longed for his regard, just a tiny morsel, was how she put it to herself now. Love, she had always known, was out of the question, but a kind word would once have been like something from God, something holy.

Not anymore.

No, her father never saw anything that did not concern him and his wants and needs. Over and over again, he demanded, "What do you mean it was supposed to be you? What do you mean? Did those niggahs put you up to it, Mary Jacob? I need to know once and for all why you came to that demonstration to humiliate me. Calm yourself down child and tell me."

"I came there to save him," she said at last.

"What do you mean, 'save him'? Save who?"

"Martin Luther King."

She saw her father's eyes widen. Even through her tears she could see he was scared like the colored man at the jewelry store, like the woman in the kitchen who wasn't Lavina.

She had to unburden herself.

"You were going to shoot Martin Luther King. And I went there to save him."

"Save him? But he never came to Murpheysfield, Mary Jacob. And even if he had, why would you do a thing like that?"

"I don't know," she said.

"Tell me, Mary Jacob." And once more he reached for her hand, but this time, she would not let him take it. He whispered, "I won't hurt you if you tell me the truth. Tell me now, child. Tell me."

She was young enough then to believe in the truth, the personal truth that sets you free. And perhaps more important than that, he was going to listen. She could see it on his face, that he wanted to understand—he was paying attention. It had never happened before. She looked into his eyes and said simply, "I love Martin Luther King. I've always loved him. I thought he had more reason to live than I did. And I'd rather you shoot me than him."

Her father did not move. Instead, he sat in his chair across from her, nodding his head. Then his head stopped moving and he stared at her. And she knew then, for the first time in her life, she had finally said something that he really heard and felt. And had to pay attention to. She knew, too, it would have been wiser to lie. His face seemed to be falling apart in front of her. She had hurt him in a way he would never forget, not if he lived to be a thousand years old. More than her grief then, she felt a sense of power welling up in her. She could wound him as he had always wounded her. And something in her rejoiced even though she knew she had lost him forever and ever, as she had lost Lavina.

"I'm sending you off to boarding school next week, Mary Jacob," he was telling her now, calmly, evenly, though his face was jumping around all over the place and his hands had turned into ugly claws that were attacking each other.

"I'm not sending you up north for obvious reasons. You'll be attending an Episcopalian boarding school in New Orleans. You'll come home Christmas and Easter, and in the summers you'll go to camp."

"I won't go," she said to him. "I'm going to stay here and look after Mama."

He lifted his hand to strike her, but she did not pull away. He could not hurt her anymore. But she could hurt him.

He was on his feet now, shouting, "You'll go where I tell you to go," and looming over her, but still she was not scared.

"You just want me out of the house so you can carry on with Van."

He began to strike her then, hard, fierce blows were coming down on her face, her shoulders, and her chest. He was hitting her with all his strength but she got to her feet in spite of the blows and thrust her face up close to his.

She said strongly, triumphantly, "If she had money, she wouldn't have anything to do with you. She does it for shoes and clothes, not because she loves you. But you don't care. Long as you get your way. Why you don't care for anybody but yourself."

He had her against the wall now. His strong hands on her shoulders and his face so close Mary Jacob could feel his hot breath on her; he smelled strongly of cigarettes. Now she knew what to say and how to win. Not with magic words or spells or incantations. Not because she was a good girl; good girls obey their fathers. Mary Jacob knew now and would never forget that there is no such thing as magic. That she had no wish to be a good girl—not on his terms. And the fairy tales she had loved all her life were lies. Lies that little children wanted to believe in. But now she was grown and had power.

"If you hit me again, I'll tell," she whispered. "I'll tell Van's mother; I'll tell my mother. I'll go to church and tell everybody. I'll tell everybody in the whole world what she does with you . . . for shoes."

Her father's hands fell and he backed away, though Mary Jacob knew, could feel it in her blood and in her bones, that the last thing on earth he wanted to do was stop. That if he had his way he would kill her with his hands, here in his office. He hated her for telling the truth. She could smell it on him: rank, sour, stronger than the cigarette smell, was the smell of his hate. Just as the kitchen that morning had been full of the smell of cinnamon and his love; that one time when he had not hated her, that morning, for a little while.

But none of that mattered. She had stopped him. And now she kept on staring at his face to see his defeat written there. Blood was flowing down from her nose into her mouth. It came to her that there was always blood between them. Blood the day he beat her in the kitchen: she could see it on the bicycle seat. And she could see it too, herself covered in Lavina's blood. She'd come home covered in blood. Though she still could not recall, even now, what had happened to the clothes with the blood and to the blood that was all over her body.

It was her own blood she could taste now and it tasted good because the blood could not stop her. Nothing could stop her. She was staring at him, with the blood flowing down, until he was the one who had to turn away.

She left him there, walking out of his office, past his secretary who stared at her and the blood running from her nose, and on to the elevators that took her down to the street. She knew where she had to go now. And as she stood at the stop, waiting for the bus that would take her to the Morehouse Road, fingering the little charm that was hanging around her neck, she wondered why it had taken her so long to look for the right person, to look for Billy Ray.

But Mary Jacob never found Billy Ray that day, no more than she kept her promise to Lavina to give her son the little golden chain with its delicate charm. Around the time her mother died, she unhooked the little thing from around her neck and buried it in an emotionless way, like a professional gravedigger, in the furthest corner of her back yard where the property was fenced off and the earth was hard as rock. Buried it in its little white box, like it was a religious relic, a toe of St. Peter, or a bit of the true cross. Though Mary Jacob said no prayer, said nothing when she patted the grass down, and brushed the dirt from her knees, and stood there for a while looking down, not even goodbye.

By the end of the next year, Billy Ray and his golden voice and harmonica playing would be resounding in the halls at her boarding school. By then Billy Ray was everywhere, where there was a radio on or hi-fi set playing. But by then she had forgotten.

Still, the kiss remained in her dreams. And she dreamed of it often, her first real kiss. She dreamed it after many men had kissed her. It was a pristine thing, complete unto itself: belonging to her.

When she left her father's office that day, she took a bus to the Morehouse Road. It was a small street of broken down houses, with just one broken down car overturned in front of one of them. She found a group of half-dressed children without shoes who ran away when she appeared at the front of the street, like she was the wicked witch or the big bad wolf.

She found bright borders of zinnias, and crops of the last fall tomatoes blooming in profusion on that miserable street, but not in front of the one house where she stood for a while. The one that was loosely boarded up. Here, the little bit of land was parched; what grass there once had been, had died now in hot, dry little patches, and the hedges were dying too. The house had a legal notice stapled to the planks that covered the door, stating that the house had been repossessed by someone called Delton Campbell. Every single window was boarded up. She peered through the wide spaces between the boards and saw bits of the kitchen with the bathtub in the corner; the bedroom that was all bed; and the shelf where the doll Pauline stood. Lavina had talked about Pauline for years. And there she was.

Mary Jacob's head was pounding when she walked down the broken front steps and into the little yard with the hedges that were parched from no one having watered them. She looked to the side. A colored woman on the next front step was staring at her. Mary Jacob waved at her, but the woman didn't wave back. Instead, she went in her house and closed her screen door.

And in some inexorable way, she was boarding up her own mind. Boarding it up like Lavina's house was boarded up. Her head began to pound. And lights were going off inside it like firecrackers. Pain, flashes of light . . . she felt any second she would throw up.

She rocked back and forth with her head in her hands, the blinding, flashing pain her whole world. She sat down on the front porch, put her head in her hands, and stayed there for a while, hoping the pain would pass.

When something touched her on the head, she jumped. She looked up and a bent old colored man who leaned on a stick was beside her, like some sort of gremlin from a fairy tale. He even knew her name.

"Mary Jacob, what you doin' here girl?"

"Looking for Billy Ray," she replied. "How do you know my name?"

The old man leaned on his cane. He was nodding his head and his body was shaking.

"Everybody here know your name, honey."

Then the shaking old man smiled at her. He didn't have any teeth.

Presently he said, "Heard Billy Ray made it to N.O. And now he in Detroit. Maybe he gonna be a big star. Maybe not. Maybe he end up in the big house."

Mary Jacob thanked him, got to her feet, and walked away.

MONTAUK

I'd also forgotten how cold and damp it could be in Louisiana in February. The day we buried Jack Long, a bone chilling rain fell on the windshield as we made our way through the grey streets lined with sodden shade trees toward downtown and the graveyard. We were in Van's big black Mercedes. Annie Hunt was sitting in front with Clyde on her lap; Van never went anywhere without her beloved Maltese in tow. We had Clyde's blanket with us and one of his toys, so he could sleep and be soothed during the burial. I was leaning forward from the back seat, glad to be near all three of them; away from Kathryn and John who were riding in the official mourning vehicle, the one following the hearse.

"Her and that old dog of hers! Did you see the way it snarled at me? I refuse to ride to Daddy's funeral with them and that's all there is to it!"

I did not reply, "And death shall have no dominion." But I was thinking it as we turned and made our way slowly through the gates of the graveyard and began to climb the hill. I had told Van all about my encounter with Kathryn's fiancé and how he had frightened me. How Billy Ray had come to the house and everything else. She didn't say much about Billy Ray, but she loved it that I had made out with a total stranger on the airplane coming to Murpheysfield. She thought it was wild and wonderful.

"I want to do that," she said. "I never do anything crazy like that. It's probably good for your marriage to feel a little guilty."

Presently, she said softly, "Mary Jacob, do you remember when we buried your mother?"

"I've been trying to remember so many things these past weeks, but I haven't gotten to that."

"Do you want to hear what I remember?"

"Yes. Please!"

"You didn't want to leave her there by herself. You said you were going to stay there with her because she was afraid to be left alone. I'll never forget it."

"Now that's the truth," little Annie said.

I was getting used to Van remembering things and telling me. Though it still held a miraculous quality, having a past, a history, and her especially as a witness. Once upon a time, she'd been my nice sister, my stepmother, and now Van was my benevolent guide. I put one hand on her shoulder and the other one on Annie's. We were all wearing cashmere sweaters from Van's shop. Mine was a plain black button down; Annie's was purple and had a fur collar— presents from Van.

"Were you there too, Annie?"

"No, darlin' but someone tole me about it. Everybody knew you were the sweetest white chile in Louisiana. Van, she were the prettiest white girl in Louisiana. And both of you is still the same!"

Van turned to Annie and smiled.

"I'm not that pretty girl anymore, Annie, and you know it. Ask Etty Mae."

Etty Mae was Van's former cook and housekeeper, a woman whom she kept "in the fanciest colored old folks home in Dallas. "I visit her every Sunday, Mary Jacob. When you come to see me, I'll take you there. Etty Mae knew Lavina, they were neighbors. She came to work for me after Lavina left."

Van did not say "left" euphemistically. It was still hard for her to readjust her thinking. Like Kathryn, all those years she had genuinely believed our father fired Lavina for drinking his whiskey. And because he was a good guy, had sent her home with a few bucks to tend her tomato plants.

It was a good story, an aristocratic southern story dripping with noblesse oblige, the kind well-suited for a gentleman's résumé. And certainly a lot more benign than what Billy Ray and I both knew happened. The truth those gentlemanly white men had hushed up so successfully.

It didn't take long to start remembering; it was a matter of hours after the singer shot out of the kitchen that afternoon, leaving me with a broken chair and a migraine. Van and Clyde arrived the next afternoon. By then, I had thrown the shattered chair in the trash, but some of the pieces of my own memory were coming back together. Like the moon, the whole had been there all along, though to this day, I'm still looking at phases, at what hasn't been obscured by trauma, migraine, and the ravages of time.

When I told Van, she covered her beautiful face in her hands and put it down on the kitchen table.

"Oh, Mary Jacob, that's just horrible!" And she'd started to cry.

It was late one night after my father had finally fallen asleep. We were down in the kitchen having a snack. After Van composed herself, she got up from her chair, leaned over, and hugged me. I was aware that it was a hug from someone who had known me my whole life. How strange and wonderful that was.

Later, Van said, "And, it explains a lot of things I've always wondered about. Why Etty Mae looked scared when she came to work for me. Who on earth would be scared of me? Why you went to pieces that summer. Why you never wanted to come home from boarding school and why you wouldn't speak to your father or barely to me. I never got in touch with you to tell you where I was because I thought you hated me for replacing your mother. Poor dear Lavina." Van shook her lovely head.

Maybe she was trying to reassure me. "You have to remember too, those were different times. Your father wasn't any different than the other men in town."

"Since when is that an excuse?"

"It's not an excuse, it's just the way things were. It was their world, Mary Jacob. But now things have changed."

On another evening, when we were up in his room as usual, I said to her, "Maybe if he had been a better guy and not like all the other men in town, you wouldn't have left. I wish you had married somebody else."

"I would have if I had stopped caring. But I never did stop loving him." Van looked across the room. "I still love him. And you in your own way love him too, Mary Jacob. All girls love their fathers."

I thought maybe she was right because I stayed to the bitter end, and I made my peace with him. Such peace as I could make.

And I finally did ask him the big question, one night when we were alone together, drinking whiskey, sitting on the bed.

"How did you get away with it? Didn't anyone ask any questions? You know, I saw her in back of the Woolworth's. I was covered in blood, do you remember that?"

My father was very short of breath. Soon, they put him in an oxygen tent. They wanted to take him to the hospital, but he refused to go.

The dying man put his hand up to his chest.

"It was a sad and terrible business, daughter. Don't tell me after all these years you still blame your poor old father?"

He started to cough. I knew he was conning me; he had a little pat rehearsed speech prepared, "the sad and terrible business, daughter." He had said that more than once. He reached for my hand then, and brought it to his lips. His lips on my hand made me shiver.

That's when I knew, all these years though I pretended to hate him, not really knowing exactly why, all along some part of me had loved him. Or certainly longed for his love. Every girl wants her father's love. Why should I be any different?

"You murdered her."

"No, child, I didn't. It was all a mistake. You should never have gone there and gotten yourself mixed up in that affair. You're not a communist anymore are you?"

I chose to ignore that idiotic question. I had my own questions to ask.

"Didn't anyone investigate her murder? How could a woman die like that and nobody gave a shit?"

"You're not to curse at me, Mary Jacob."

I wanted to shake his frail, dying body. The old bastard had blood on his hands and he was lecturing me on cursing?

But of course, what else should I expect?

"But how did you get away with it?"

"It was a police matter. The communist agitators from up north were sent back to where they belonged. And Lavina was left behind. She resisted arrest. You know it's a crime to assault a police officer."

"Lavina never assaulted anyone in her whole life. She was as gentle as a lamb."

"Child, I only know what I was told. It was a long time ago. Won't you show some mercy to a dying man?"

He started to cough. He coughed and he coughed and I gave up.

No, he never did tell me how they got away with murder. Maybe it didn't matter enough for him to remember. He wouldn't be held accountable for that or for whatever else had passed between us. To this day, I don't understand why they had to kill her. Wouldn't it have been enough to put Lavina in jail? Or fire her without her references? Wouldn't that have been enough? Why hadn't she told me? Had she told Billy Ray? Was that why he was at the sit-in? Because he knew his mother was inside?

I'm quite sure my father was telling the truth and he wasn't the one who pulled the trigger on the gun that shot Lavina. That he was just as surprised as I was to find out it was his cook and housekeeper who had sat down that day at Woolworth's. That his belief system, his way of life, his very DNA was complicit in her murder implicated him in my young eyes. And still does.

When we reached the grave site, Van stopped the car, Clyde started to bark furiously. Van scolded him, "Clyde, mind your manners, do you hear me?"

Clyde minded his manners and stopped barking. He was a well-behaved southern dog.

"Were you at Lavina's funeral, Annie?"

Annie paused. She looked over at Van.

"Yes'm."

I was still trying to get her out of the habit of saying "yes'm" to me by saying "yes'm" back to her, but there were too many years of conditioning working against my P.C. principals.

"Everybody came to Lavina's funeral, Mary Jacob, except for Billy Ray."

"I know; I was there too."

"Why honey, I didn't know that."

"I was hiding behind a tree. I was worried somebody was going to see me and send me home to Jack. I can remember hiding behind that tree as though it were yesterday."

Annie was nodding her head. If she couldn't understand the intricacies of a traumatic memory block, she knew all too well what being sent home to Jack would have meant. Unfortunately, all of us sitting in that car did. Yet two of us had loved him.

We left the car, the three of us. Then we stood under umbrellas and buried my father.

Van, Kathryn, and some of the mourners cried. Annie Hunt and I were stone faced. Would I ever forget how Jack Long cried when Van stood by his bed, leaned over, and kissed him?

Van had cried too. They'd cried in each other's arms like long lost lovers, which they were. The room was filled with their love.

"So why did you leave?" I asked her that night or the next night. "I could tell when you walked in the door you still feel the same. You two look at each other the same way you did when I was little. I used to think you looked like a king and queen."

Van reached out with her soft hand and put it in mine.

"Bless you for that, Mary Jacob. I want to tell you why I left, but not now."

It was late at night when I finally got the story. The two of us were sitting upstairs in Jack's big bedroom. The bedroom that had once been hers. By this point, round-the-clock nurses had come; the hospital bed and the I.V. drip were standard features. It was bringing me back to when my mother died. And it was bringing Van back too.

The room was dimly lit. In the soft light Van didn't look all that different than she had when we were growing up, if you looked at her above the neck. Her body had thickened, like mine was going to do if I stayed down here in Louisiana smoking, drinking, and not running. The oxygen tent arrived the next day, but that night we could still smoke in Jack's room. Both of us kept expecting him to wake up and ask us for a smoke and a cocktail.

I was leaving the next day to go back home for a few days. And to dry out, I told myself. Kathryn was coming back from Atlanta to hold down the fort and Van was going home to Dallas. All these arrangements! My stepdaughter Lizzie was at the apartment in New York for Spring break and was being there for Josh. But they missed me. Their father missed me too. It was the longest I'd ever been away.

"Okay, so why did you leave? What happened? Did you fall in love with someone your age? The tennis pro at the country club or something?"

My former stepmother blew out a long stream of smoke.

"No Mary Jacob. I don't think you know about right and wrong when you're young. Not really. But no, I never cheated on Jack. I guess I've still never cheated on him."

"Get out of here! You've never been with anyone else?"

"No, that's not what I mean, but I haven't loved anyone else, because I did wrong. I won't let myself. Do you know what I'm trying to say?"

"I think children do the right thing because it is in their hearts to do so. I know my children do, if that's what you mean about right and wrong. My stepdaughter is the same age you were when you married Jack. You were hardly more than a child."

"Did you know we had a son?"

We were sitting close together so I could easily lean over and give her a hug.

"Kathryn told me. I didn't know before."

"I visited his grave on the way in from Dallas.

I wanted to give him a name and to honor my brother who never lived so I said "Jack Lynam Long III."

Van sighed. Then she lit another cigarette with the butt she was smoking.

"I didn't realize it was wrong, what we were doing to your mother. I loved Jack, so I thought it was right. He was the world to me, you know."

"I spied on you. I guess you could say it was my introduction to sex. Y'all were in the library."

Van smiled, "You're getting your southern accent back, Mary Jacob."

I smiled back at her.

"How old were you when you spied on us?"

"Twelve, I guess. It was the summer Lavina died. A lot happened that summer!"

"So I would have been seventeen. You know we started up when I just turned fifteen."

I looked across the room, where the dying man lay, unmoved, protected in death as he had been in life. What would be the point of shouting? And too, he was so doped up I could stab him and he wouldn't feel pain.

"That's disgusting!"

"No, Mary Jacob, you're not to say that. It wasn't disgusting at all. Jack was wonderful to me. The most romantic man in the world. He worshiped me and I worshiped him. I cherish every memory I have of him. And us. Besides, Mary Jacob, It was a different time back then. We were all different."

"Do you want to tell me about it?

"About Jack and I?"

"Jack and *me*, for heaven's sake, Van!"

"You and Jack?" Van look scared.

"Jack and me, not Jack and I."

"Oh." Van sounded tremendously relieved. "Well grammar doesn't really matter, does it?"

"It does to me. I'm a writer."

Van sighed deeply. "And your mother would have been so proud of you! Remember her up in that bed over there, reading and reading? Remember her talking about Mrs. Wharton and Mr. Trollope? And how she loved that book on housekeeping, what was it called? And how she thought John O'Hara was vulgar? Your mother was always so good to me too. She was such a cultured person. Not like anyone else I knew growing up. I liked her so much better than my mother."

"Your mother wasn't horrified when you told her you were going to marry my father?"

"She was in hog heaven! Your father was rich in those days. And he was high society. That's what I was on this earth to do. Marry a rich man. She was still alive when my store started becoming a success, but that didn't make her proud. She kept asking me if I was going out with anybody, and if I said yes, she'd ask me if he came from a good family."

I couldn't make out the expression on Van's beautiful face. I was convinced by that point that Van's mother had sold her to my father. I wondered how large a sum of money had been exchanged. My father would have gladly paid a king's ransom to own Van.

"After our baby died, I started realizing what I'd done. It's not as if I thought God had punished me for loving Jack. But I understood about suffering. Your mother suffered because Jack loved me. Maybe it killed her even more than she was already dying. But I was too young to realize that back when it started."

"Do you think she knew?"

"I think she knew he didn't love her. And she was scared of him."

"I remember how scared she was of him. I was too."

We sat there in the semi-dark in companionable silence. Finally Van said, "Did you know your mother was Jewish? She didn't go to the temple but she was born Jewish. Her father was from somewhere in Europe and barely spoke English. He must have been plenty smart to have made all that money, and him not speaking English very well. I don't think her mother spoke English at all. Anyway, Jack was ashamed of that. He made her hide it. It was easy to do because they died very early on and after the War people scattered and moved to different places. She was their only child. But I think that's why she was scared of him."

I was too overcome to speak. If my mother was Jewish, that meant I was Jewish too. How peculiar life is. I was thinking of my father saying, "The Jewish race is conducted on the matrilineal line." The vile remark about ritual sacrifice. And also of Mrs. Beeton. When my mother had told me her own mother gave her the book—indeed so many of my mother's stories were wishful thinking—she was trying to create an upper-class mythology. Perhaps that whole futile struggle had worn her down and eventually killed her.

"How do you know this?"

"Jack told me. We told each other everything, you know. He made me swear I'd never tell a soul, but I thought you'd want to know. Especially since you told me you are raising Joshua Jewish. I go to those Bar Mitzvah things all the time! I'm always dressing my customers up for the parties. In fact, promise me you'll let me dress you when the time comes. And of course I expect to be invited! Everybody has a ball! They're so cute! I can't imagine why Jack was so hell-bent on hiding things."

"Van, you've got to tell me everything you know. This is really important."

"There isn't much to tell. Jack was insane on the subject. He said it was a curse and his children were never to know of it. That none of you would be accepted in good society. I never understood it, I think there were half a dozen Jewish people in my high school graduating class, but now I have so many nice Jewish friends in Dallas. They're so warm and generous. They take me to their country club for brunch. The food is fabulous."

If you are an outsider all your life, you don't suddenly start being an insider once you technically belong. Still, I knew it would make

Joshua happy I was a Jew. It was sort of miraculous, finding all this out just short of his Bar Mitzvah; it was a good story, anyway. I could stand up next to him on the altar and say the insider prayers, the ones only Jews get to say, because my mother was Jewish. It was an idiotic exclusionary law, but it would make my son happy. Maybe it would even make my husband happy on some level. Peter wanted me back in a big way and called me every day to say so. I was even sort of starting to believe him.

The real question was, if I decided to believe him, what would that mean for me? Was I any different because I had a past? Because I now knew the family secret? And now that I finally belonged somewhere, would that make me happy? Possibly, momentarily. I'd been an outsider my whole life. Now I would have the appearance of belonging. Still, you can't undo a life's habit of mind just by revealing a secret. The psyche is far more complicated than that.

"So is that why you left? So you could brunch on Jew food at the country club?"

"Now, Mary Jacob, you're being sarcastic, of course not. Like I said, when my baby died, I understood about suffering. I left him when I realized what I'd done to your poor mother was wrong. I shouldn't have carried on with Jack while she was here, in this very room, suffering like that. Anyway, that's why I left. I couldn't stay when I realized what I'd done. No matter how much I loved him. No matter how much I wanted to stay."

༄

A man of the cloth, a few men my father's age, and quite a number of well-dressed middle-aged women were there at the graveyard. We buried Jack Lynam Long Jr. next to Jack Lynam Long III. Mother was buried there too. Later, one by one, the ladies appeared at the house to pay their respects. Van caught on first. "They're his lady friends, Mary Jacob. All the women loved Jack. He was so charming, wasn't he?"

I squeezed her hand. I was thinking of another graveyard, as I stood there in the rain in between Van and Annie Hunt. I was trying to recall how I had escaped the house and gotten to Lavina's service. How had I found out where and when the service was? By then they would have been watching me, my father, the nurse, maybe even Van. Still, I'd been there at the funeral, hiding behind a tree. I could see myself, mouthing a hymn . . .

There is a balm in Gilead,
That makes the wounded whole.
There is a balm in Gilead, to heal the sin-sick soul.

Because, of course, the mind is capricious. It remembers what it wants to remember. What it can bear to remember. And ironically, even then, the truth was difficult to accept. It's still hard, even now, to put the "me" back into what I remember. It's so much easier to imagine how things were for Billy Ray and for Lavina. To imagine what happened to us all through their eyes.

To be conscious is not to be in time.
But only in time can the moment in the rose garden,
The moment in the arbor where the rain beat,
The moment in the draughty church at smokefall
Be remembered; involved with past and present.
Only through time, time is conquered.

By the time I caught up with Billy Ray again, one summer's night in Montauk, months later, I had to some extent conquered time. I had imposed a certain order on things. My headaches were getting better too, and I was starting to believe what I remembered as being true. At least true for me.

We were renting a house for the month of August. One morning, I opened up the local paper and there it was, the same picture of Billy Ray I had seen in the Murpheysfield paper: Billy Ray live. It does not matter whether I believed an unseen hand was guiding me to take an August rental on that house in East Hampton, a short drive from the club where he would be performing that night. Or even as I told myself Billy Ray and I were bound to meet again. Maybe they're both true. Maybe neither is true. Still we did meet again, and on that particular night, as I stood outside the nightclub, I was as nervous about going in as I was about stepping off the plane in Murpheysfield all those months ago.

It took me quite a while to get up the courage to go inside. Once I parked my car, I walked up and down a little pier that smelled of fish near the club and stared at the boats and at the waning of that fine August day in the sky. There were a million subtle colors in the sky that early evening, as though the same unseen hand that had brought me to Montauk had painted the sky just for this meeting.

Billy Ray wasn't expecting me, here in a little club on the eastern tip of Long Island, no more than I had been expecting to meet him when I returned to visit my dying father. But I had something real to give Billy Ray: as real as gold.

It had taken some digging and sifting to find it. And had I perhaps been like my own fictional sleuth, little Vina, or even a trained forensics expert, I might have been filled with glee when I unearthed the thing that day in the back yard of the big white house. But I wasn't. I was stunned, incredulous, and even then, saying, no, it can't be. Still, finding the golden harmonica charm on its delicate little chain was at last positive proof of the crime. Prima facie evidence. The box it had come in had long gone by way of the worms. Still, there were little strands of that soft white stuff they put in jewelry boxes all entangled in its little links. Once I had it in my hand, I held the little thing up to the sunlight and moved it back and forth, back and forth, as it dangled and spun. I brought it in, took some painkiller, and showed the thing to Van and told her the story.

The little chain with its delicate little charm was clean now, and nearly as shiny as it was the day I held it in my hand the first time. It was August now as it was August then. But this time, I would get it right and return the gold harmonica chain to its rightful owner. Or so I told myself as I turned and entered the club.

The place had a low ceiling and smelled of beer and, at eight fifteen that Saturday night, was all but empty. According to the local paper, the show would not start until nine. Still, the emptiness of the place worried me. Surely, a big star like Billy Ray could command better than this, even if he wasn't a big star anymore. And I had a wild desire suddenly to call the few people I knew who were out here for August to get over here and help fill up the club. The place had such a mournful air with its smell of beer, and its little makeshift stage where a large black man and a skinny white boy were setting up instruments in a half-hearted way. The heavy black man seemed far more interested in his bag of chips than in the equipment.

I wanted more for the former boy wonder who I regarded then, as my brother. Not "yo, bro" kind of a brother, but my real brother. For at that particular time in my recollection, I had come to the perhaps sentimental point of believing Billy Ray and I were brother and sister. We were raised and loved by the same woman after all. And along with the little gold harmonica chain I had in my purse, I wanted to give Billy Ray my take on the situation, a take that went something like this: She made us both. And whatever good there is in us is because of her, because of Lavina. And that makes us belong to each other.

I also wanted, I suppose, at least I imagined, that Billy Ray would smile and we would hug or something. I guess you could say, I wanted a happy ending. Or if not that, then at least, as they say on the talk shows, "closure."

Still, I kept stalling, perhaps knowing that a happy ending wasn't what I was going to get from Billy Ray. That night or any night, come to that. I went to the bar, ordered a vodka on the rocks, and spent a few minutes drinking it. I thought about ordering another one, but decided against it. Van was coming to visit the next week and I'd be drinking plenty enough then.

A few more people drifted in the bar before I finished up my vodka. By then I guess I knew there wasn't going to be a magic moment when it would be perfect to confront Billy Ray. But I told myself, he at least was one person who would know what really happened to Lavina. Billy Ray had been there, after all.

The bartender pointed in the direction of the ocean to a door. When I opened it and stepped in a narrow corridor, I bumped into the large man I'd seen setting up for the show. He was emerging from the men's room, buttoning his pants.

I went in the ladies room and stayed in there for another few minutes, killing time, and when I came out, I knocked timidly on the one door that wasn't labeled as a bathroom. I imagined how it must have been for Billy Ray that day when he stood at my father's door and rang the bell. I thought if he could do it, then so, by God, could I. And once again I told myself, he's your brother, Mary Jacob. And you've got to go in there for Lavina's sake.

I knocked again. Louder this time. And a man's voice called out, "it ain't locked."

I opened the door and stepped inside. The place was queerly lit: almost dark. The only illumination other than from the dim hallway light behind me came from the little bulbs on the makeup mirror. When my eyes adjusted themselves to the dimness, I saw Billy Ray. Shirtless, he was sitting down in front of his makeshift dressing table peering intently at the mirror. A pair of half glasses rested on the very tip of his nose and he was holding a wand of mascara in his hand. His shirt and a blue spangled jacket were hanging up in their dry cleaning plastic from the top of a floor lamp near his makeup table. Billy Ray looked skinny and old and, with the yellow bulbs, slightly green in color. Nothing like the golden boy of my memories who stood in the sun that day in front of Woolworth's and took the whole world in his hand.

He was making it as hard on me as I must have made it for him that day when he arrived at my father's house. Still, in my mind, I had an excuse. What was his excuse, I wondered as I stood there unnoticed. Billy Ray didn't have a traumatic block. Billy Ray remembered. At least he once had. But as I stood there, minutes going by, still unnoticed, it occurred to me that maybe that scene in my father's house might have traumatized him: the last straw in a series of psychic shocks starting thirty years ago. Was it possible that he blocked the whole thing out? His coming to the house, the big red-faced man in the front hall, and dreadful Kathryn asking him what he was doing at her door? Anything was possible. I had learned that the hard way, hadn't I?

It was then that I heard a little scuffling sound coming from some dark corner of that little room that somehow made me think of a puppy. A little boy's voice, very southern, called out in a sleepy little voice, "Billy Ray? Is your show over yet? Where's Mom? Can we get us somethin' to eat now?"

And to this voice, Billy Ray answered right away, "Show ain't happened yet, Connor. Why don't you get yourself some more sleep and I'll wake you up when it's time to eat."

"Okay," he said. "But where's Mom?"

As if on cue, a blond woman appeared in the doorway holding a tray with a glass and a bottle of Perrier. I liked her face immediately.

She looked at me, then at Billy Ray.

"They didn't have Evian, this is the best I could do."

Billy Ray picked up the glass, then poured himself a generous helping and tossed it off in a couple of thirsty gulps. He sighed afterwards, which seemed to be his way of saying thank you.

Facing the mirror again, he started working some powder on his face. Although I had prepared myself, I expected something better than this. For Billy Ray still wouldn't acknowledge my presence.

The woman came out of the shadows and offered her right hand. On the left, she wore an enormous diamond ring on her engagement finger; it kept catching stray bits of light.

"I'm Sarah," she said. "Billy Ray doesn't like to talk before he plays."

The silent harmonica player stood up then, stripped the wrappings from his jacket and shirt and wadded the plastic in a neat ball and tossed it on the floor. Sarah picked it up and held the balled up plastic in her hand. We both watched Billy Ray slip his shirt on. While he was buttoning up, he finally spoke.

"You are maybe the last person I expected to see here tonight." Then he leaned over and checked himself out in the mirror, smoothed his hair back with one hand. He went on then, more to himself than to me, "I take it back, you're the next to last person I expected to see here tonight."

I said, casually, trying to match his tone, "My family and I are renting a house near here and I thought I'd stop by and say hello." I was about to say something about being sorry about how weirdly I'd acted last time when Billy Ray cut me off.

"Ain't that nice," he said. Only it didn't sound so nice. He was obviously pissed. And who wouldn't be, given the way I'd acted that afternoon?

I had a lot to say, really too much to say, and not nearly enough time to get even the important parts in. I was already beginning to see how ridiculous it would be trying to give Billy Ray even an abbreviated version of my own memory loss—particularly when my memory loss wasn't what we had between us. What we had between us was Lavina. And the gold harmonica charm, of course. I reached in my purse and I took it out.

"Look." I said, "I know you're in a rush, but your mother bought this for you a few days before she died and she made me promise that if something happened to her, I'd get this to you. It's been buried in my father's back yard all these years. After you came to see me that day, I remembered about it and found it."

"Anyway," I said, finally, "From your mother to you, thirty years late." And I walked over to Billy Ray, grabbed one of his long, graceful hands, and dropped the little thing in it.

Billy Ray looked down at his hand. Then up at me. I knew I was leaving something out. Something very important out—but I could not for the life of me remember what it was. Instead, I said the first thing that popped into my head. "She was the best person I ever met in my whole life. And I'll miss her till the day I die."

Billy Ray didn't answer me. I saw him lift the little charm up in the air with his long thumb and forefinger as he swung the little thing back and forth, back and forth, just like I had done that day I found it.

We were both staring at the little souvenir of that lost summer dangling and spinning in Billy Ray's hand. It seemed to me we were both hypnotizing ourselves, staring at the movement of the chain and its tiny little charm as it moved back and forth, back and forth, and Billy Ray and I were together again that day at the Woolworth's, with the crowds in front of the store; in that cool dark place on the side of the store where we kissed before we found Lavina. And then it came to me, what I wanted to know. What I'd been dying to know since I remembered. I wanted to ask Billy Ray how he had ended up there that day. And had he known that Lavina was in there at the sit-in? And if so, what had made her do it?

I was about to ask this when the little boy appeared in our small circle of light. He went to stand between his mother and Billy Ray. Then he reached for both their hands, shooting me a fierce look. A look that told me I had overstayed my welcome, if indeed I had been welcome at all.

He stared at the gold harmonica on its delicate chain.

"What's that, Billy Ray?"

"I'll tell you later," Billy Ray told him, and his mother said "hush, you know Billy Ray doesn't like to talk before the show."

Sarah was looking at me, waiting. But I had already taken the hint. I left the three of them standing in the circle of light: mother, child, and harmonica player.

The last thing I heard was, "Woncha just let me look at it, Billly Ray?"

That and Billy Ray's good-natured reply, "You can wear it if you want. Here, turn yourself around."

Just then "Diamond Buttons" began blasting out of the speakers, filling up that drab honkytonk joint with energy and motion. And when I stepped out in the club, it was no longer empty, but full of people dancing. People of all ages. Summer-looking people my age, kids my stepdaughter Lizzie's age, black kids, white kids, a few Asian kids—I thought Lavina would have liked the crowd, the ease of it. Would have liked that I had come to give Billy Ray the charm.

The parking lot was full and lots of people were milling about outside. Excitement was definitely in the air as surely as the faint smell of fish wafting off the docks. When I finally pulled out of the lot, someone with a flashlight was directing the steady stream of cars, cars that were backed up for miles on that two-lane stretch of highway leading into Montauk. The stars were out now and I was headed home with the moon in front of me, though not a single car. All the cars on that stretch of road were headed toward Montauk and the harmonica player. As I passed them, one by one, the cars filled with people, I raised my eyes to the moon and the starry night, everything seemed to point to a genuine comeback for Billy Ray.

And, in a way I was only beginning to understand, a way without the fanfare of music or even a mild burst of applause; by writing this down, I've started making my own sort of comeback as well.

ABOUT THE AUTHOR

Mary Marcus grew up in Louisiana, raised by her mother's housekeeper, during the turbulent end of the Jim Crow South. She is the author of the novel *The New Me*. Her short fiction has appeared in numerous literary magazines, including The North Atlantic Review, Fiction, and Karamu, among others.

She lives in Los Angeles and the East End of Long Island.